DOUBLE D BOOK 1: JUST DESSERTS

WRITTEN BY EDDIE ARGOS

ART BY STEVEN HORRY

COLOURS BY DAVID COOPER

LETTERS BY COLIN BELL

DESIGN AND CHAPTER 1 COLOUR FLATS BY VICTORIA HORRY

EDITED BY ALEX SARLL

CHAPTER 1

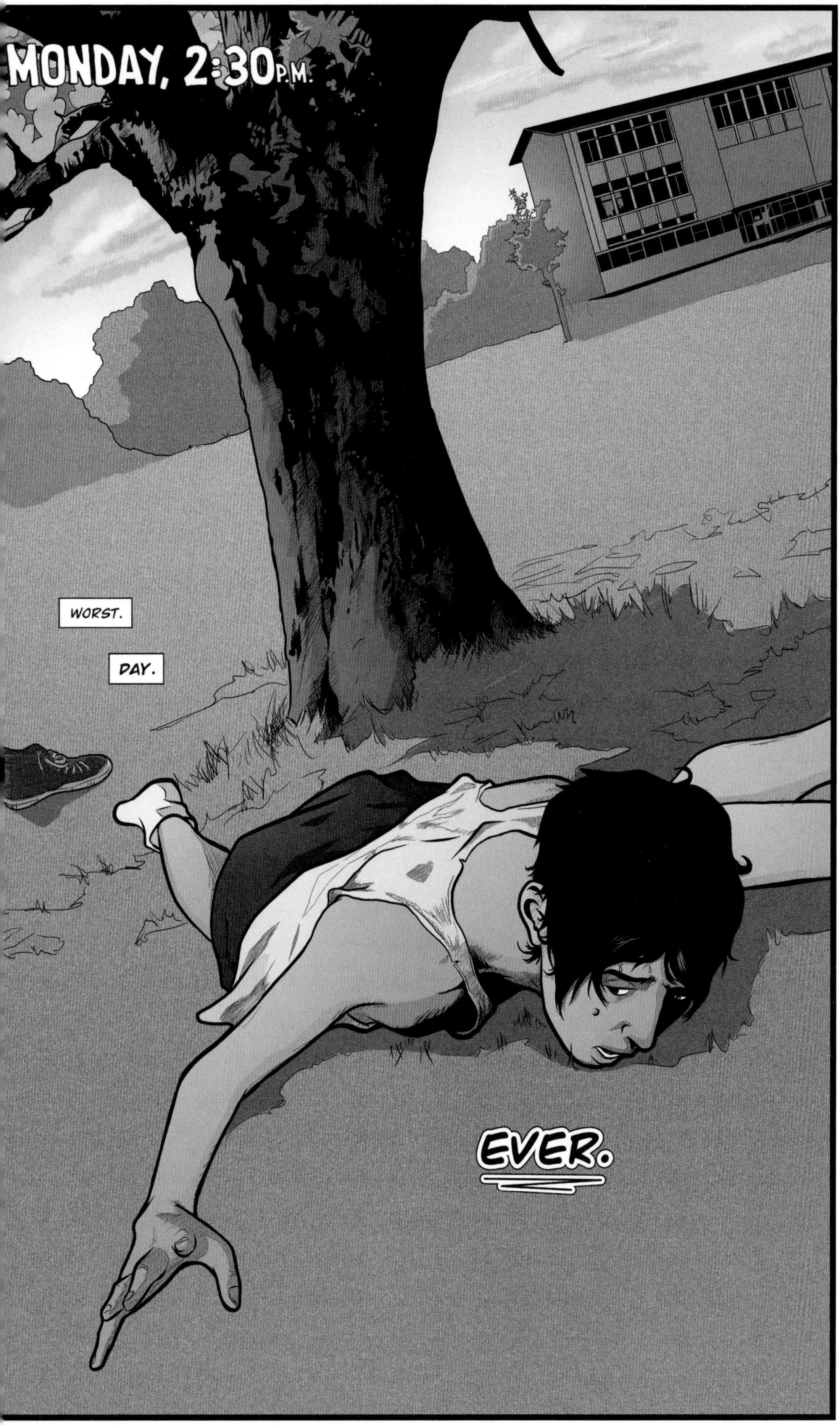
MONDAY, 2:30P.M.
WORST.
DAY.
EVER.

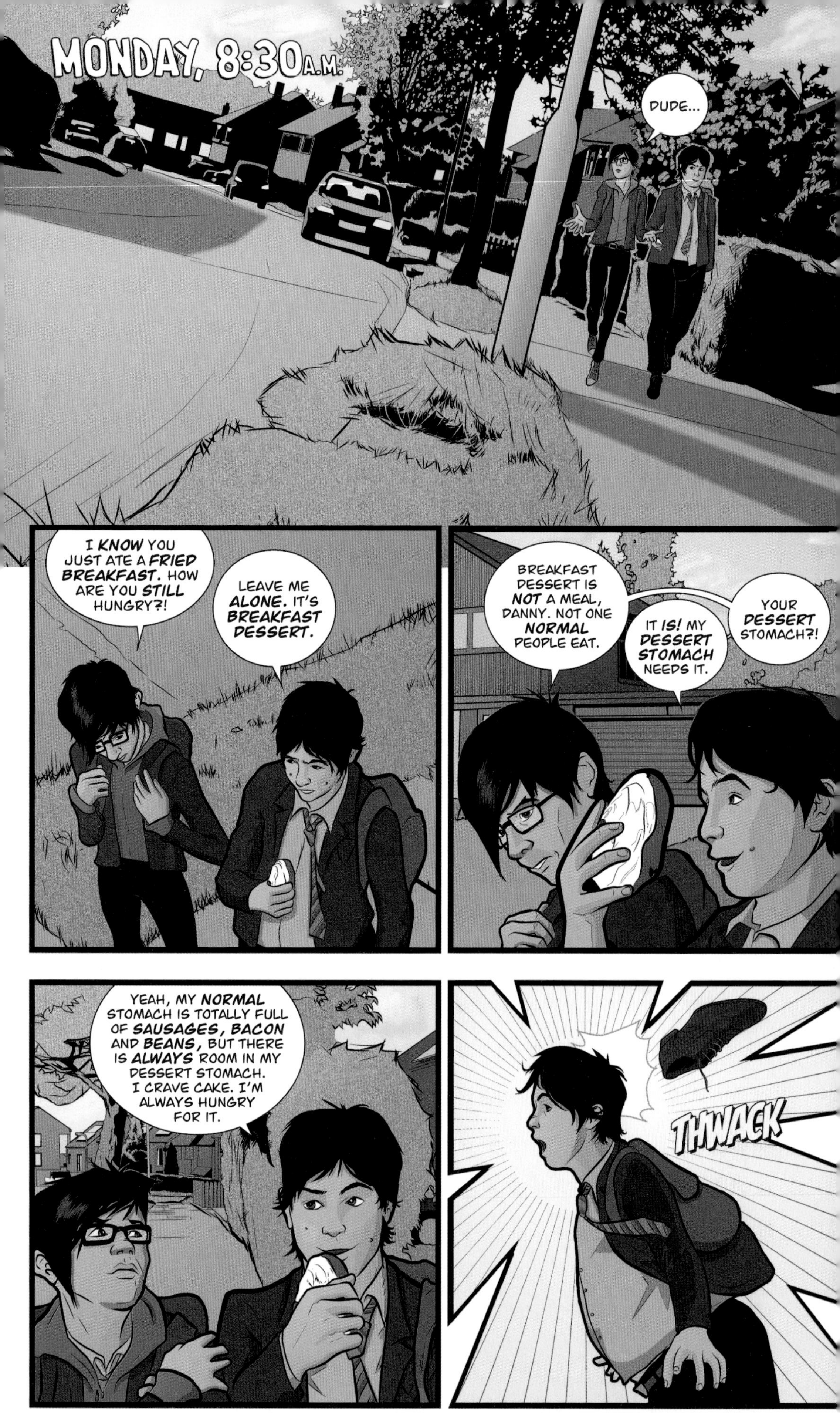
MONDAY, 8:30 A.M.
DUDE...
I KNOW YOU JUST ATE A FRIED BREAKFAST. HOW ARE YOU STILL HUNGRY?!
LEAVE ME ALONE. IT'S BREAKFAST DESSERT.
BREAKFAST DESSERT IS NOT A MEAL, DANNY. NOT ONE NORMAL PEOPLE EAT.
IT IS! MY DESSERT STOMACH NEEDS IT.
YOUR DESSERT STOMACH?!
YEAH, MY NORMAL STOMACH IS TOTALLY FULL OF SAUSAGES, BACON AND BEANS, BUT THERE IS ALWAYS ROOM IN MY DESSERT STOMACH. I CRAVE CAKE. I'M ALWAYS HUNGRY FOR IT.
THWACK

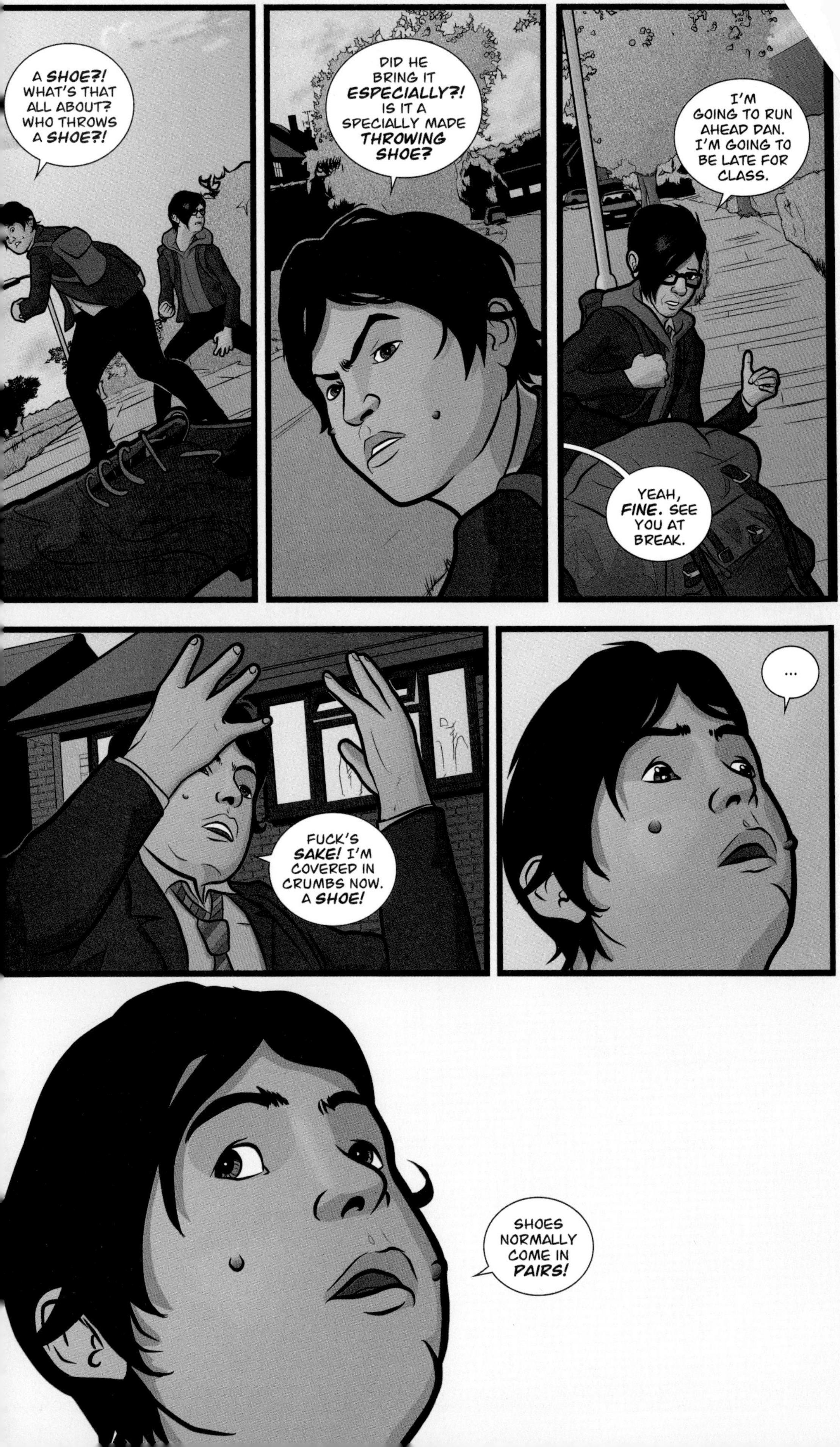
A SHOE?! WHAT'S THAT ALL ABOUT? WHO THROWS A SHOE?!
DID HE BRING IT ESPECIALLY?! IS IT A SPECIALLY MADE THROWING SHOE?
I'M GOING TO RUN AHEAD DAN. I'M GOING TO BE LATE FOR CLASS.
YEAH, FINE. SEE YOU AT BREAK.
FUCK'S SAKE! I'M COVERED IN CRUMBS NOW. A SHOE!
...
SHOES NORMALLY COME IN PAIRS!

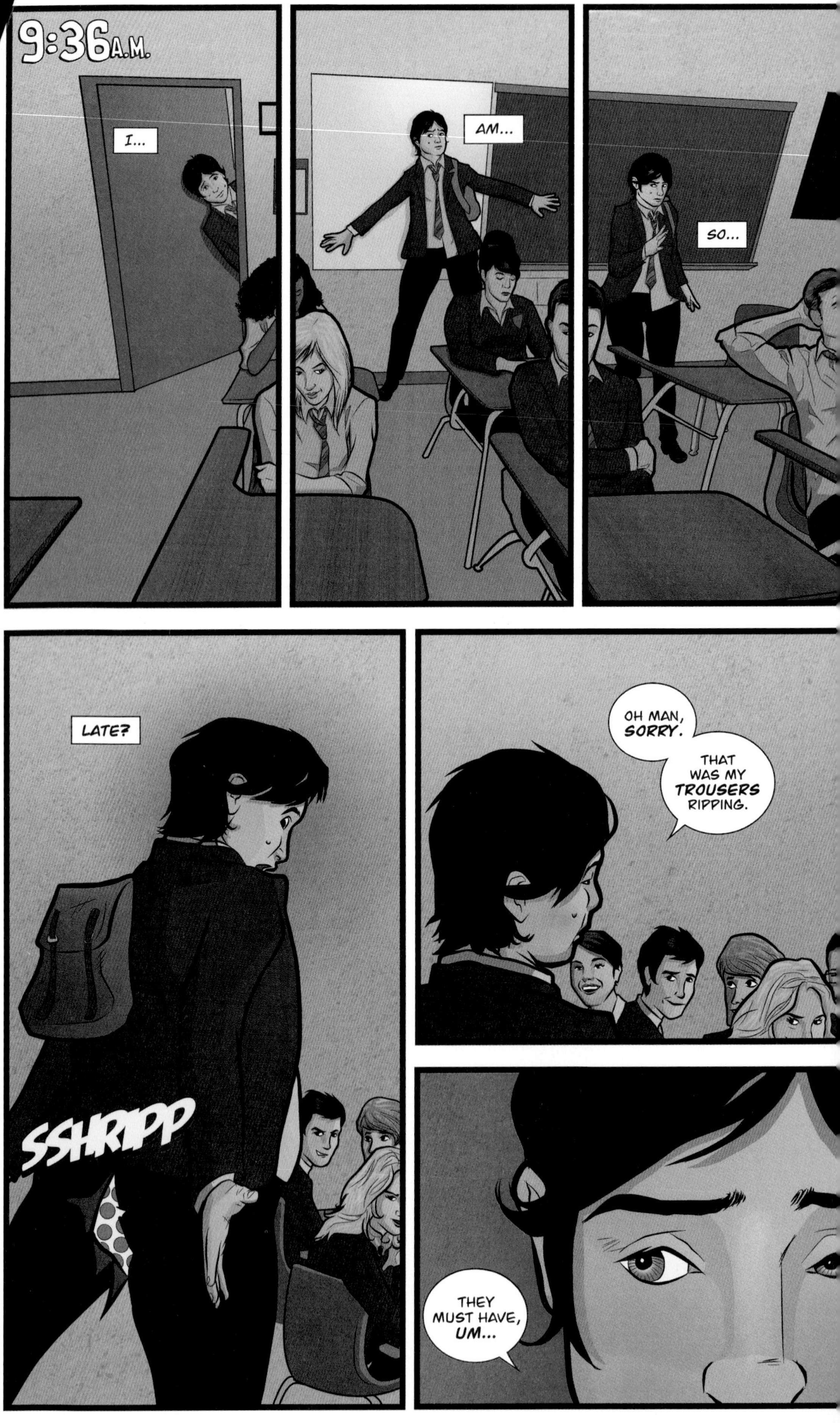
9:36A.M.
I...
AM...
SO...
LATE?
SSHRIPP
OH MAN, SORRY.
THAT WAS MY TROUSERS RIPPING.
THEY MUST HAVE, UM...

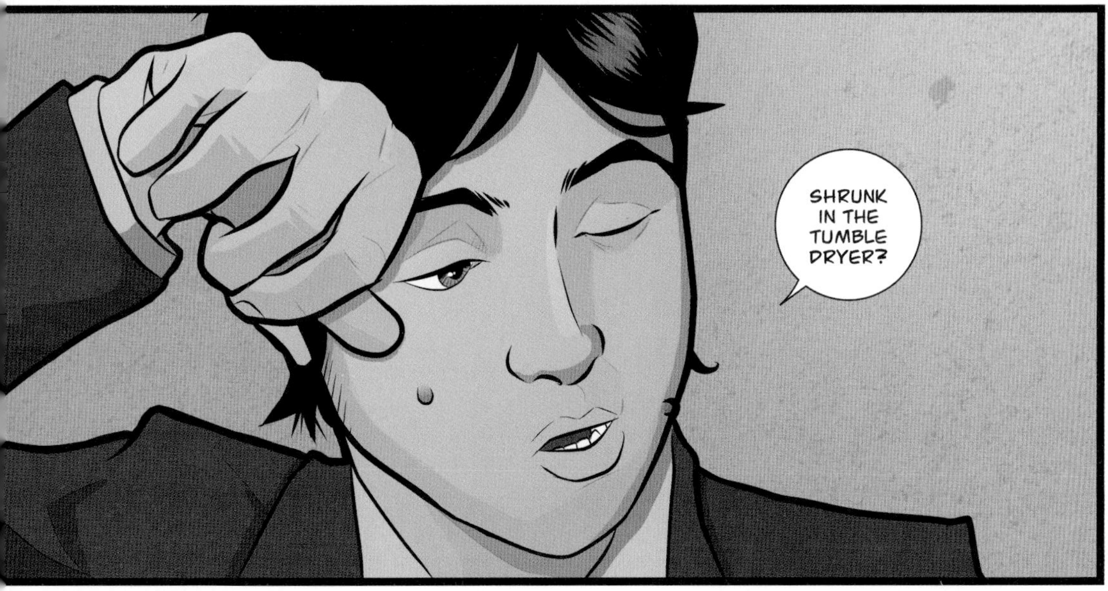
SHRUNK
IN THE
TUMBLE
DRYER?

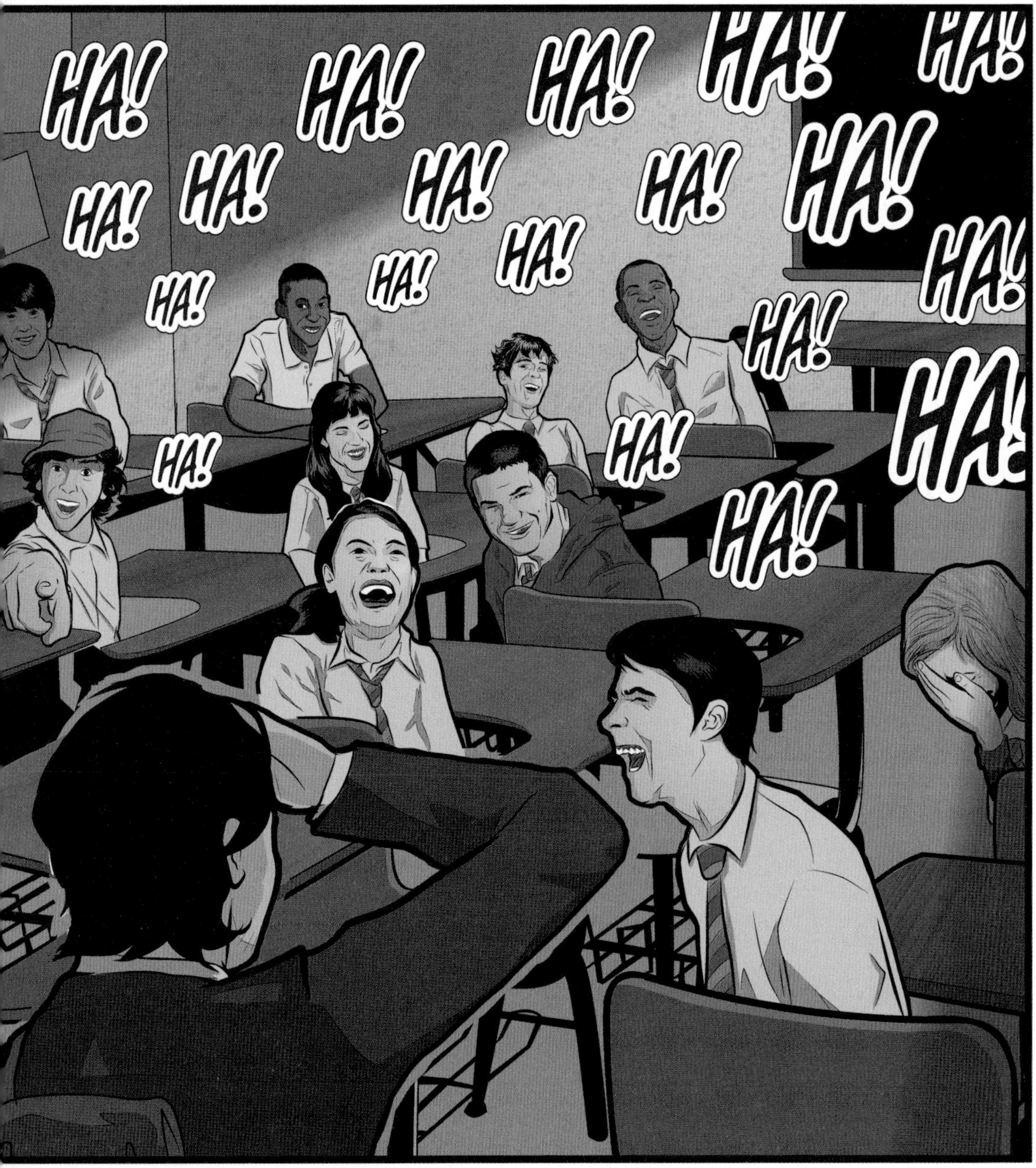
HA!
HA!
HA!
HA!
HA!
HA!
HA!
HA!
HA!
HA!
HA!
HA!
HA!
HA!
HA!
HA!
HA!
HA!
HA!

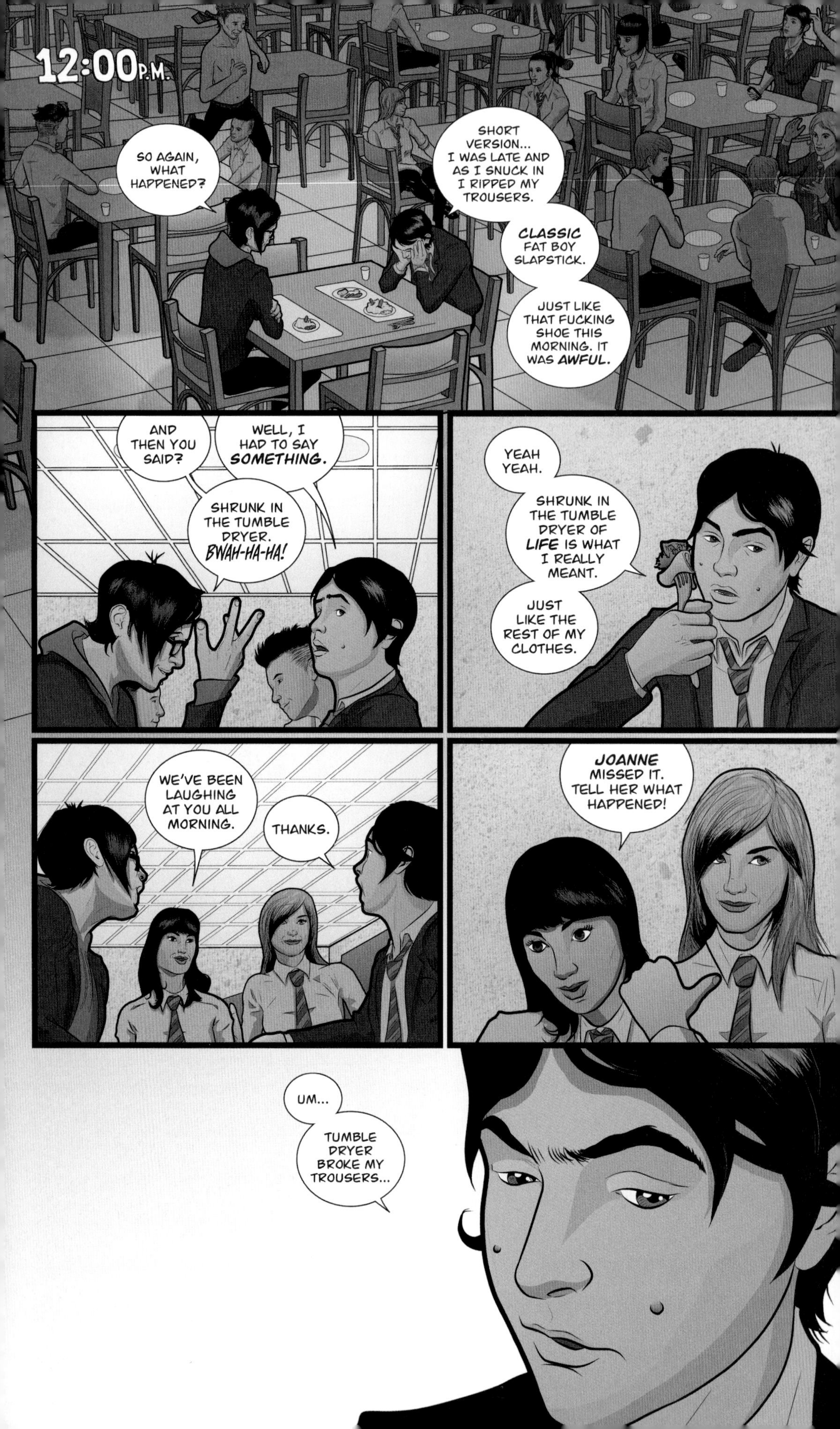

12:00P.M.
SO AGAIN, WHAT HAPPENED?
SHORT VERSION... I WAS LATE AND AS I SNUCK IN I RIPPED MY TROUSERS.
CLASSIC FAT BOY SLAPSTICK.
JUST LIKE THAT FUCKING SHOE THIS MORNING. IT WAS AWFUL.
AND THEN YOU SAID?
WELL, I HAD TO SAY SOMETHING.
SHRUNK IN THE TUMBLE DRYER. BWAH-HA-HA!
YEAH YEAH.
SHRUNK IN THE TUMBLE DRYER OF LIFE IS WHAT I REALLY MEANT.
JUST LIKE THE REST OF MY CLOTHES.
WE'VE BEEN LAUGHING AT YOU ALL MORNING.
THANKS.
JOANNE MISSED IT. TELL HER WHAT HAPPENED!
UM...
TUMBLE DRYER BROKE MY TROUSERS...

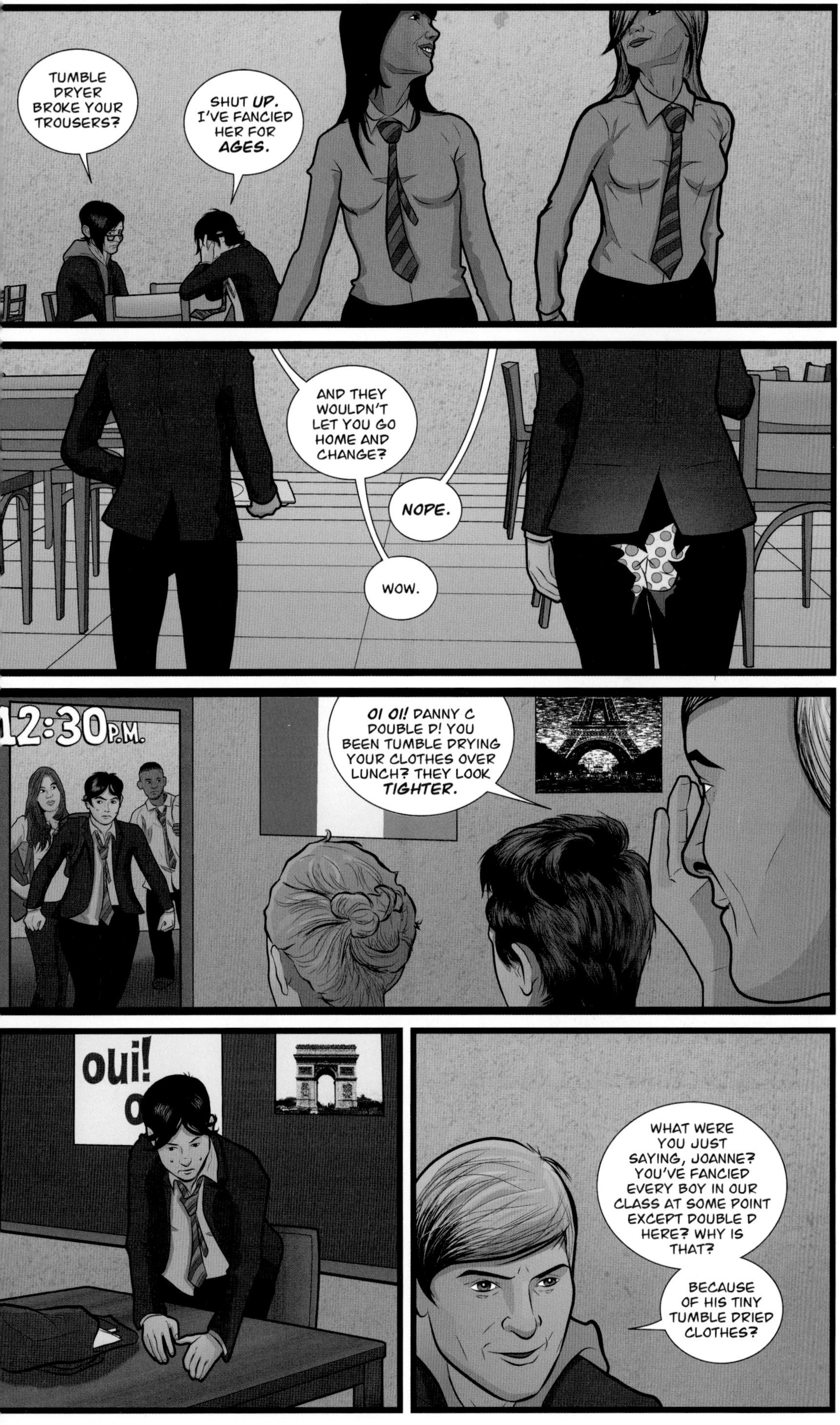
TUMBLE DRYER BROKE YOUR TROUSERS?
SHUT UP. I'VE FANCIED HER FOR AGES.
AND THEY WOULDN'T LET YOU GO HOME AND CHANGE?
NOPE.
WOW.
12:30P.M.
OI OI! DANNY C DOUBLE D! YOU BEEN TUMBLE DRYING YOUR CLOTHES OVER LUNCH? THEY LOOK TIGHTER.
oui!
WHAT WERE YOU JUST SAYING, JOANNE? YOU'VE FANCIED EVERY BOY IN OUR CLASS AT SOME POINT EXCEPT DOUBLE D HERE? WHY IS THAT?
BECAUSE OF HIS TINY TUMBLE DRIED CLOTHES?

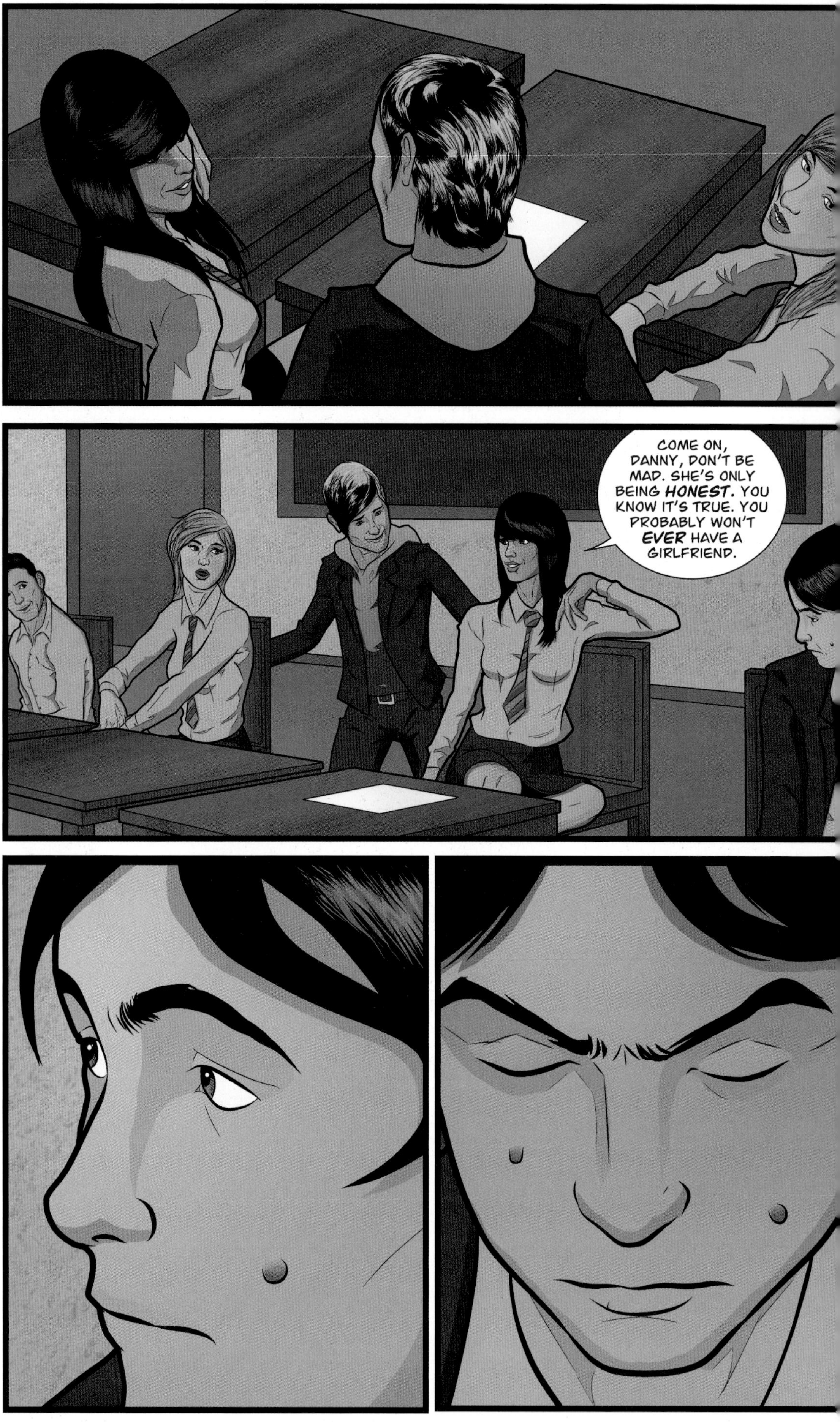
COME ON, DANNY, DON'T BE MAD. SHE'S ONLY BEING HONEST. YOU KNOW IT'S TRUE. YOU PROBABLY WON'T EVER HAVE A GIRLFRIEND.

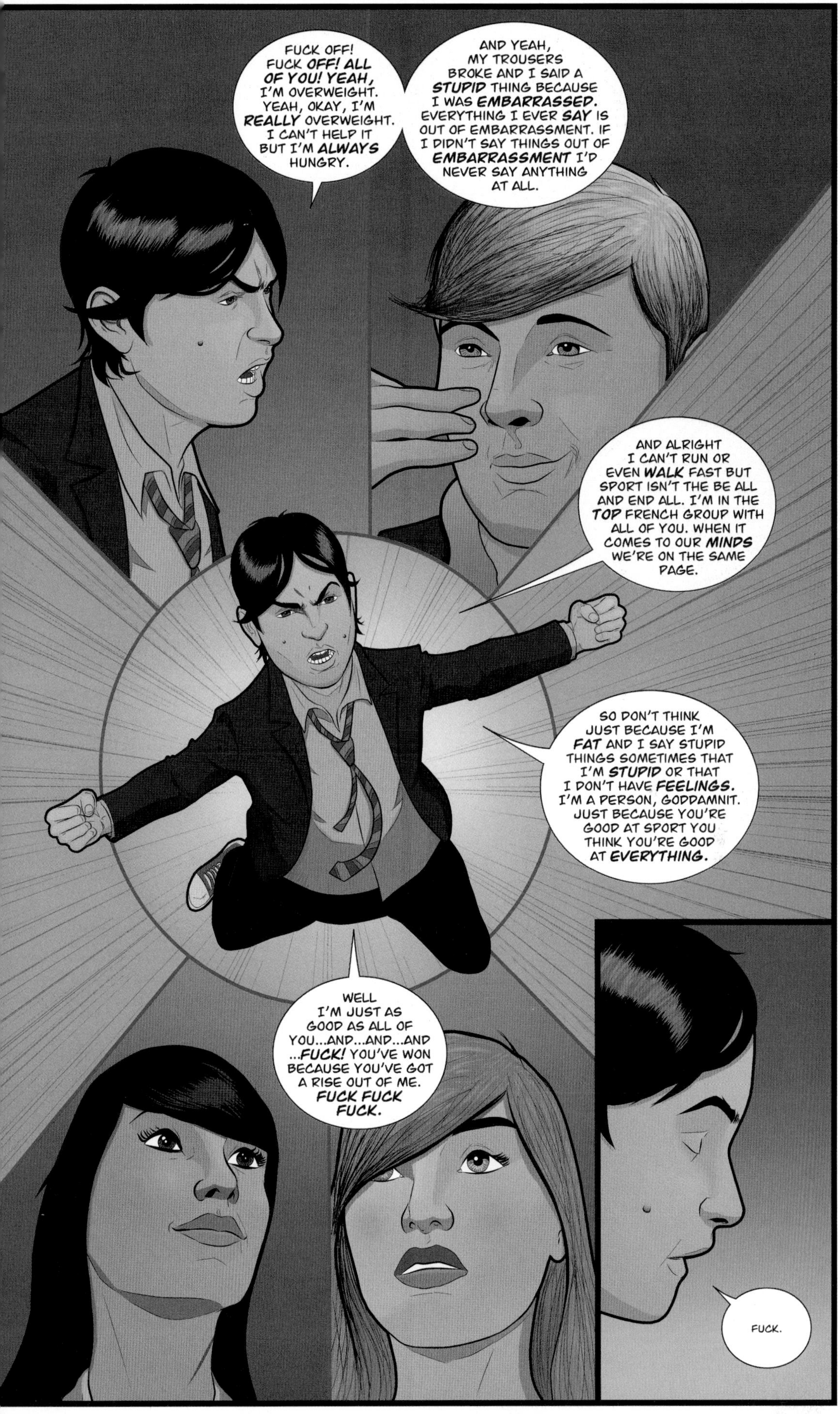
FUCK OFF! FUCK OFF! ALL OF YOU! YEAH, I'M OVERWEIGHT. YEAH, OKAY, I'M REALLY OVERWEIGHT. I CAN'T HELP IT BUT I'M ALWAYS HUNGRY.
AND YEAH, MY TROUSERS BROKE AND I SAID A STUPID THING BECAUSE I WAS EMBARRASSED. EVERYTHING I EVER SAY IS OUT OF EMBARRASSMENT. IF I DIDN'T SAY THINGS OUT OF EMBARRASSMENT I'D NEVER SAY ANYTHING AT ALL.
AND ALRIGHT I CAN'T RUN OR EVEN WALK FAST BUT SPORT ISN'T THE BE ALL AND END ALL. I'M IN THE TOP FRENCH GROUP WITH ALL OF YOU. WHEN IT COMES TO OUR MINDS WE'RE ON THE SAME PAGE.
SO DON'T THINK JUST BECAUSE I'M FAT AND I SAY STUPID THINGS SOMETIMES THAT I'M STUPID OR THAT I DON'T HAVE FEELINGS. I'M A PERSON, GODDAMNIT. JUST BECAUSE YOU'RE GOOD AT SPORT YOU THINK YOU'RE GOOD AT EVERYTHING.
WELL I'M JUST AS GOOD AS ALL OF YOU...AND...AND...AND ...FUCK! YOU'VE WON BECAUSE YOU'VE GOT A RISE OUT OF ME. FUCK FUCK FUCK.
FUCK.

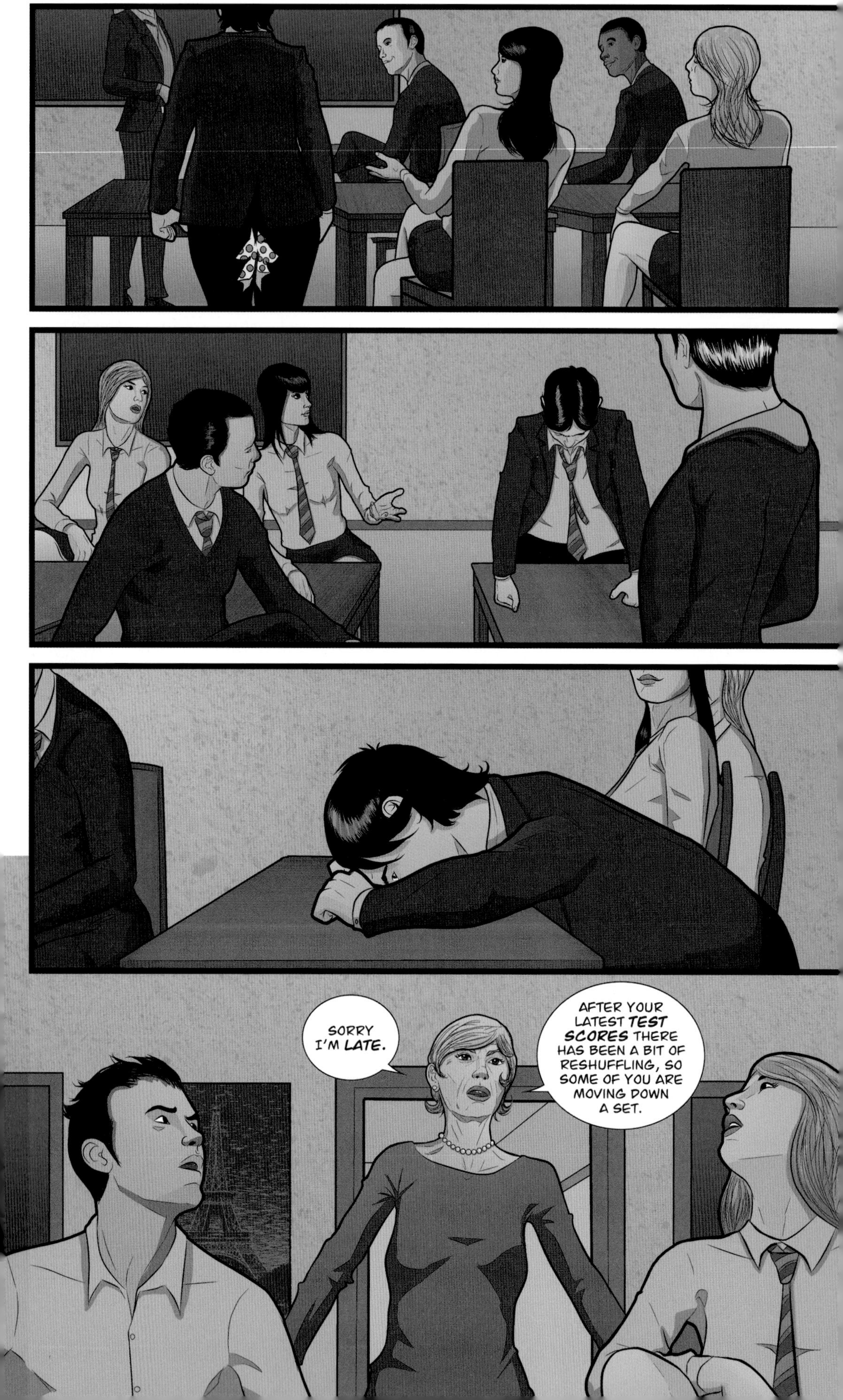
SORRY I'M LATE.
AFTER YOUR LATEST TEST SCORES THERE HAS BEEN A BIT OF RESHUFFLING, SO SOME OF YOU ARE MOVING DOWN A SET.

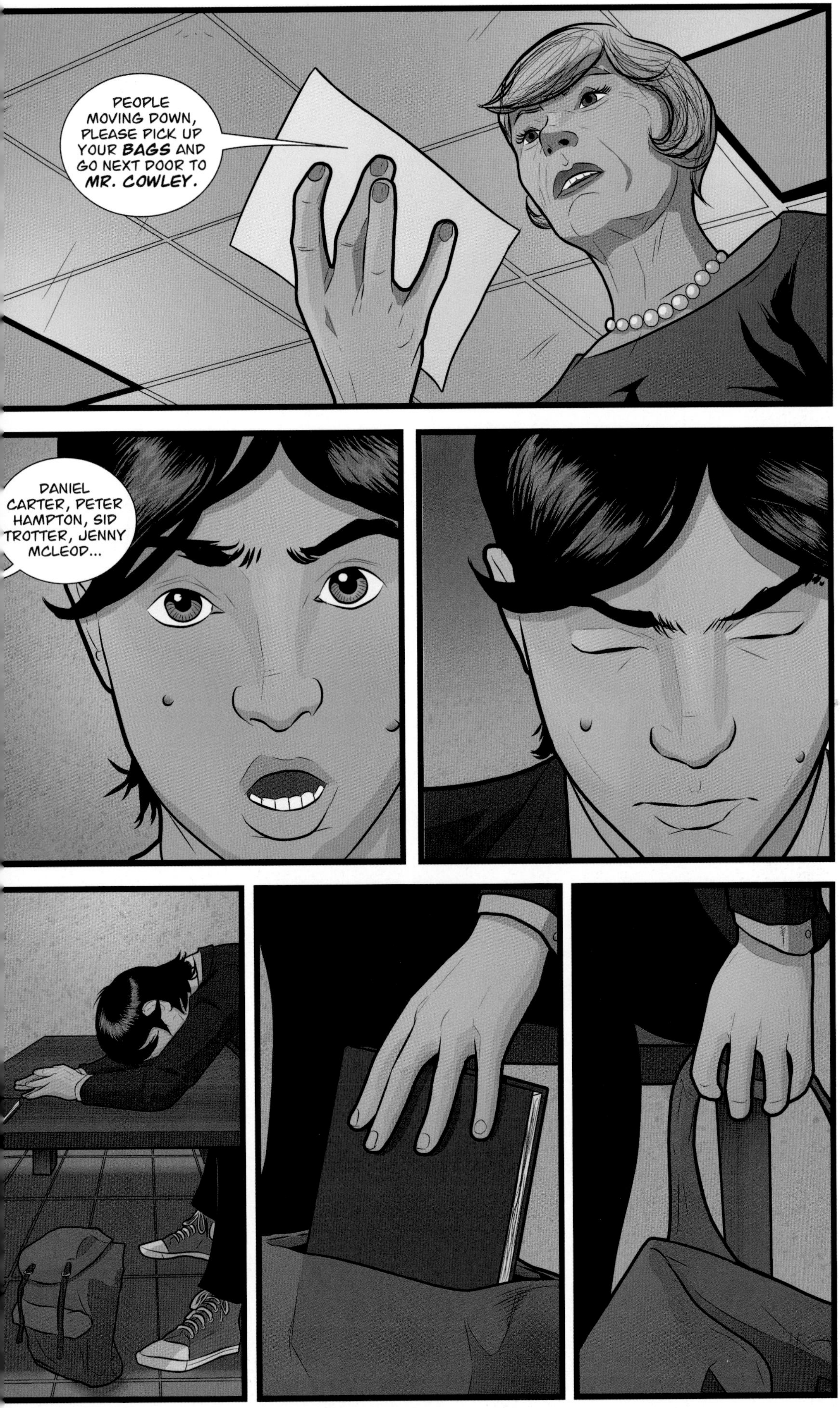
PEOPLE MOVING DOWN, PLEASE PICK UP YOUR **BAGS** AND GO NEXT DOOR TO **MR. COWLEY**.
DANIEL CARTER, PETER HAMPTON, SID TROTTER, JENNY MCLEOD...

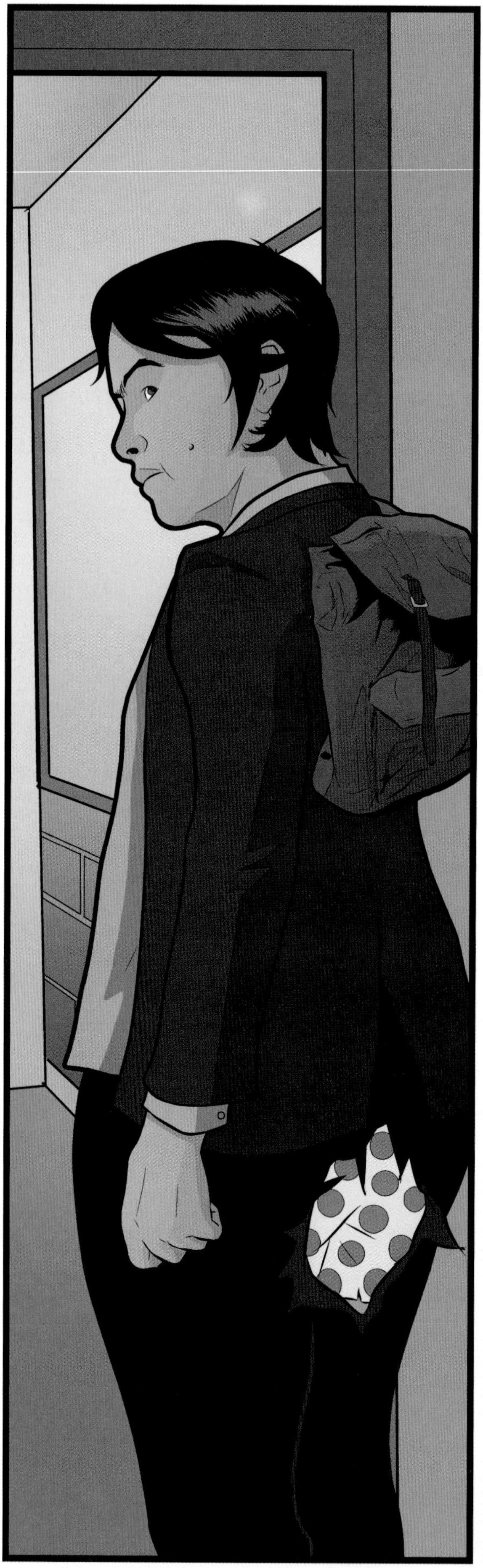
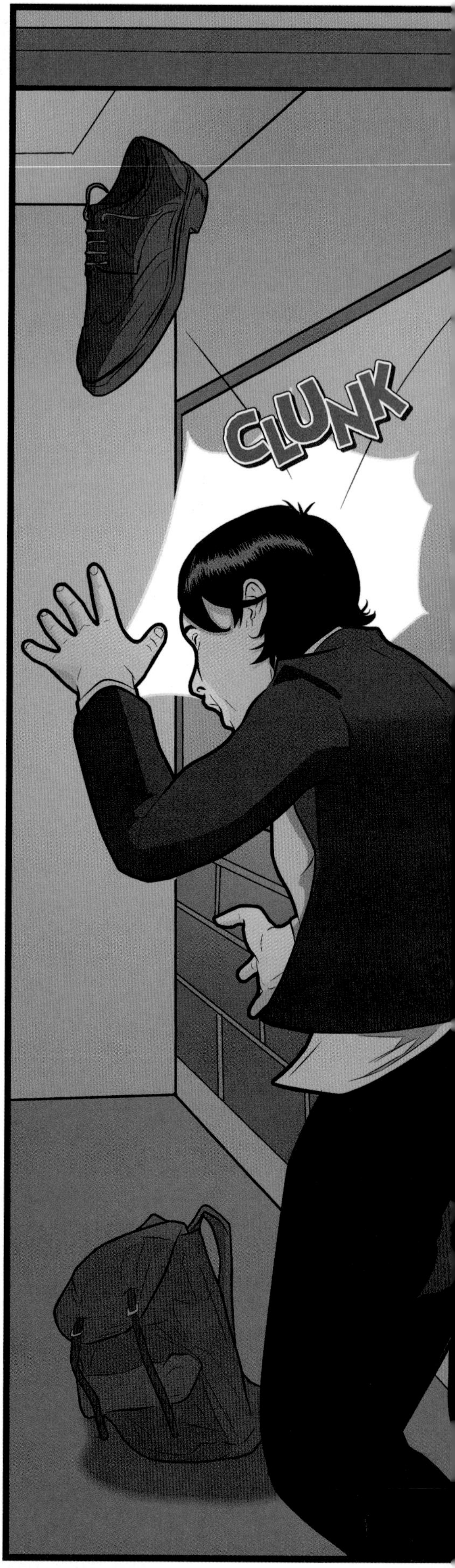
CLUNK

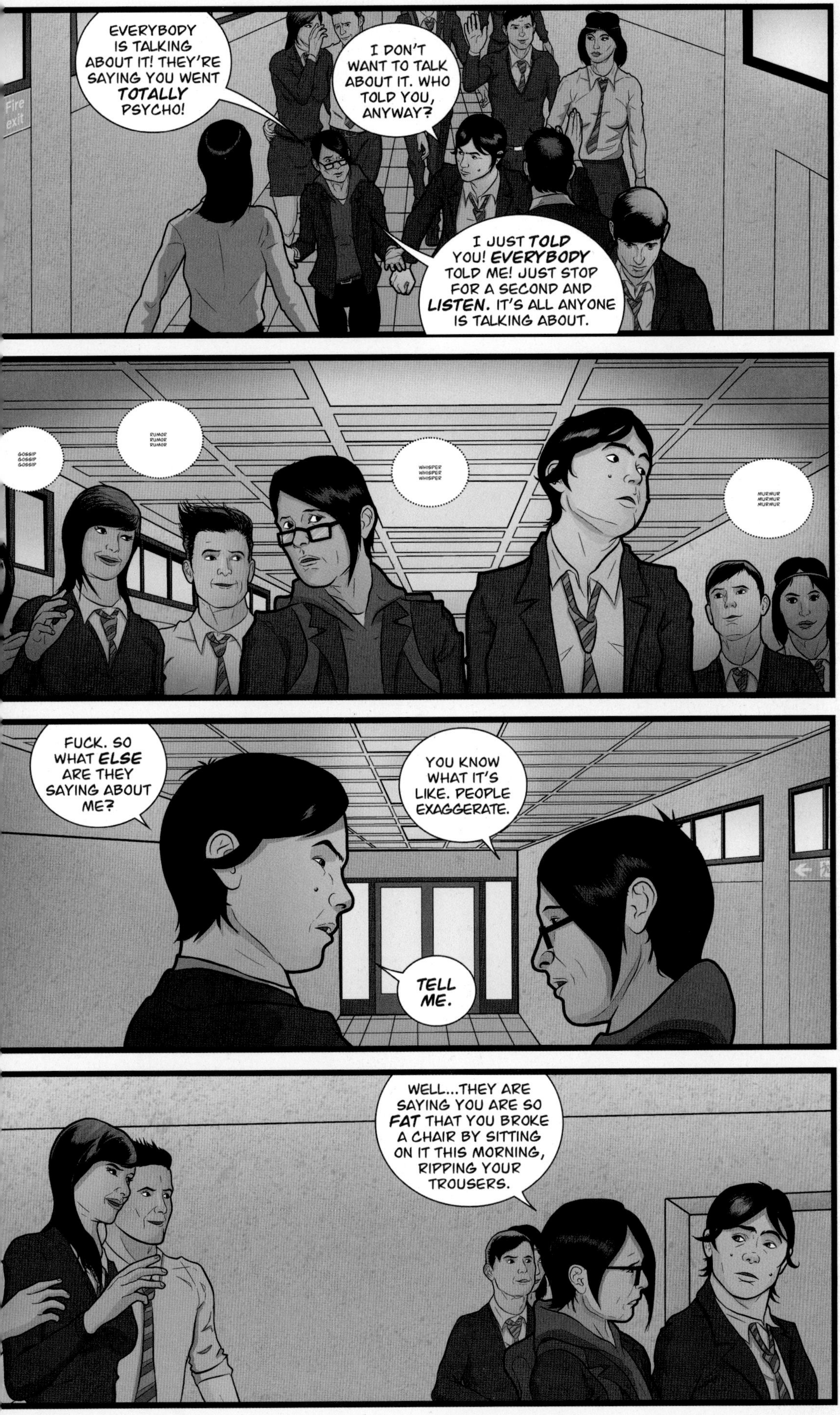
Fire exit
EVERYBODY IS TALKING ABOUT IT! THEY'RE SAYING YOU WENT TOTALLY PSYCHO!
I DON'T WANT TO TALK ABOUT IT. WHO TOLD YOU, ANYWAY?
I JUST TOLD YOU! EVERYBODY TOLD ME! JUST STOP FOR A SECOND AND LISTEN. IT'S ALL ANYONE IS TALKING ABOUT.
GOSSIP GOSSIP GOSSIP
RUMOR RUMOR RUMOR
WHISPER WHISPER WHISPER
MURMUR MURMUR MURMUR
FUCK. SO WHAT ELSE ARE THEY SAYING ABOUT ME?
YOU KNOW WHAT IT'S LIKE. PEOPLE EXAGGERATE.
TELL ME.
WELL...THEY ARE SAYING YOU ARE SO FAT THAT YOU BROKE A CHAIR BY SITTING ON IT THIS MORNING, RIPPING YOUR TROUSERS.

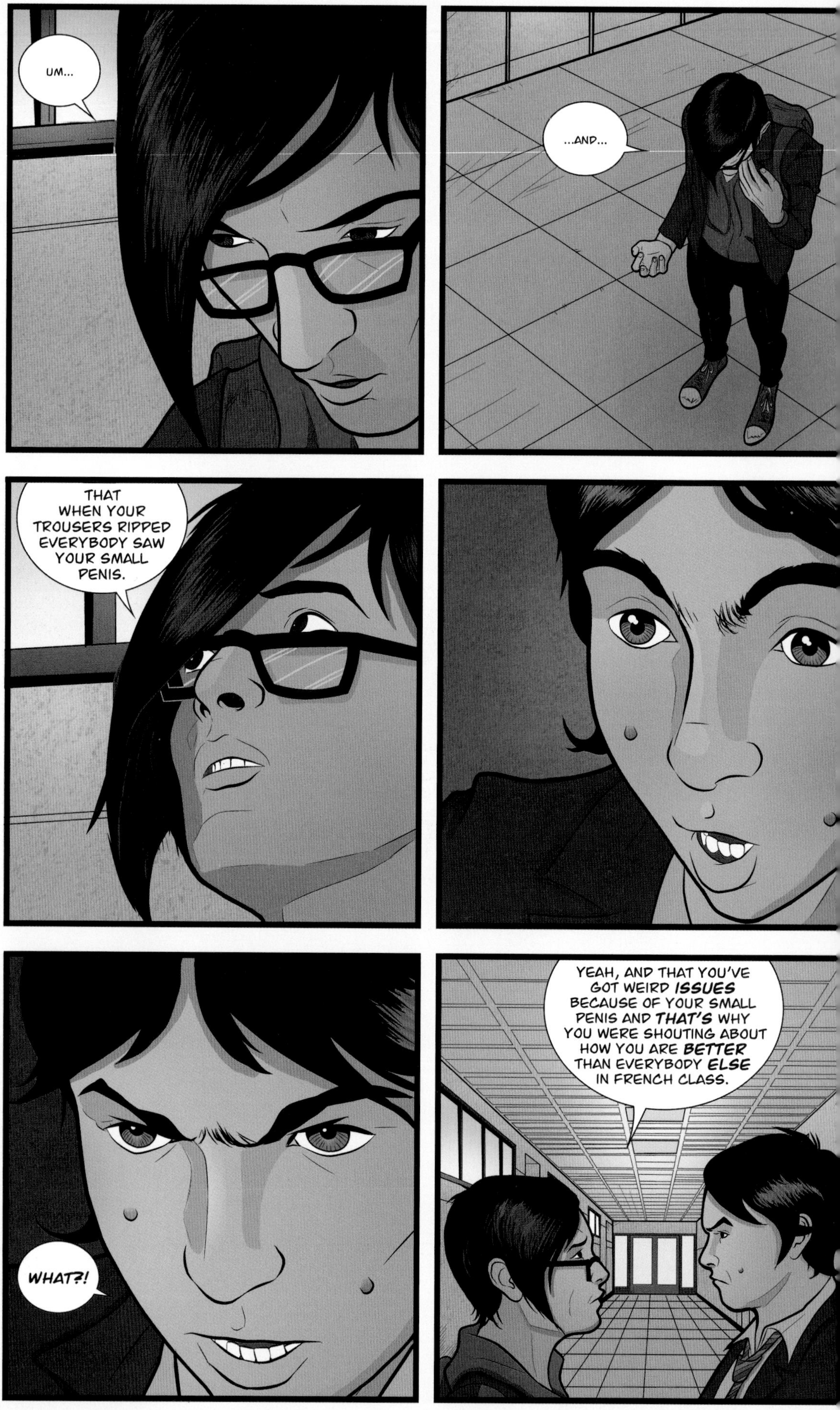
UM...
...AND...
THAT WHEN YOUR TROUSERS RIPPED EVERYBODY SAW YOUR SMALL PENIS.
WHAT?!
YEAH, AND THAT YOU'VE GOT WEIRD ISSUES BECAUSE OF YOUR SMALL PENIS AND THAT'S WHY YOU WERE SHOUTING ABOUT HOW YOU ARE BETTER THAN EVERYBODY ELSE IN FRENCH CLASS.

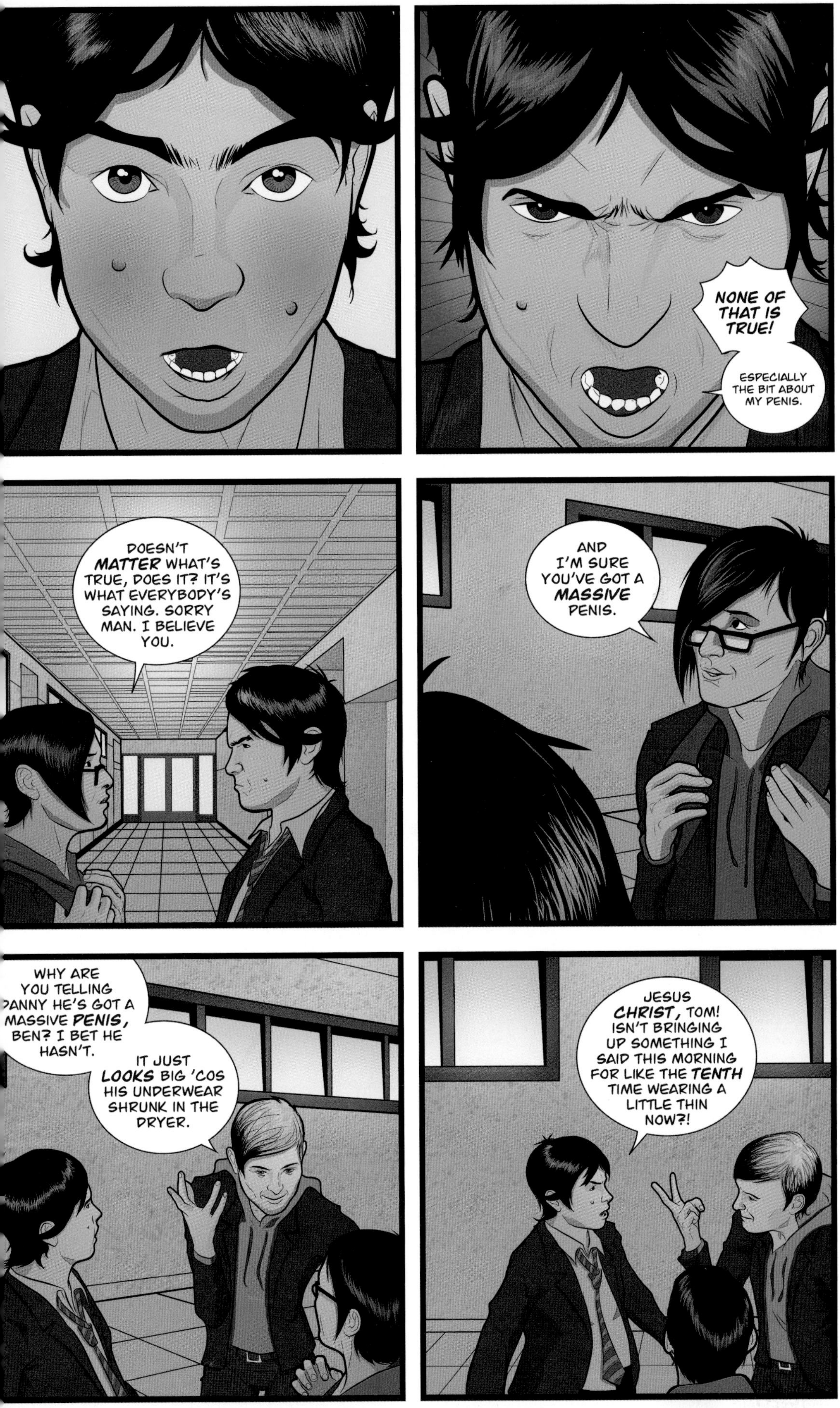
NONE OF THAT IS TRUE!
ESPECIALLY THE BIT ABOUT MY PENIS.
DOESN'T MATTER WHAT'S TRUE, DOES IT? IT'S WHAT EVERYBODY'S SAYING. SORRY MAN. I BELIEVE YOU.
AND I'M SURE YOU'VE GOT A MASSIVE PENIS.
WHY ARE YOU TELLING DANNY HE'S GOT A MASSIVE PENIS, BEN? I BET HE HASN'T.
IT JUST LOOKS BIG 'COS HIS UNDERWEAR SHRUNK IN THE DRYER.
JESUS CHRIST, TOM! ISN'T BRINGING UP SOMETHING I SAID THIS MORNING FOR LIKE THE TENTH TIME WEARING A LITTLE THIN NOW?!

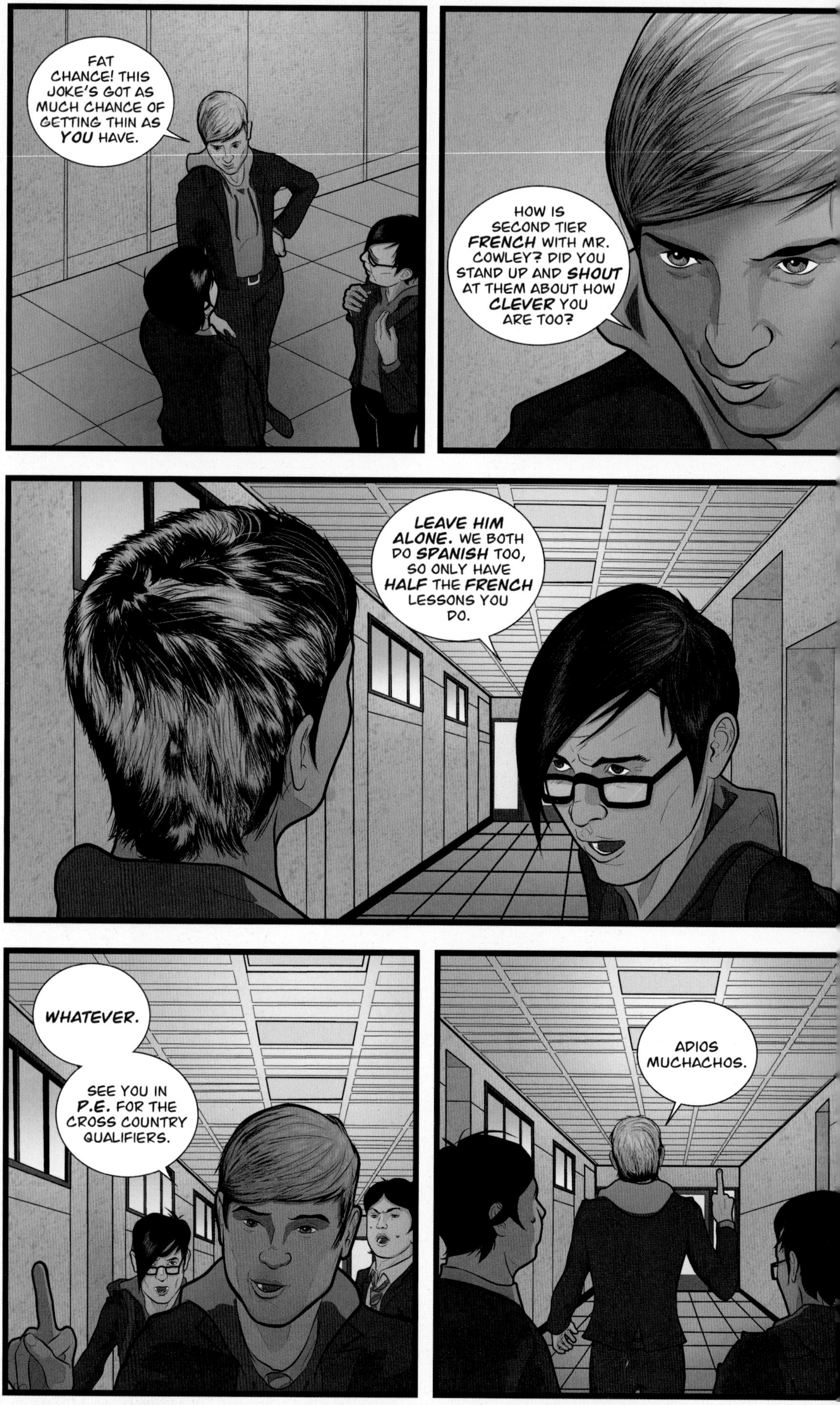
FAT CHANCE! THIS JOKE'S GOT AS MUCH CHANCE OF GETTING THIN AS YOU HAVE.
HOW IS SECOND TIER FRENCH WITH MR. COWLEY? DID YOU STAND UP AND SHOUT AT THEM ABOUT HOW CLEVER YOU ARE TOO?
LEAVE HIM ALONE. WE BOTH DO SPANISH TOO, SO ONLY HAVE HALF THE FRENCH LESSONS YOU DO.
WHATEVER.
SEE YOU IN P.E. FOR THE CROSS COUNTRY QUALIFIERS.
ADIOS MUCHACHOS.

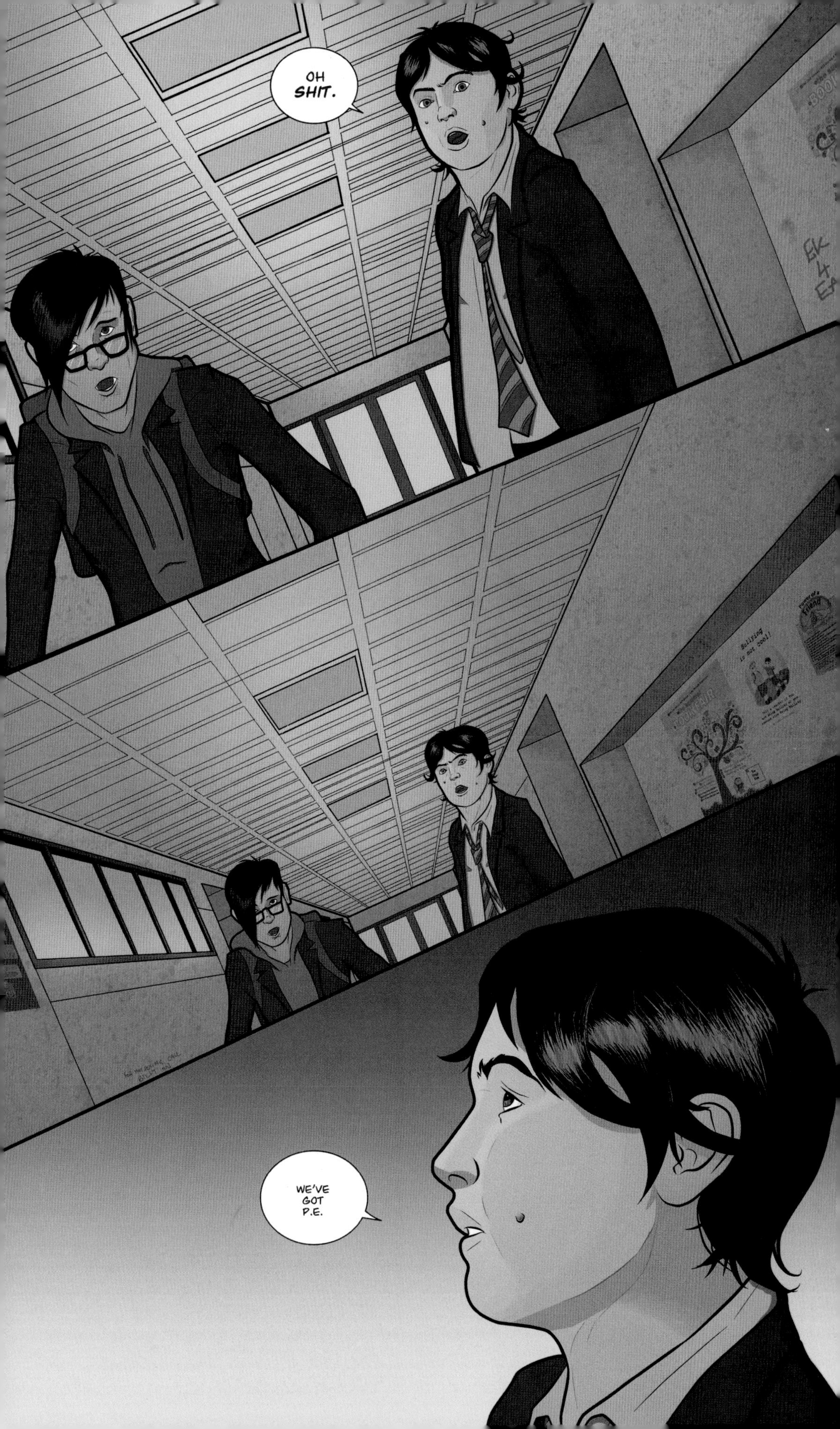
OH SHIT.
Bullying is not cool!
WE'VE GOT P.E.

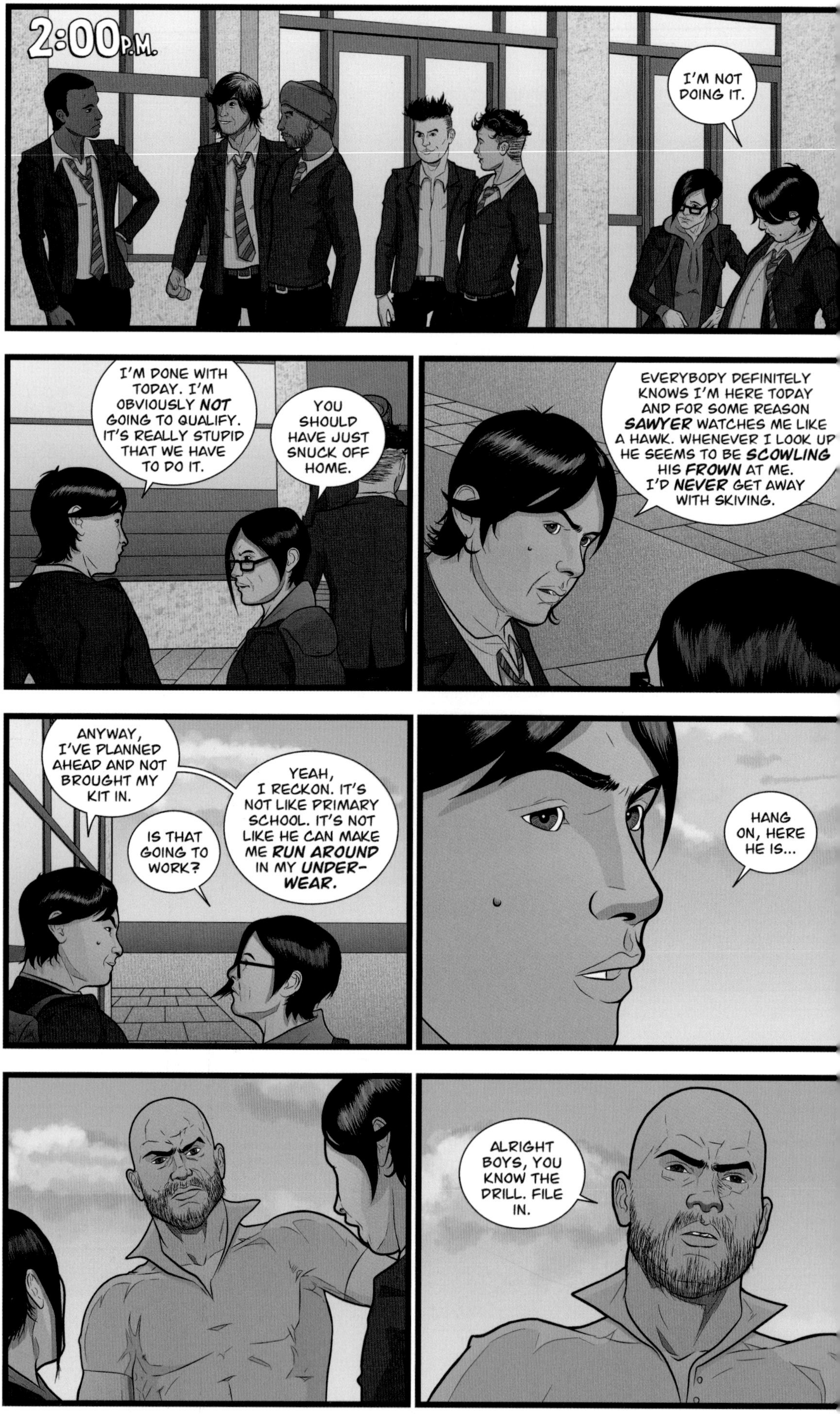
2:00P.M.
I'M NOT DOING IT.
I'M DONE WITH TODAY. I'M OBVIOUSLY NOT GOING TO QUALIFY. IT'S REALLY STUPID THAT WE HAVE TO DO IT.
YOU SHOULD HAVE JUST SNUCK OFF HOME.
EVERYBODY DEFINITELY KNOWS I'M HERE TODAY AND FOR SOME REASON SAWYER WATCHES ME LIKE A HAWK. WHENEVER I LOOK UP HE SEEMS TO BE SCOWLING HIS FROWN AT ME. I'D NEVER GET AWAY WITH SKIVING.
ANYWAY, I'VE PLANNED AHEAD AND NOT BROUGHT MY KIT IN.
IS THAT GOING TO WORK?
YEAH, I RECKON. IT'S NOT LIKE PRIMARY SCHOOL. IT'S NOT LIKE HE CAN MAKE ME RUN AROUND IN MY UNDER-WEAR.
HANG ON, HERE HE IS...
ALRIGHT BOYS, YOU KNOW THE DRILL. FILE IN.

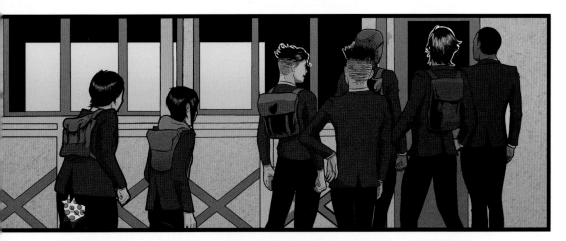

SORRY SIR, I LEFT MY KIT AT HOME.

WHAT?! YOU "ACCIDENTALLY" FORGOT IT?

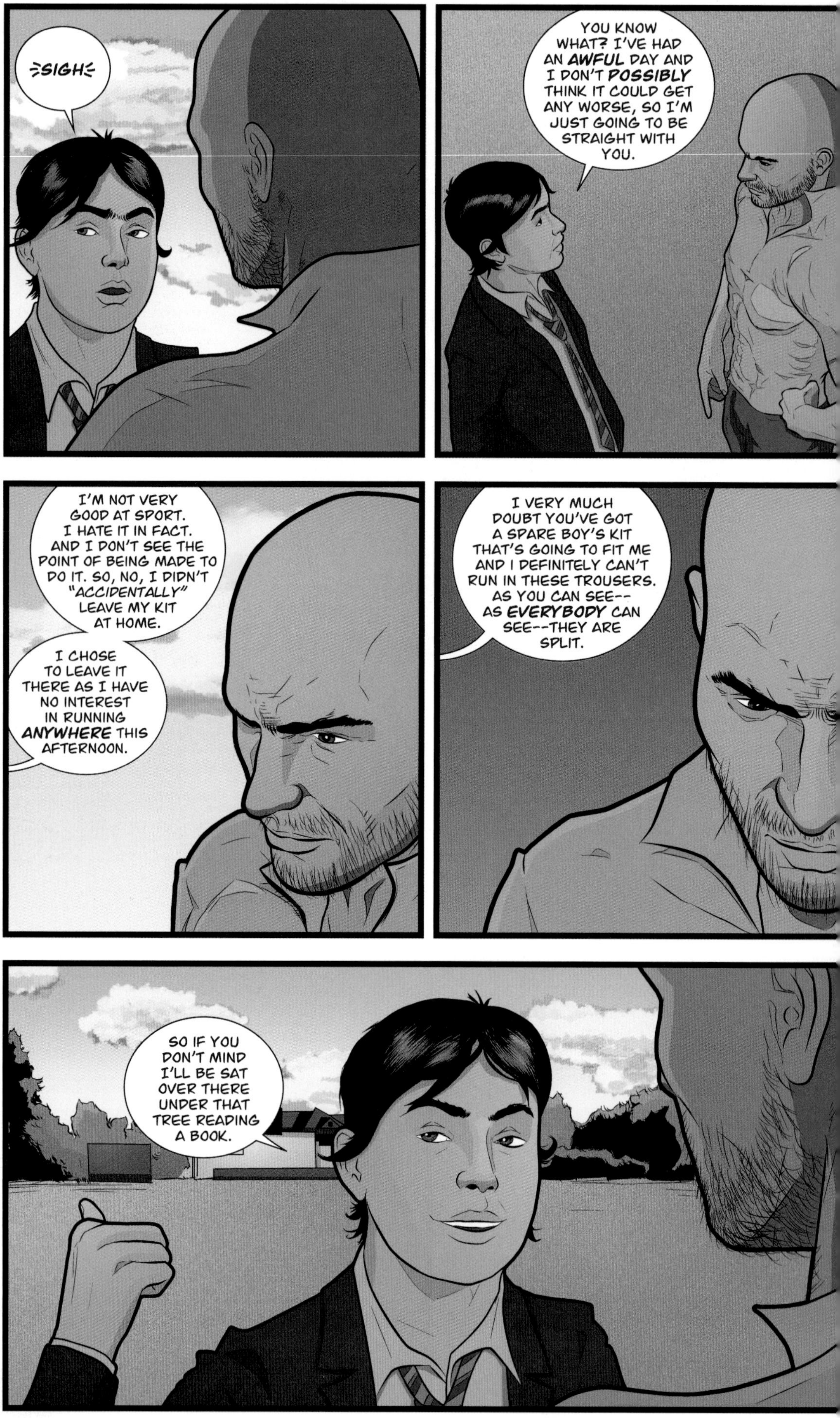
SIGH
YOU KNOW WHAT? I'VE HAD AN AWFUL DAY AND I DON'T POSSIBLY THINK IT COULD GET ANY WORSE, SO I'M JUST GOING TO BE STRAIGHT WITH YOU.
I'M NOT VERY GOOD AT SPORT. I HATE IT IN FACT. AND I DON'T SEE THE POINT OF BEING MADE TO DO IT. SO, NO, I DIDN'T "ACCIDENTALLY" LEAVE MY KIT AT HOME.
I CHOSE TO LEAVE IT THERE AS I HAVE NO INTEREST IN RUNNING ANYWHERE THIS AFTERNOON.
I VERY MUCH DOUBT YOU'VE GOT A SPARE BOY'S KIT THAT'S GOING TO FIT ME AND I DEFINITELY CAN'T RUN IN THESE TROUSERS. AS YOU CAN SEE-- AS EVERYBODY CAN SEE--THEY ARE SPLIT.
SO IF YOU DON'T MIND I'LL BE SAT OVER THERE UNDER THAT TREE READING A BOOK.

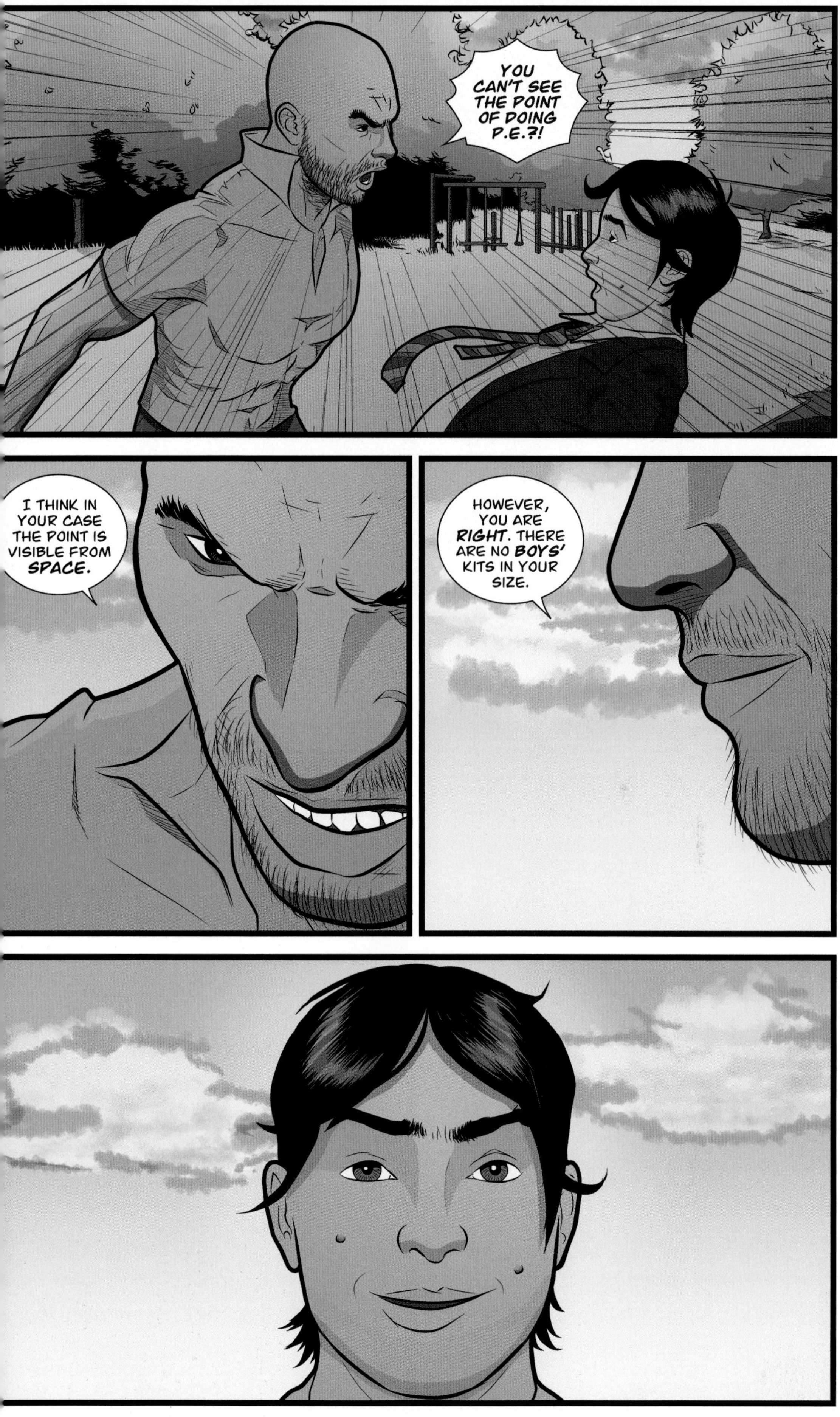
YOU CAN'T SEE THE POINT OF DOING P.E.?!
I THINK IN YOUR CASE THE POINT IS VISIBLE FROM SPACE.
HOWEVER, YOU ARE RIGHT. THERE ARE NO BOYS' KITS IN YOUR SIZE.

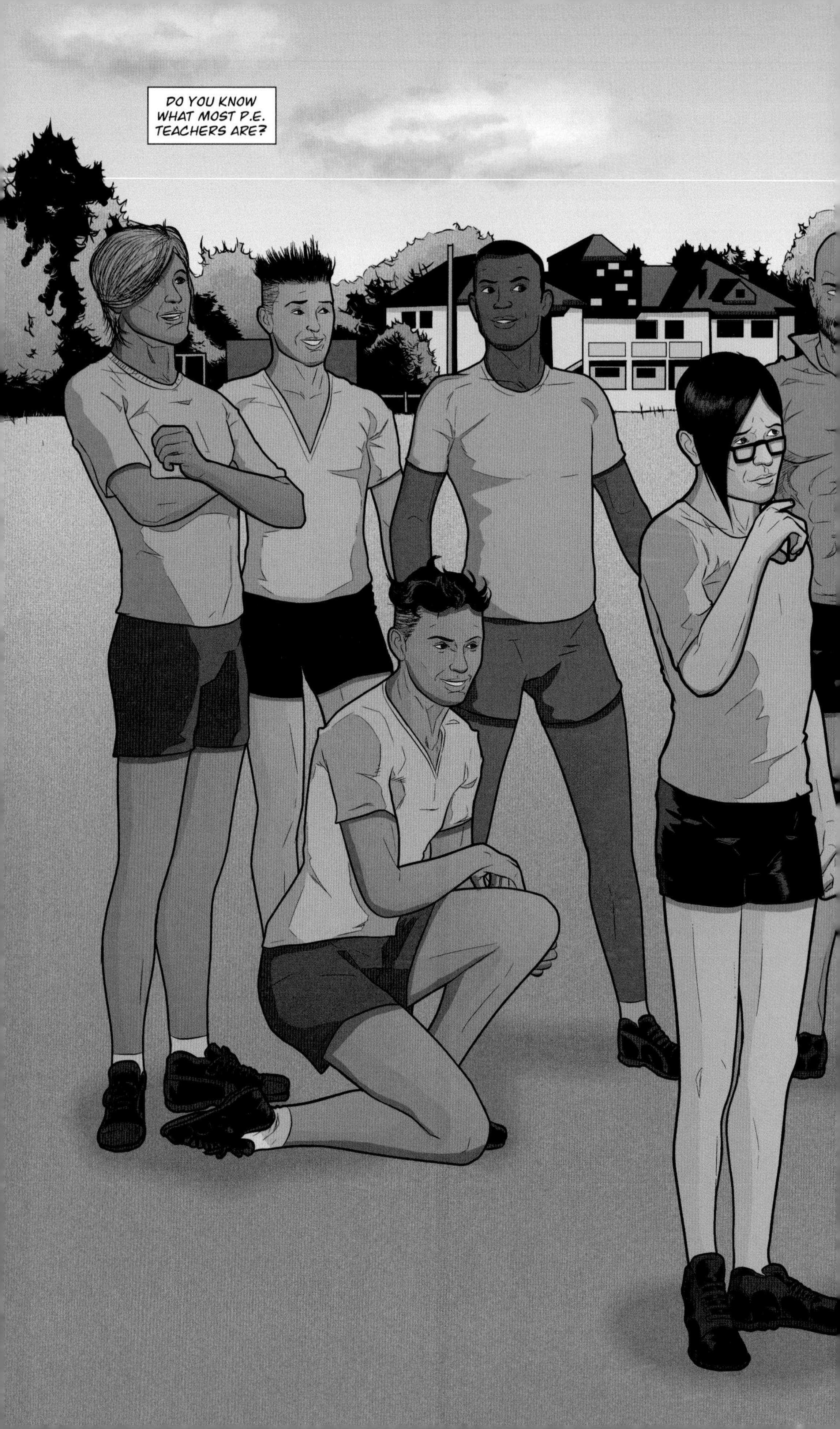
DO YOU KNOW WHAT MOST P.E. TEACHERS ARE?

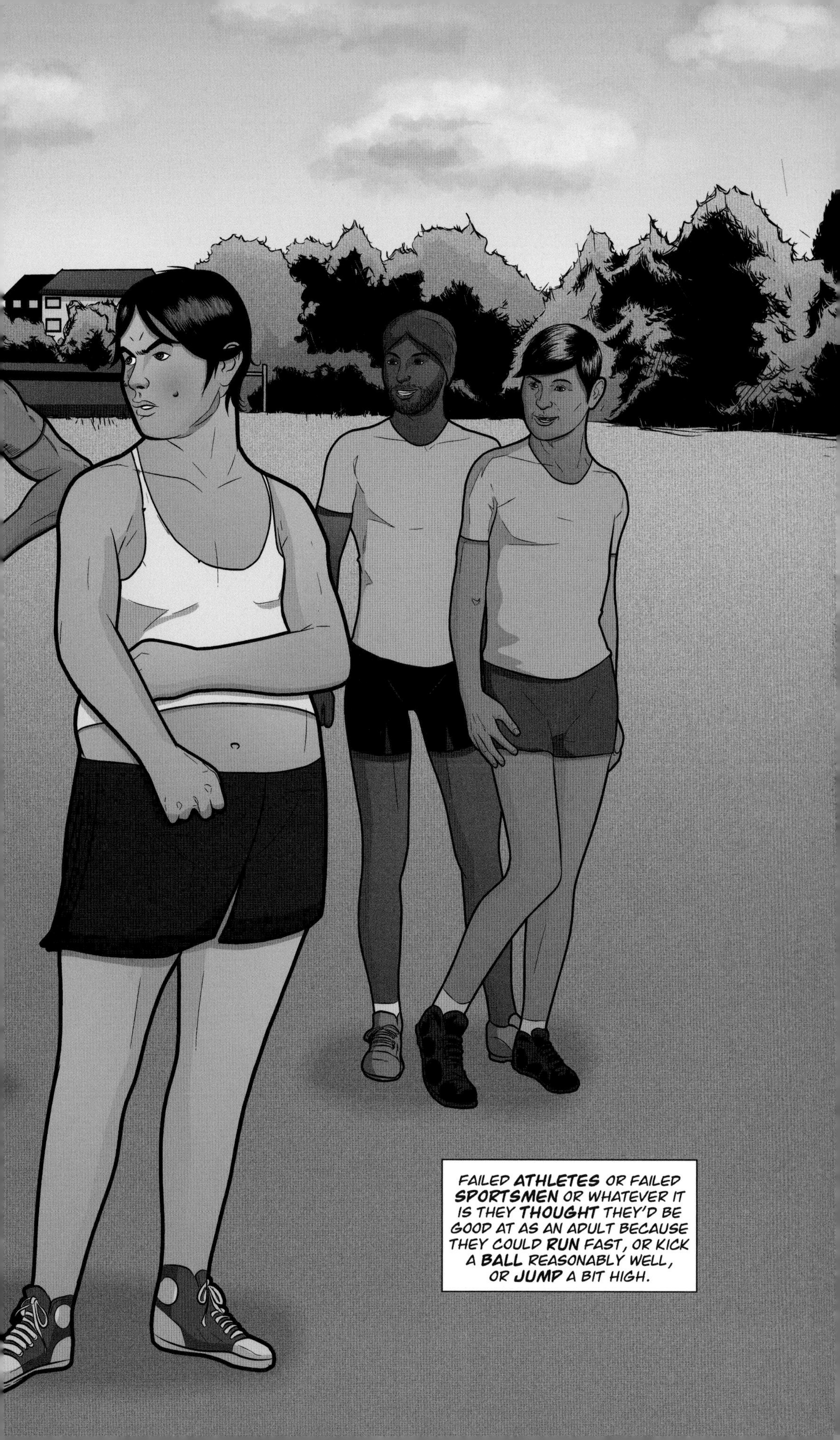
FAILED **ATHLETES** OR FAILED **SPORTSMEN** OR WHATEVER IT IS THEY **THOUGHT** THEY'D BE GOOD AT AS AN ADULT BECAUSE THEY COULD **RUN** FAST, OR KICK A **BALL** REASONABLY WELL, OR **JUMP** A BIT HIGH.

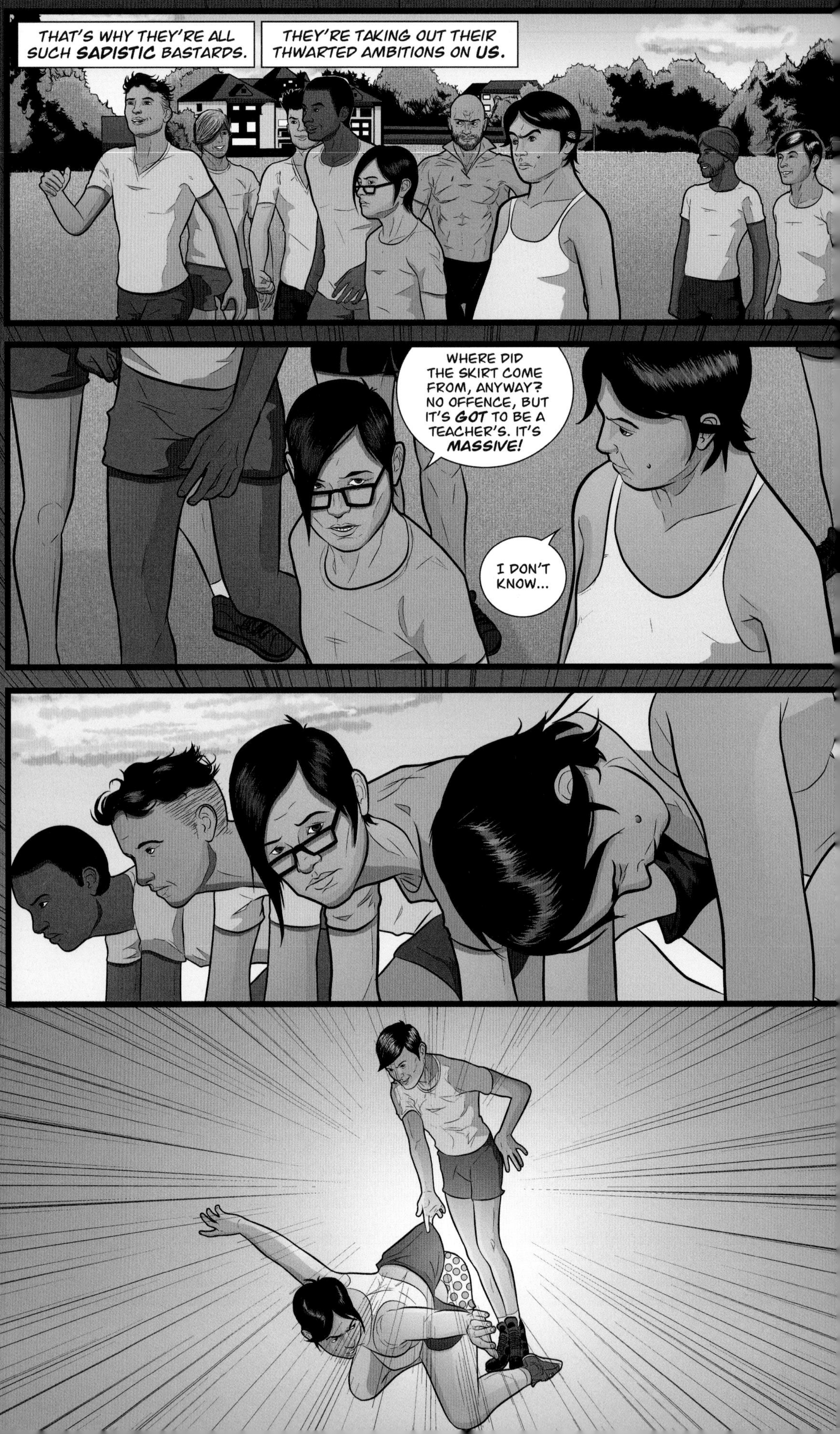
THAT'S WHY THEY'RE ALL SUCH SADISTIC BASTARDS.
THEY'RE TAKING OUT THEIR THWARTED AMBITIONS ON US.
WHERE DID THE SKIRT COME FROM, ANYWAY? NO OFFENCE, BUT IT'S GOT TO BE A TEACHER'S. IT'S MASSIVE!
I DON'T KNOW...

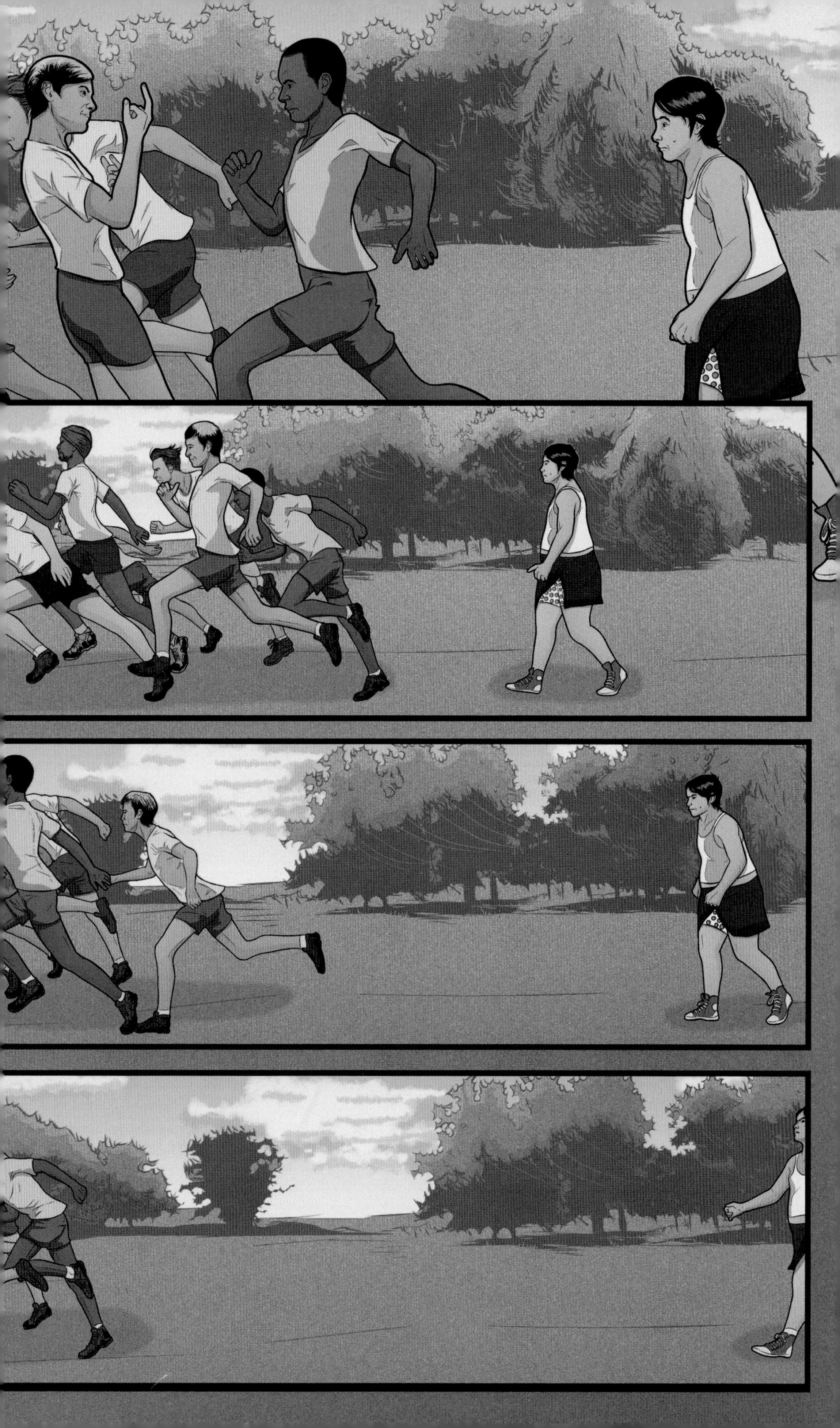

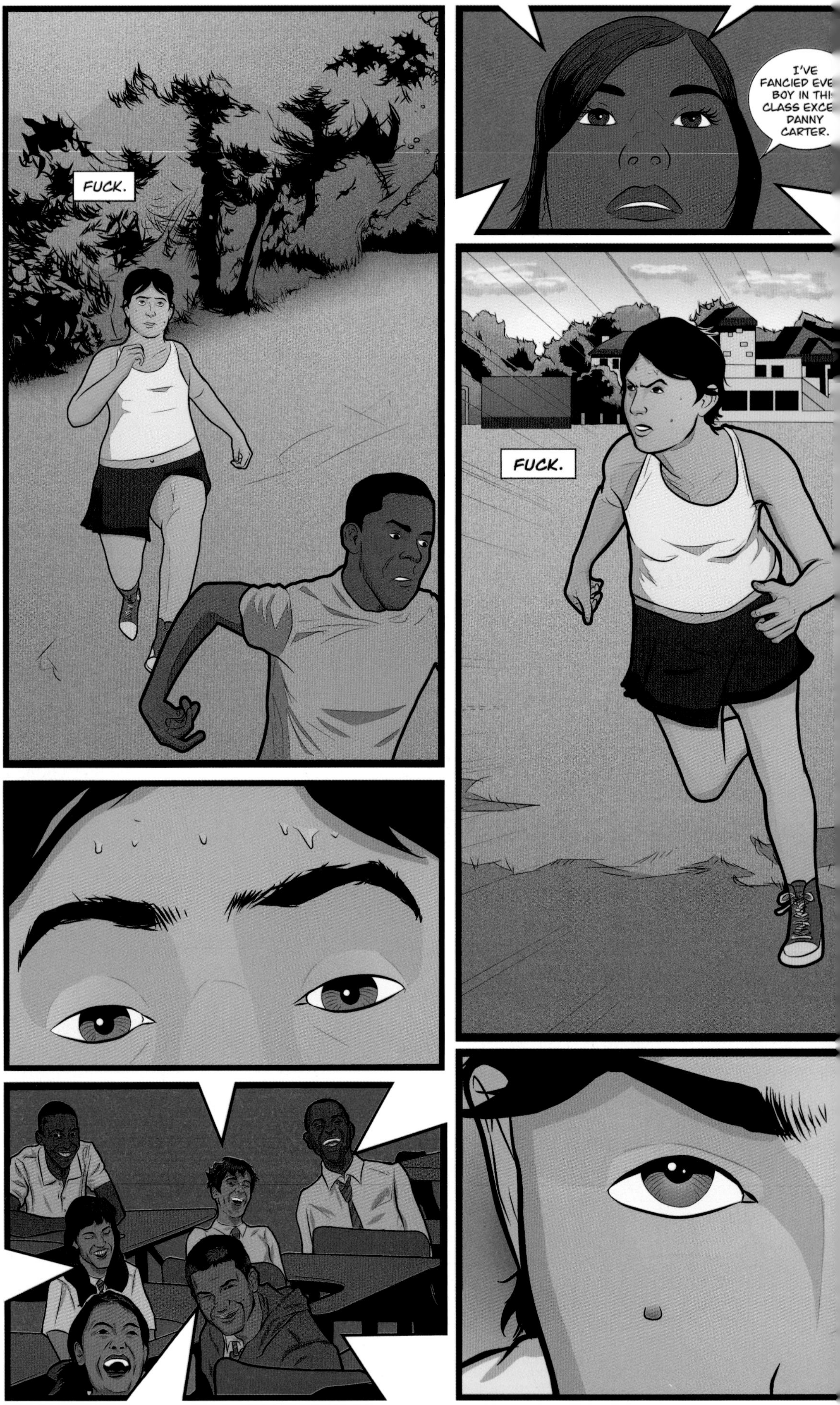
FUCK.
I'VE FANCIED EVE BOY IN THI CLASS EXCE DANNY CARTER.
FUCK.

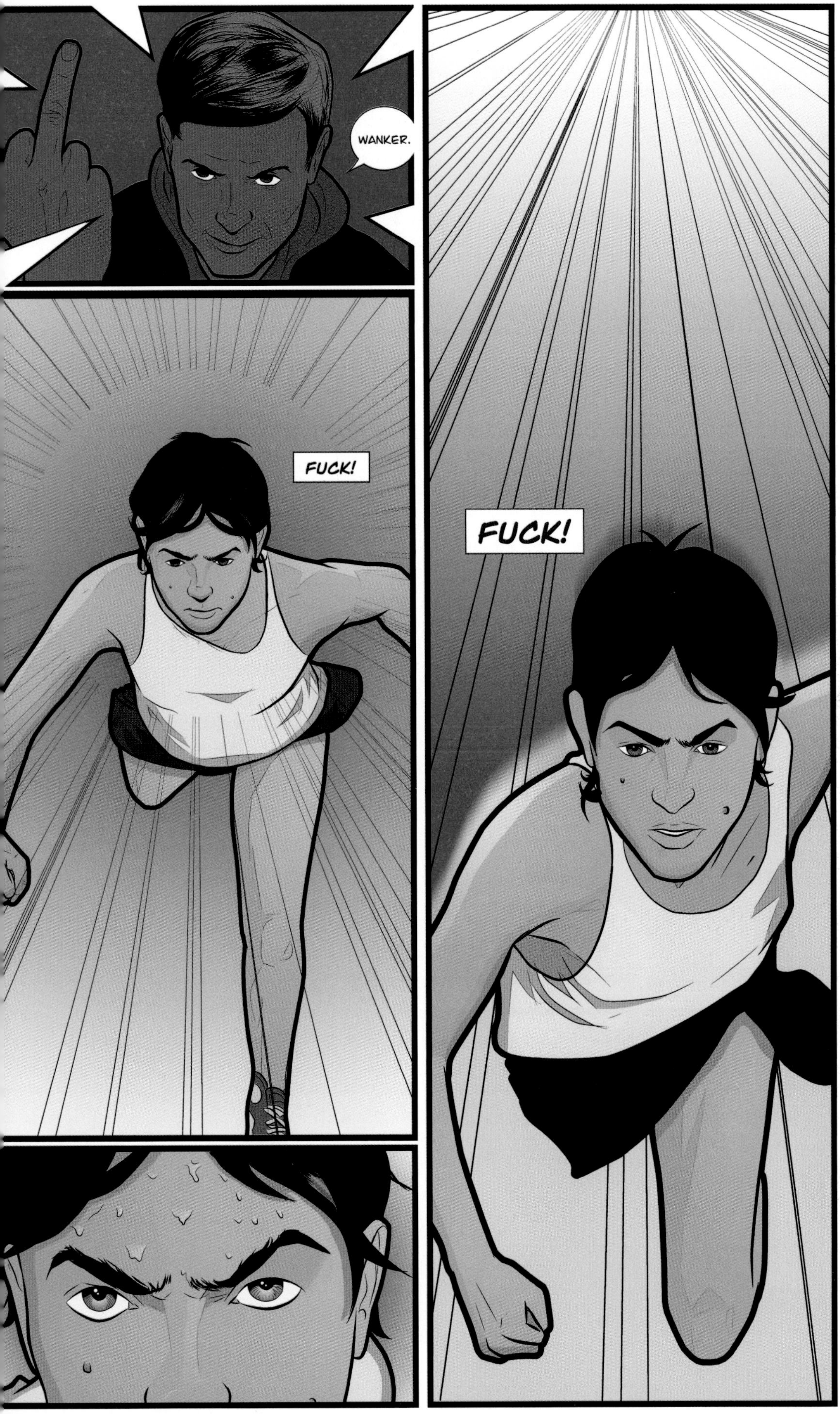
WANKER.
FUCK!
FUCK!

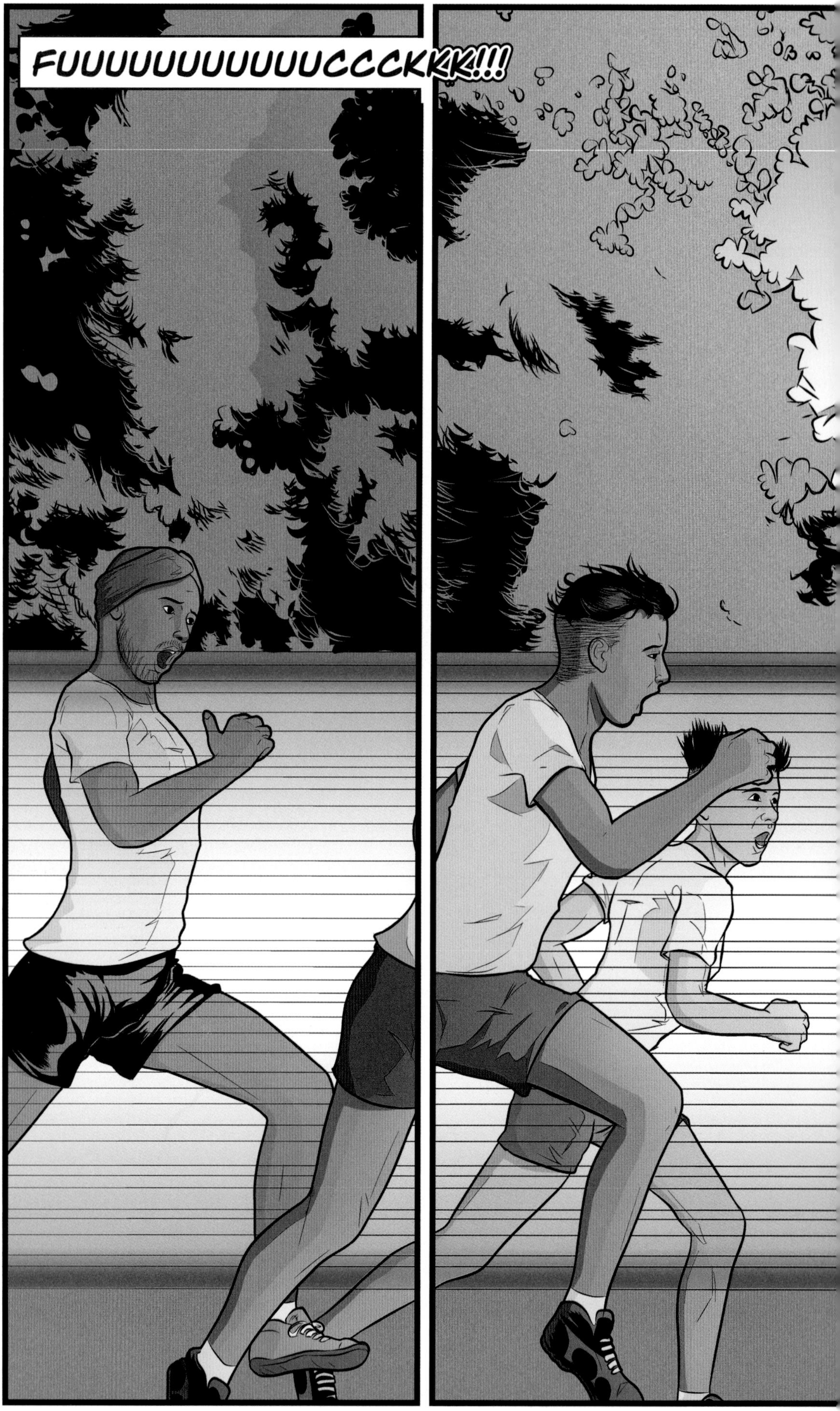
FUUUUUUUUUUUCCCCKKK!!!

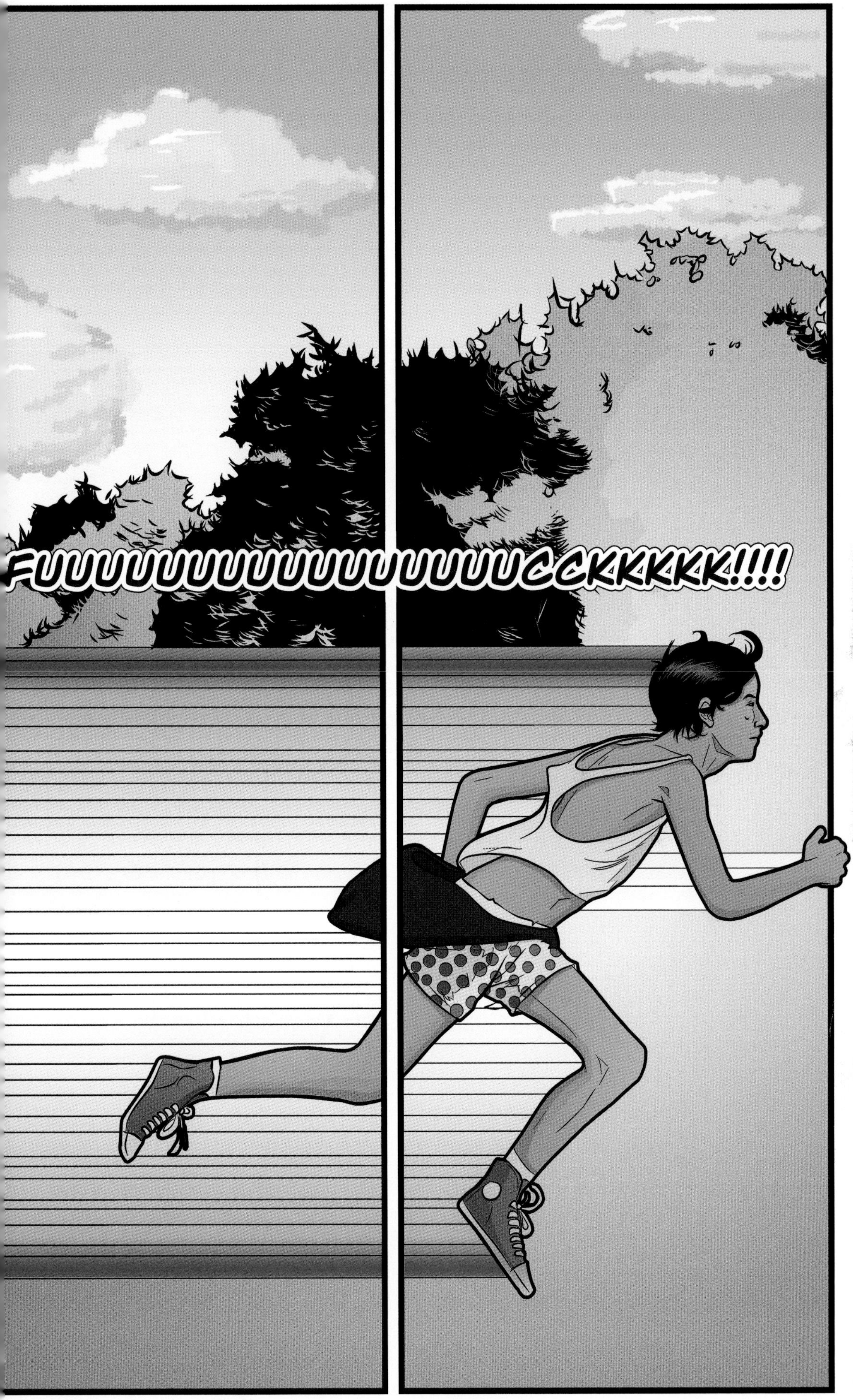
FUUUUUUUUUUUUUUUUUUCCKKKKKK!!!!

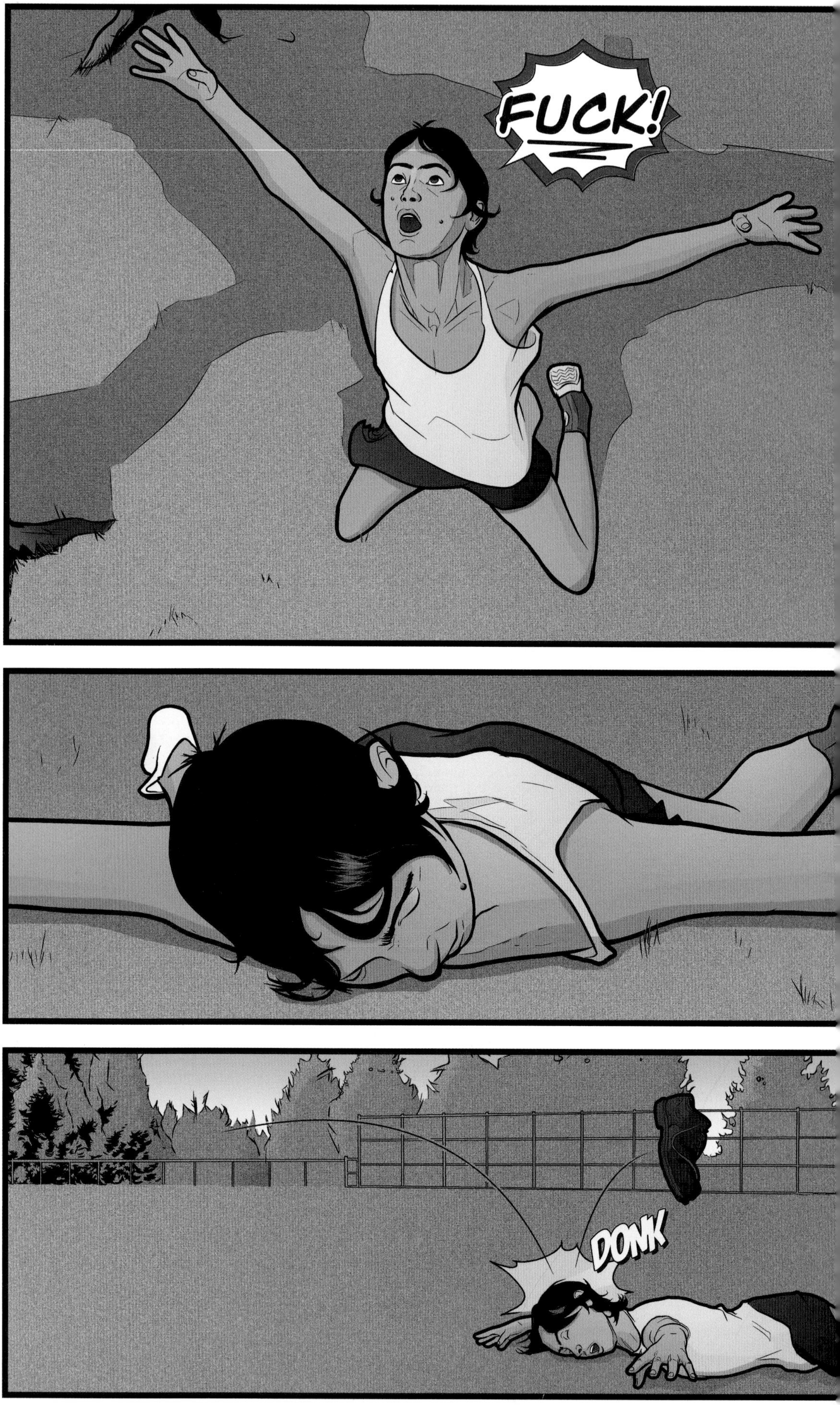
FUCK!
DONK

CHAPTER 2

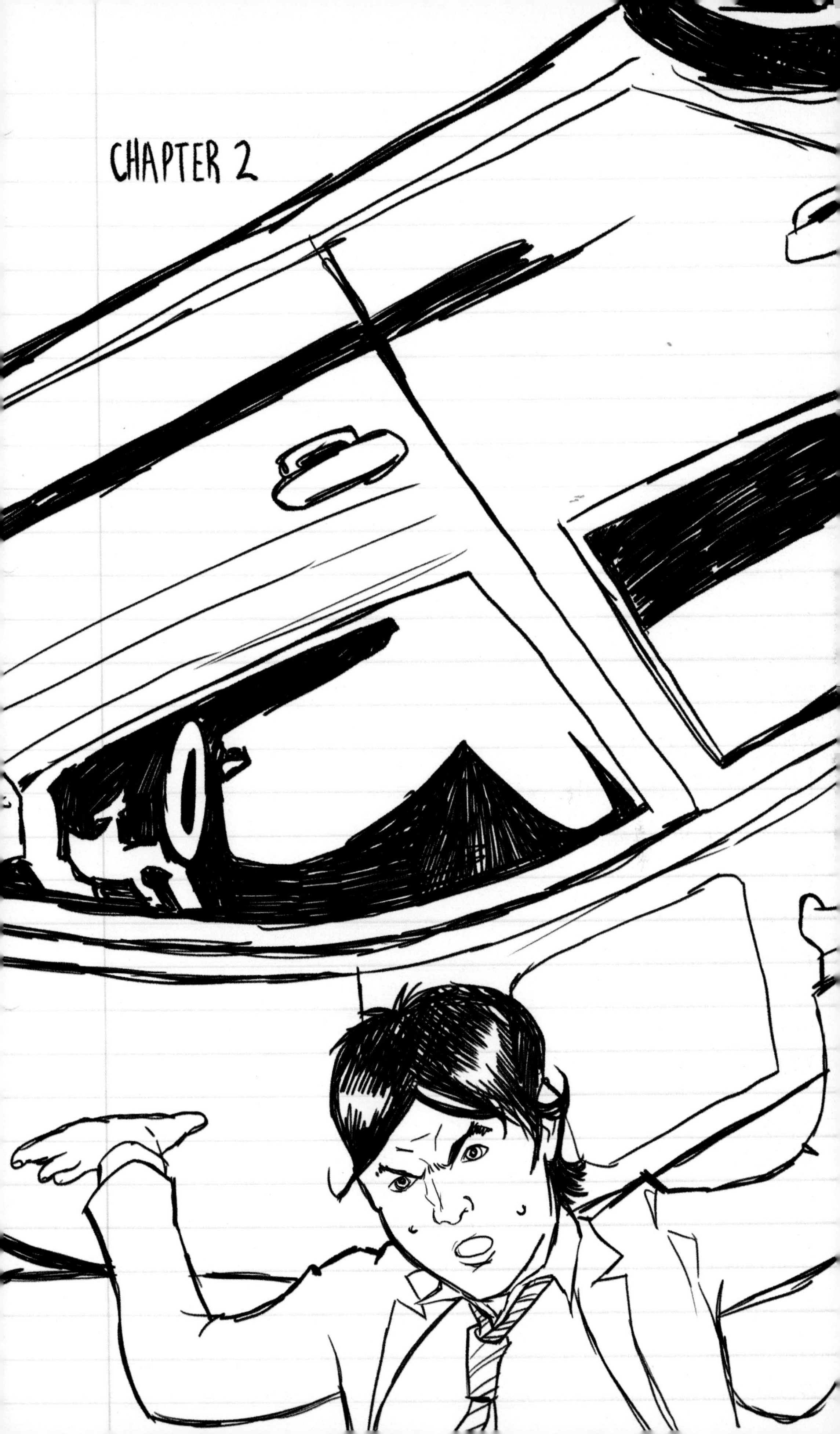

TWO

WEEKS

LATER...

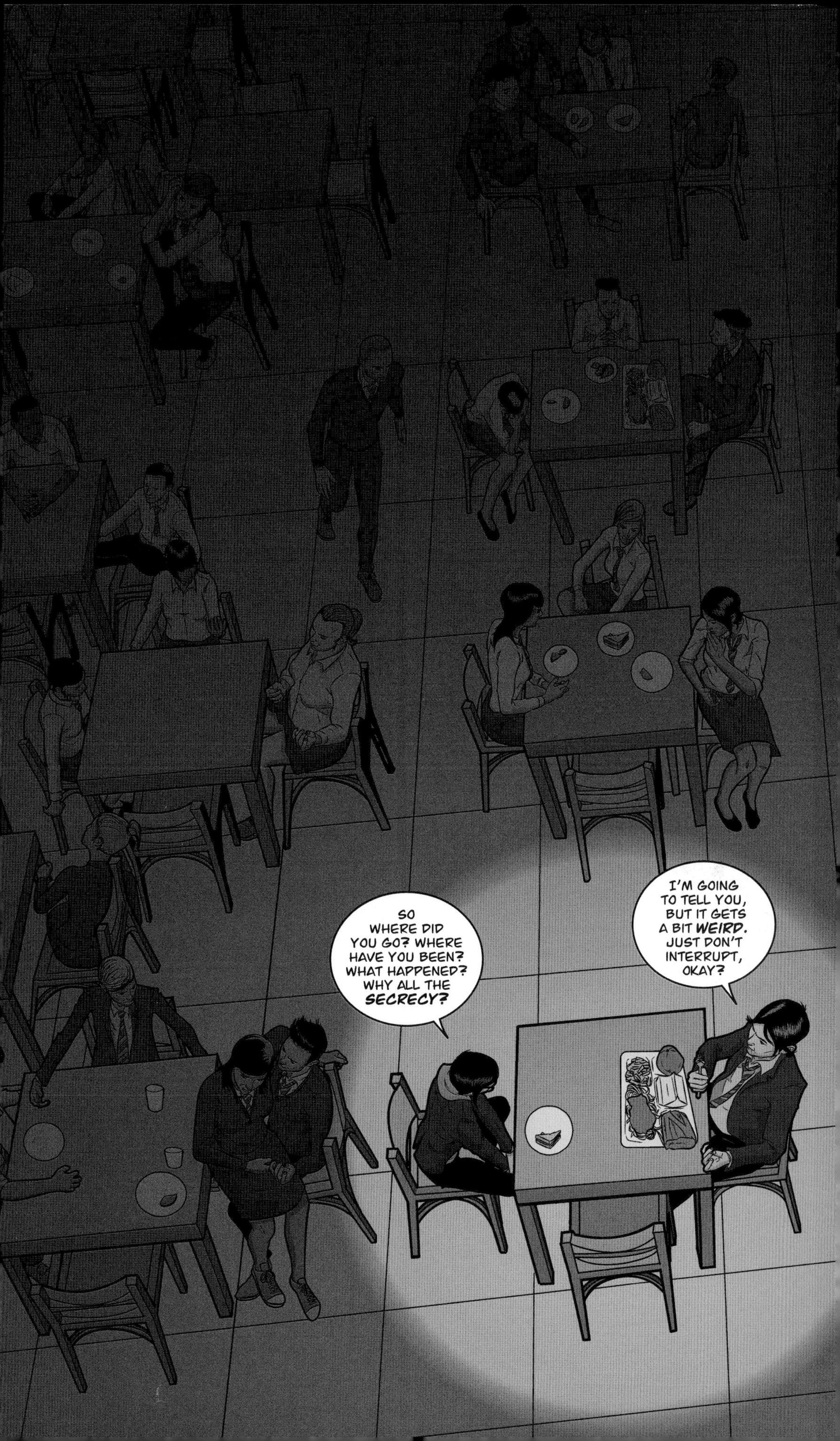
SO WHERE DID YOU GO? WHERE HAVE YOU BEEN? WHAT HAPPENED? WHY ALL THE SECRECY?
I'M GOING TO TELL YOU, BUT IT GETS A BIT WEIRD. JUST DON'T INTERRUPT, OKAY?

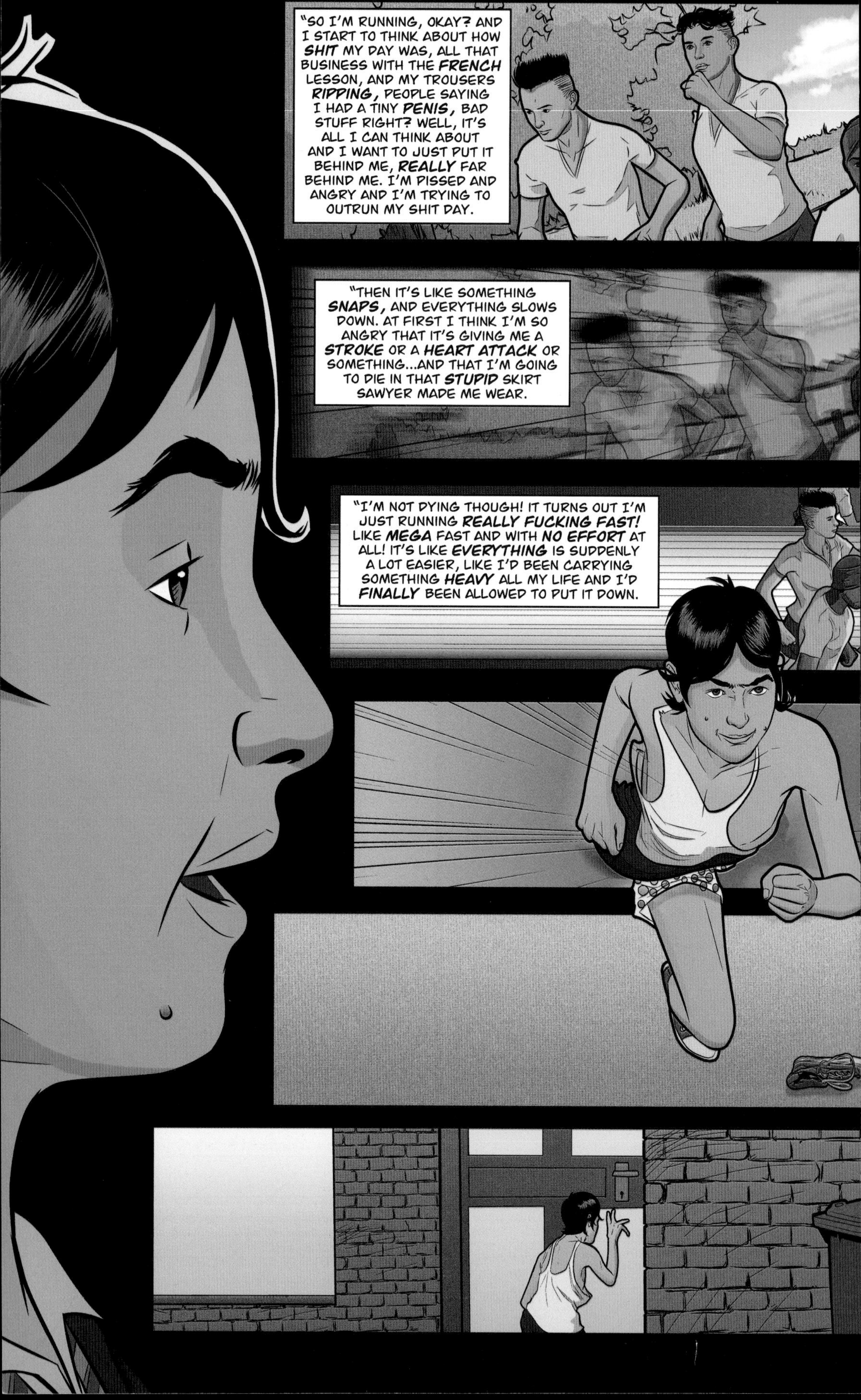
"SO I'M RUNNING, OKAY? AND I START TO THINK ABOUT HOW SHIT MY DAY WAS, ALL THAT BUSINESS WITH THE FRENCH LESSON, AND MY TROUSERS RIPPING, PEOPLE SAYING I HAD A TINY PENIS, BAD STUFF RIGHT? WELL, IT'S ALL I CAN THINK ABOUT AND I WANT TO JUST PUT IT BEHIND ME, REALLY FAR BEHIND ME. I'M PISSED AND ANGRY AND I'M TRYING TO OUTRUN MY SHIT DAY.
"THEN IT'S LIKE SOMETHING SNAPS, AND EVERYTHING SLOWS DOWN. AT FIRST I THINK I'M SO ANGRY THAT IT'S GIVING ME A STROKE OR A HEART ATTACK OR SOMETHING...AND THAT I'M GOING TO DIE IN THAT STUPID SKIRT SAWYER MADE ME WEAR.
"I'M NOT DYING THOUGH! IT TURNS OUT I'M JUST RUNNING REALLY FUCKING FAST! LIKE MEGA FAST AND WITH NO EFFORT AT ALL! IT'S LIKE EVERYTHING IS SUDDENLY A LOT EASIER, LIKE I'D BEEN CARRYING SOMETHING HEAVY ALL MY LIFE AND I'D FINALLY BEEN ALLOWED TO PUT IT DOWN.

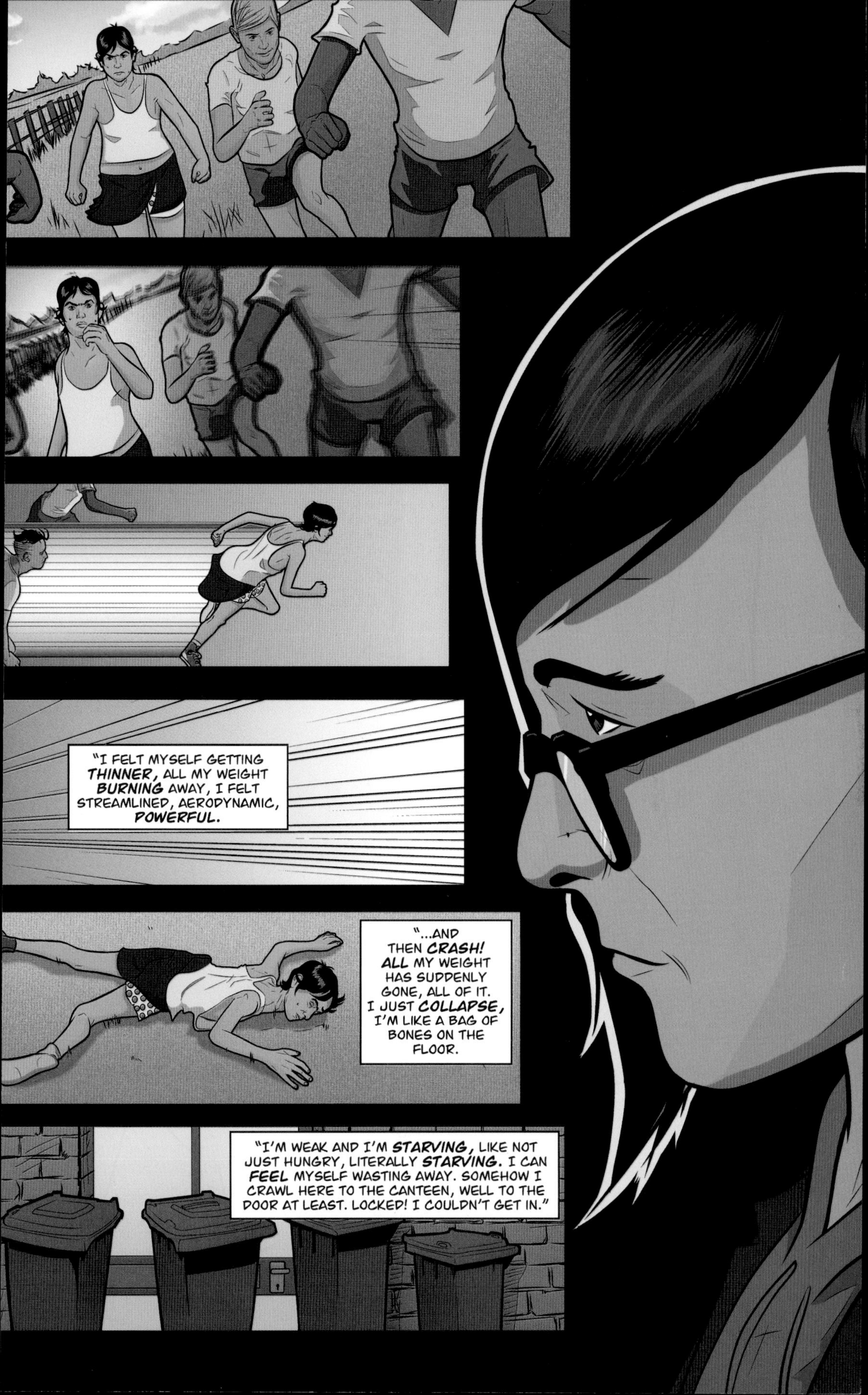
"I FELT MYSELF GETTING THINNER, ALL MY WEIGHT BURNING AWAY, I FELT STREAMLINED, AERODYNAMIC, POWERFUL.
"...AND THEN CRASH! ALL MY WEIGHT HAS SUDDENLY GONE, ALL OF IT. I JUST COLLAPSE, I'M LIKE A BAG OF BONES ON THE FLOOR.
"I'M WEAK AND I'M STARVING, LIKE NOT JUST HUNGRY, LITERALLY STARVING. I CAN FEEL MYSELF WASTING AWAY. SOMEHOW I CRAWL HERE TO THE CANTEEN, WELL TO THE DOOR AT LEAST. LOCKED! I COULDN'T GET IN."

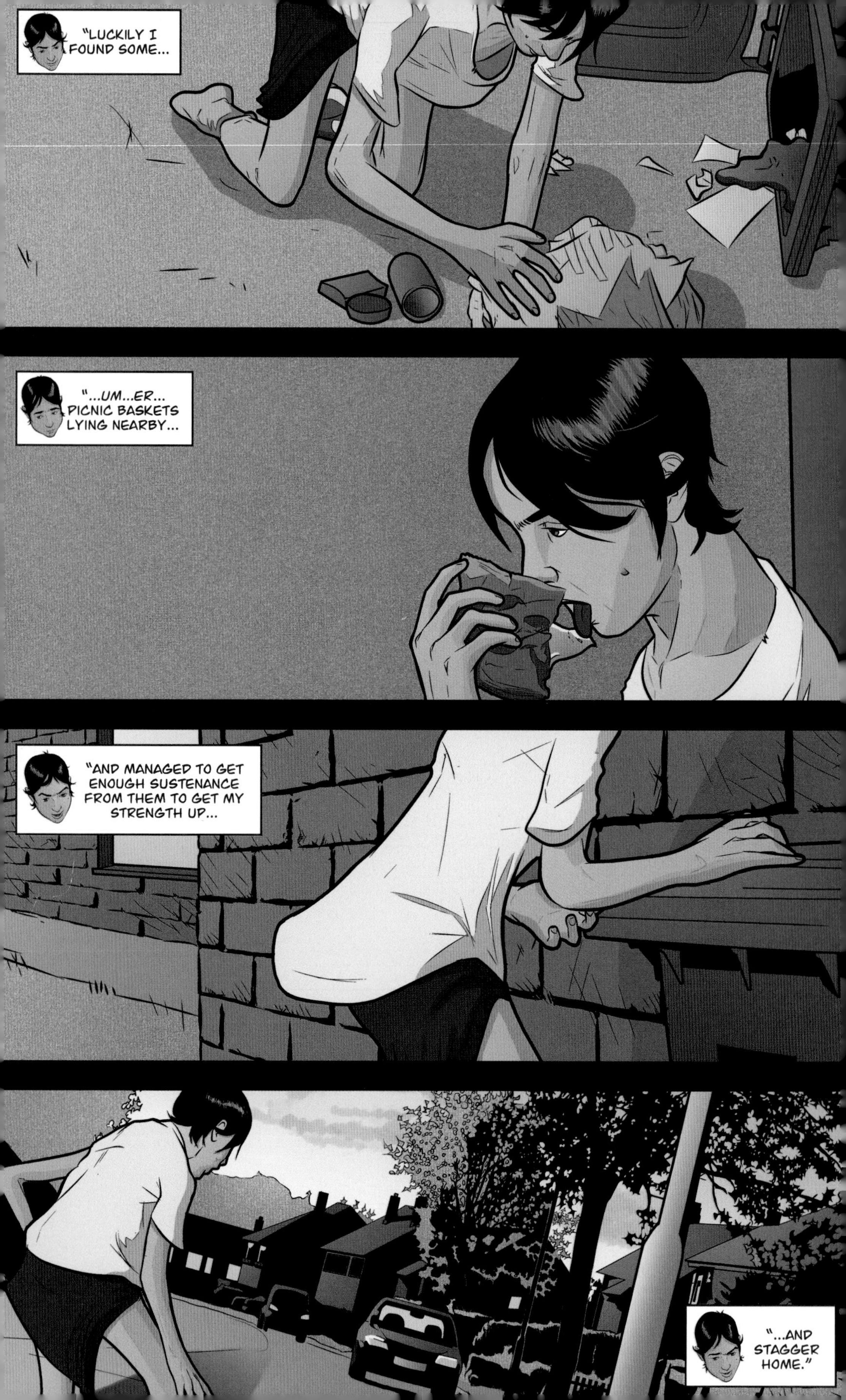
"LUCKILY I FOUND SOME...
"...UM...ER... PICNIC BASKETS LYING NEARBY...
"AND MANAGED TO GET ENOUGH SUSTENANCE FROM THEM TO GET MY STRENGTH UP...
"...AND STAGGER HOME."

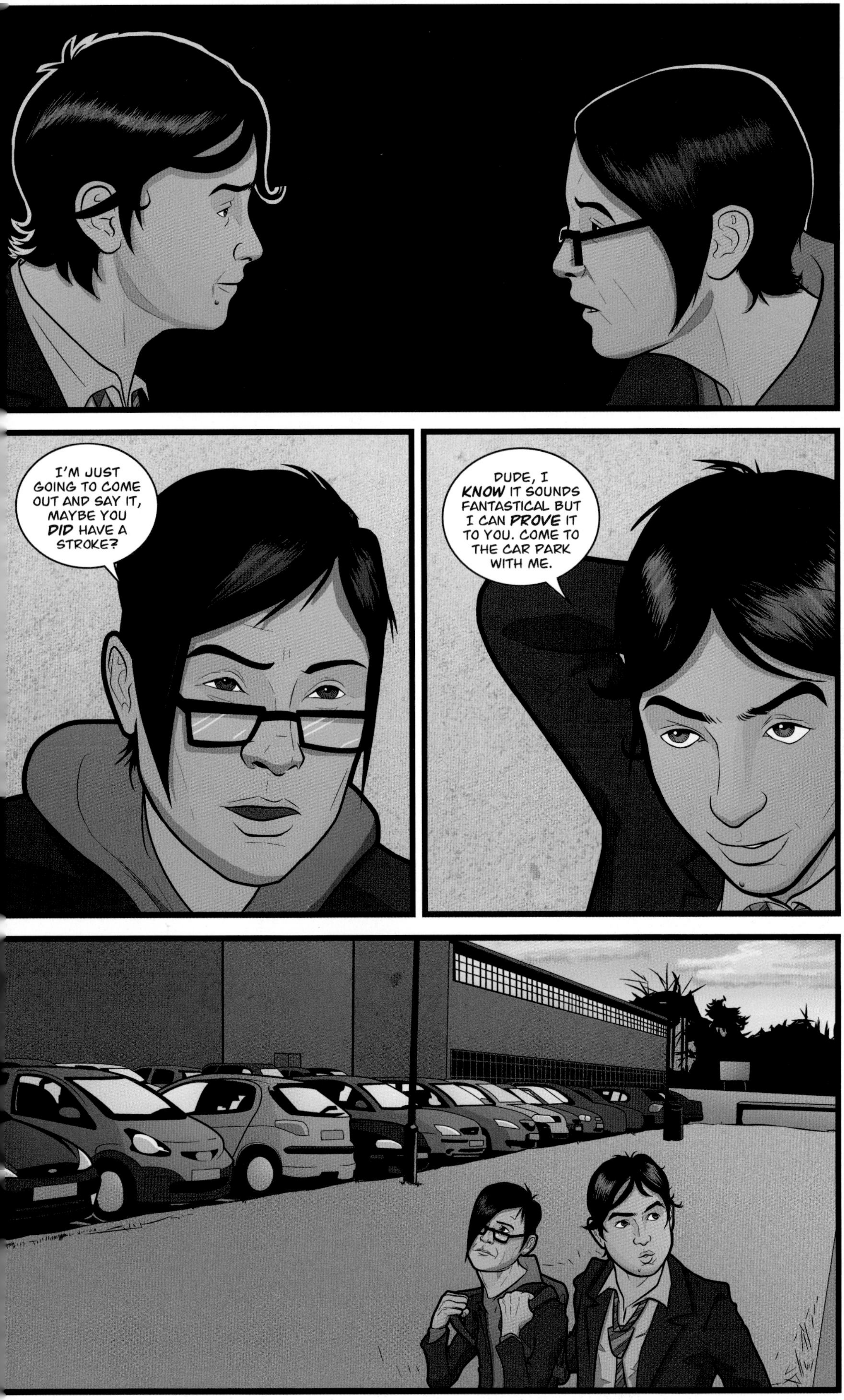
I'M JUST GOING TO COME OUT AND SAY IT, MAYBE YOU DID HAVE A STROKE?
DUDE, I KNOW IT SOUNDS FANTASTICAL BUT I CAN PROVE IT TO YOU. COME TO THE CAR PARK WITH ME.

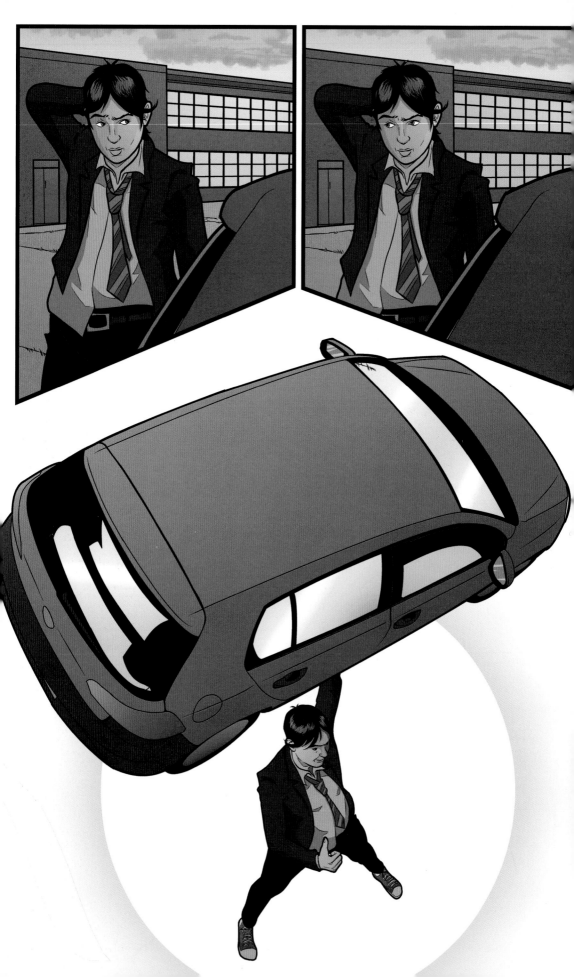

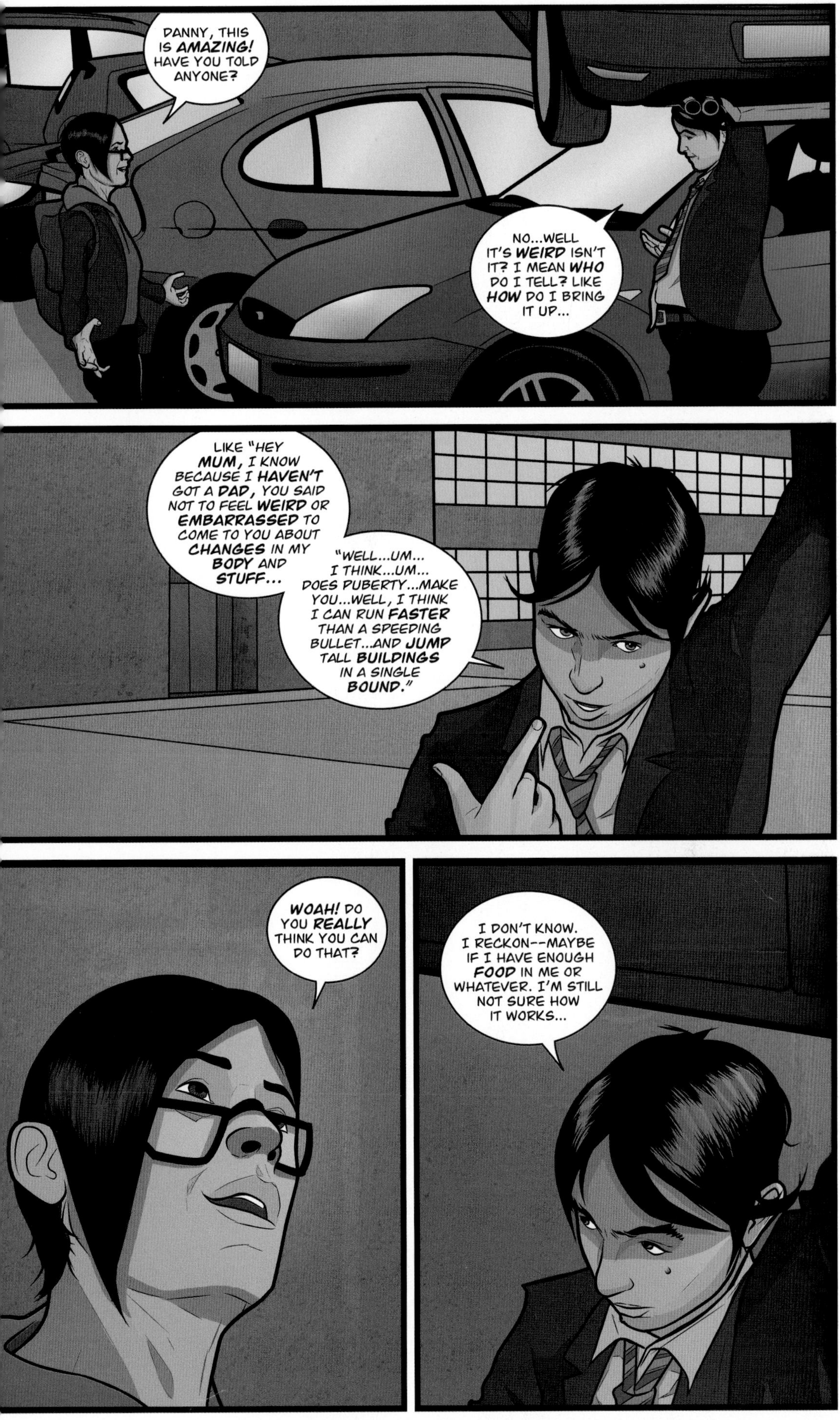
DANNY, THIS IS AMAZING! HAVE YOU TOLD ANYONE?
NO...WELL IT'S WEIRD ISN'T IT? I MEAN WHO DO I TELL? LIKE HOW DO I BRING IT UP...
LIKE "HEY MUM, I KNOW BECAUSE I HAVEN'T GOT A DAD, YOU SAID NOT TO FEEL WEIRD OR EMBARRASSED TO COME TO YOU ABOUT CHANGES IN MY BODY AND STUFF...
"WELL...UM... I THINK...UM... DOES PUBERTY...MAKE YOU...WELL, I THINK I CAN RUN FASTER THAN A SPEEDING BULLET...AND JUMP TALL BUILDINGS IN A SINGLE BOUND."
WOAH! DO YOU REALLY THINK YOU CAN DO THAT?
I DON'T KNOW. I RECKON--MAYBE IF I HAVE ENOUGH FOOD IN ME OR WHATEVER. I'M STILL NOT SURE HOW IT WORKS...

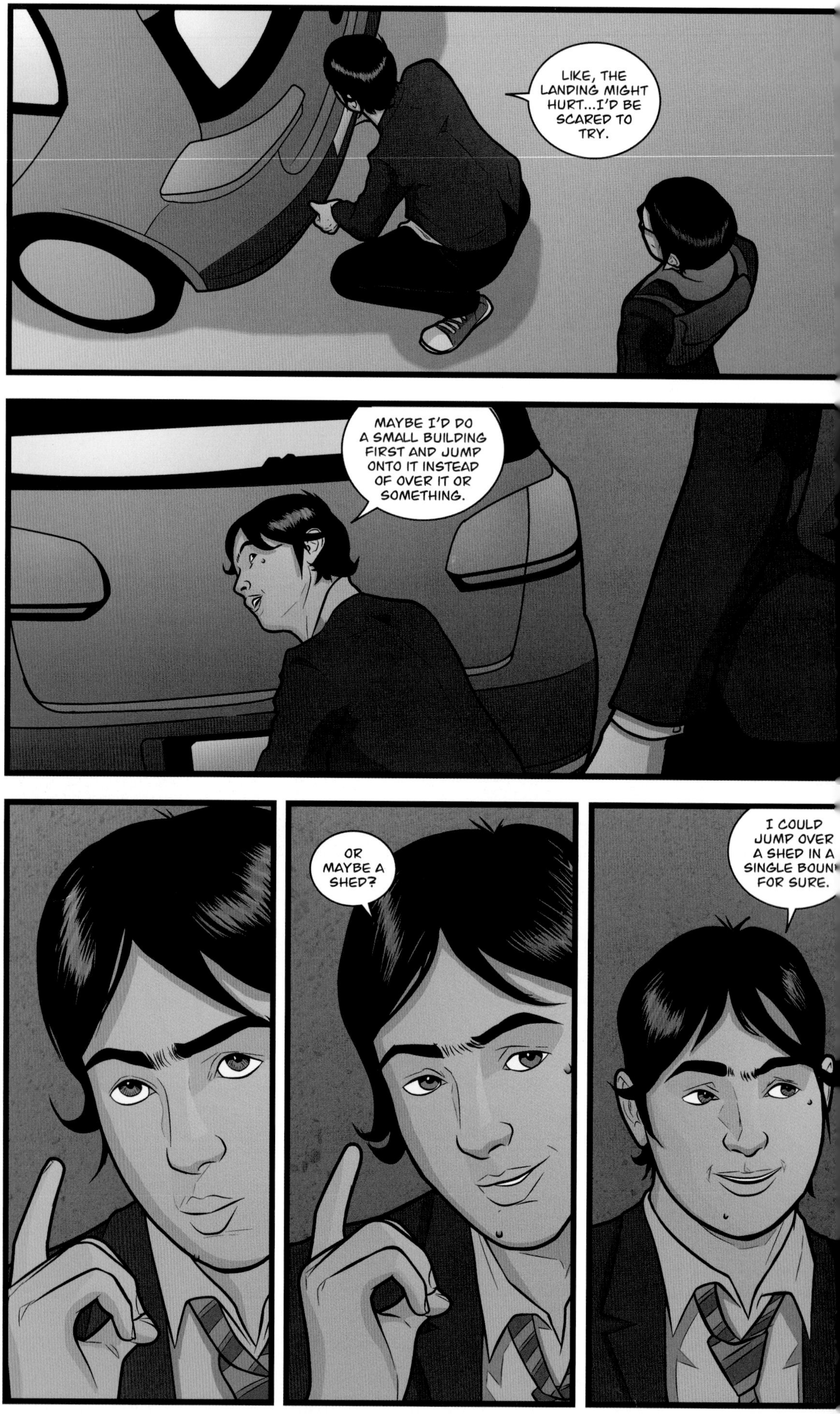
LIKE, THE LANDING MIGHT HURT...I'D BE SCARED TO TRY.
MAYBE I'D DO A SMALL BUILDING FIRST AND JUMP ONTO IT INSTEAD OF OVER IT OR SOMETHING.
OR MAYBE A SHED?
I COULD JUMP OVER A SHED IN A SINGLE BOUN FOR SURE.

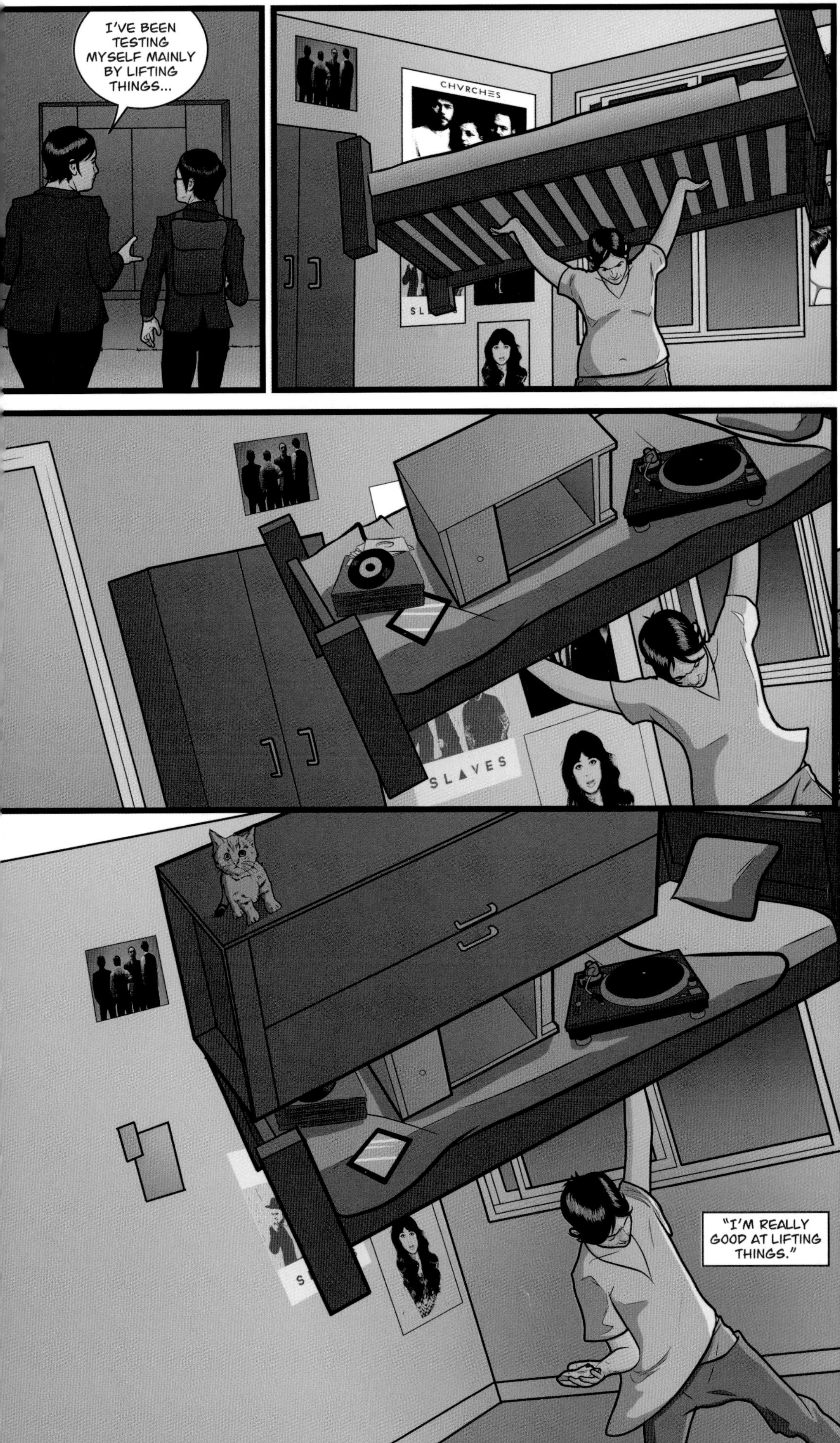
I'VE BEEN TESTING MYSELF MAINLY BY LIFTING THINGS...
CHVRCHES
SLAVES
"I'M REALLY GOOD AT LIFTING THINGS."

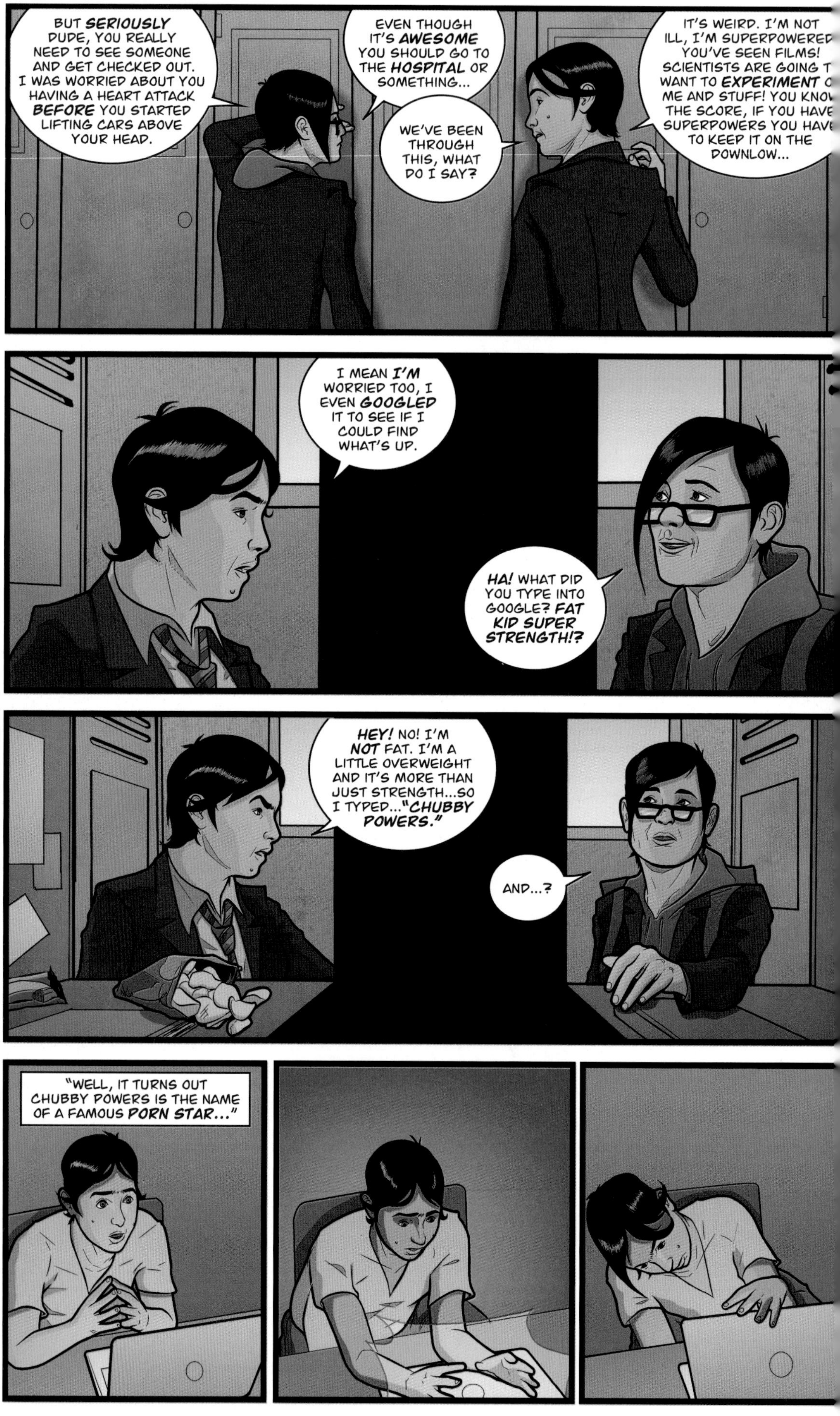
BUT SERIOUSLY DUDE, YOU REALLY NEED TO SEE SOMEONE AND GET CHECKED OUT. I WAS WORRIED ABOUT YOU HAVING A HEART ATTACK BEFORE YOU STARTED LIFTING CARS ABOVE YOUR HEAD.
EVEN THOUGH IT'S AWESOME YOU SHOULD GO TO THE HOSPITAL OR SOMETHING...
WE'VE BEEN THROUGH THIS, WHAT DO I SAY?
IT'S WEIRD. I'M NOT ILL, I'M SUPERPOWERED YOU'VE SEEN FILMS! SCIENTISTS ARE GOING T WANT TO EXPERIMENT O ME AND STUFF! YOU KNOW THE SCORE, IF YOU HAVE SUPERPOWERS YOU HAVE TO KEEP IT ON THE DOWNLOW...
I MEAN I'M WORRIED TOO, I EVEN GOOGLED IT TO SEE IF I COULD FIND WHAT'S UP.
HA! WHAT DID YOU TYPE INTO GOOGLE? FAT KID SUPER STRENGTH!?
HEY! NO! I'M NOT FAT. I'M A LITTLE OVERWEIGHT AND IT'S MORE THAN JUST STRENGTH...SO I TYPED..."CHUBBY POWERS."
AND...?
"WELL, IT TURNS OUT CHUBBY POWERS IS THE NAME OF A FAMOUS PORN STAR..."

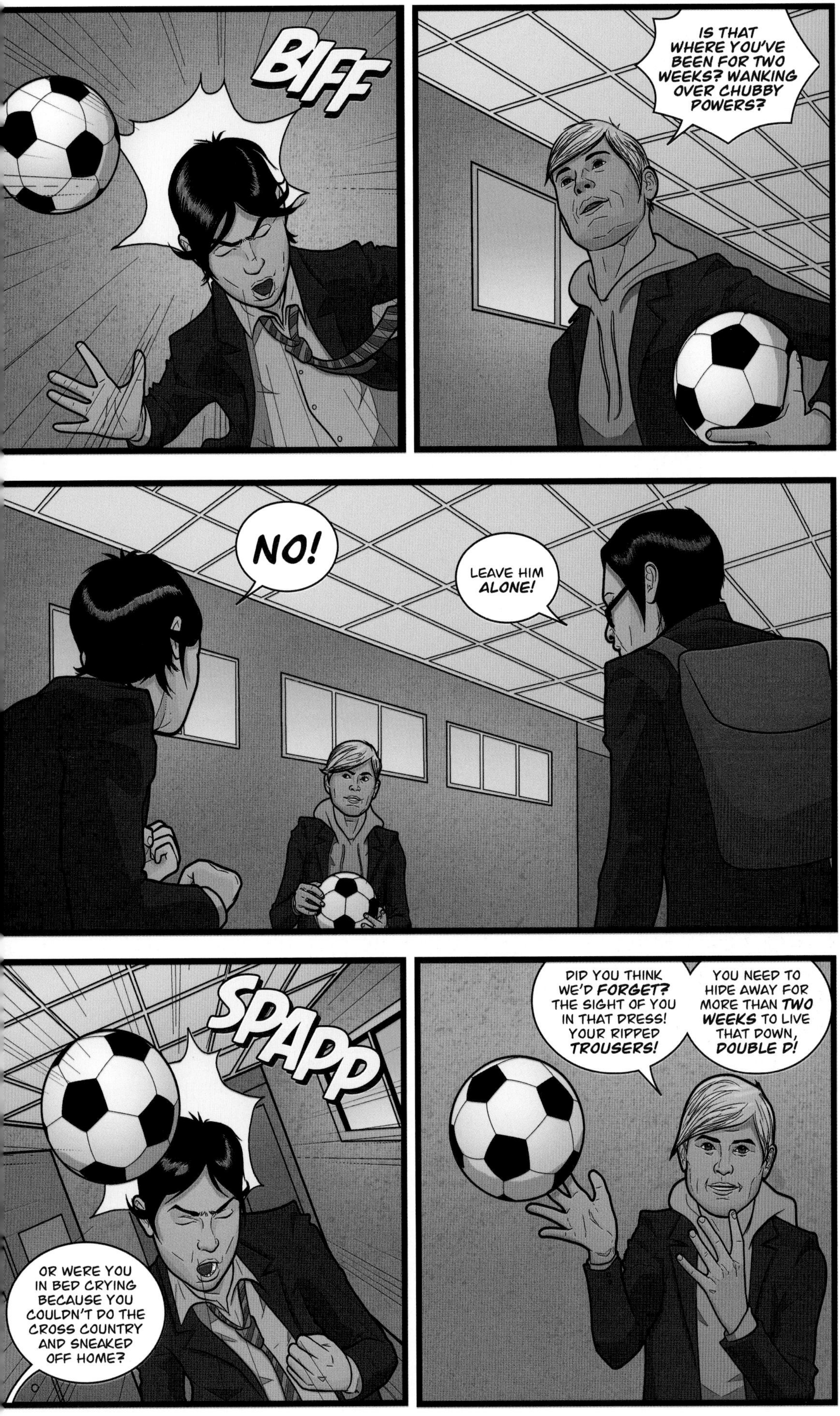
BIFF
IS THAT WHERE YOU'VE BEEN FOR TWO WEEKS? WANKING OVER CHUBBY POWERS?
NO!
LEAVE HIM ALONE!
SPAPP
OR WERE YOU IN BED CRYING BECAUSE YOU COULDN'T DO THE CROSS COUNTRY AND SNEAKED OFF HOME?
DID YOU THINK WE'D FORGET? THE SIGHT OF YOU IN THAT DRESS! YOUR RIPPED TROUSERS!
YOU NEED TO HIDE AWAY FOR MORE THAN TWO WEEKS TO LIVE THAT DOWN, DOUBLE D!

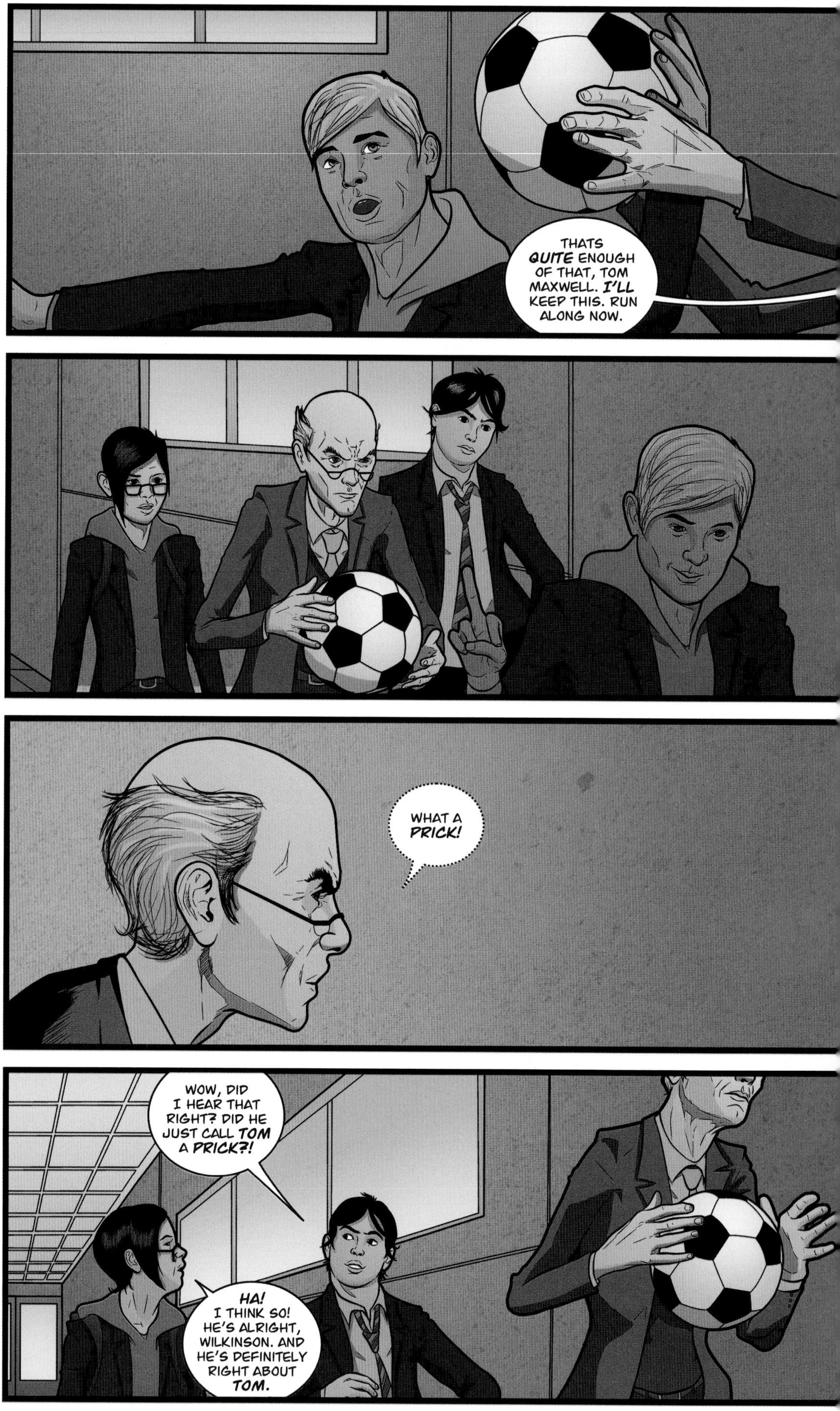
THATS QUITE ENOUGH OF THAT, TOM MAXWELL. I'LL KEEP THIS. RUN ALONG NOW.
WHAT A PRICK!
WOW, DID I HEAR THAT RIGHT? DID HE JUST CALL TOM A PRICK?!
HA! I THINK SO! HE'S ALRIGHT, WILKINSON. AND HE'S DEFINITELY RIGHT ABOUT TOM.

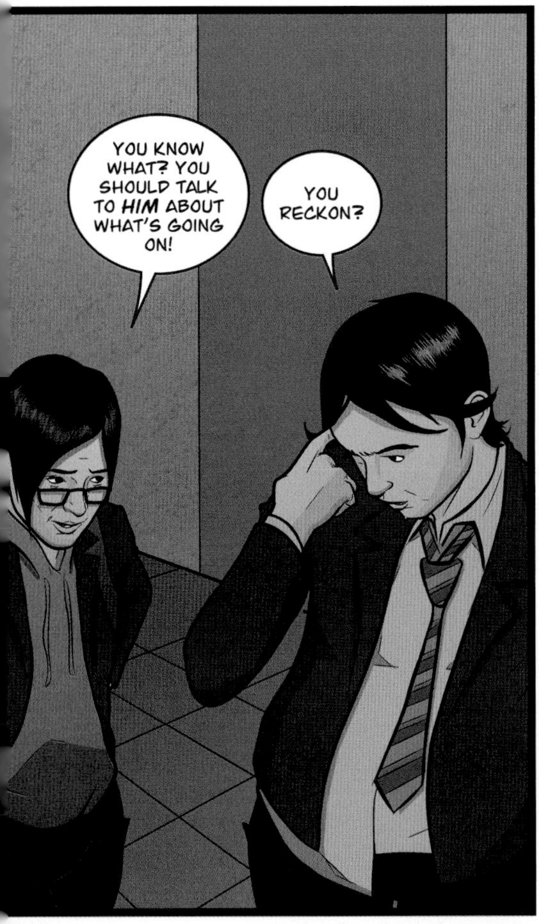
YOU KNOW WHAT? YOU SHOULD TALK TO HIM ABOUT WHAT'S GOING ON!
YOU RECKON?

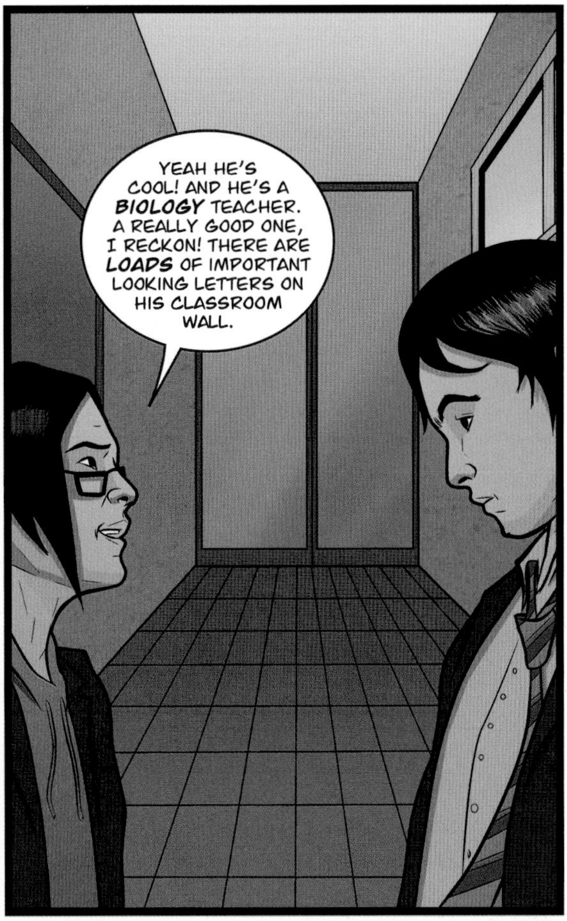
YEAH HE'S COOL! AND HE'S A BIOLOGY TEACHER. A REALLY GOOD ONE, I RECKON! THERE ARE LOADS OF IMPORTANT LOOKING LETTERS ON HIS CLASSROOM WALL.

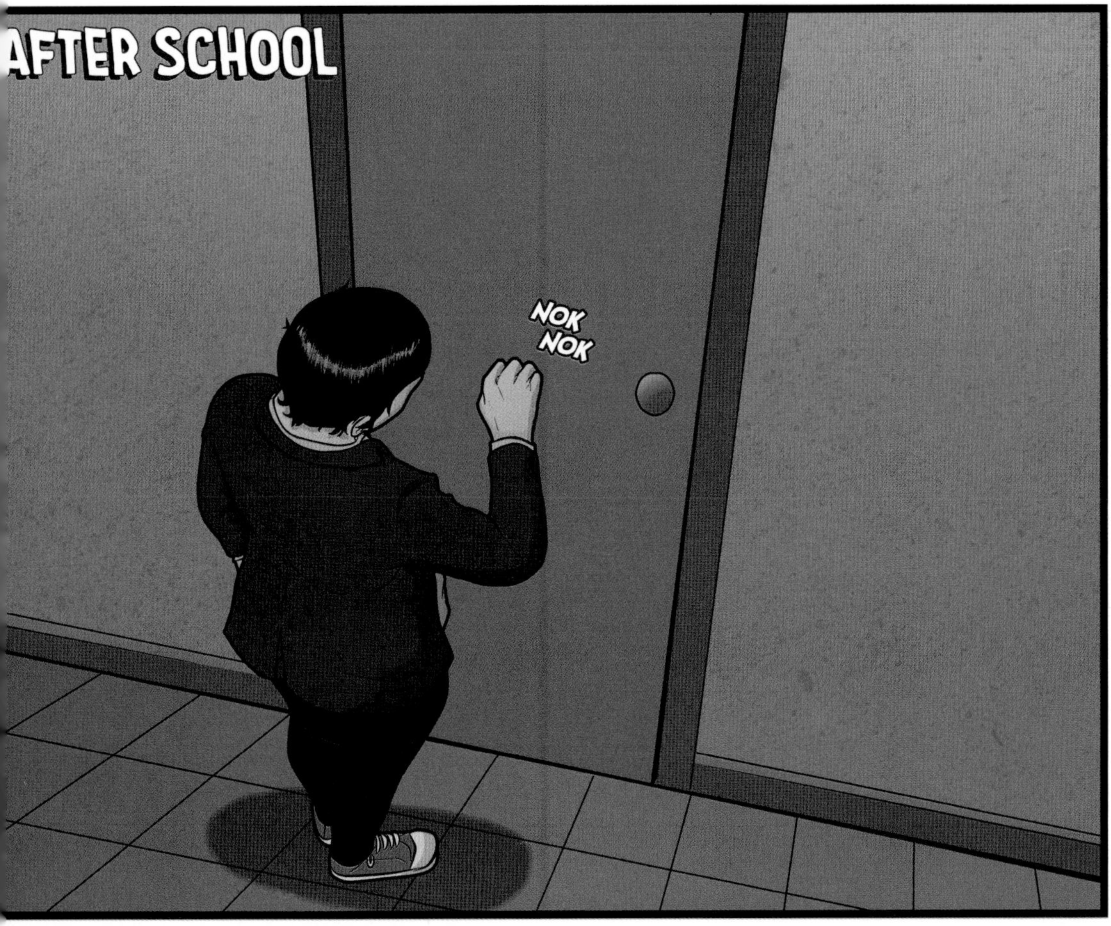
AFTER SCHOOL
NOK NOK

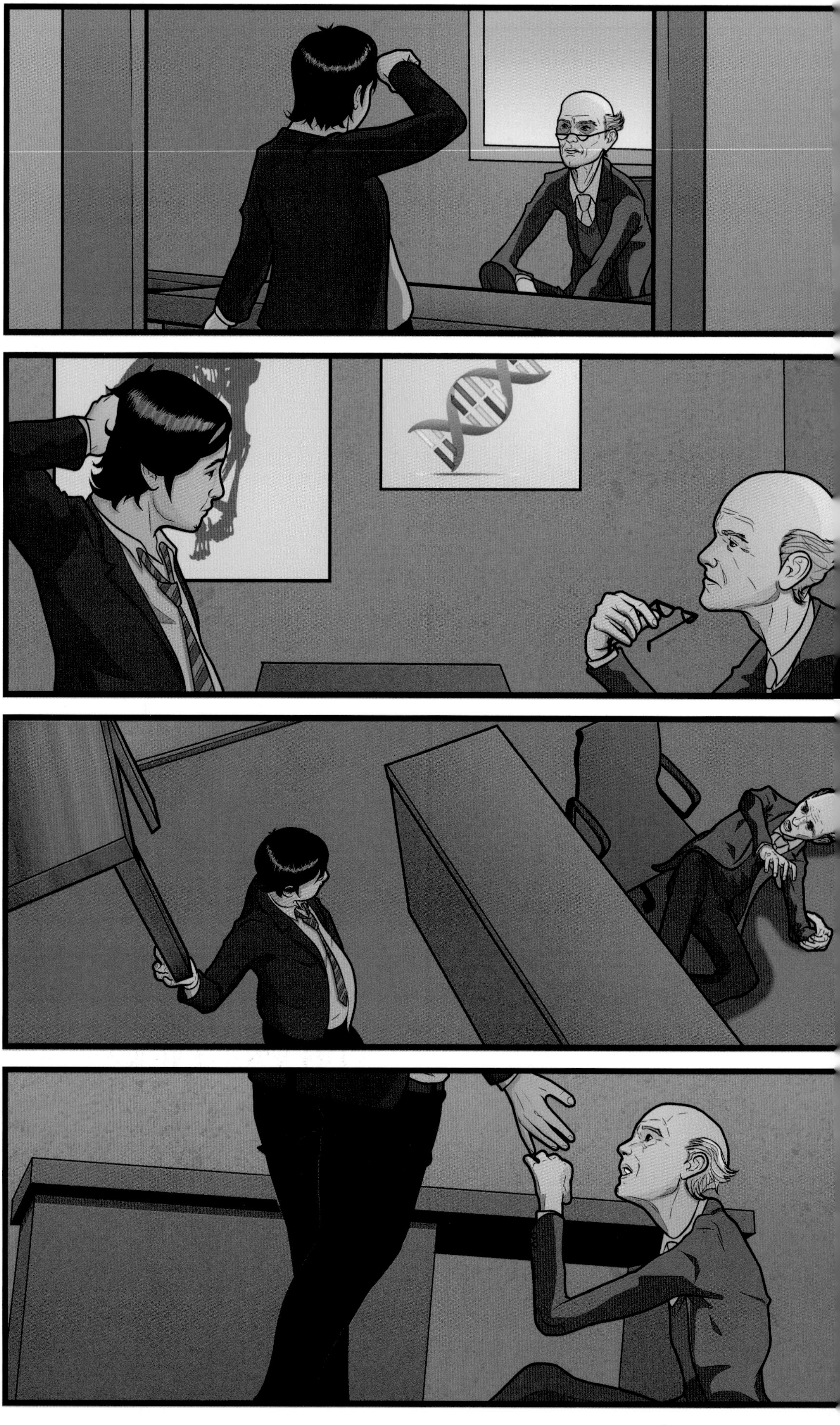

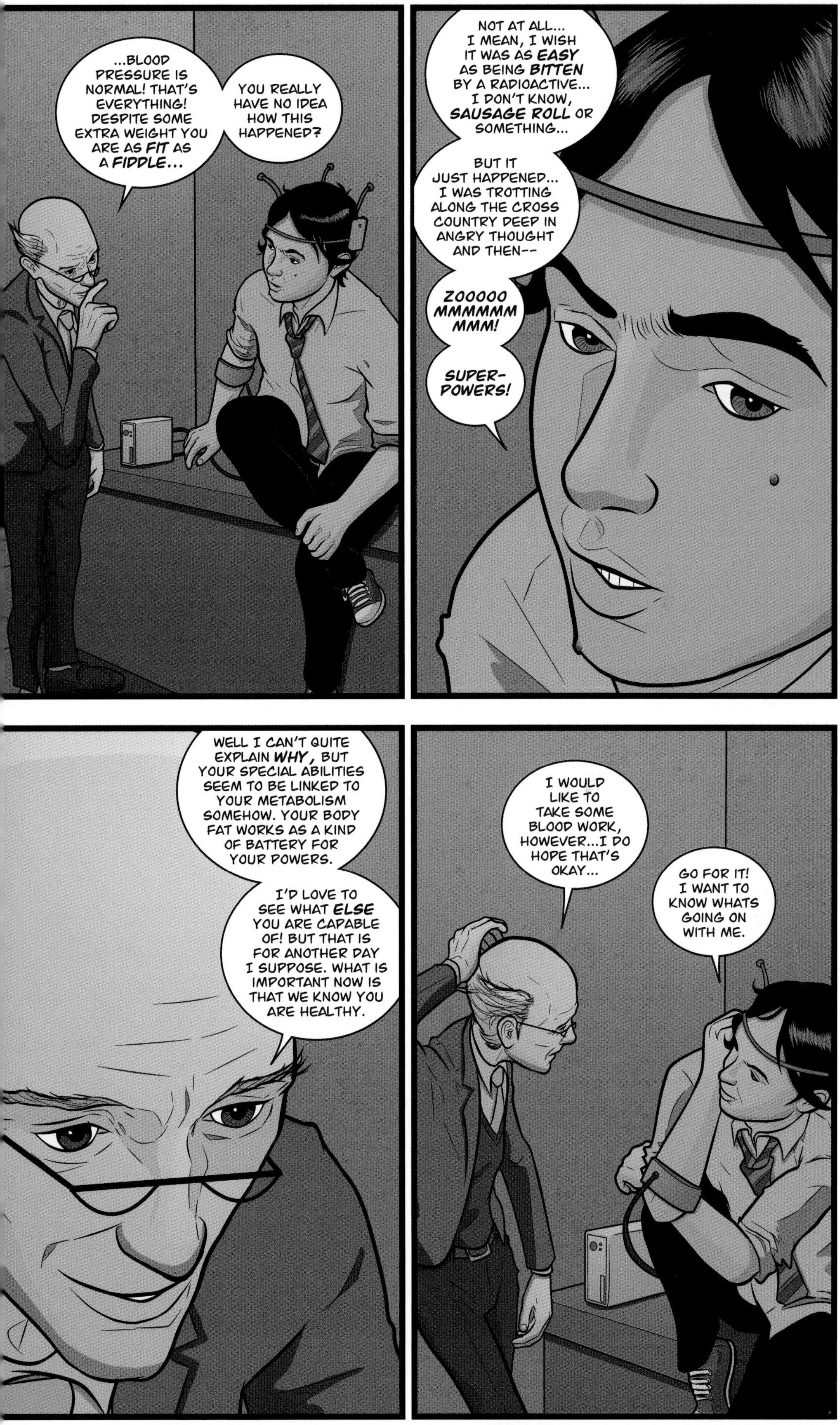
...BLOOD PRESSURE IS NORMAL! THAT'S EVERYTHING! DESPITE SOME EXTRA WEIGHT YOU ARE AS FIT AS A FIDDLE...
YOU REALLY HAVE NO IDEA HOW THIS HAPPENED?
NOT AT ALL... I MEAN, I WISH IT WAS AS EASY AS BEING BITTEN BY A RADIOACTIVE... I DON'T KNOW, SAUSAGE ROLL OR SOMETHING...
BUT IT JUST HAPPENED... I WAS TROTTING ALONG THE CROSS COUNTRY DEEP IN ANGRY THOUGHT AND THEN--
ZOOOOO MMMMMM MMM!
SUPER-POWERS!
WELL I CAN'T QUITE EXPLAIN WHY, BUT YOUR SPECIAL ABILITIES SEEM TO BE LINKED TO YOUR METABOLISM SOMEHOW. YOUR BODY FAT WORKS AS A KIND OF BATTERY FOR YOUR POWERS.
I'D LOVE TO SEE WHAT ELSE YOU ARE CAPABLE OF! BUT THAT IS FOR ANOTHER DAY I SUPPOSE. WHAT IS IMPORTANT NOW IS THAT WE KNOW YOU ARE HEALTHY.
I WOULD LIKE TO TAKE SOME BLOOD WORK, HOWEVER...I DO HOPE THAT'S OKAY...
GO FOR IT! I WANT TO KNOW WHATS GOING ON WITH ME.

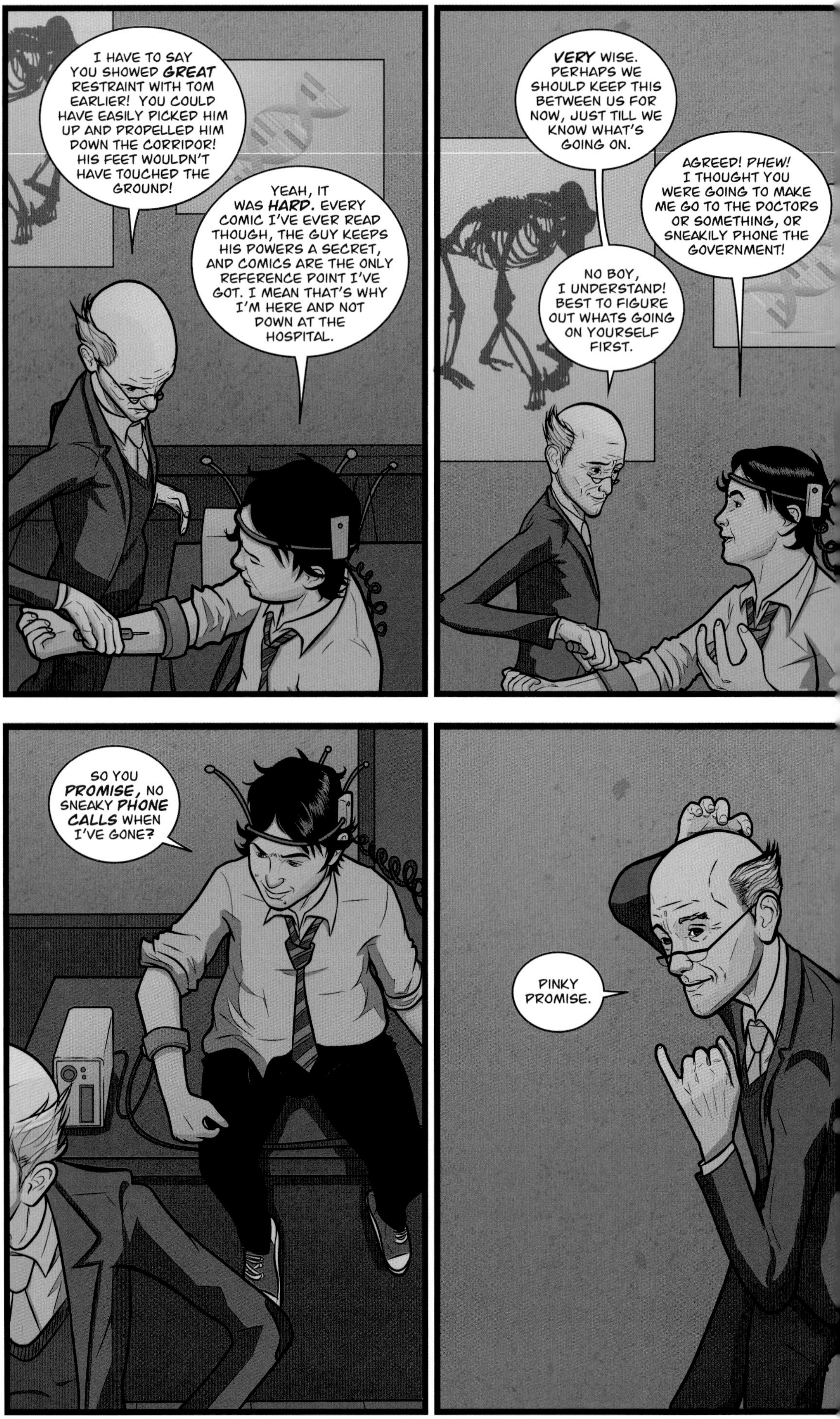
I HAVE TO SAY YOU SHOWED GREAT RESTRAINT WITH TOM EARLIER! YOU COULD HAVE EASILY PICKED HIM UP AND PROPELLED HIM DOWN THE CORRIDOR! HIS FEET WOULDN'T HAVE TOUCHED THE GROUND!
YEAH, IT WAS HARD. EVERY COMIC I'VE EVER READ THOUGH, THE GUY KEEPS HIS POWERS A SECRET, AND COMICS ARE THE ONLY REFERENCE POINT I'VE GOT. I MEAN THAT'S WHY I'M HERE AND NOT DOWN AT THE HOSPITAL.
VERY WISE. PERHAPS WE SHOULD KEEP THIS BETWEEN US FOR NOW, JUST TILL WE KNOW WHAT'S GOING ON.
AGREED! PHEW! I THOUGHT YOU WERE GOING TO MAKE ME GO TO THE DOCTORS OR SOMETHING, OR SNEAKILY PHONE THE GOVERNMENT!
NO BOY, I UNDERSTAND! BEST TO FIGURE OUT WHATS GOING ON YOURSELF FIRST.
SO YOU PROMISE, NO SNEAKY PHONE CALLS WHEN I'VE GONE?
PINKY PROMISE.

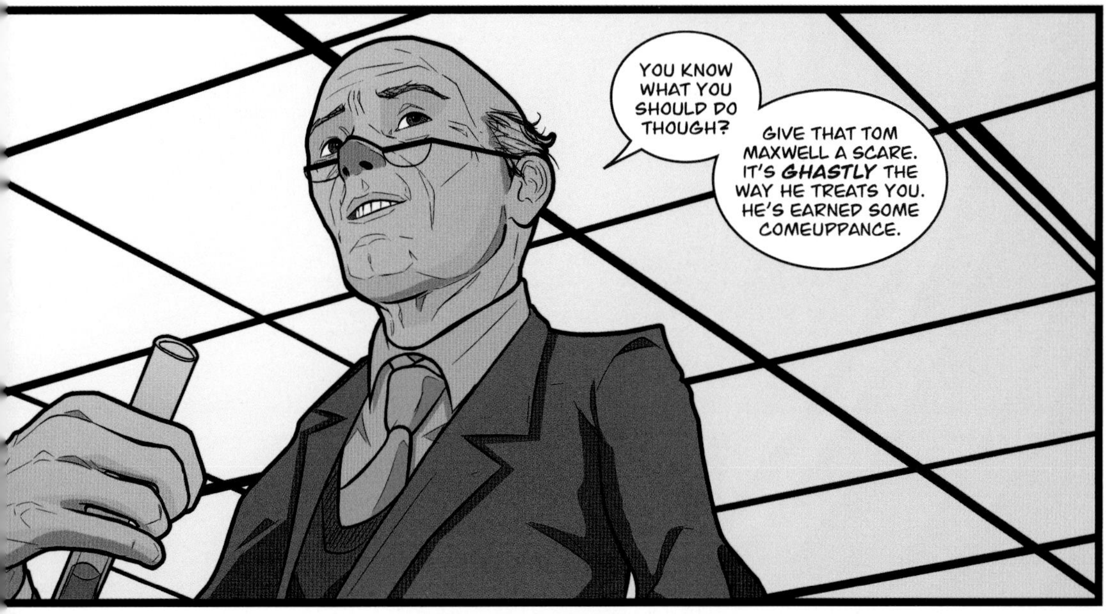
YOU KNOW WHAT YOU SHOULD DO THOUGH?
GIVE THAT TOM MAXWELL A SCARE. IT'S **GHASTLY** THE WAY HE TREATS YOU. HE'S EARNED SOME COMEUPPANCE.

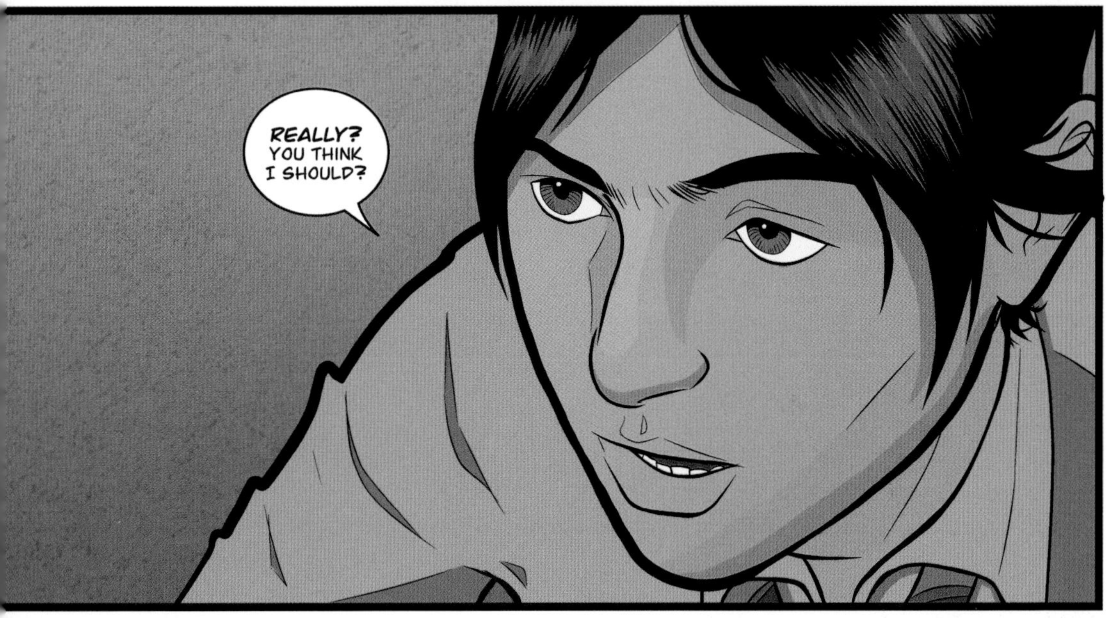
REALLY? YOU THINK I SHOULD?

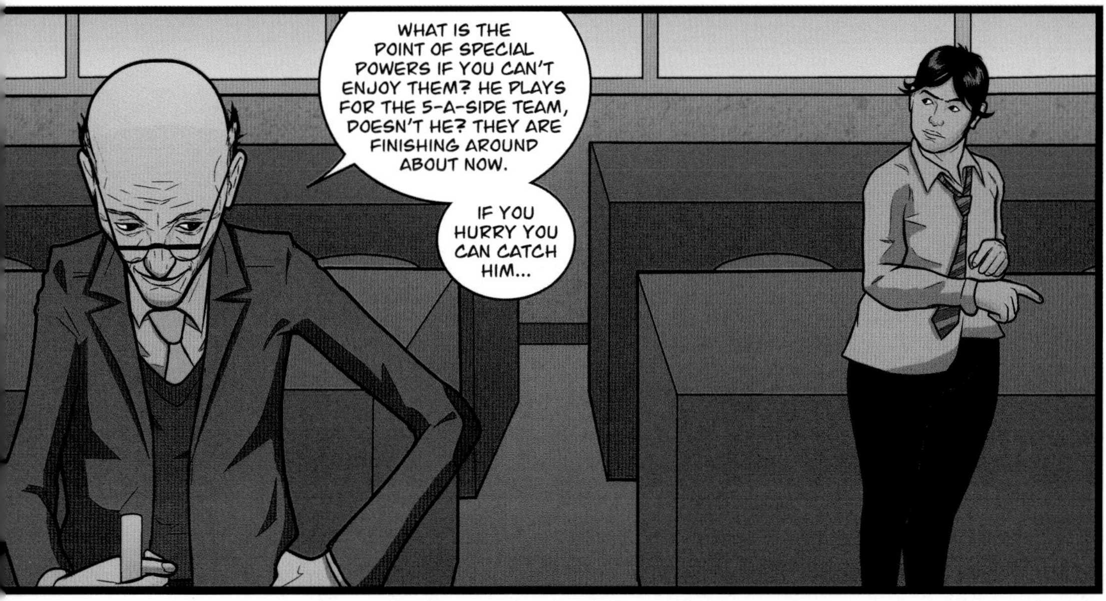
WHAT IS THE POINT OF SPECIAL POWERS IF YOU CAN'T ENJOY THEM? HE PLAYS FOR THE 5-A-SIDE TEAM, DOESN'T HE? THEY ARE FINISHING AROUND ABOUT NOW.
IF YOU HURRY YOU CAN CATCH HIM...

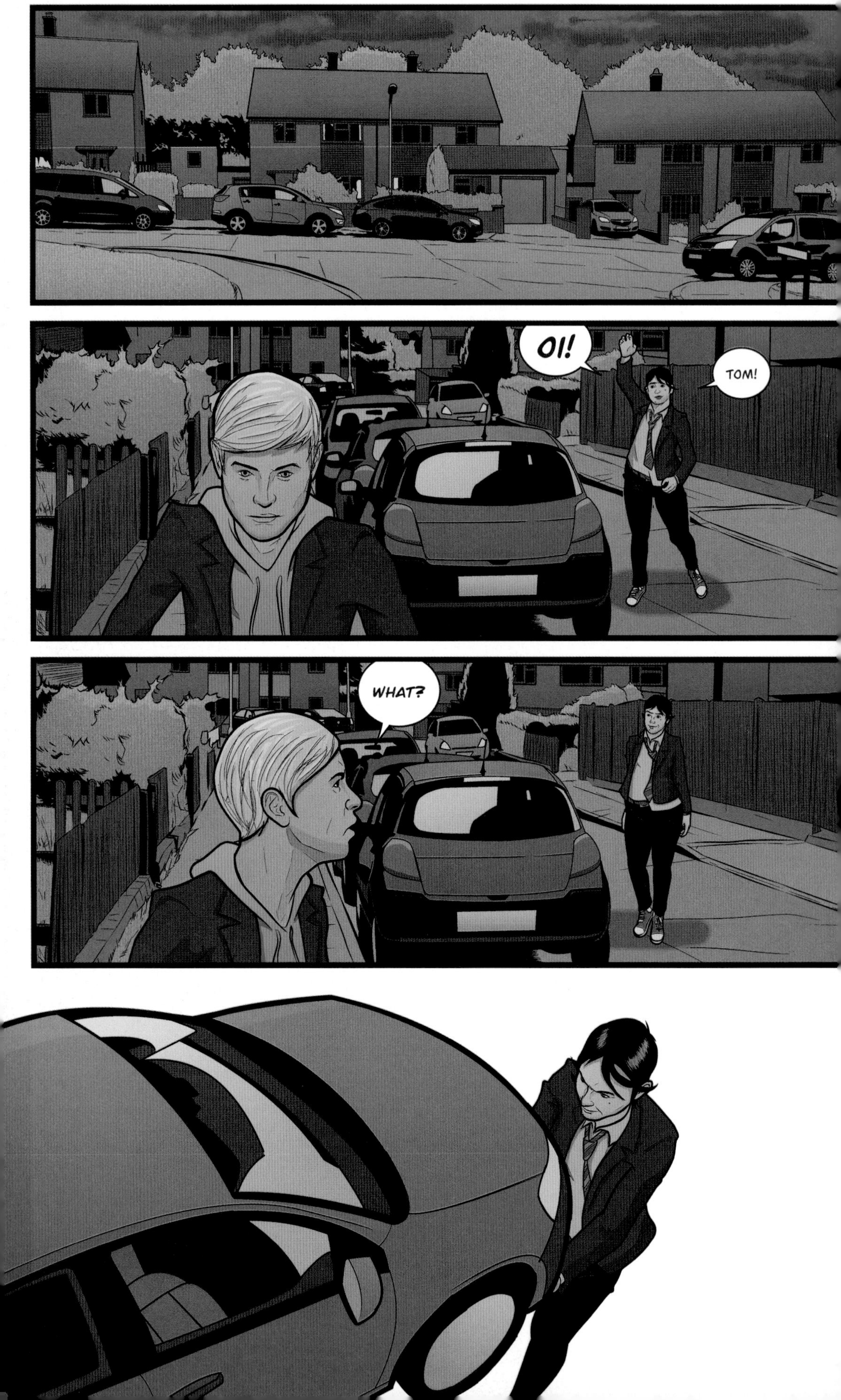
OI!
TOM!
WHAT?

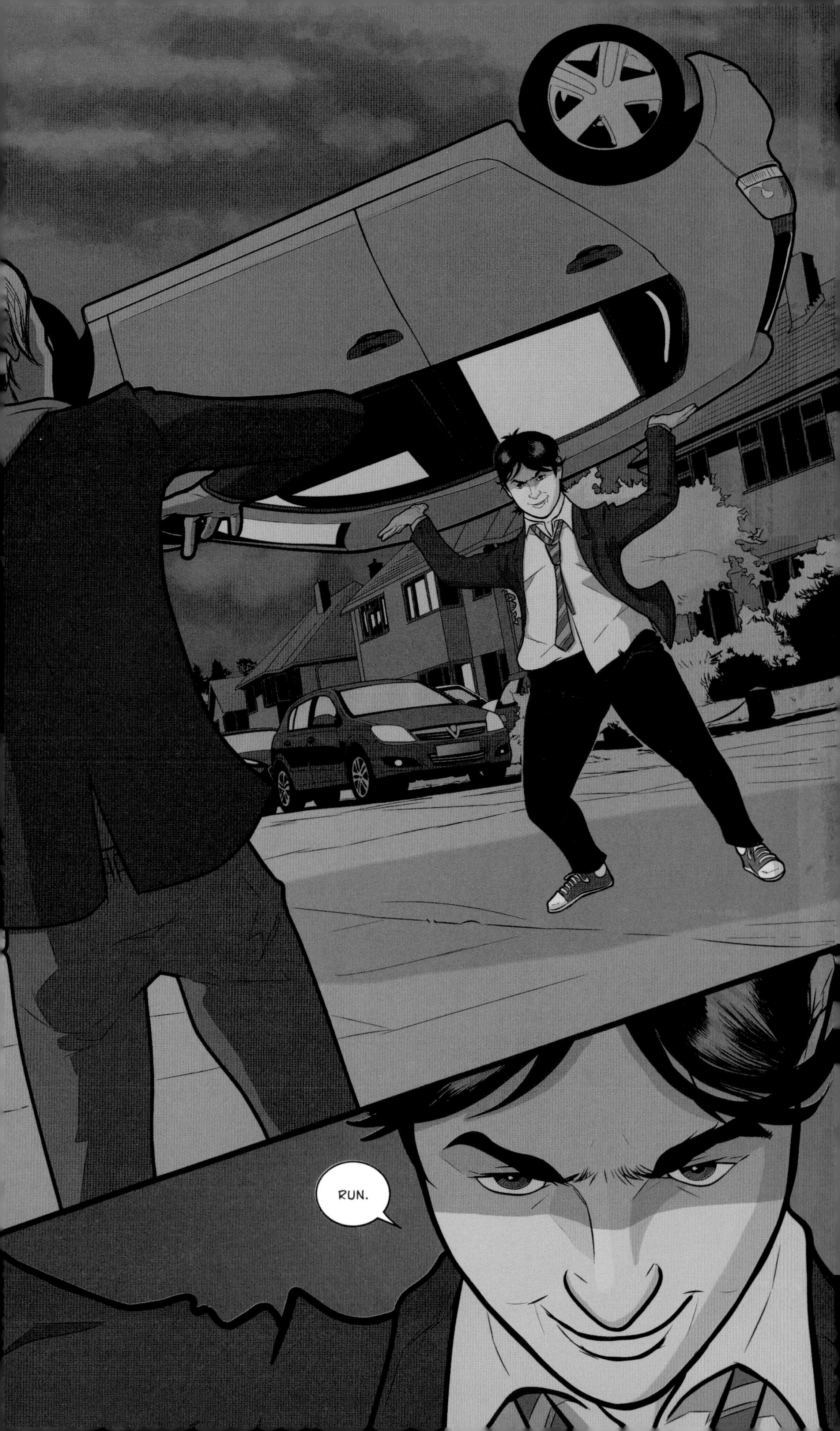
RUN.

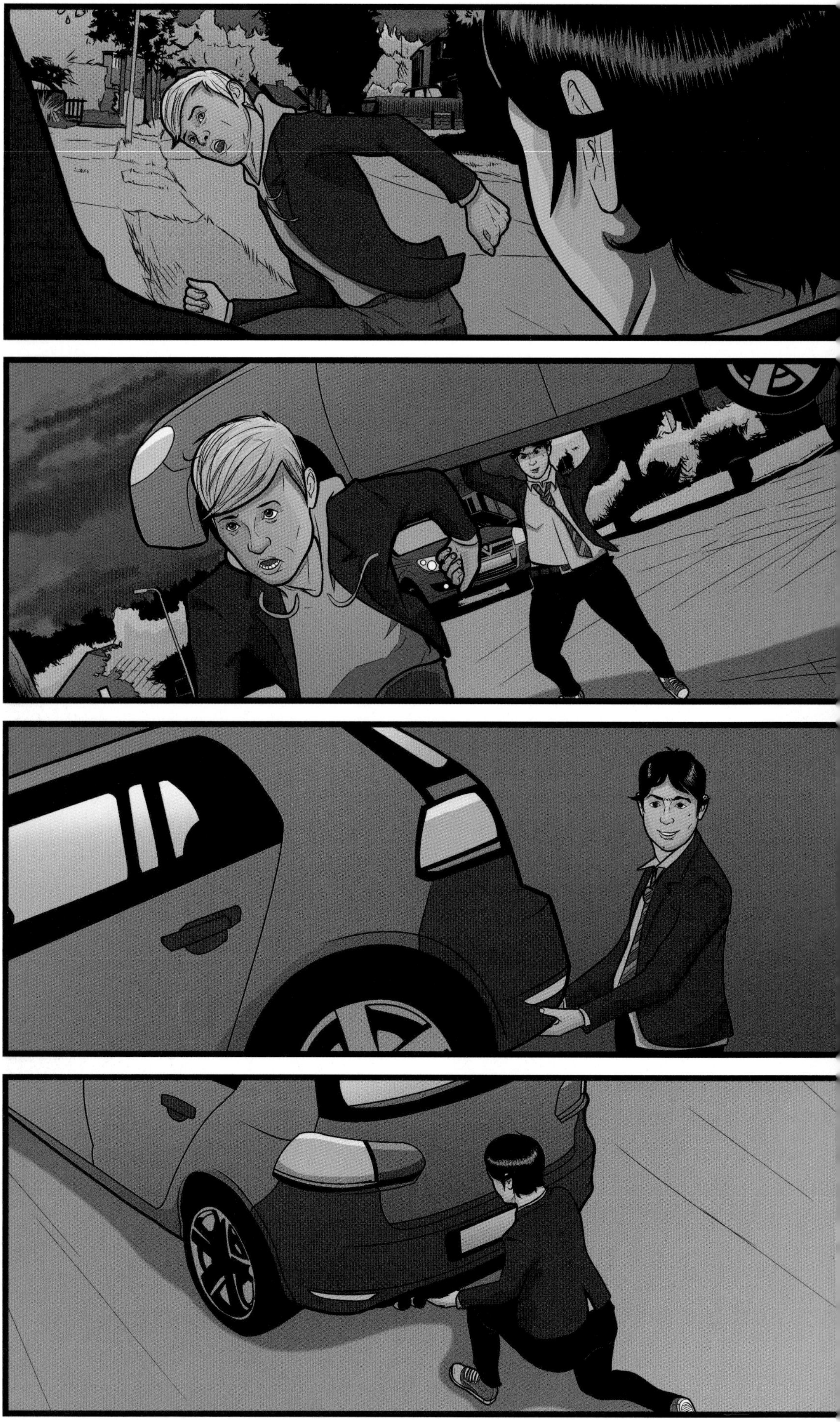

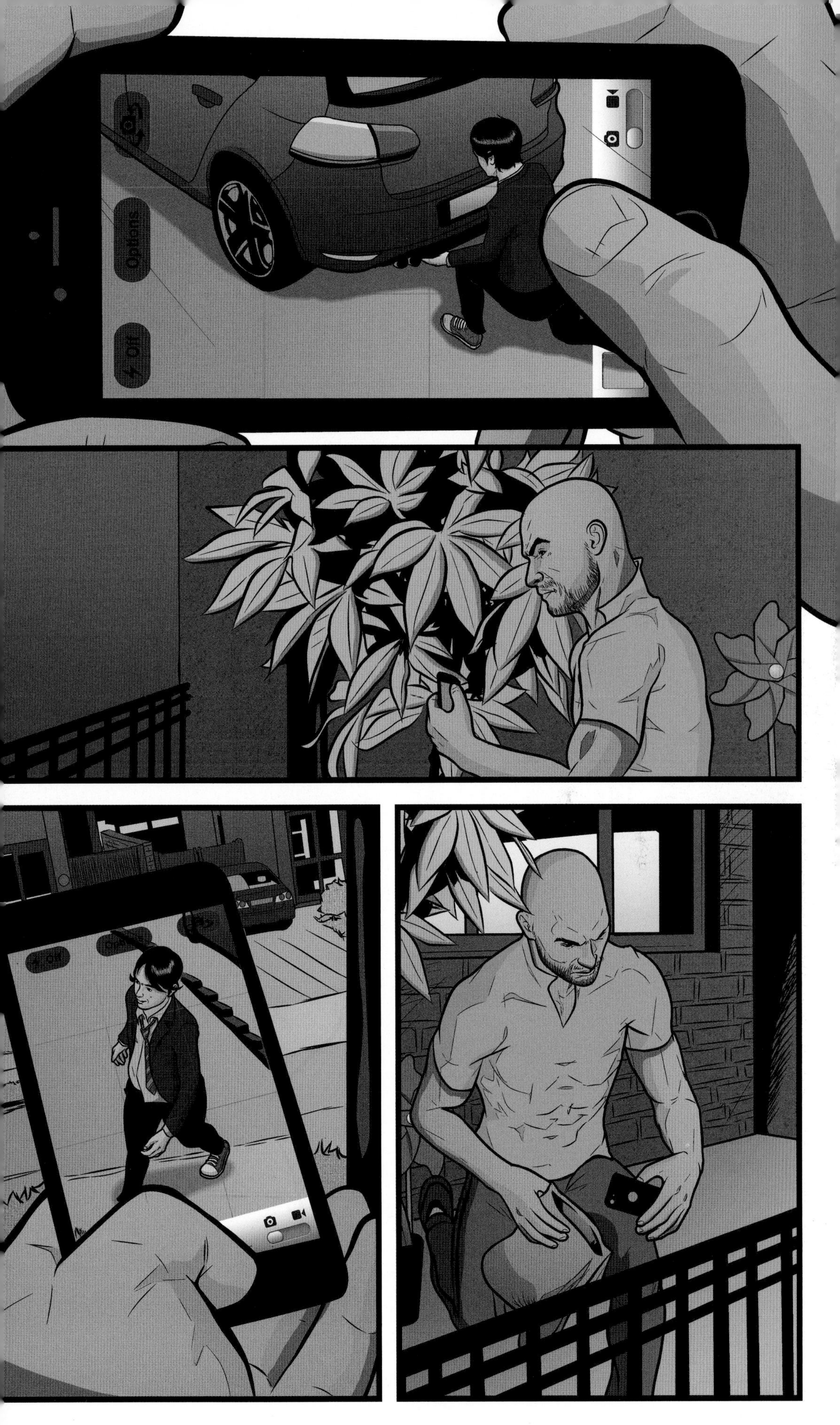
Options
Off

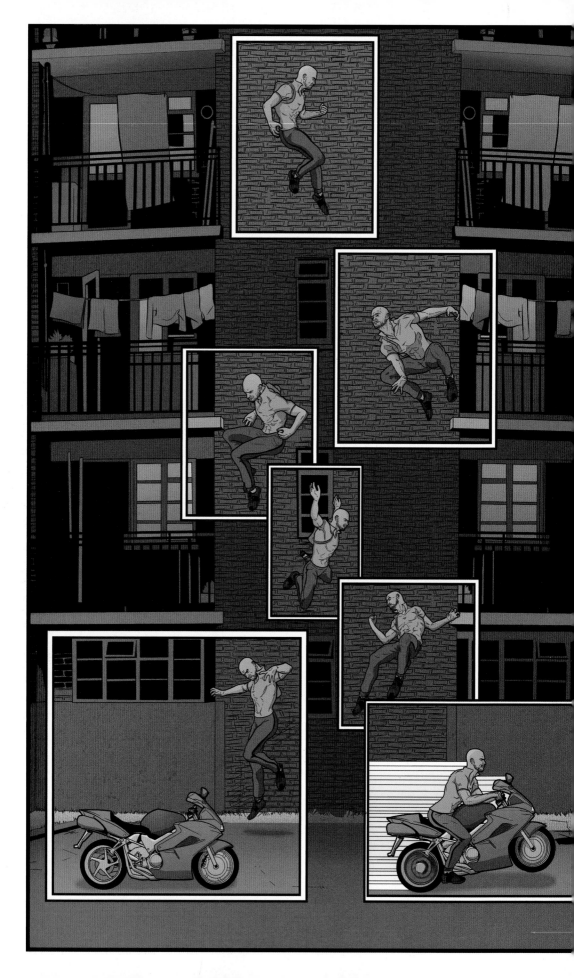

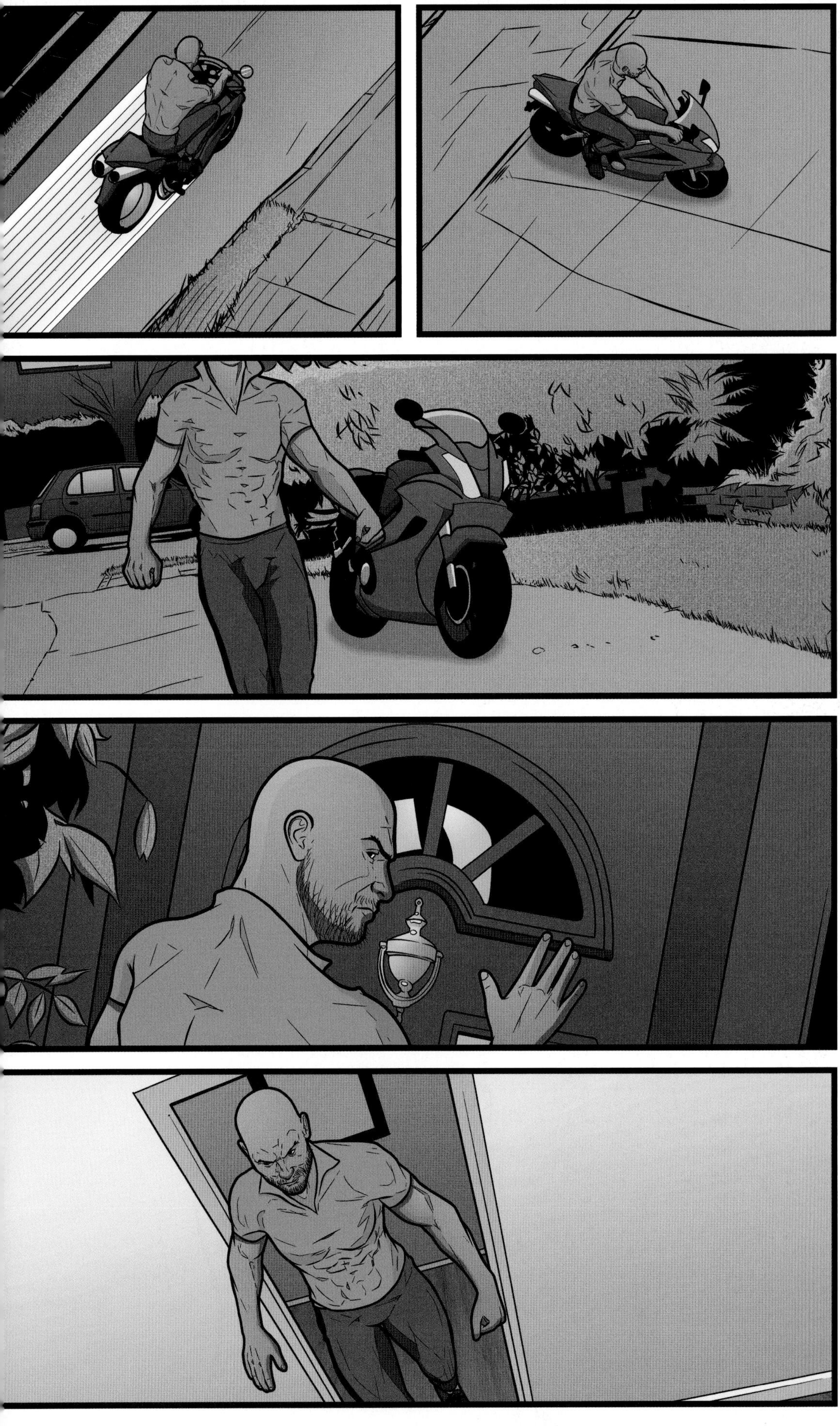

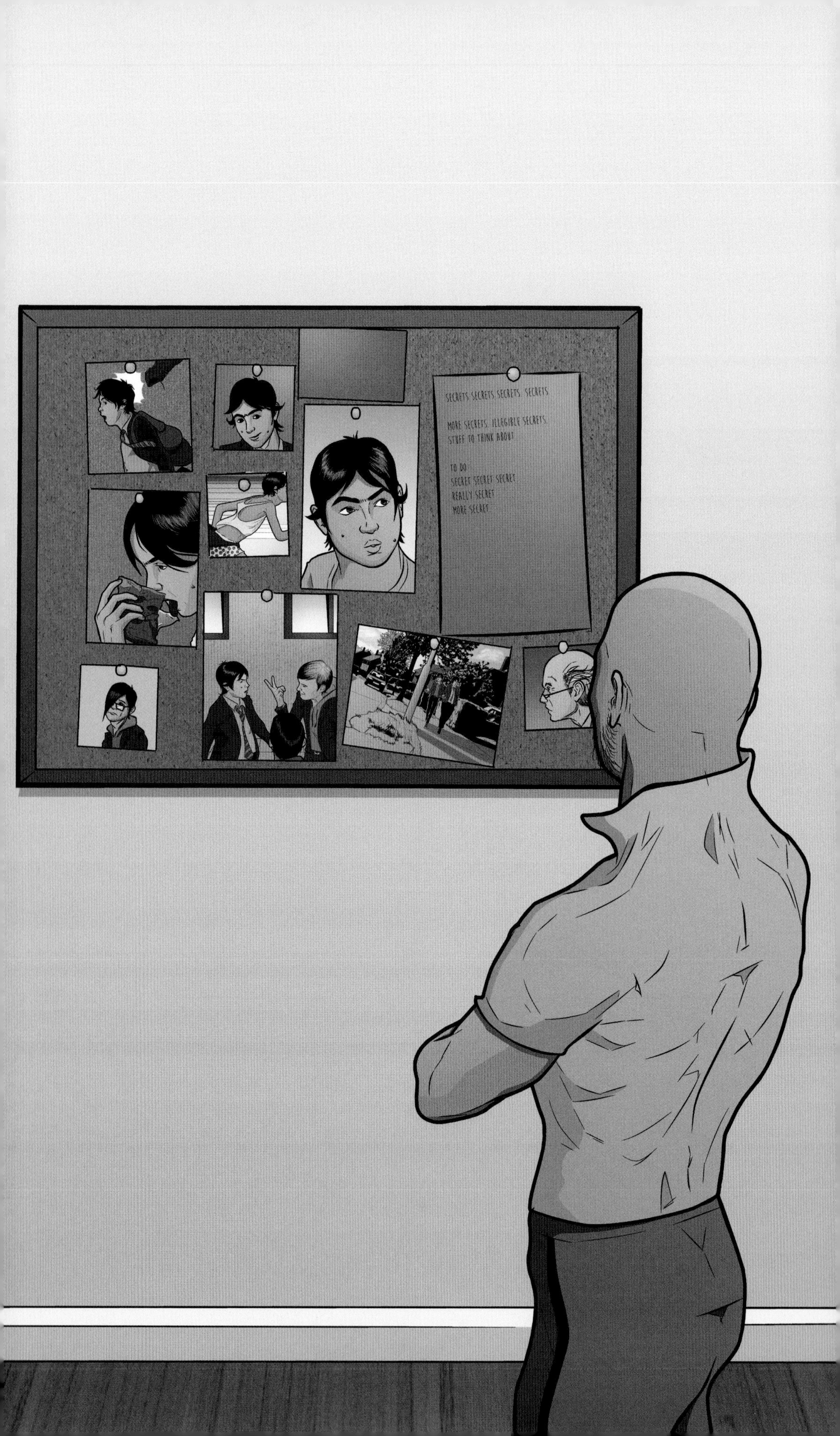
SECRETS SECRETS SECRETS. SECRETS.
MORE SECRETS. ILLEGIBLE SECRETS.
STUFF TO THINK ABOUT
TO DO:
SECRET SECRET SECRET
REALLY SECRET
MORE SECRET

CHAPTER 3

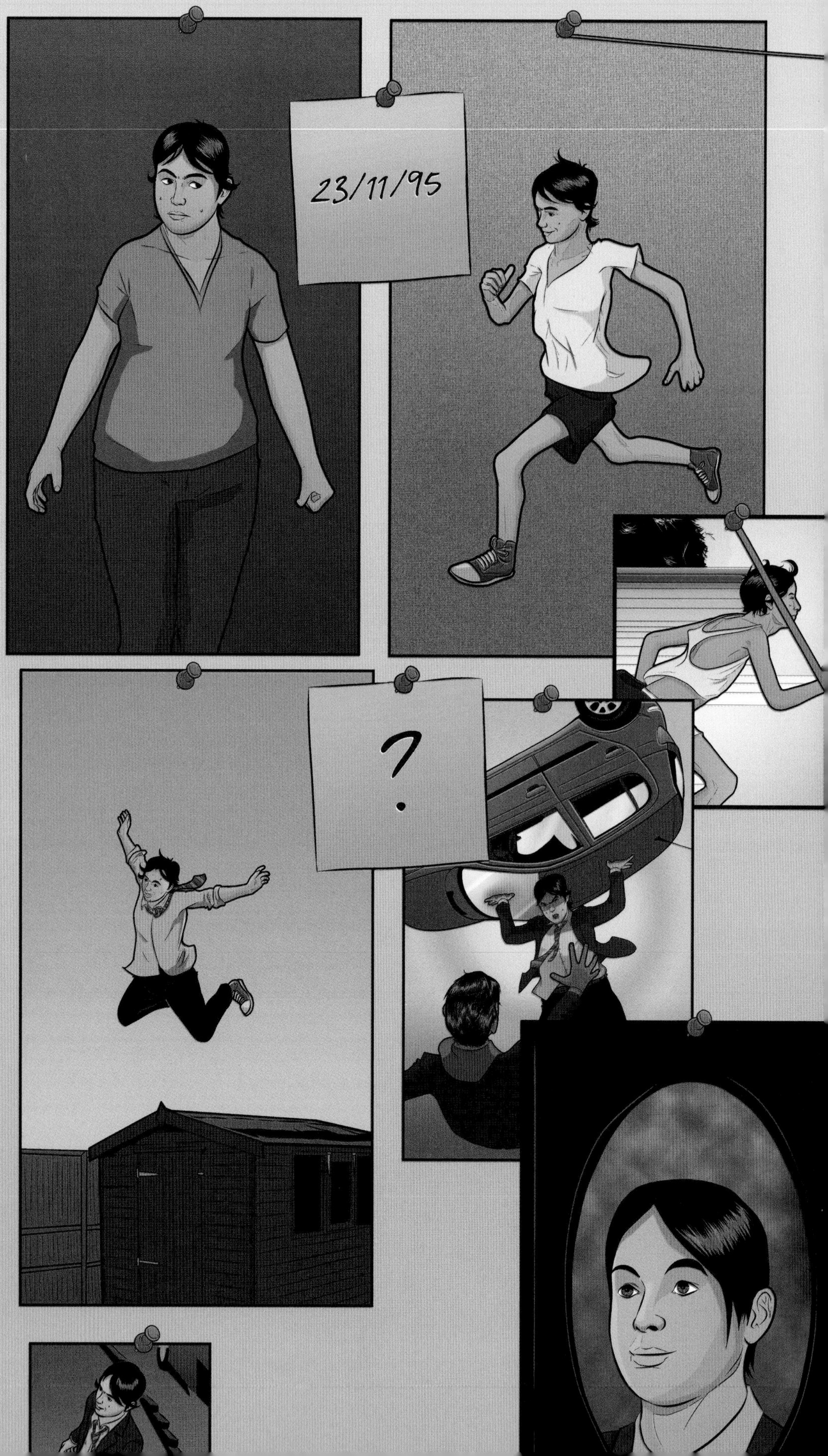
23/11/95
?

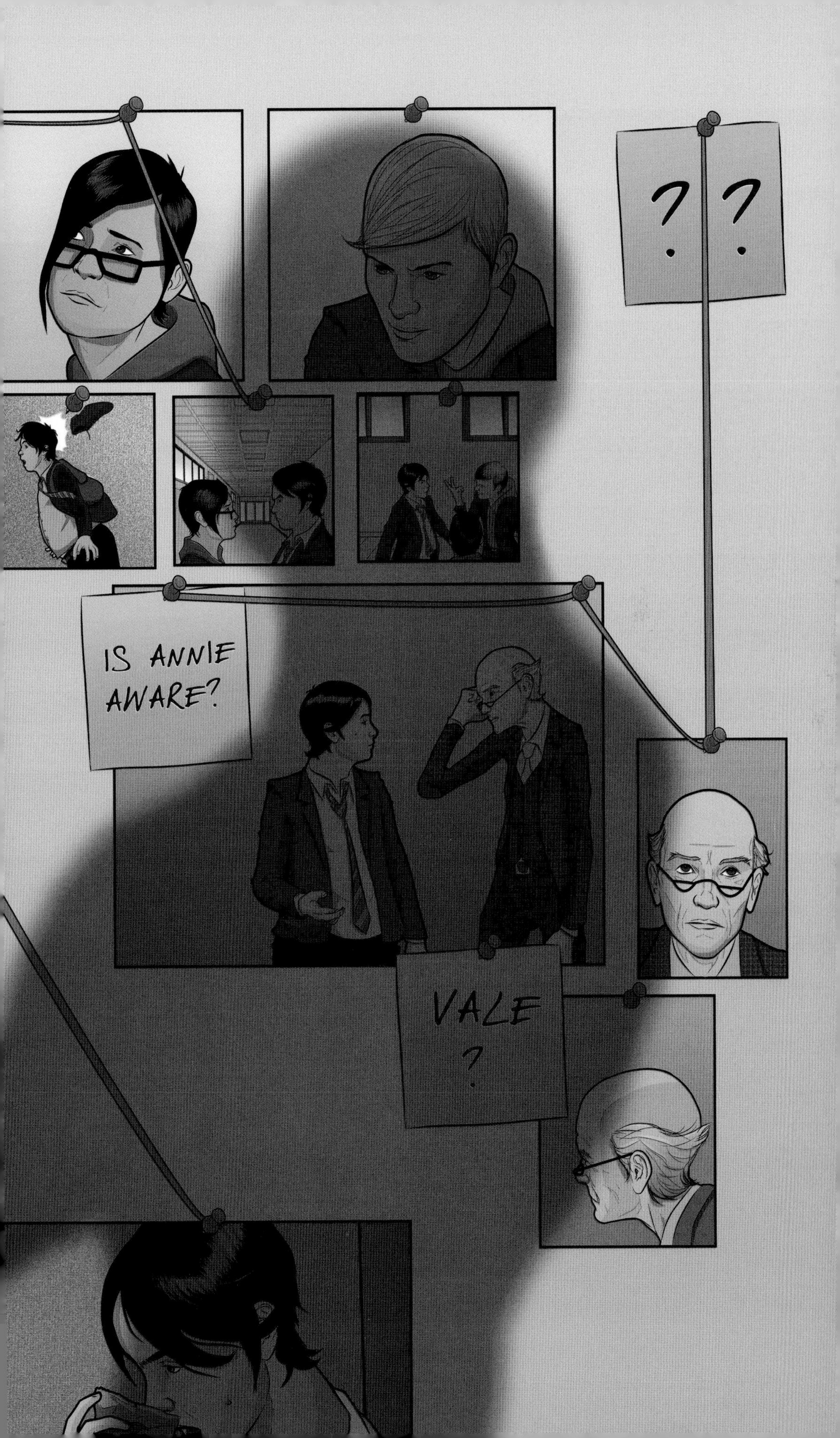
??
IS ANNIE AWARE?
VALE ?

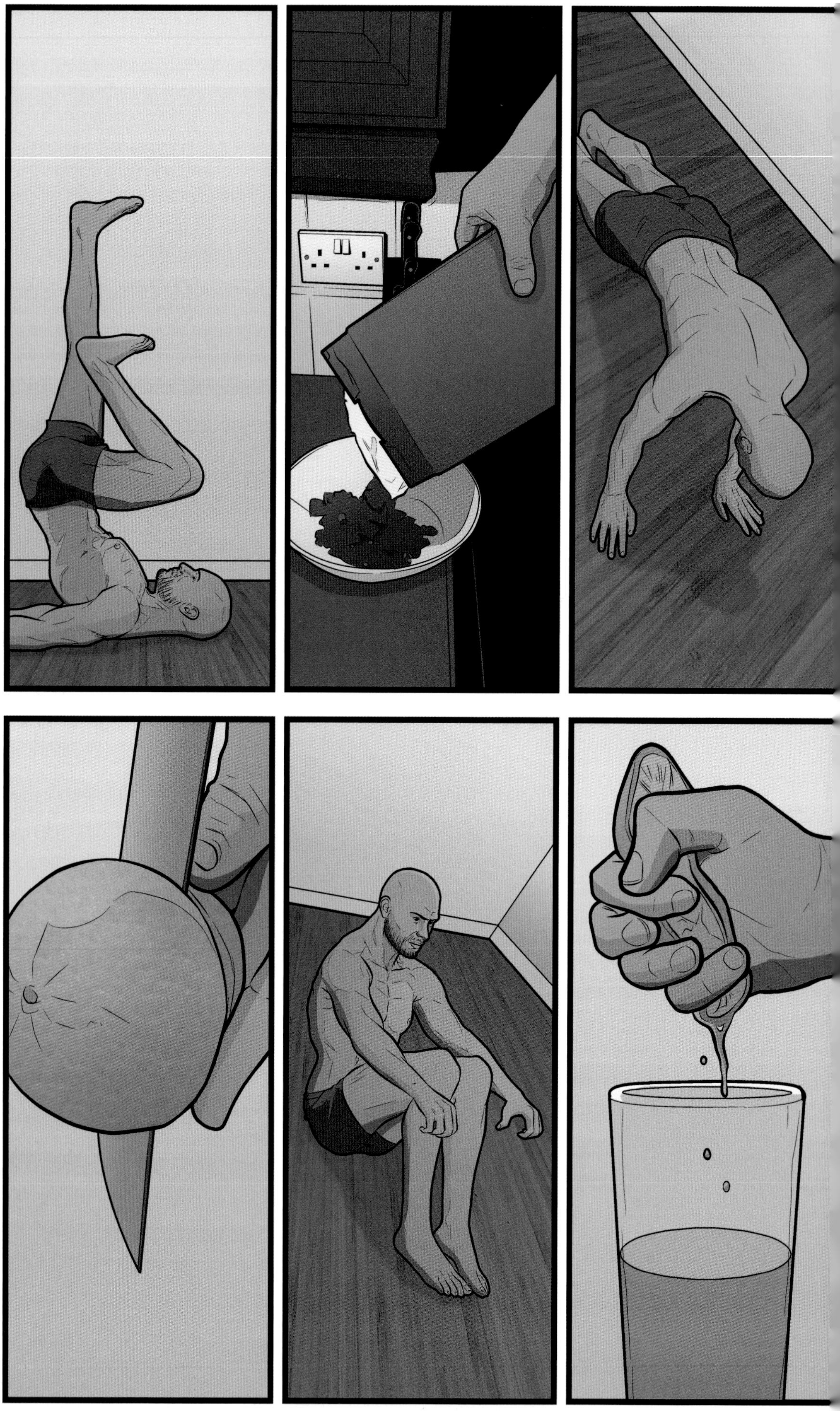

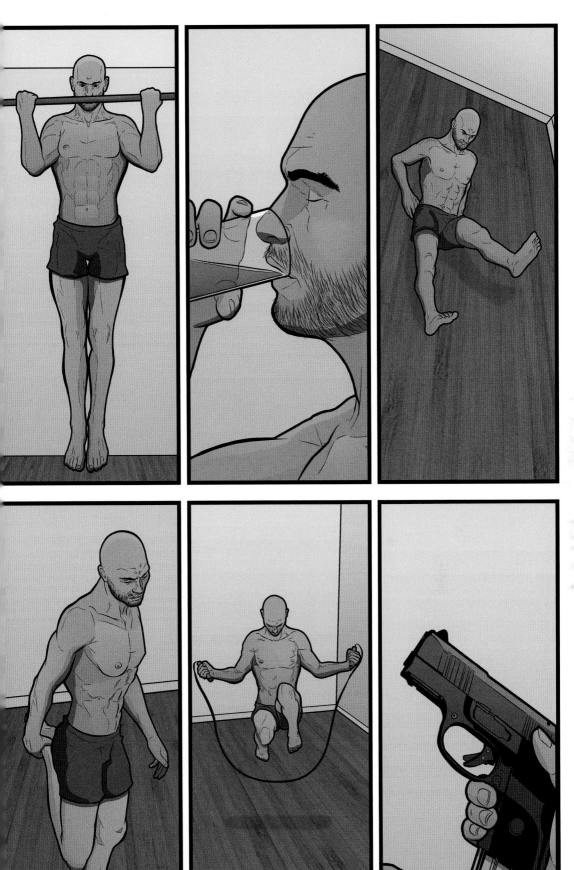

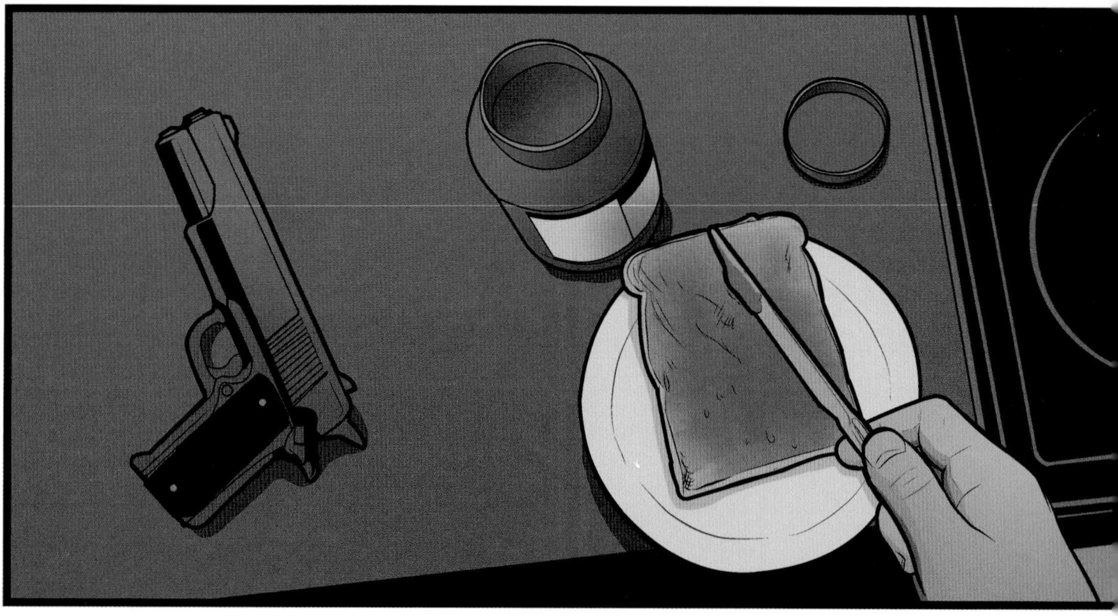
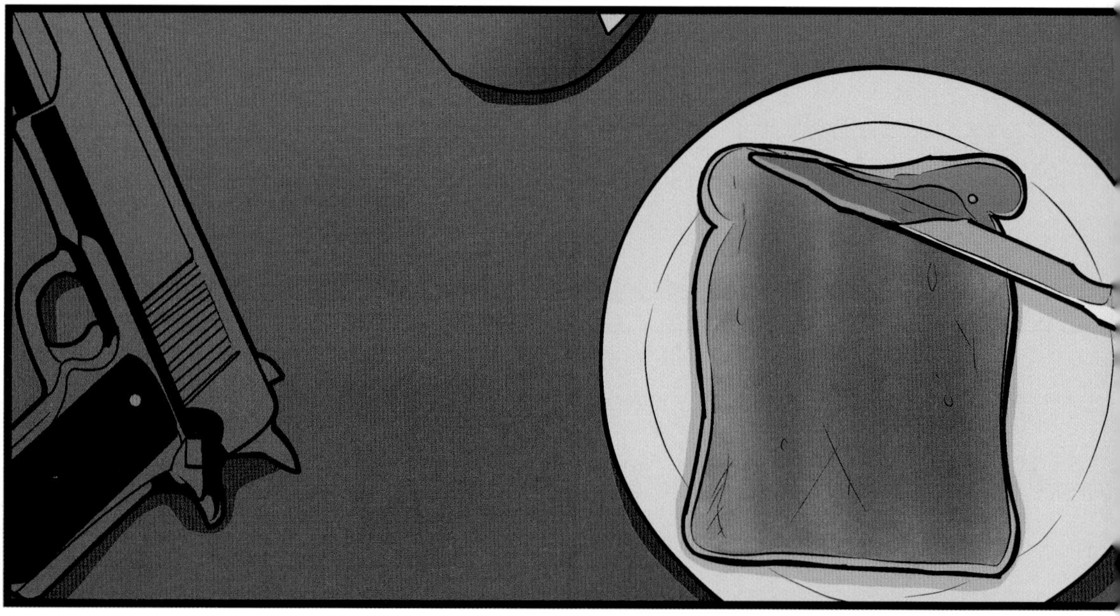
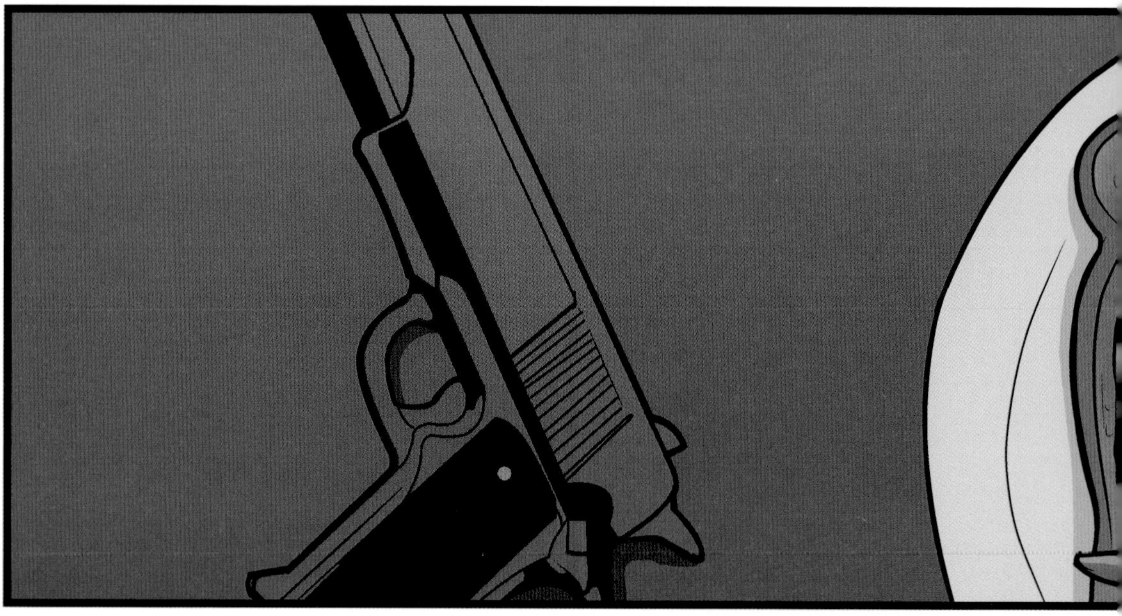

LIVE FEED ACTIVE

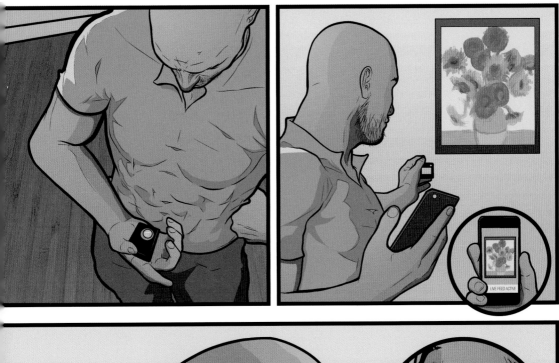

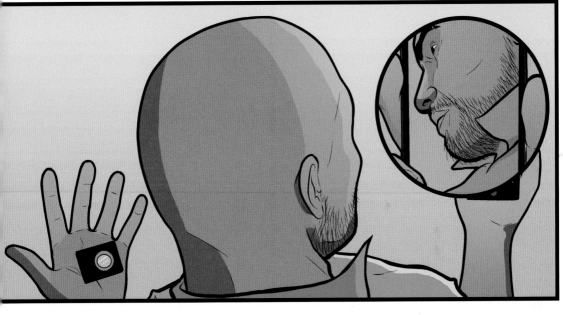

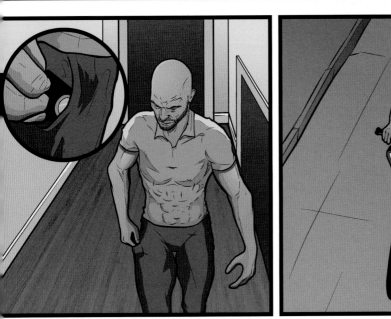

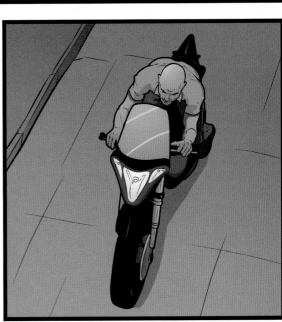

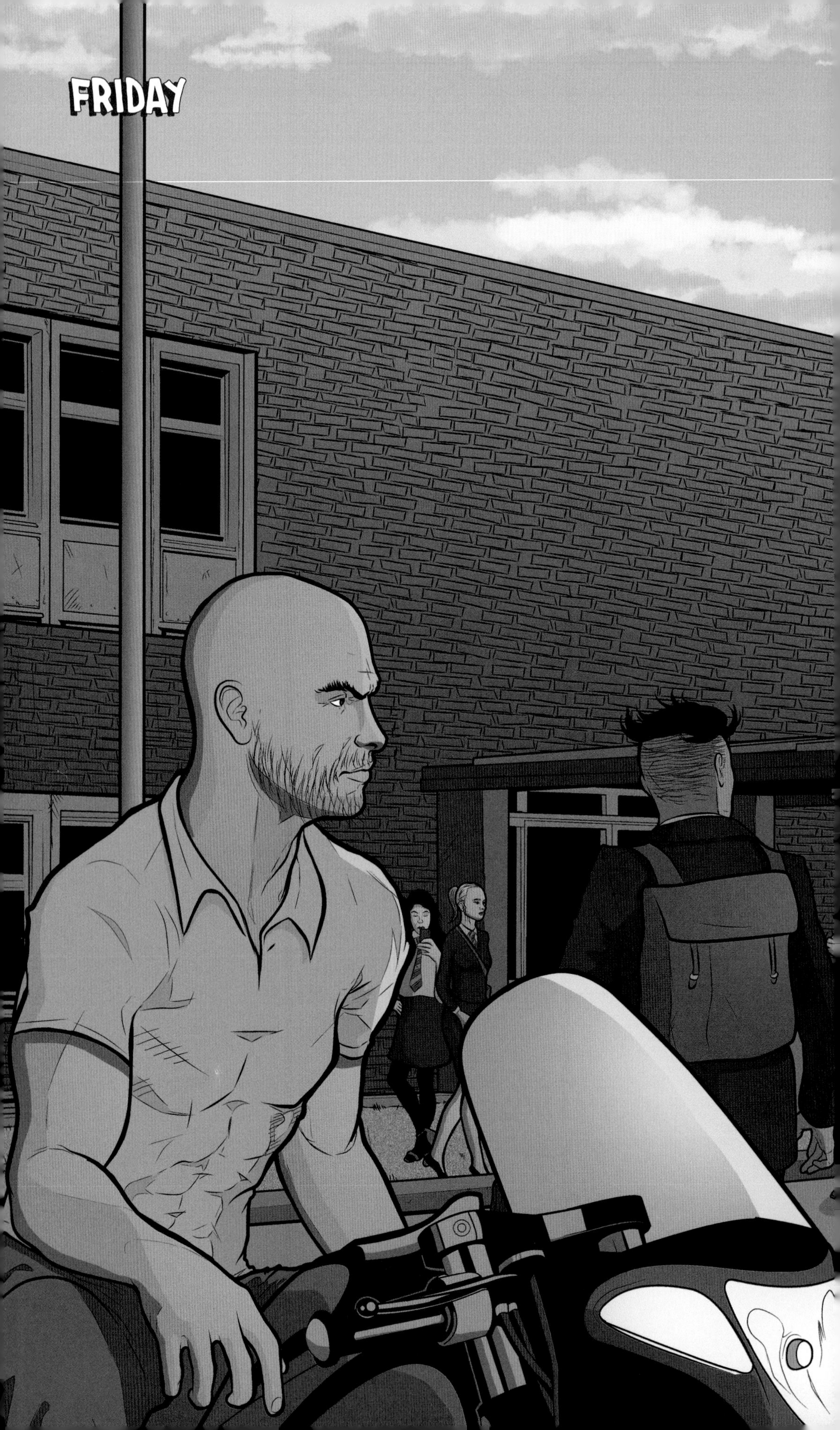
FRIDAY

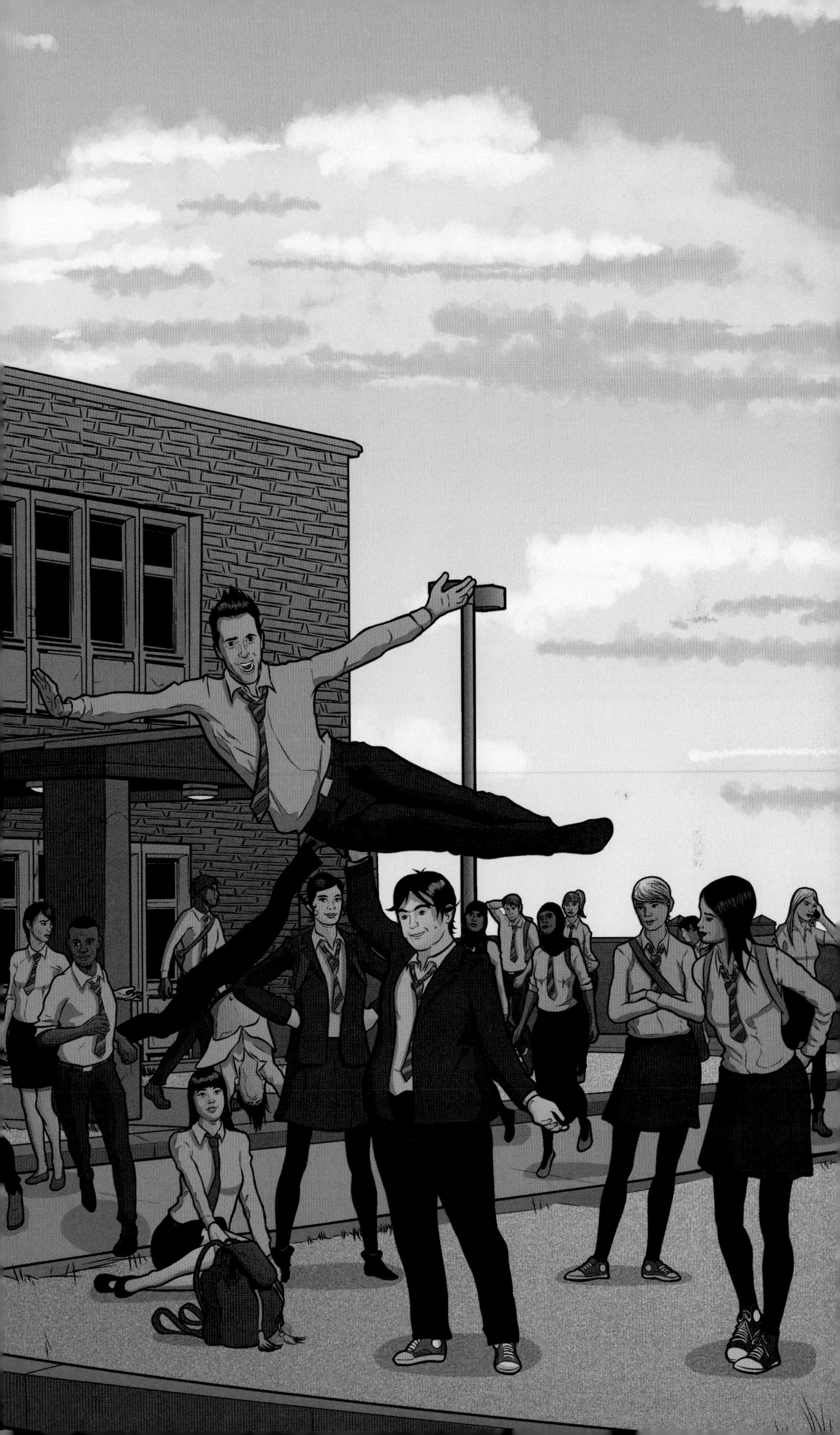

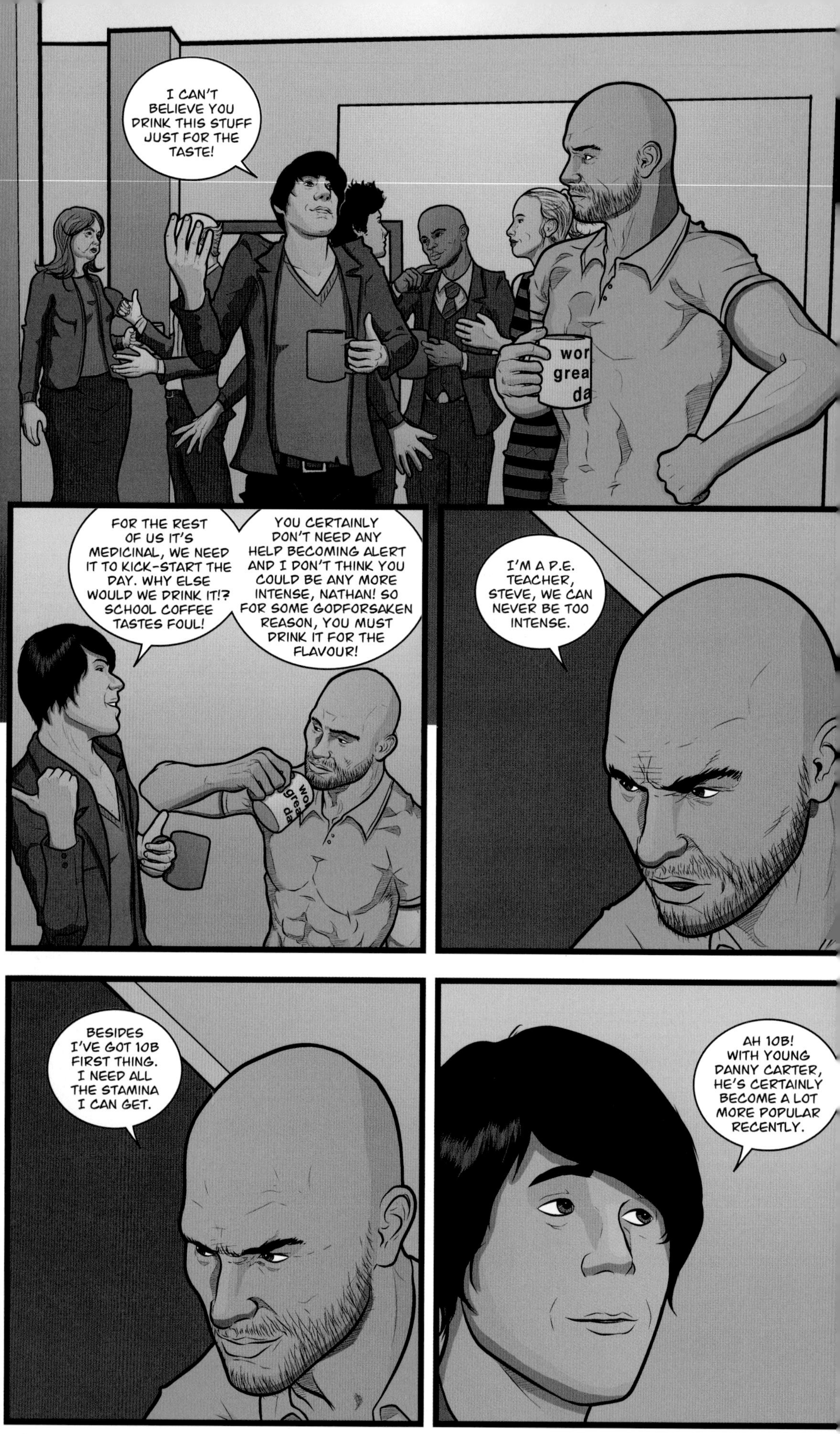

I CAN'T BELIEVE YOU DRINK THIS STUFF JUST FOR THE TASTE!
wor grea da
FOR THE REST OF US IT'S MEDICINAL, WE NEED IT TO KICK-START THE DAY. WHY ELSE WOULD WE DRINK IT!? SCHOOL COFFEE TASTES FOUL!
YOU CERTAINLY DON'T NEED ANY HELP BECOMING ALERT AND I DON'T THINK YOU COULD BE ANY MORE INTENSE, NATHAN! SO FOR SOME GODFORSAKEN REASON, YOU MUST DRINK IT FOR THE FLAVOUR!
I'M A P.E. TEACHER, STEVE, WE CAN NEVER BE TOO INTENSE.
BESIDES I'VE GOT 10B FIRST THING. I NEED ALL THE STAMINA I CAN GET.
AH 10B! WITH YOUNG DANNY CARTER, HE'S CERTAINLY BECOME A LOT MORE POPULAR RECENTLY.

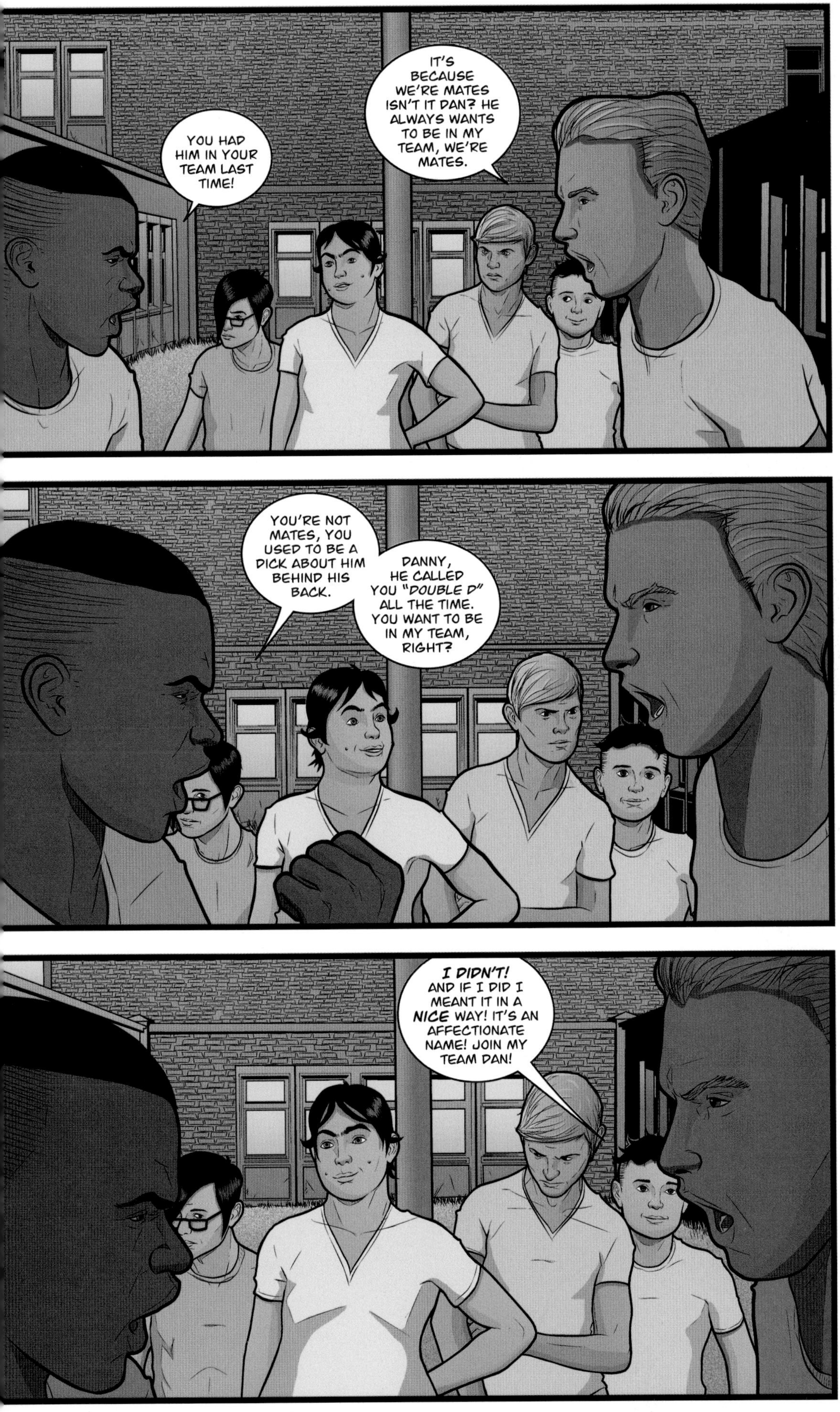
YOU HAD HIM IN YOUR TEAM LAST TIME!
IT'S BECAUSE WE'RE MATES ISN'T IT DAN? HE ALWAYS WANTS TO BE IN MY TEAM, WE'RE MATES.
YOU'RE NOT MATES, YOU USED TO BE A DICK ABOUT HIM BEHIND HIS BACK.
DANNY, HE CALLED YOU "DOUBLE D" ALL THE TIME. YOU WANT TO BE IN MY TEAM, RIGHT?
I DIDN'T! AND IF I DID I MEANT IT IN A NICE WAY! IT'S AN AFFECTIONATE NAME! JOIN MY TEAM DAN!

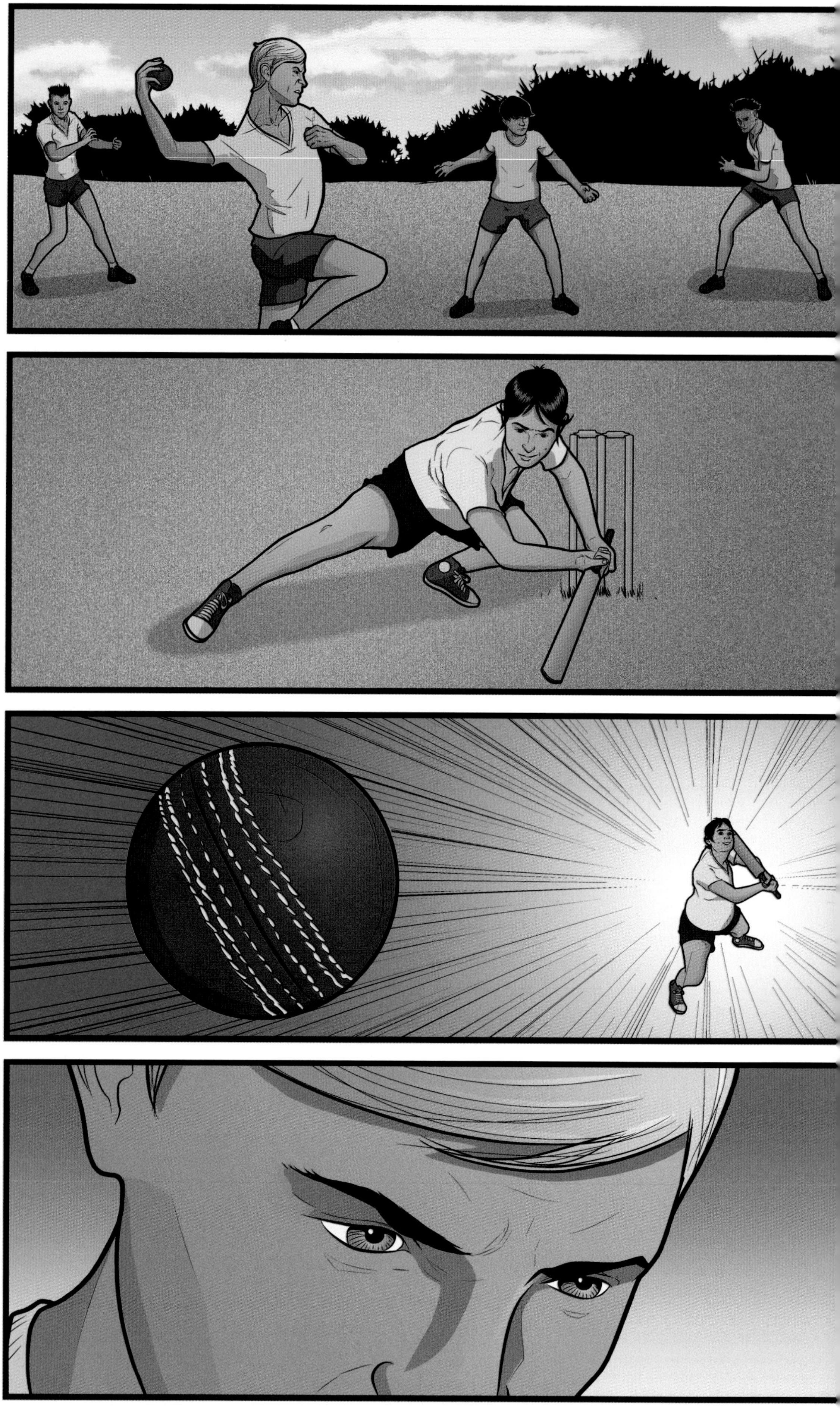

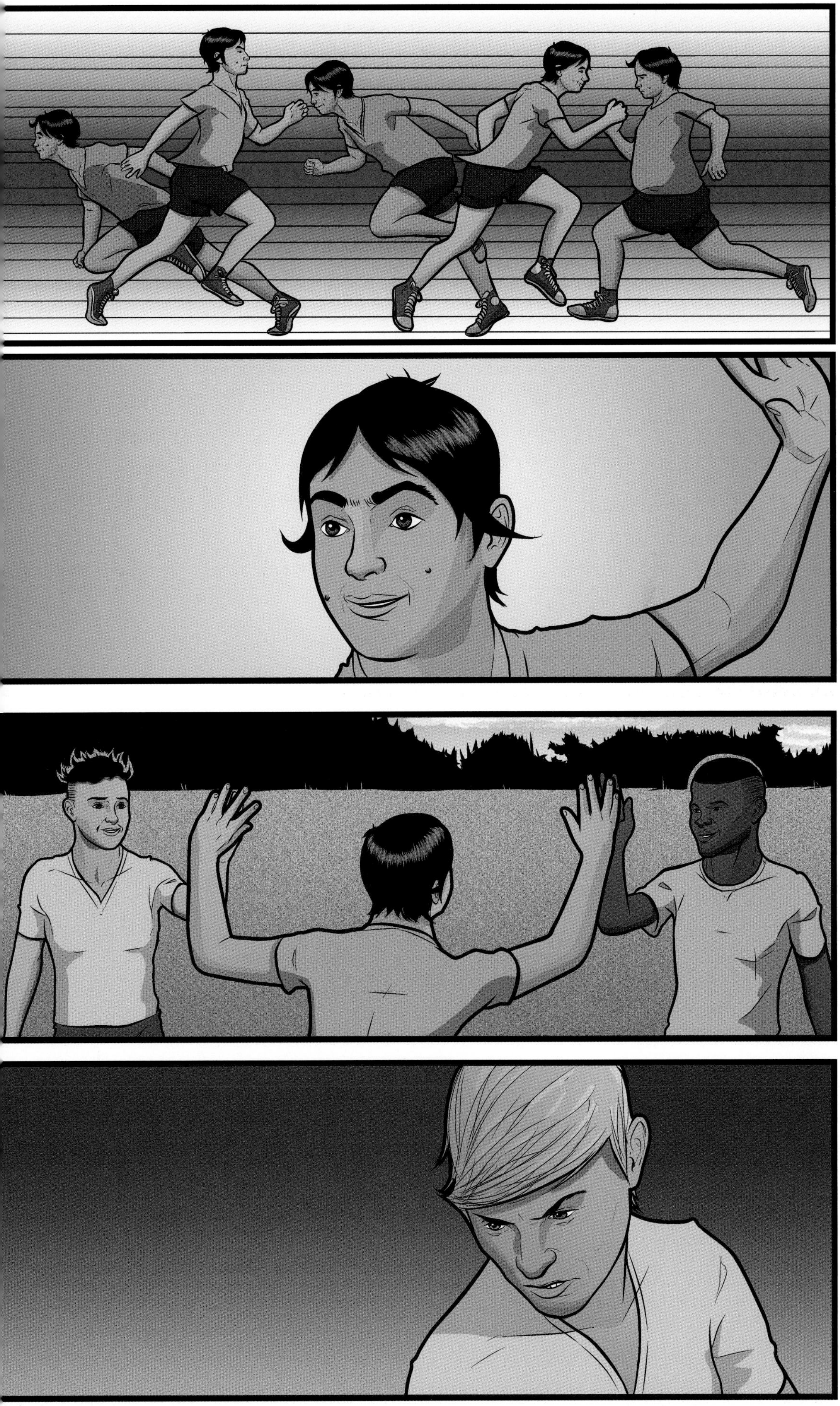

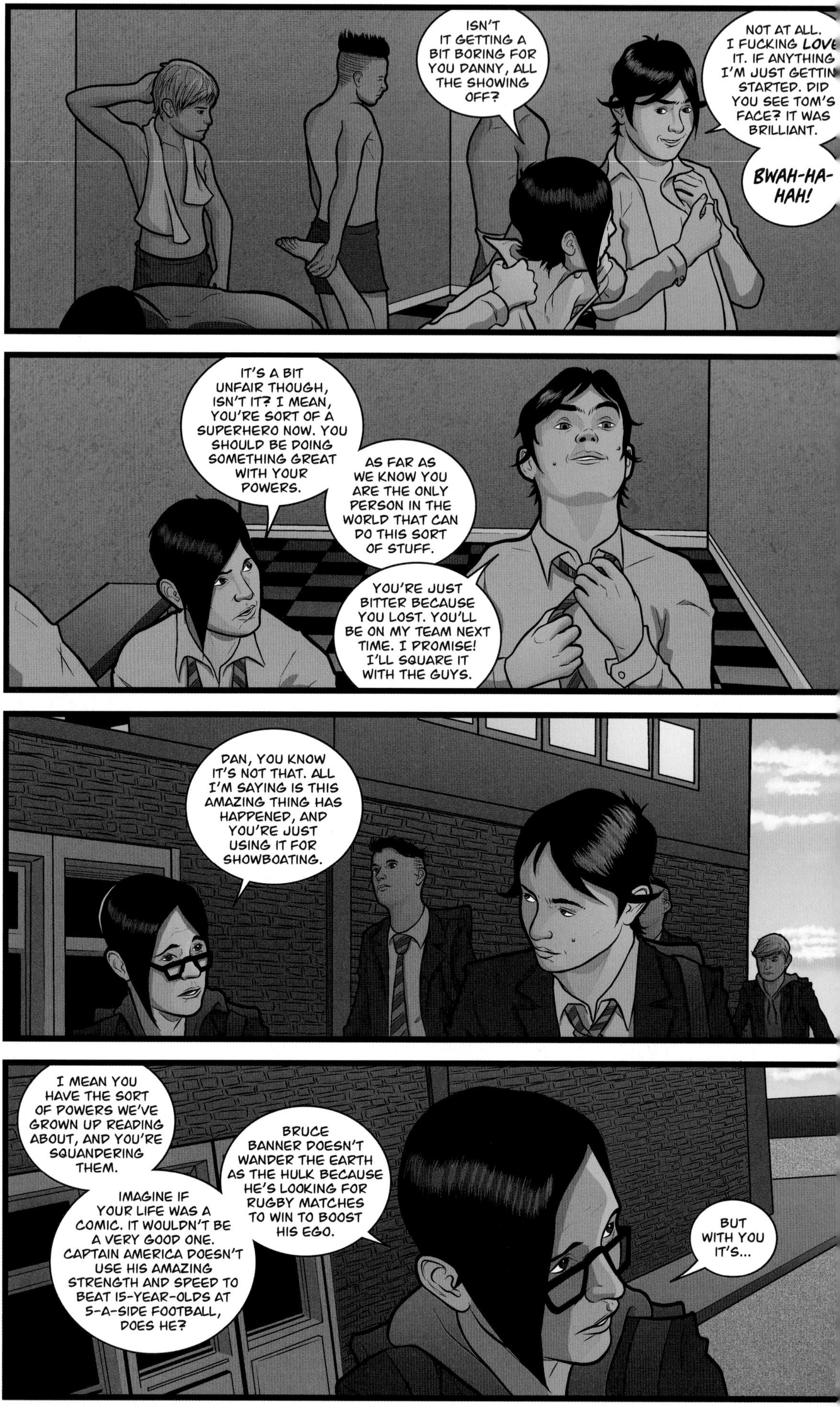
ISN'T IT GETTING A BIT BORING FOR YOU DANNY, ALL THE SHOWING OFF?
NOT AT ALL. I FUCKING LOVE IT. IF ANYTHING I'M JUST GETTING STARTED. DID YOU SEE TOM'S FACE? IT WAS BRILLIANT.
BWAH-HA-HAH!
IT'S A BIT UNFAIR THOUGH, ISN'T IT? I MEAN, YOU'RE SORT OF A SUPERHERO NOW. YOU SHOULD BE DOING SOMETHING GREAT WITH YOUR POWERS.
AS FAR AS WE KNOW YOU ARE THE ONLY PERSON IN THE WORLD THAT CAN DO THIS SORT OF STUFF.
YOU'RE JUST BITTER BECAUSE YOU LOST. YOU'LL BE ON MY TEAM NEXT TIME. I PROMISE! I'LL SQUARE IT WITH THE GUYS.
DAN, YOU KNOW IT'S NOT THAT. ALL I'M SAYING IS THIS AMAZING THING HAS HAPPENED, AND YOU'RE JUST USING IT FOR SHOWBOATING.
I MEAN YOU HAVE THE SORT OF POWERS WE'VE GROWN UP READING ABOUT, AND YOU'RE SQUANDERING THEM.
IMAGINE IF YOUR LIFE WAS A COMIC. IT WOULDN'T BE A VERY GOOD ONE. CAPTAIN AMERICA DOESN'T USE HIS AMAZING STRENGTH AND SPEED TO BEAT 15-YEAR-OLDS AT 5-A-SIDE FOOTBALL, DOES HE?
BRUCE BANNER DOESN'T WANDER THE EARTH AS THE HULK BECAUSE HE'S LOOKING FOR RUGBY MATCHES TO WIN TO BOOST HIS EGO.
BUT WITH YOU IT'S...

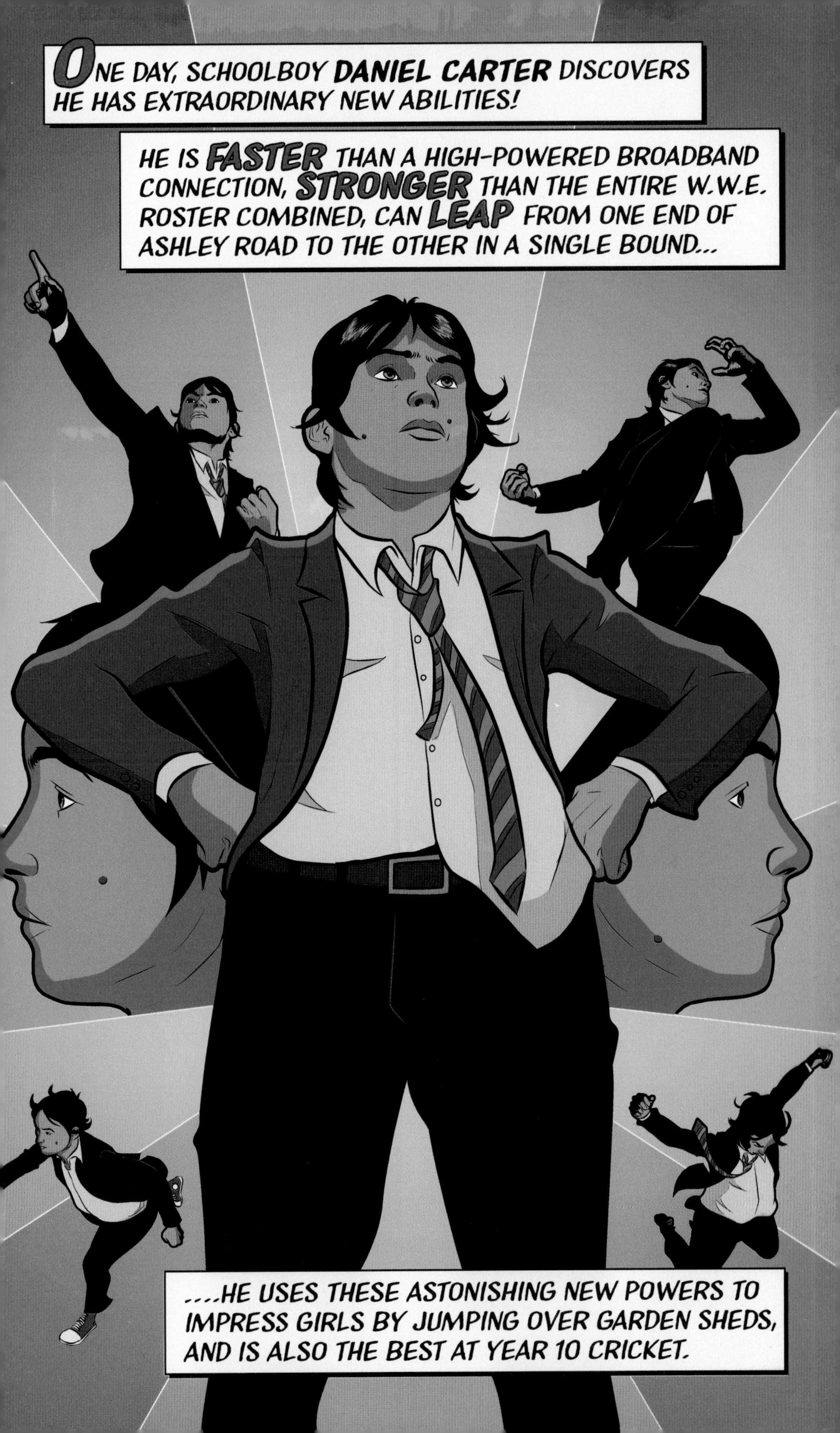
ONE DAY, SCHOOLBOY DANIEL CARTER DISCOVERS HE HAS EXTRAORDINARY NEW ABILITIES!
HE IS FASTER THAN A HIGH-POWERED BROADBAND CONNECTION, STRONGER THAN THE ENTIRE W.W.E. ROSTER COMBINED, CAN LEAP FROM ONE END OF ASHLEY ROAD TO THE OTHER IN A SINGLE BOUND...
....HE USES THESE ASTONISHING NEW POWERS TO IMPRESS GIRLS BY JUMPING OVER GARDEN SHEDS, AND IS ALSO THE BEST AT YEAR 10 CRICKET.

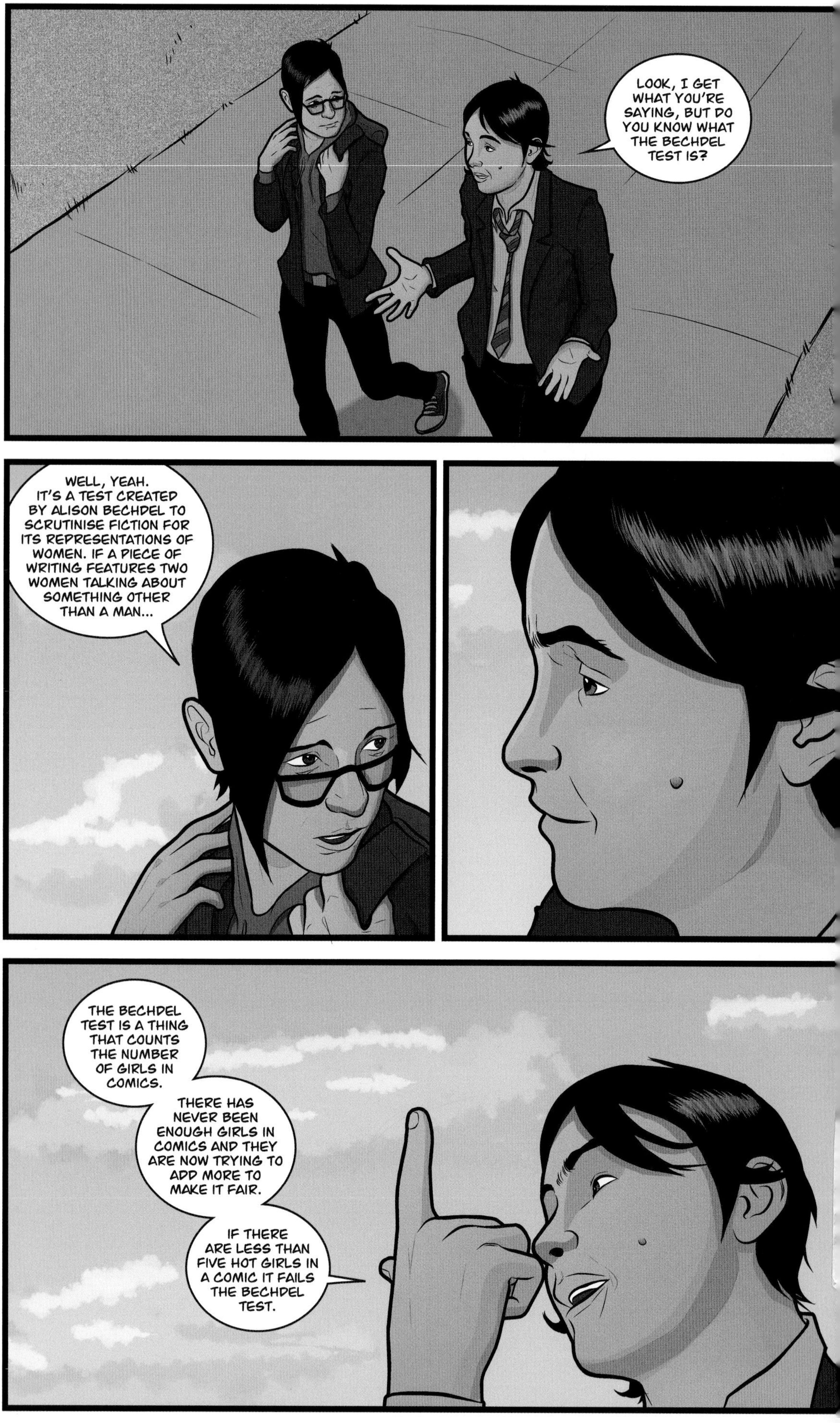
LOOK, I GET WHAT YOU'RE SAYING, BUT DO YOU KNOW WHAT THE BECHDEL TEST IS?
WELL, YEAH. IT'S A TEST CREATED BY ALISON BECHDEL TO SCRUTINISE FICTION FOR ITS REPRESENTATIONS OF WOMEN. IF A PIECE OF WRITING FEATURES TWO WOMEN TALKING ABOUT SOMETHING OTHER THAN A MAN...
THE BECHDEL TEST IS A THING THAT COUNTS THE NUMBER OF GIRLS IN COMICS.
THERE HAS NEVER BEEN ENOUGH GIRLS IN COMICS AND THEY ARE NOW TRYING TO ADD MORE TO MAKE IT FAIR.
IF THERE ARE LESS THAN FIVE HOT GIRLS IN A COMIC IT FAILS THE BECHDEL TEST.

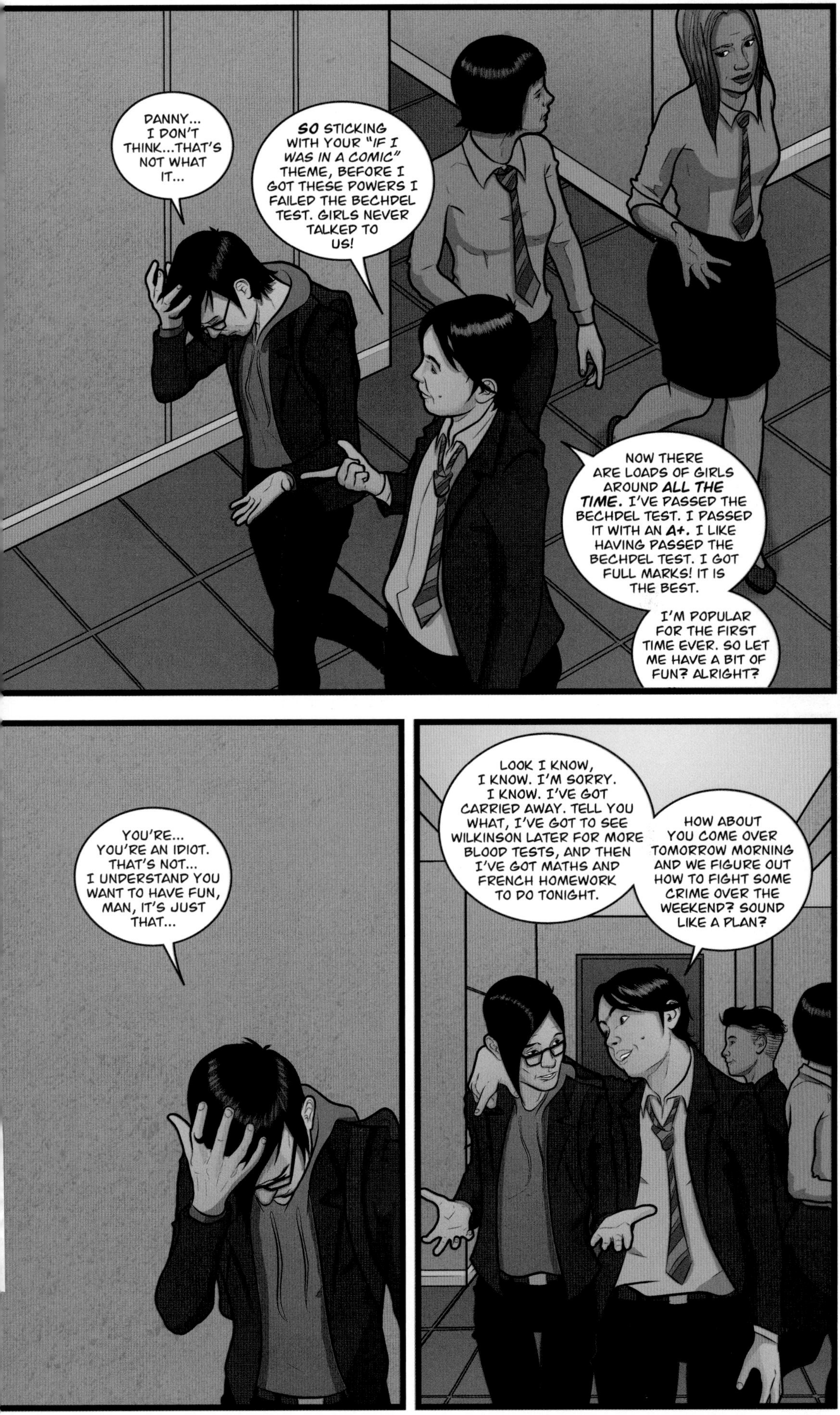

DANNY... I DON'T THINK...THAT'S NOT WHAT IT...
SO STICKING WITH YOUR "IF I WAS IN A COMIC" THEME, BEFORE I GOT THESE POWERS I FAILED THE BECHDEL TEST. GIRLS NEVER TALKED TO US!
NOW THERE ARE LOADS OF GIRLS AROUND ALL THE TIME. I'VE PASSED THE BECHDEL TEST. I PASSED IT WITH AN A+. I LIKE HAVING PASSED THE BECHDEL TEST. I GOT FULL MARKS! IT IS THE BEST.
I'M POPULAR FOR THE FIRST TIME EVER. SO LET ME HAVE A BIT OF FUN? ALRIGHT?
YOU'RE... YOU'RE AN IDIOT. THAT'S NOT... I UNDERSTAND YOU WANT TO HAVE FUN, MAN, IT'S JUST THAT...
LOOK I KNOW, I KNOW. I'M SORRY. I KNOW. I'VE GOT CARRIED AWAY. TELL YOU WHAT, I'VE GOT TO SEE WILKINSON LATER FOR MORE BLOOD TESTS, AND THEN I'VE GOT MATHS AND FRENCH HOMEWORK TO DO TONIGHT.
HOW ABOUT YOU COME OVER TOMORROW MORNING AND WE FIGURE OUT HOW TO FIGHT SOME CRIME OVER THE WEEKEND? SOUND LIKE A PLAN?

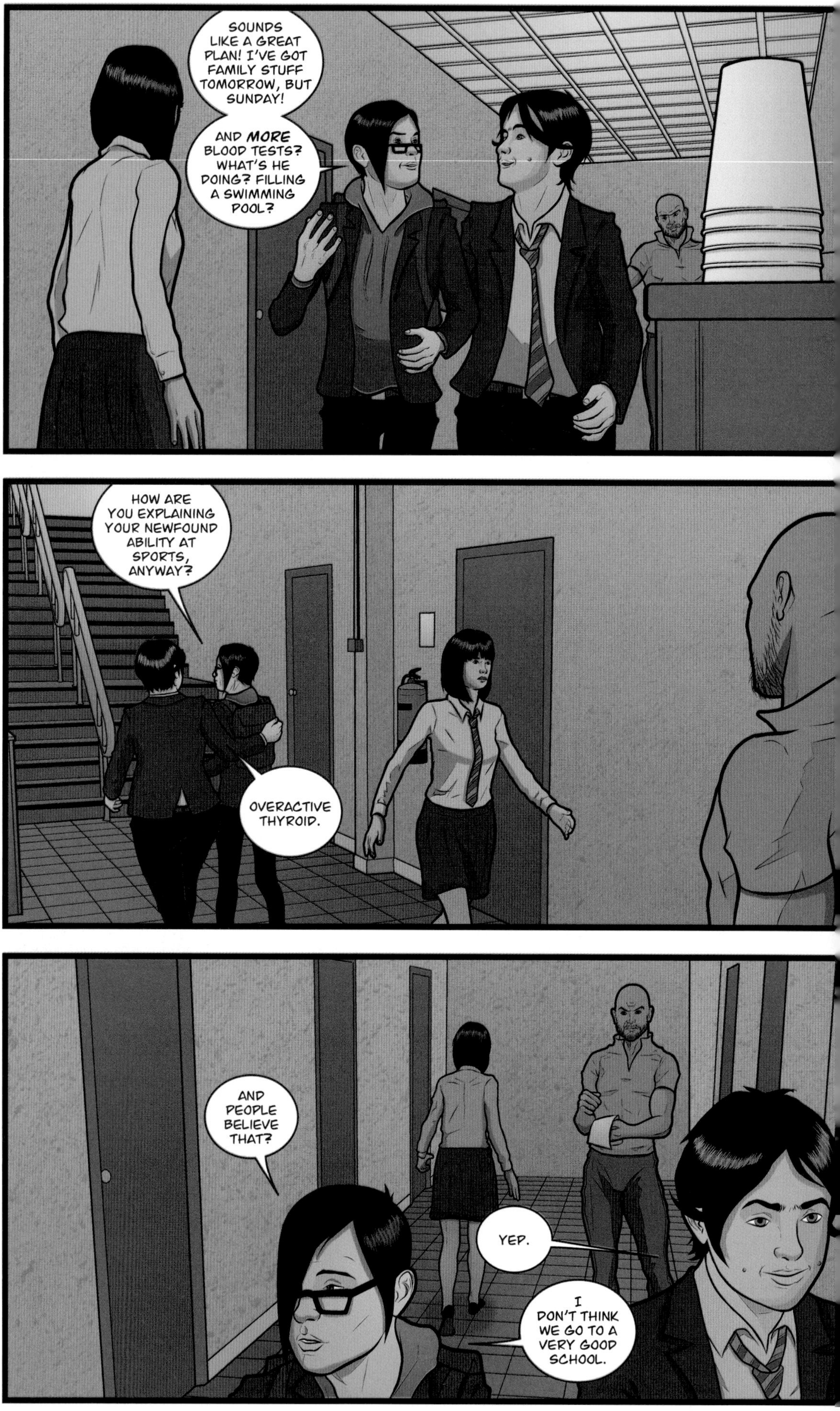
SOUNDS LIKE A GREAT PLAN! I'VE GOT FAMILY STUFF TOMORROW, BUT SUNDAY!
AND MORE BLOOD TESTS? WHAT'S HE DOING? FILLING A SWIMMING POOL?
HOW ARE YOU EXPLAINING YOUR NEWFOUND ABILITY AT SPORTS, ANYWAY?
OVERACTIVE THYROID.
AND PEOPLE BELIEVE THAT?
YEP.
I DON'T THINK WE GO TO A VERY GOOD SCHOOL.

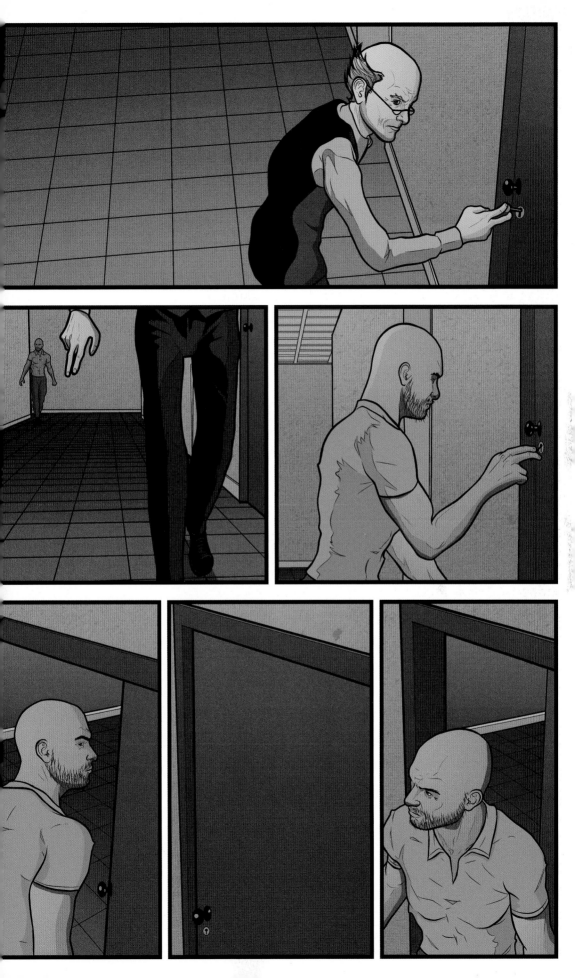

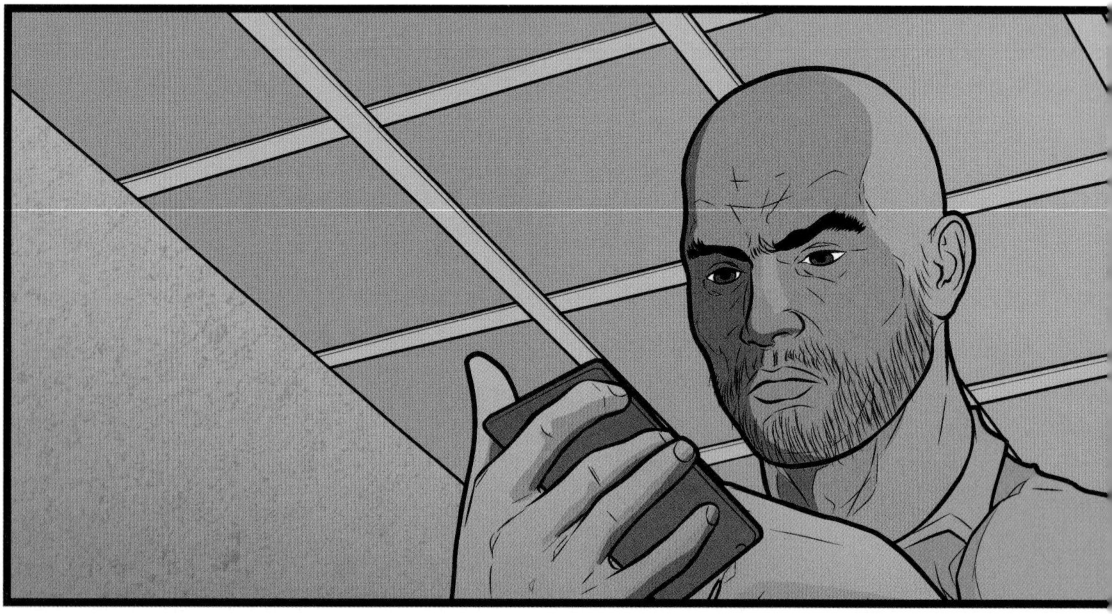

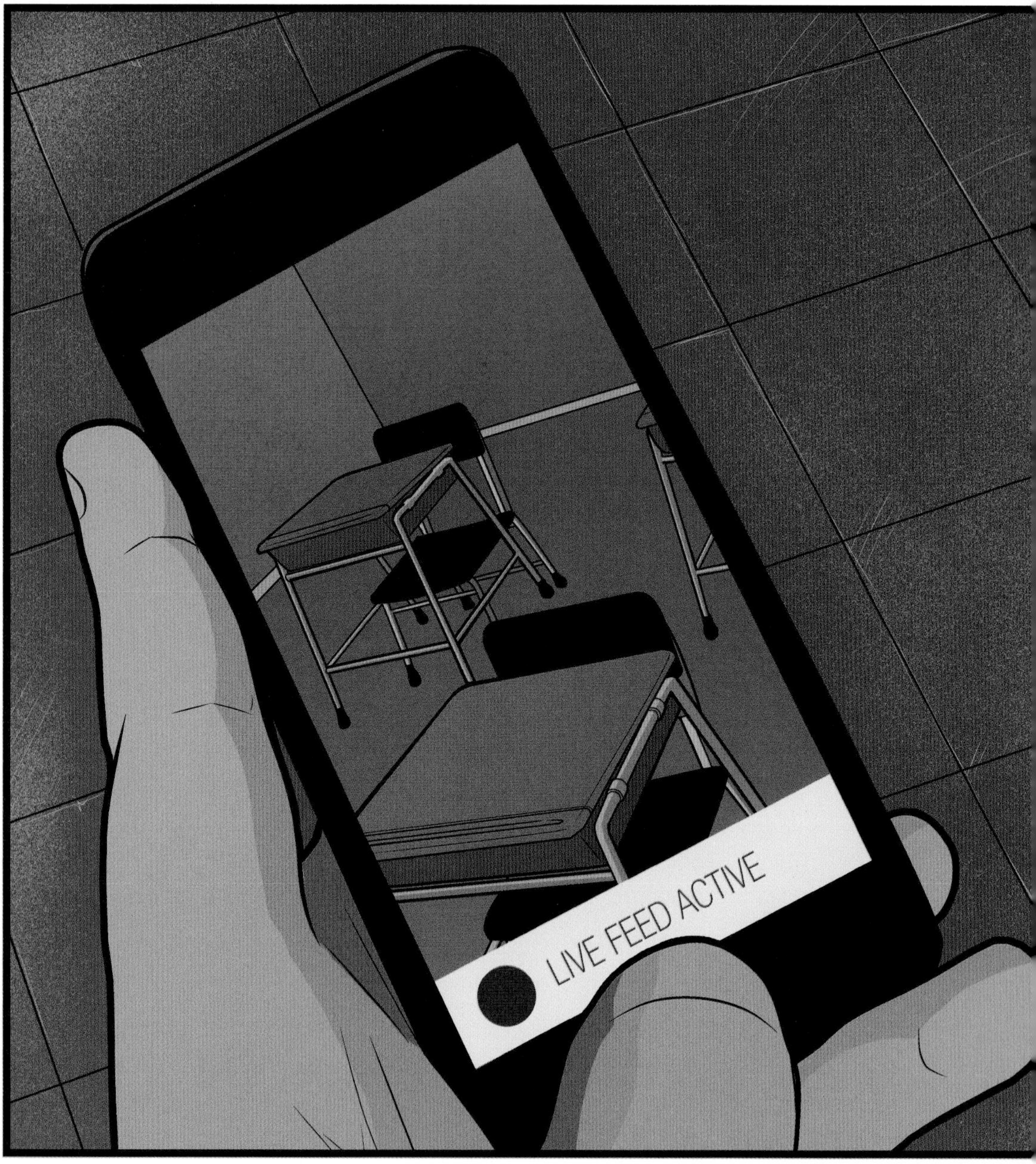
LIVE FEED ACTIVE

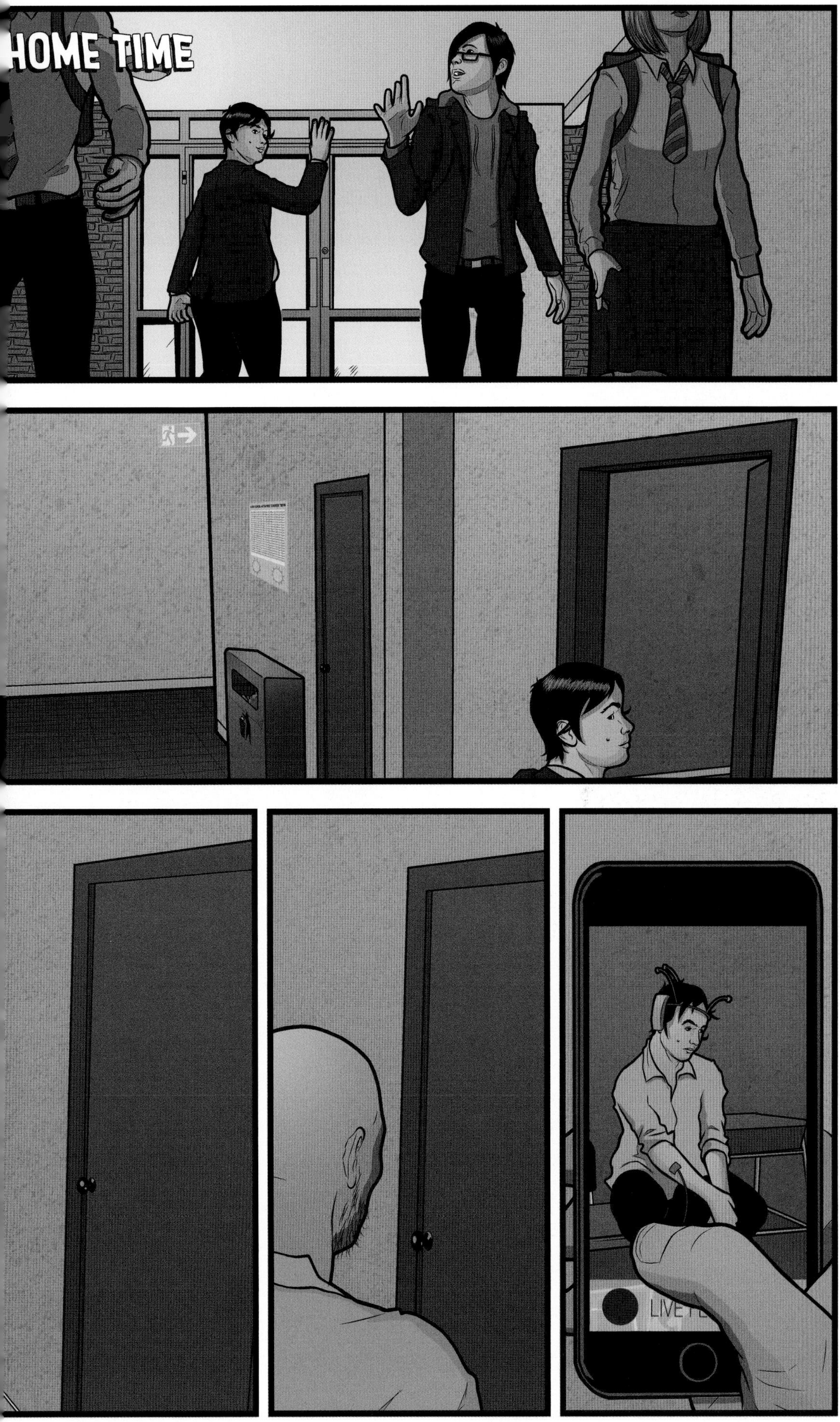
HOME TIME
LIVE

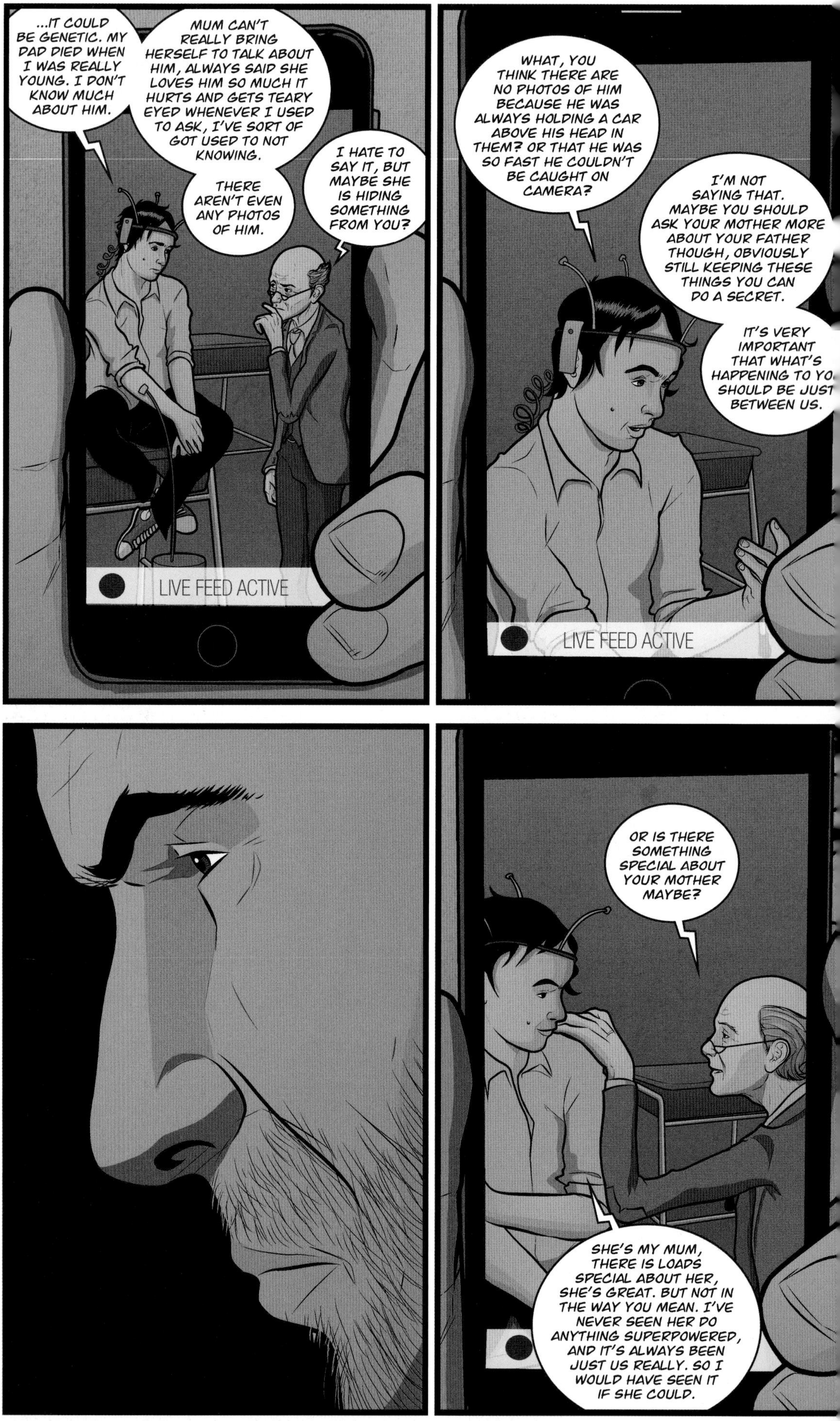
...IT COULD BE GENETIC. MY DAD DIED WHEN I WAS REALLY YOUNG. I DON'T KNOW MUCH ABOUT HIM.
MUM CAN'T REALLY BRING HERSELF TO TALK ABOUT HIM, ALWAYS SAID SHE LOVES HIM SO MUCH IT HURTS AND GETS TEARY EYED WHENEVER I USED TO ASK, I'VE SORT OF GOT USED TO NOT KNOWING.
THERE AREN'T EVEN ANY PHOTOS OF HIM.
I HATE TO SAY IT, BUT MAYBE SHE IS HIDING SOMETHING FROM YOU?
LIVE FEED ACTIVE
WHAT, YOU THINK THERE ARE NO PHOTOS OF HIM BECAUSE HE WAS ALWAYS HOLDING A CAR ABOVE HIS HEAD IN THEM? OR THAT HE WAS SO FAST HE COULDN'T BE CAUGHT ON CAMERA?
I'M NOT SAYING THAT. MAYBE YOU SHOULD ASK YOUR MOTHER MORE ABOUT YOUR FATHER THOUGH, OBVIOUSLY STILL KEEPING THESE THINGS YOU CAN DO A SECRET.
IT'S VERY IMPORTANT THAT WHAT'S HAPPENING TO YO SHOULD BE JUST BETWEEN US.
LIVE FEED ACTIVE
OR IS THERE SOMETHING SPECIAL ABOUT YOUR MOTHER MAYBE?
SHE'S MY MUM, THERE IS LOADS SPECIAL ABOUT HER, SHE'S GREAT. BUT NOT IN THE WAY YOU MEAN. I'VE NEVER SEEN HER DO ANYTHING SUPERPOWERED, AND IT'S ALWAYS BEEN JUST US REALLY. SO I WOULD HAVE SEEN IT IF SHE COULD.

SEE YOU ON MONDAY.

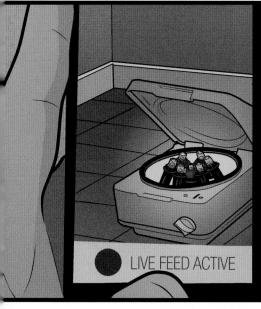

LIVE FEED ACTIVE

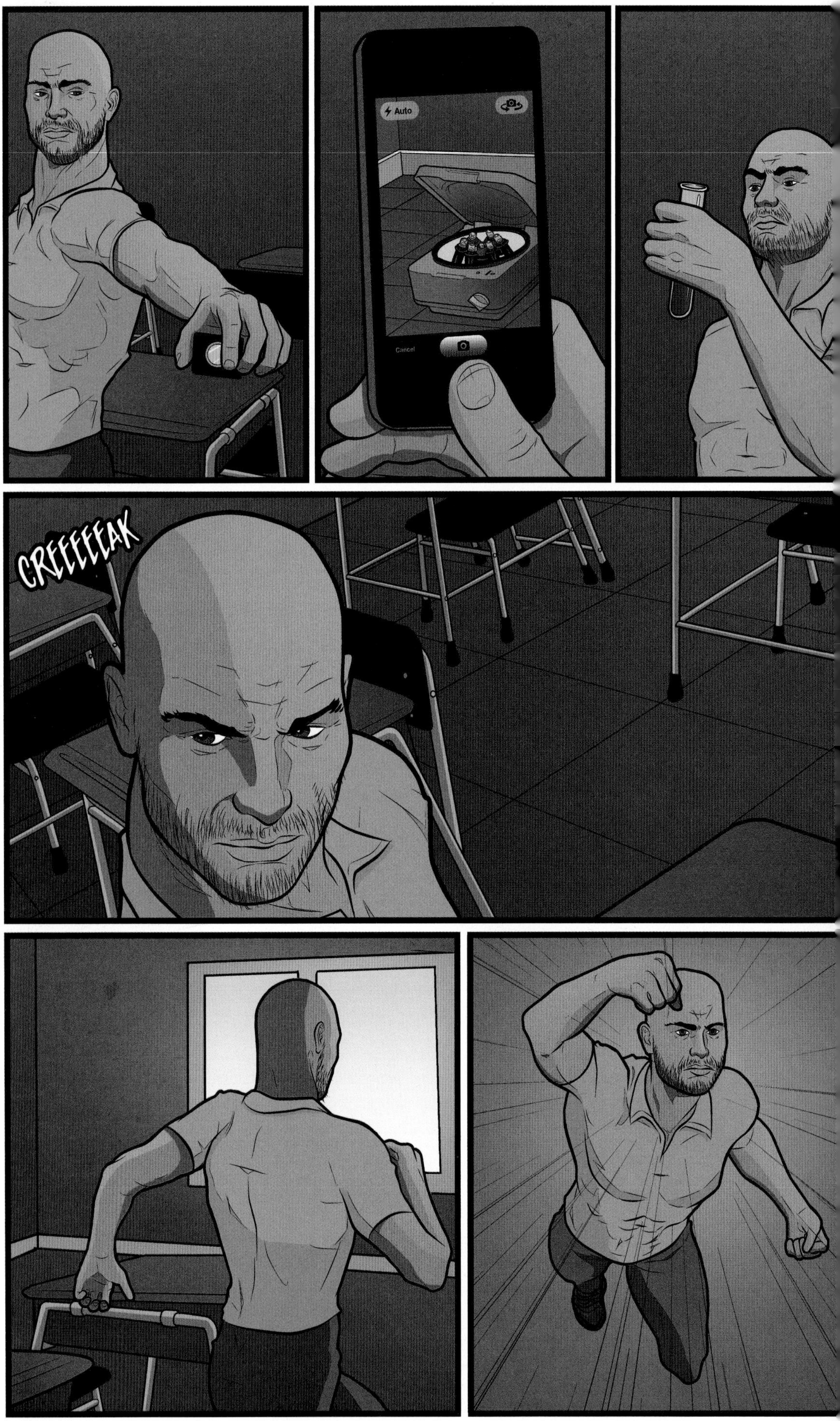

Auto
Cancel
CREEEEEAK

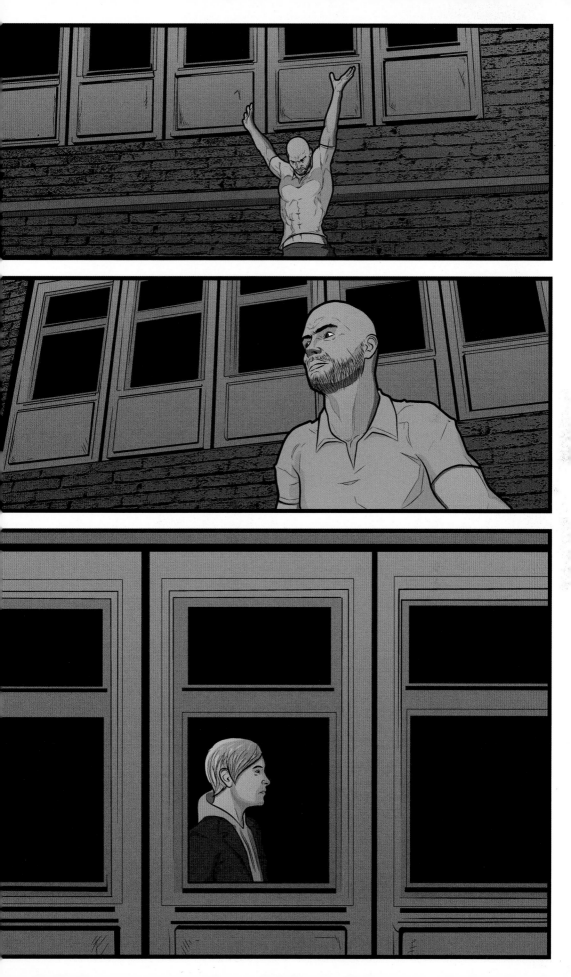

CHAPTER 4

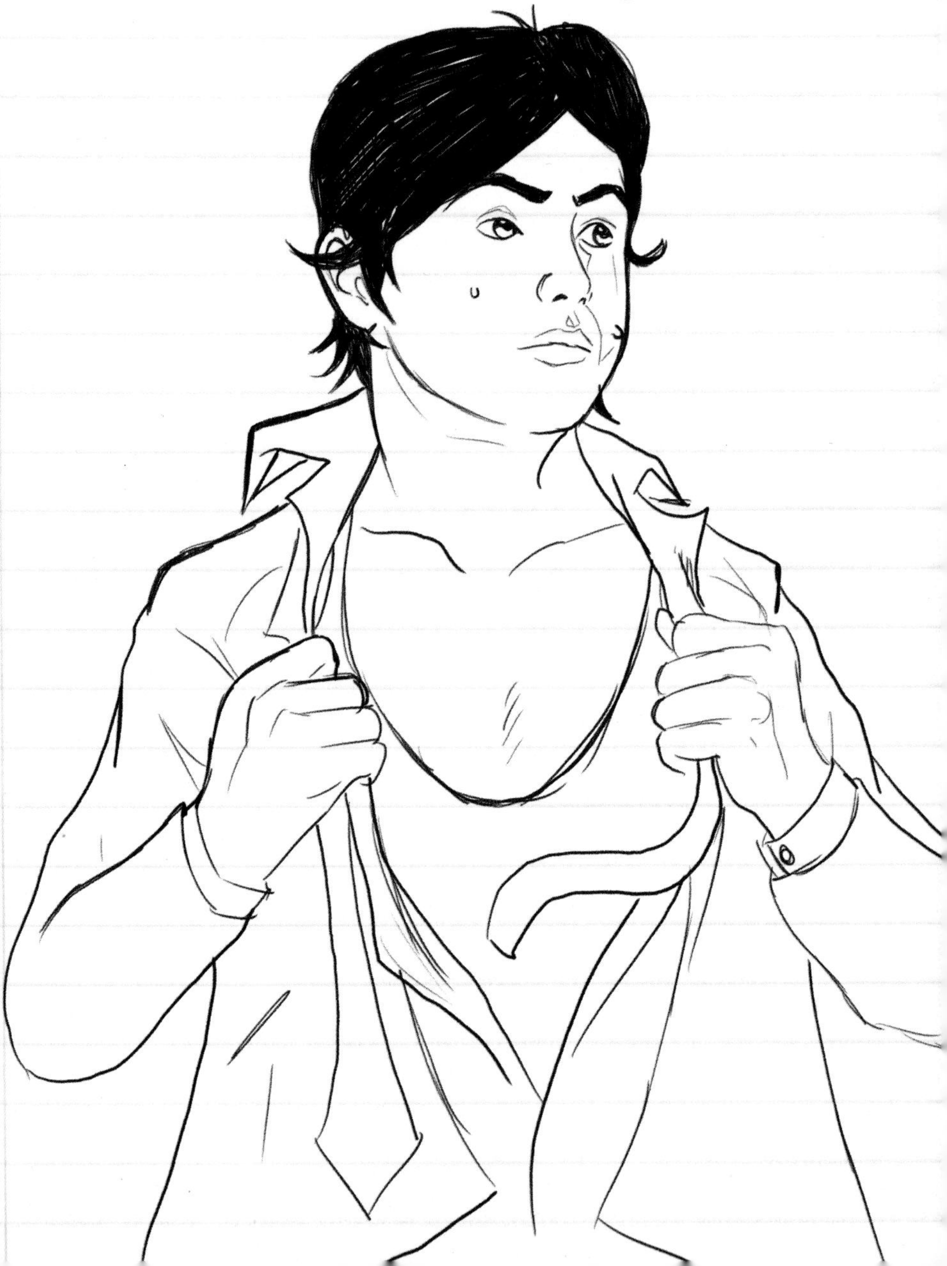

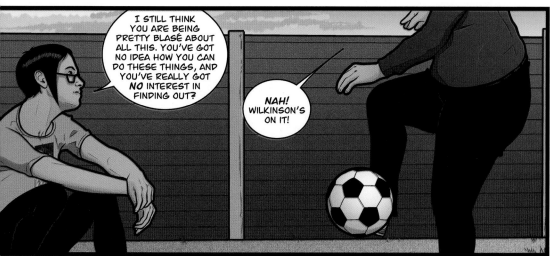

I STILL THINK YOU ARE BEING PRETTY BLASÉ ABOUT ALL THIS. YOU'VE GOT NO IDEA HOW YOU CAN DO THESE THINGS, AND YOU'VE REALLY GOT *NO* INTEREST IN FINDING OUT?

NAH! WILKINSON'S ON IT!

I'M WORRIED THAT IF I QUESTION IT TOO MUCH, IT WILL GO AWAY.

SOMEONE IS BOUND TO FIGURE OUT IT'S NOT NORMAL SOON, YOU'VE NOT REALLY BEEN VERY SECRETIVE ABOUT HAVING AMAZING NEW ABILITIES.

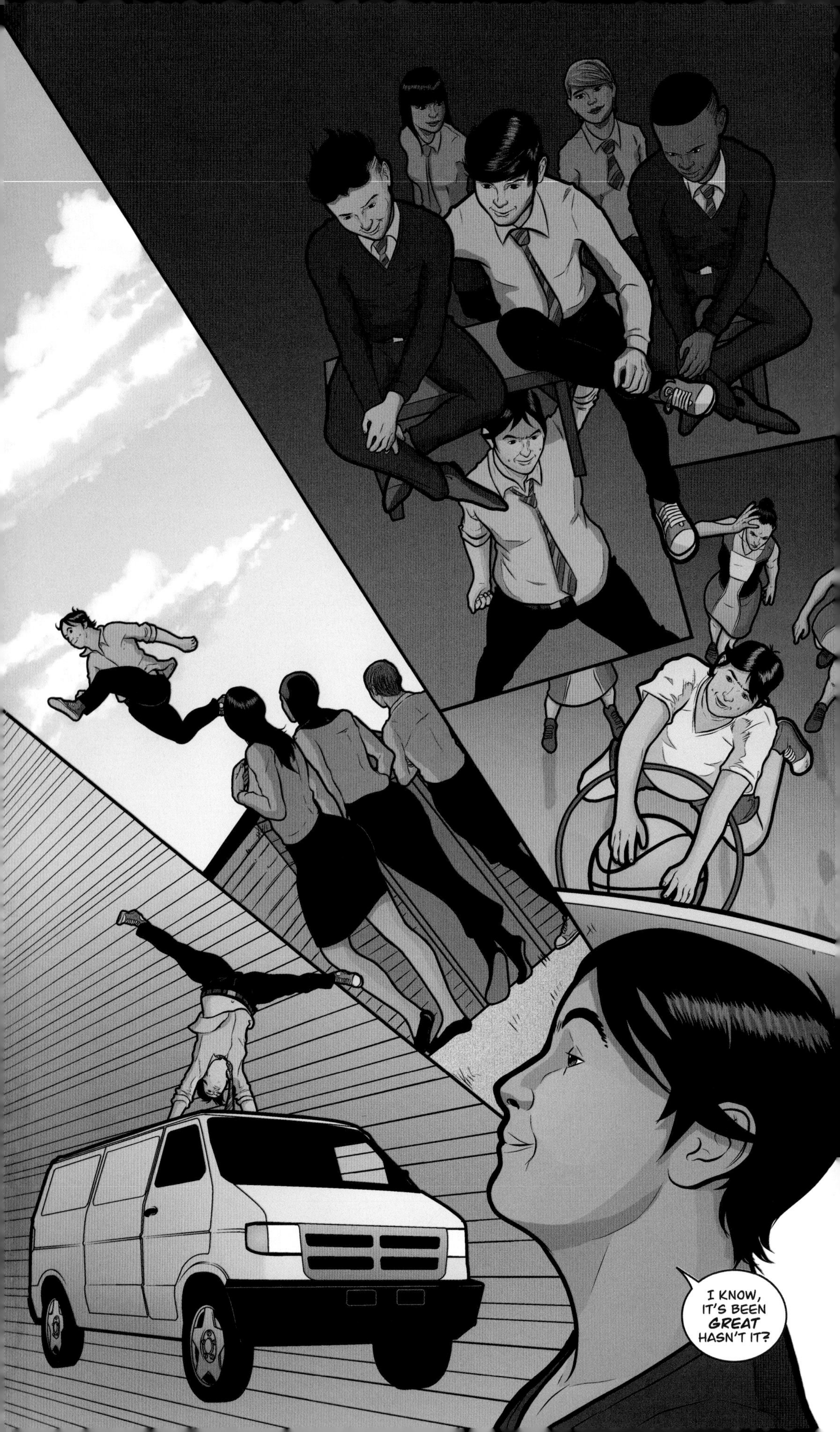
I KNOW, IT'S BEEN GREAT HASN'T IT?

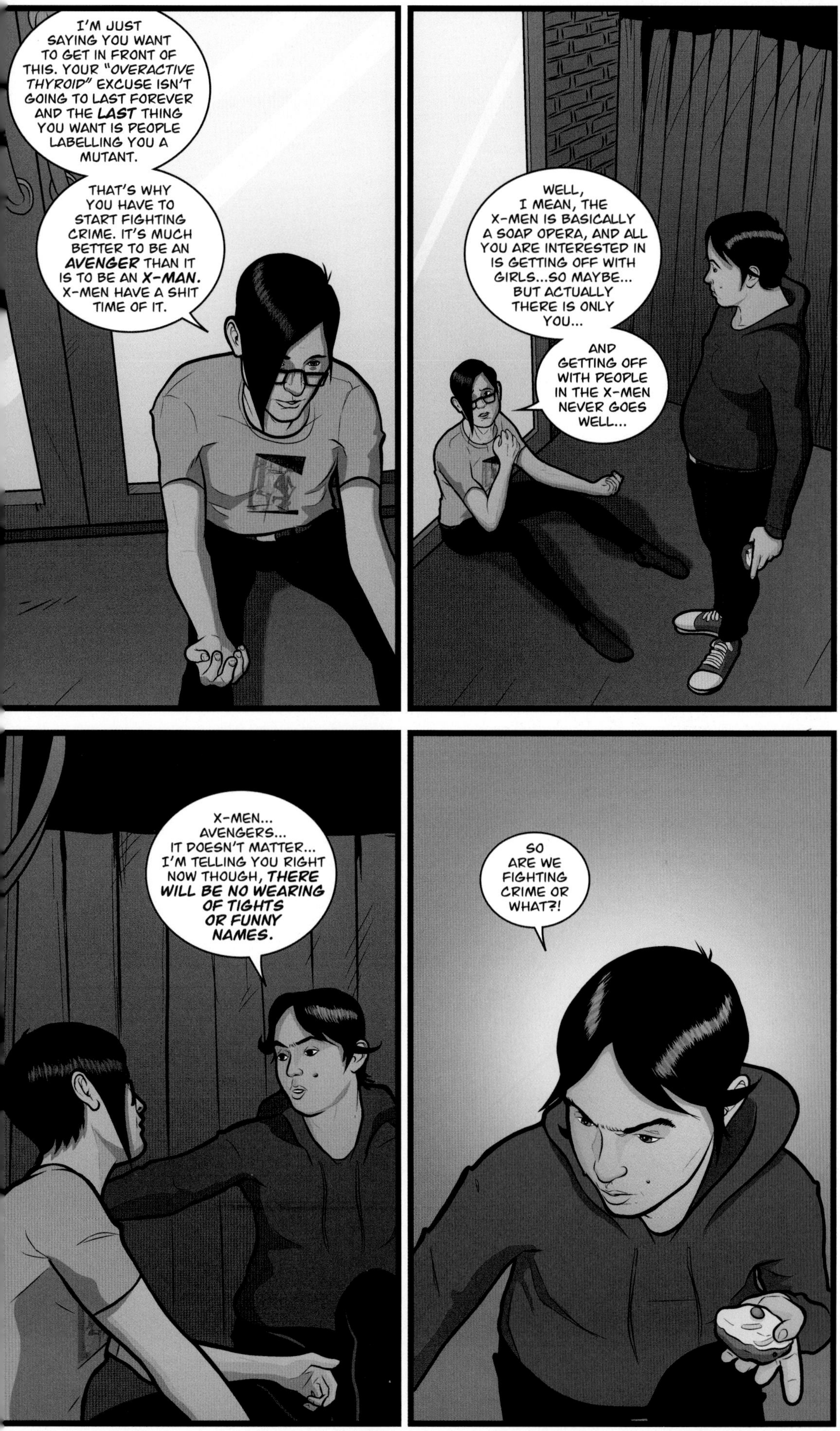
I'M JUST SAYING YOU WANT TO GET IN FRONT OF THIS. YOUR "OVERACTIVE THYROID" EXCUSE ISN'T GOING TO LAST FOREVER AND THE LAST THING YOU WANT IS PEOPLE LABELLING YOU A MUTANT.
THAT'S WHY YOU HAVE TO START FIGHTING CRIME. IT'S MUCH BETTER TO BE AN AVENGER THAN IT IS TO BE AN X-MAN. X-MEN HAVE A SHIT TIME OF IT.
WELL, I MEAN, THE X-MEN IS BASICALLY A SOAP OPERA, AND ALL YOU ARE INTERESTED IN IS GETTING OFF WITH GIRLS...SO MAYBE... BUT ACTUALLY THERE IS ONLY YOU...
AND GETTING OFF WITH PEOPLE IN THE X-MEN NEVER GOES WELL...
X-MEN... AVENGERS... IT DOESN'T MATTER... I'M TELLING YOU RIGHT NOW THOUGH, THERE WILL BE NO WEARING OF TIGHTS OR FUNNY NAMES.
SO ARE WE FIGHTING CRIME OR WHAT?!

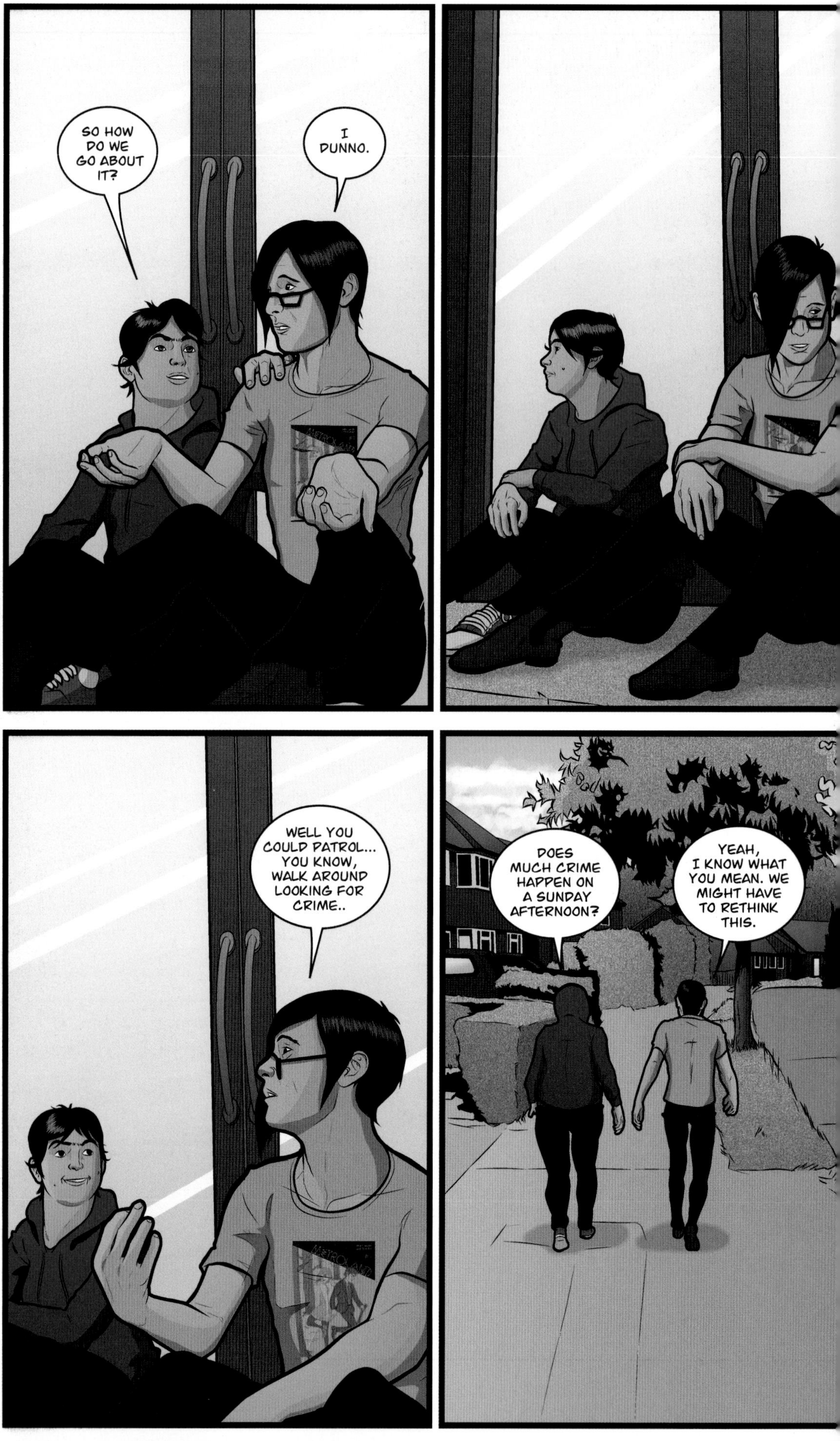
SO HOW DO WE GO ABOUT IT?
I DUNNO.
WELL YOU COULD PATROL... YOU KNOW, WALK AROUND LOOKING FOR CRIME..
DOES MUCH CRIME HAPPEN ON A SUNDAY AFTERNOON?
YEAH, I KNOW WHAT YOU MEAN. WE MIGHT HAVE TO RETHINK THIS.

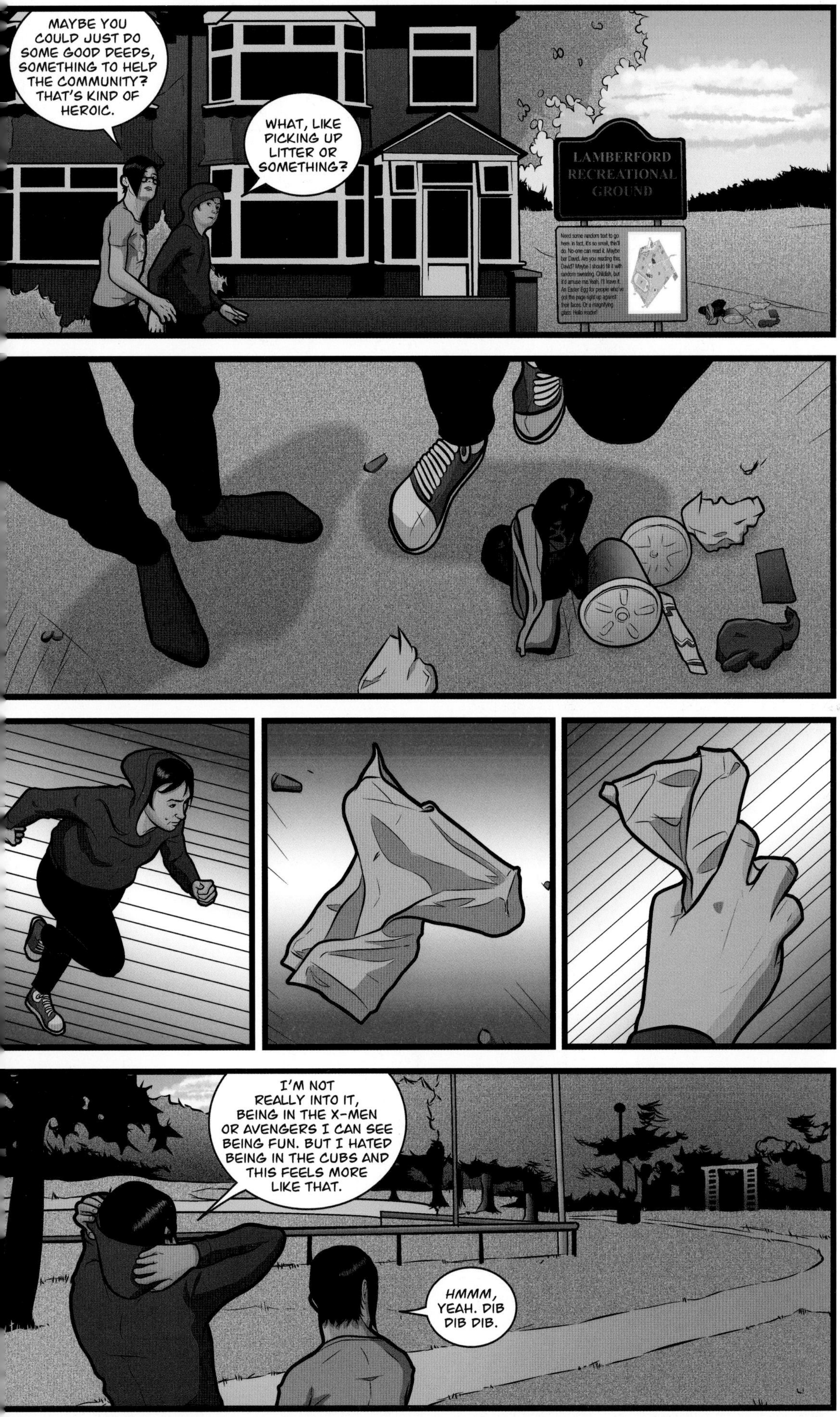
MAYBE YOU COULD JUST DO SOME GOOD DEEDS, SOMETHING TO HELP THE COMMUNITY? THAT'S KIND OF HEROIC.
WHAT, LIKE PICKING UP LITTER OR SOMETHING?
LAMBERFORD RECREATIONAL GROUND
Need some random text to go here. In fact, it's so small, this'll do. No-one can read it. Maybe bar David. Are you reading this, David? Maybe I should fill it with random swearing. Childish, but it'd amuse me. Yeah, I'll leave it. An Easter Egg for people who've got the page right up against their faces. Or a magnifying glass. Hello reader!
I'M NOT REALLY INTO IT, BEING IN THE X-MEN OR AVENGERS I CAN SEE BEING FUN. BUT I HATED BEING IN THE CUBS AND THIS FEELS MORE LIKE THAT.
HMMM, YEAH. DIB DIB DIB.

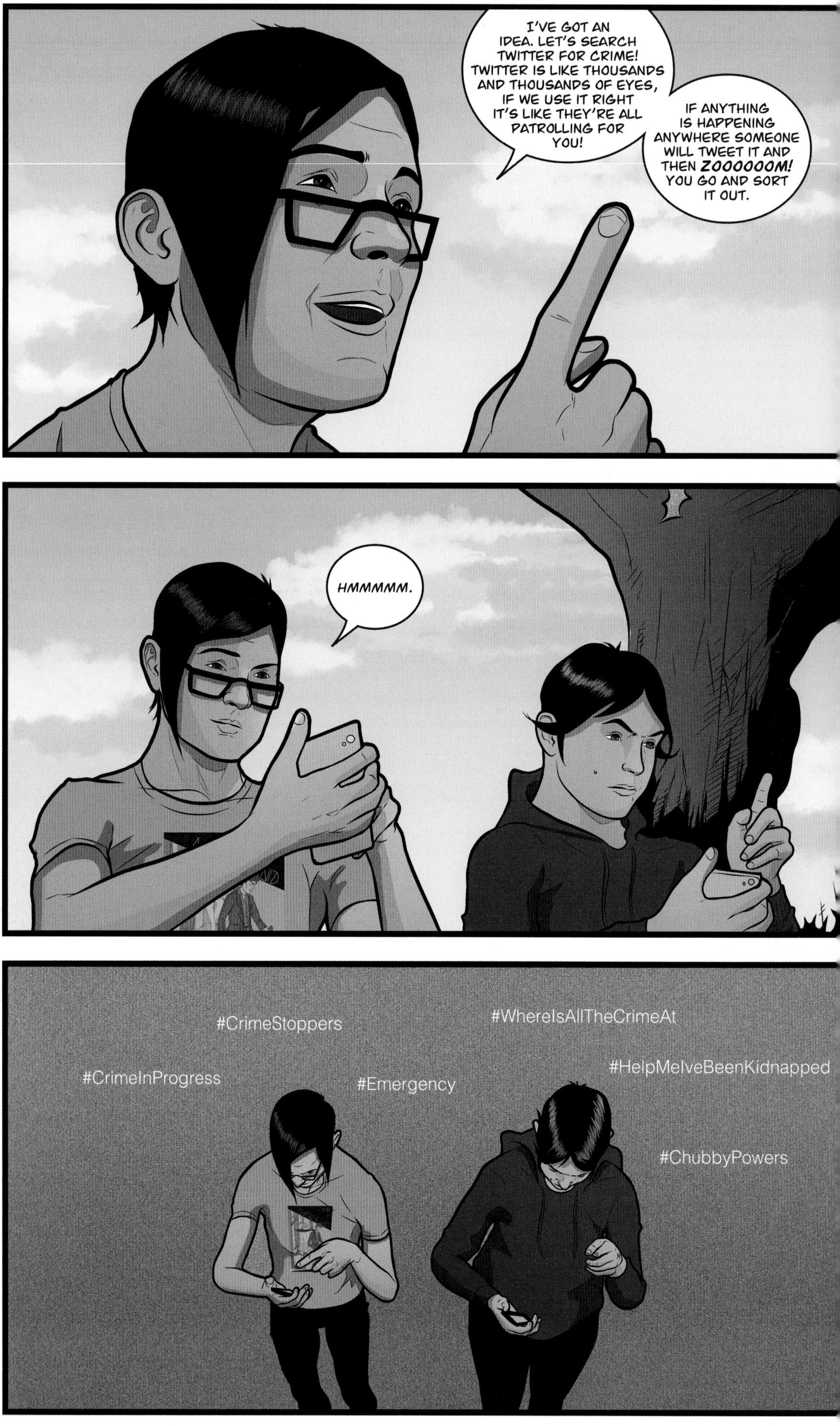
I'VE GOT AN IDEA. LET'S SEARCH TWITTER FOR CRIME! TWITTER IS LIKE THOUSANDS AND THOUSANDS OF EYES, IF WE USE IT RIGHT IT'S LIKE THEY'RE ALL PATROLLING FOR YOU!
IF ANYTHING IS HAPPENING ANYWHERE SOMEONE WILL TWEET IT AND THEN ZOOOOOOM! YOU GO AND SORT IT OUT.
HMMMMM.
#CrimeStoppers
#WhereIsAllTheCrimeAt
#CrimeInProgress
#Emergency
#HelpMeIveBeenKidnapped
#ChubbyPowers

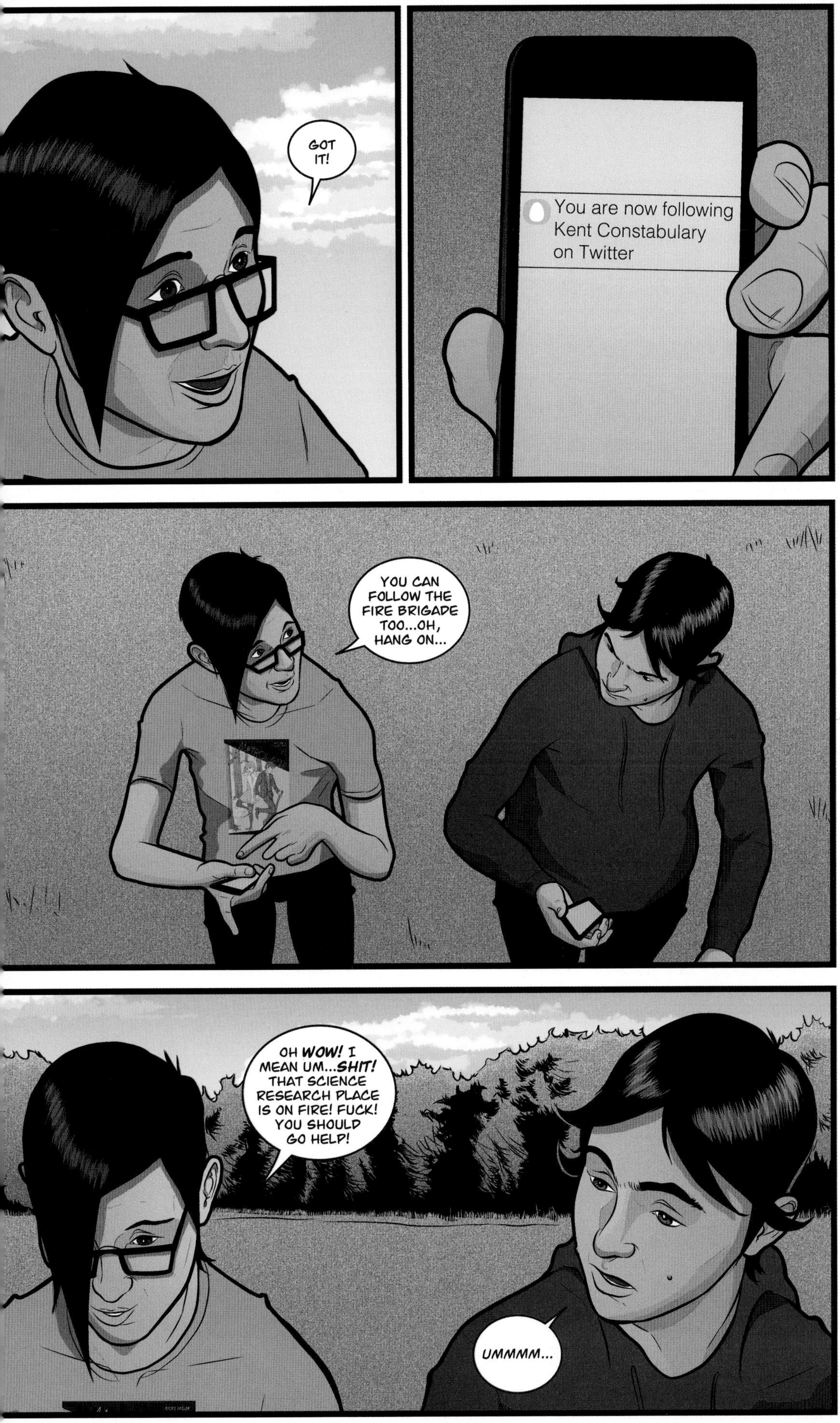
GOT IT!
You are now following Kent Constabulary on Twitter
YOU CAN FOLLOW THE FIRE BRIGADE TOO...OH, HANG ON...
OH *WOW!* I MEAN UM...*SHIT!* THAT SCIENCE RESEARCH PLACE IS ON FIRE! FUCK! YOU SHOULD GO HELP!
UMMMM...

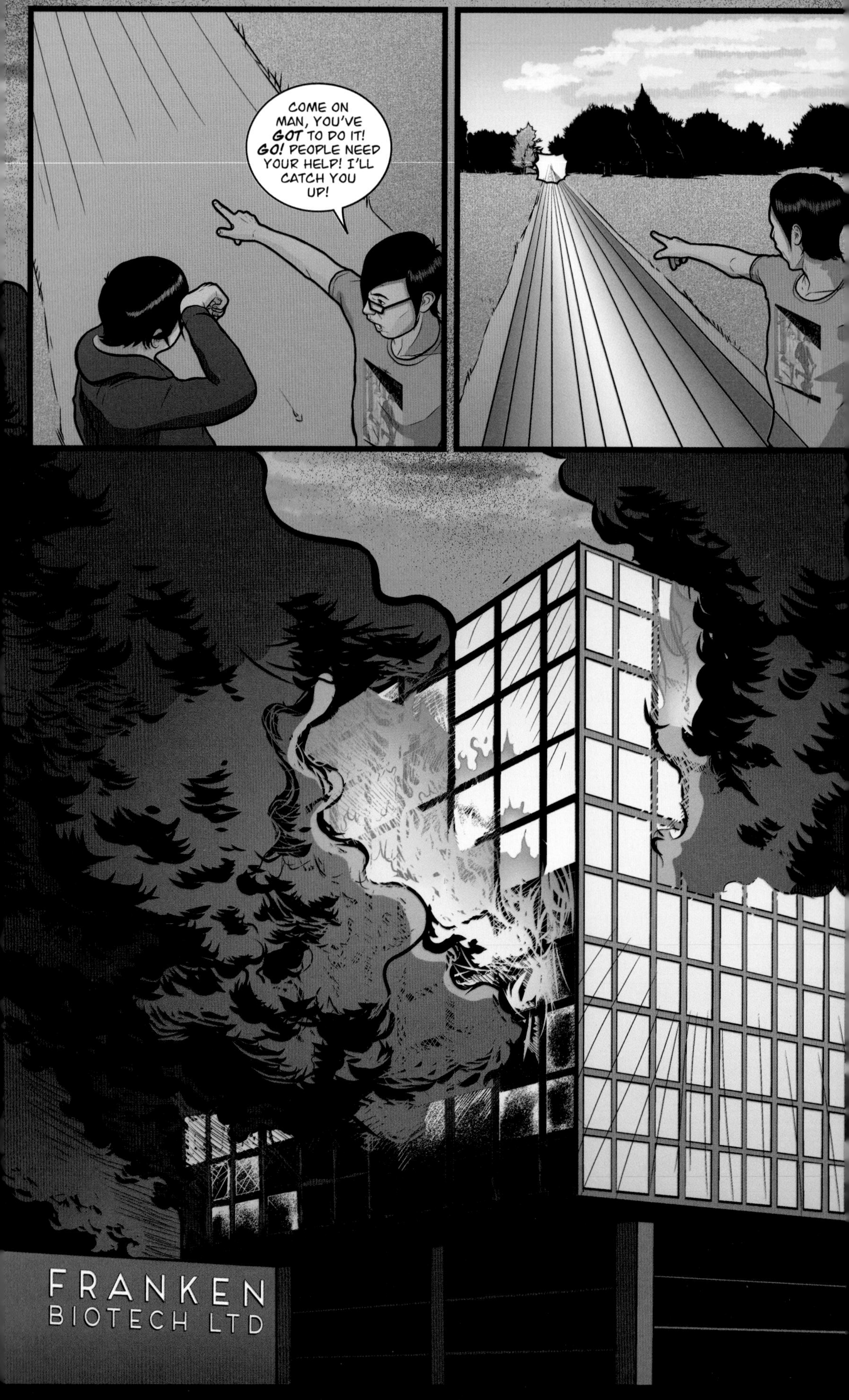
COME ON MAN, YOU'VE GOT TO DO IT! GO! PEOPLE NEED YOUR HELP! I'LL CATCH YOU UP!
FRANKEN BIOTECH LTD

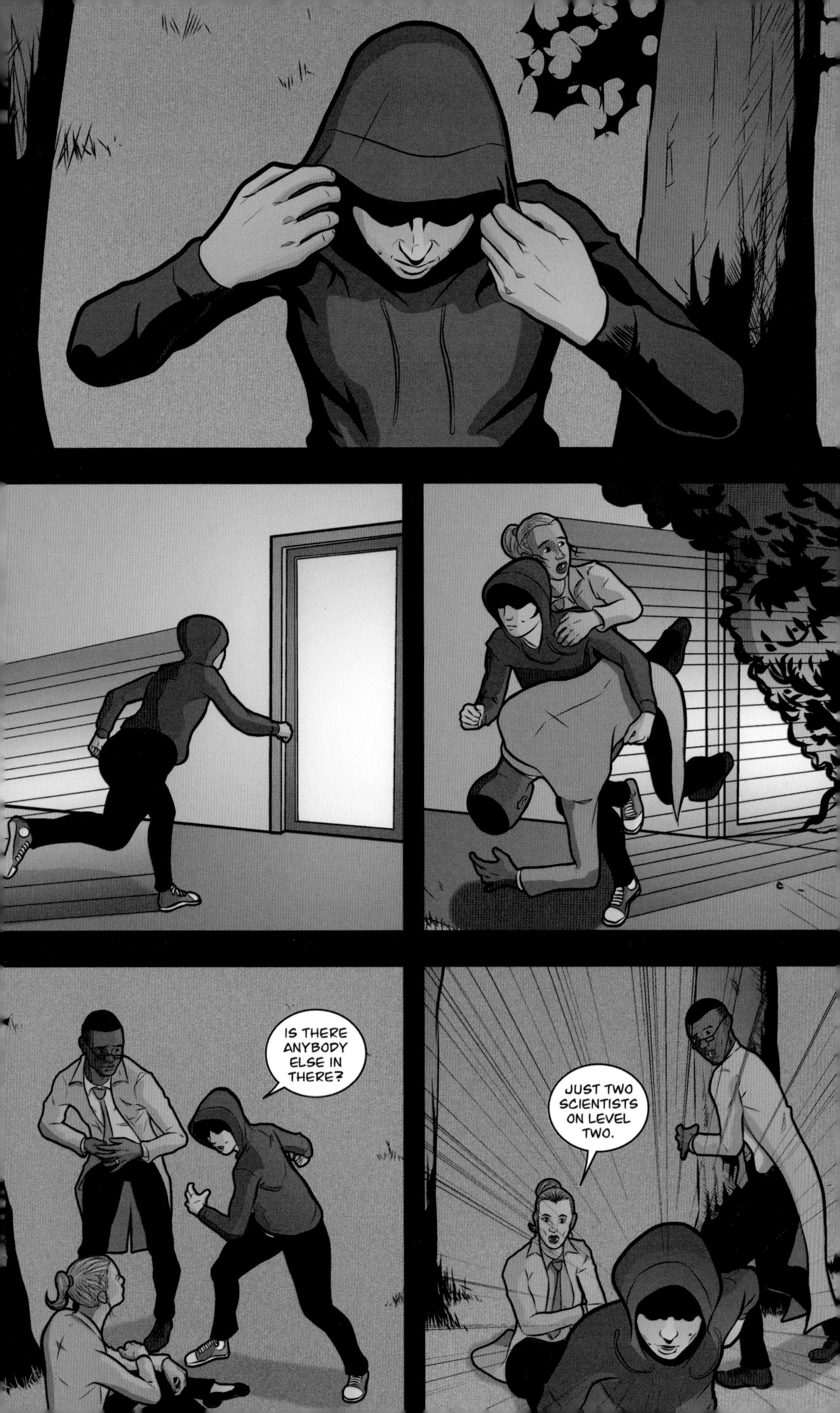
IS THERE ANYBODY ELSE IN THERE?
JUST TWO SCIENTISTS ON LEVEL TWO.

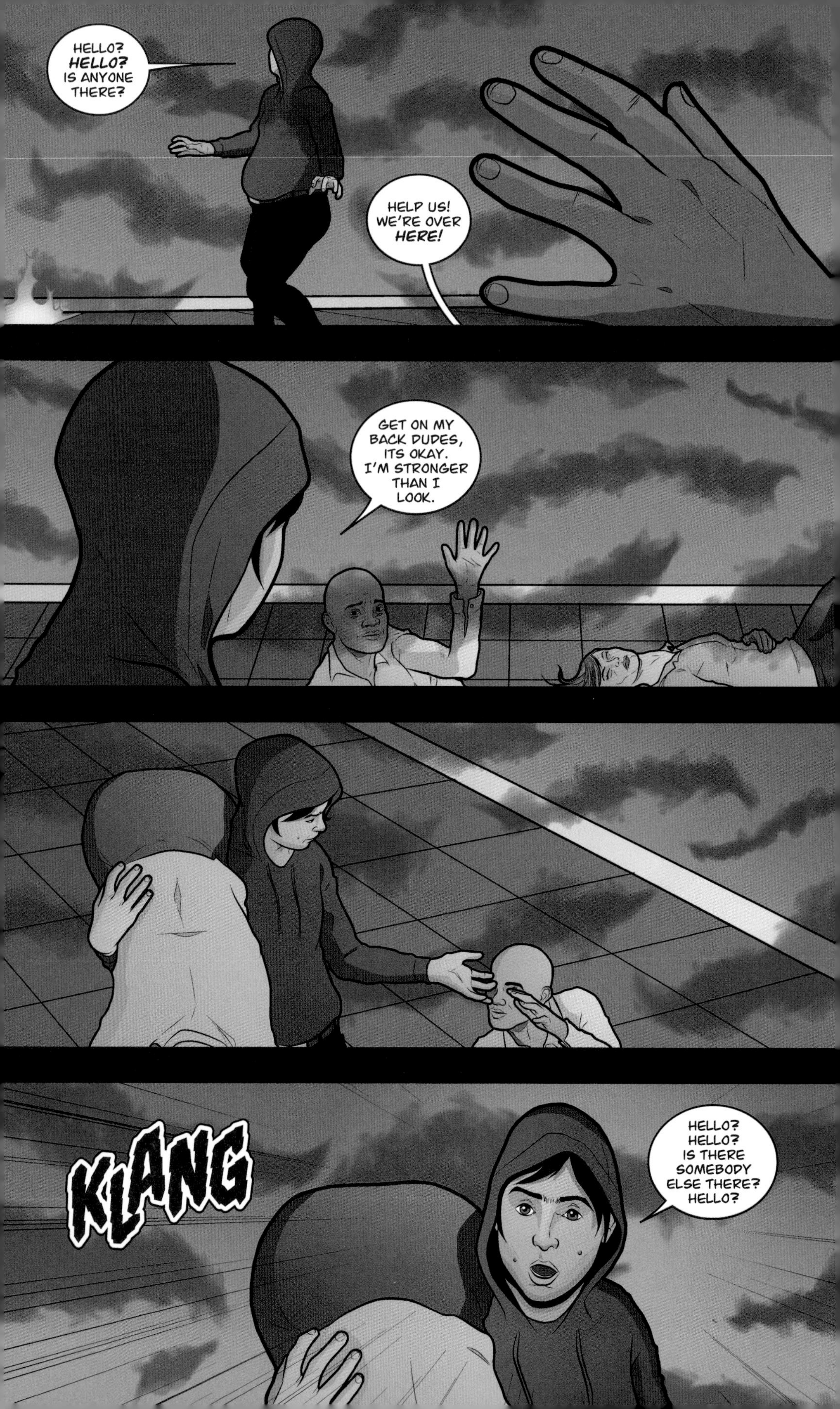
HELLO?
HELLO?
IS ANYONE
THERE?
HELP US!
WE'RE OVER
HERE!
GET ON MY
BACK DUDES,
ITS OKAY.
I'M STRONGER
THAN I
LOOK.
KLANG
HELLO?
HELLO?
IS THERE
SOMEBODY
ELSE THERE?
HELLO?

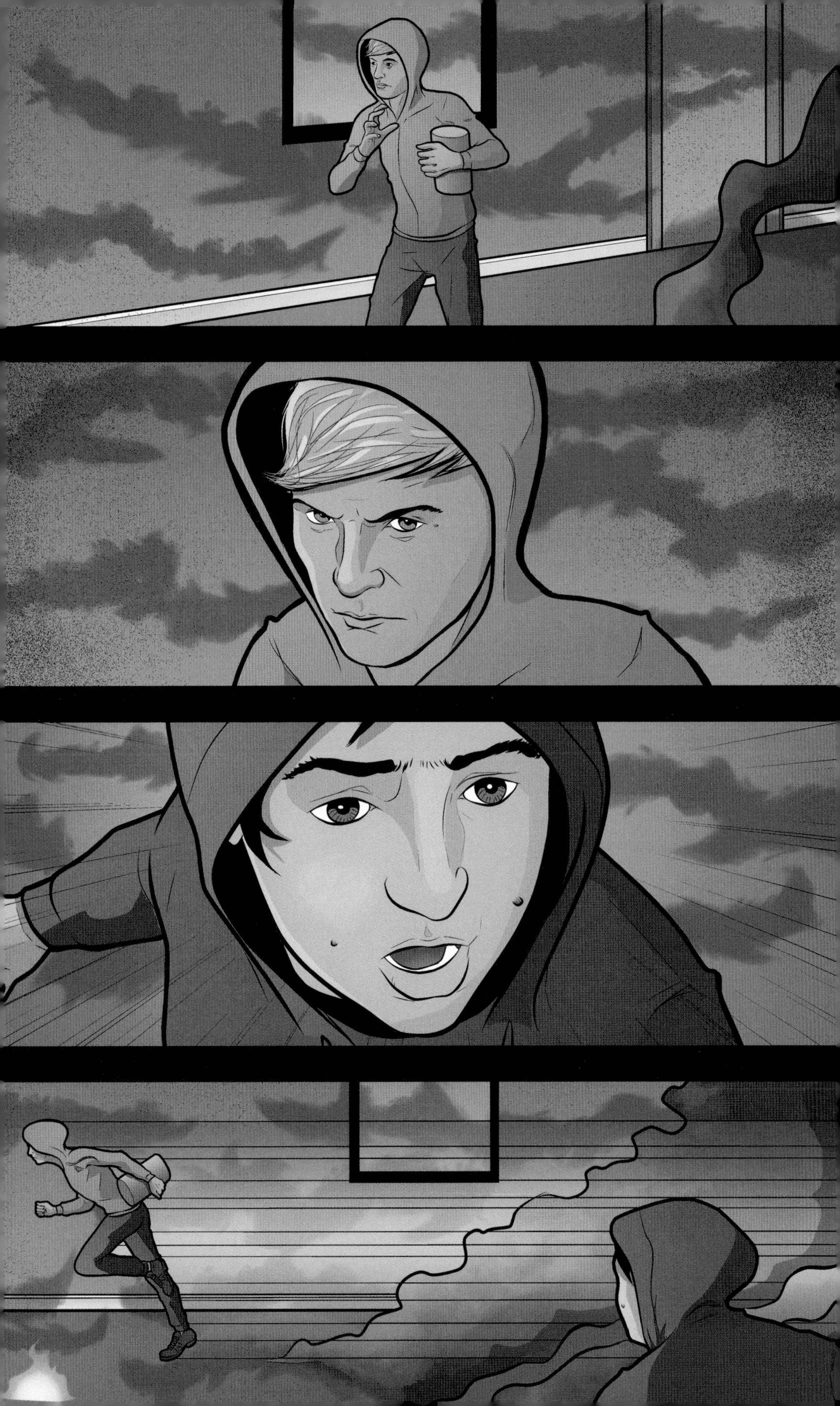

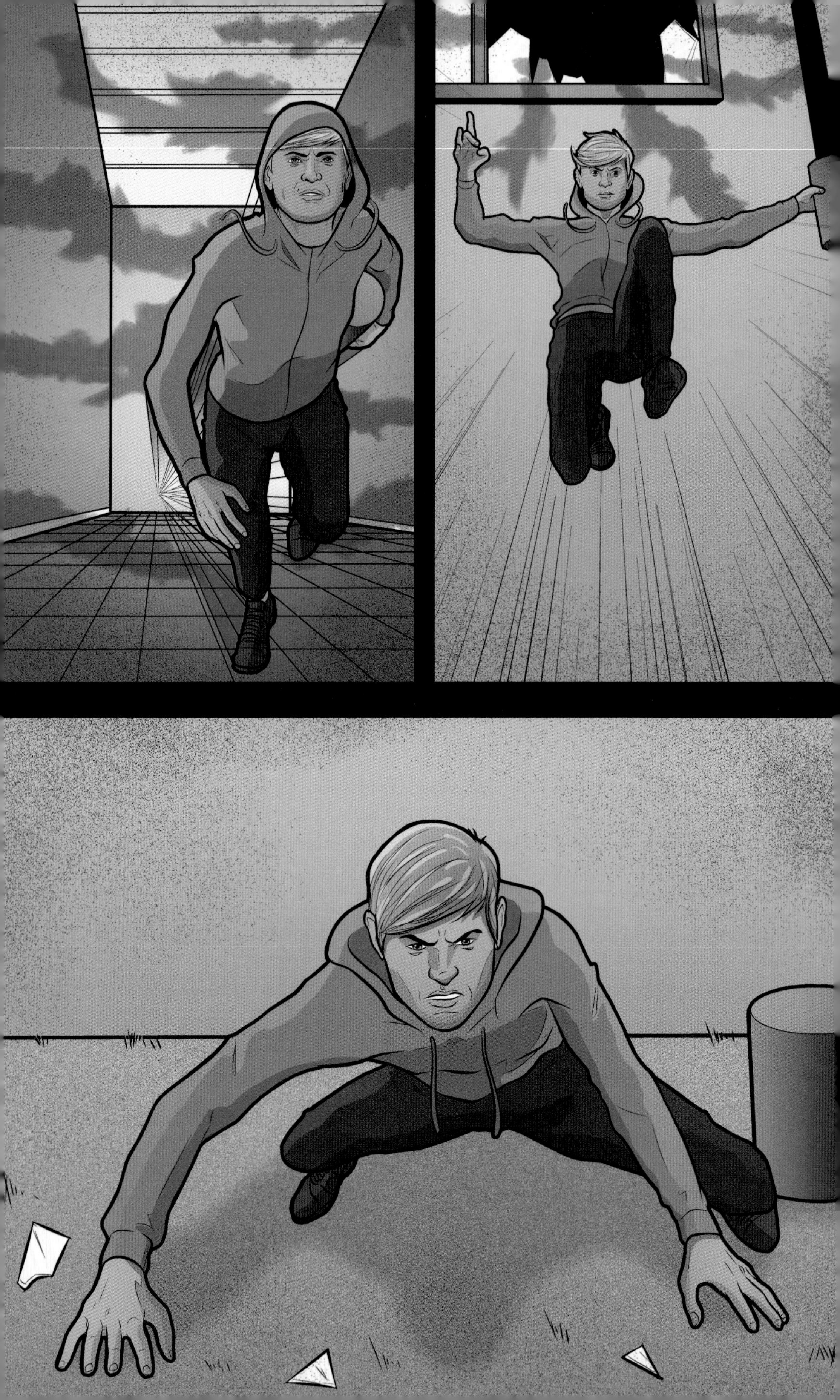

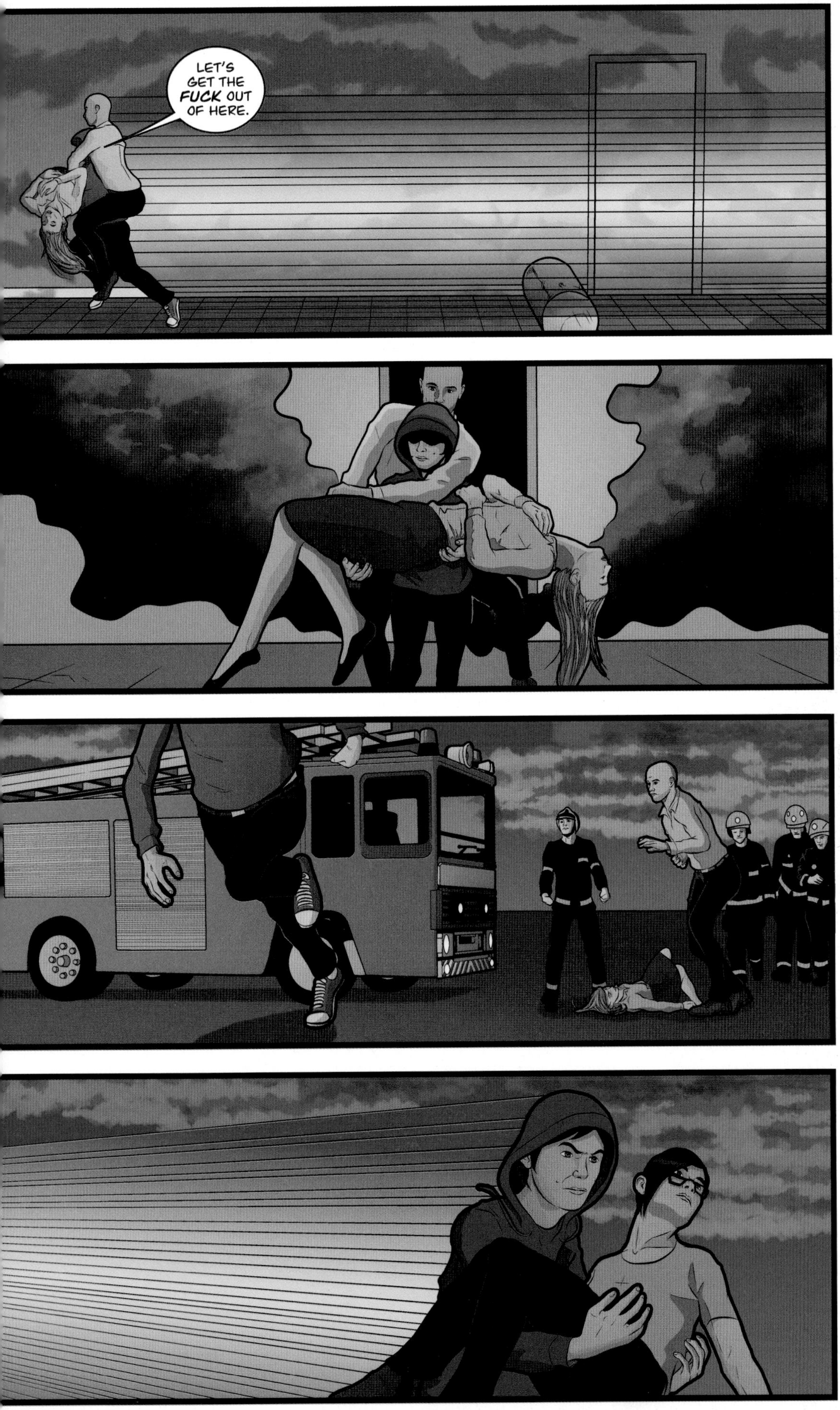
LET'S GET THE FUCK OUT OF HERE.

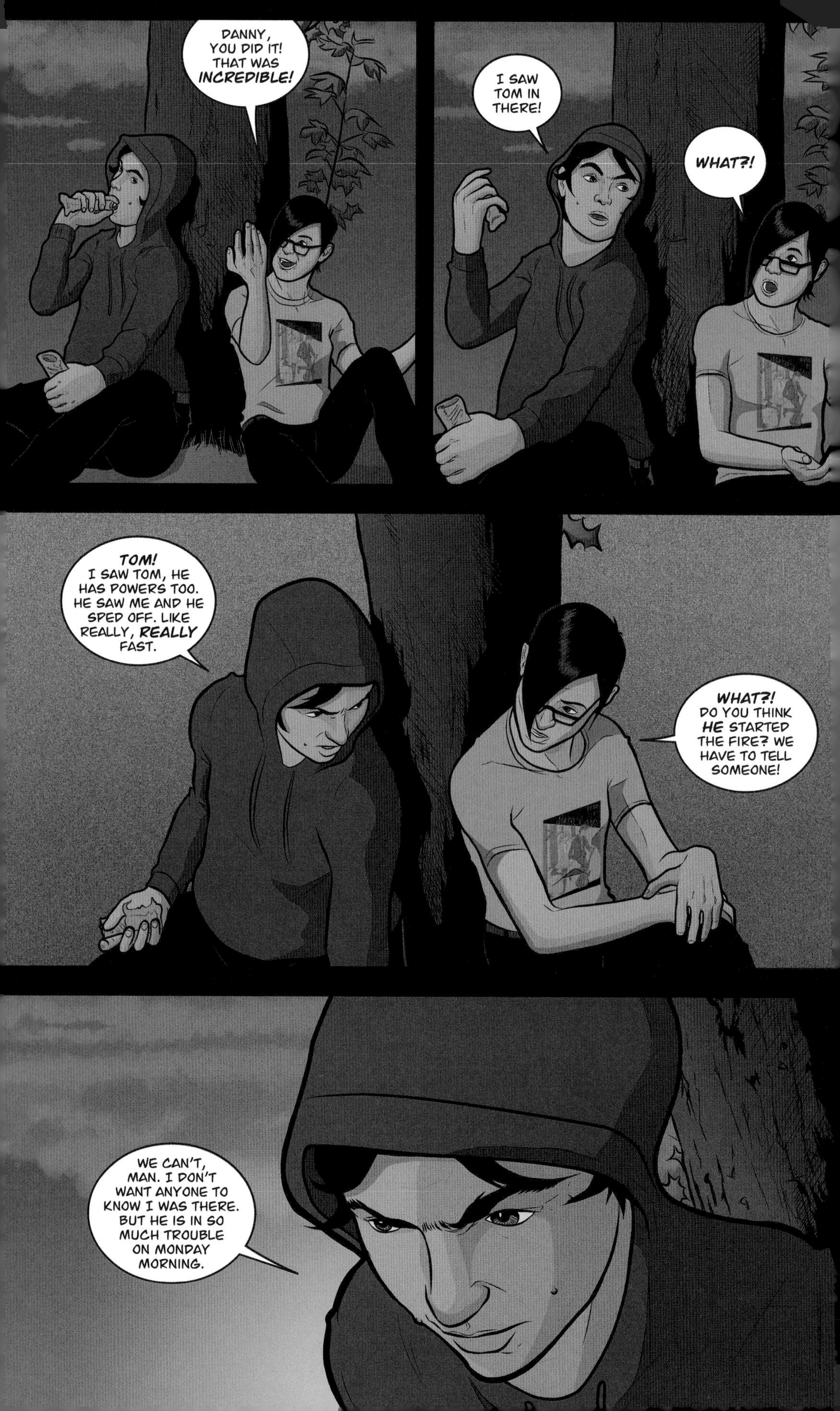
DANNY, YOU DID IT! THAT WAS INCREDIBLE!
I SAW TOM IN THERE!
WHAT?!
TOM! I SAW TOM, HE HAS POWERS TOO. HE SAW ME AND HE SPED OFF. LIKE REALLY, REALLY FAST.
WHAT?! DO YOU THINK HE STARTED THE FIRE? WE HAVE TO TELL SOMEONE!
WE CAN'T, MAN. I DON'T WANT ANYONE TO KNOW I WAS THERE. BUT HE IS IN SO MUCH TROUBLE ON MONDAY MORNING.

CHAPTER 5

CLASSIFIED

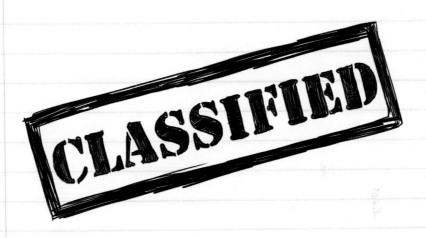

17 YEARS EARLIER

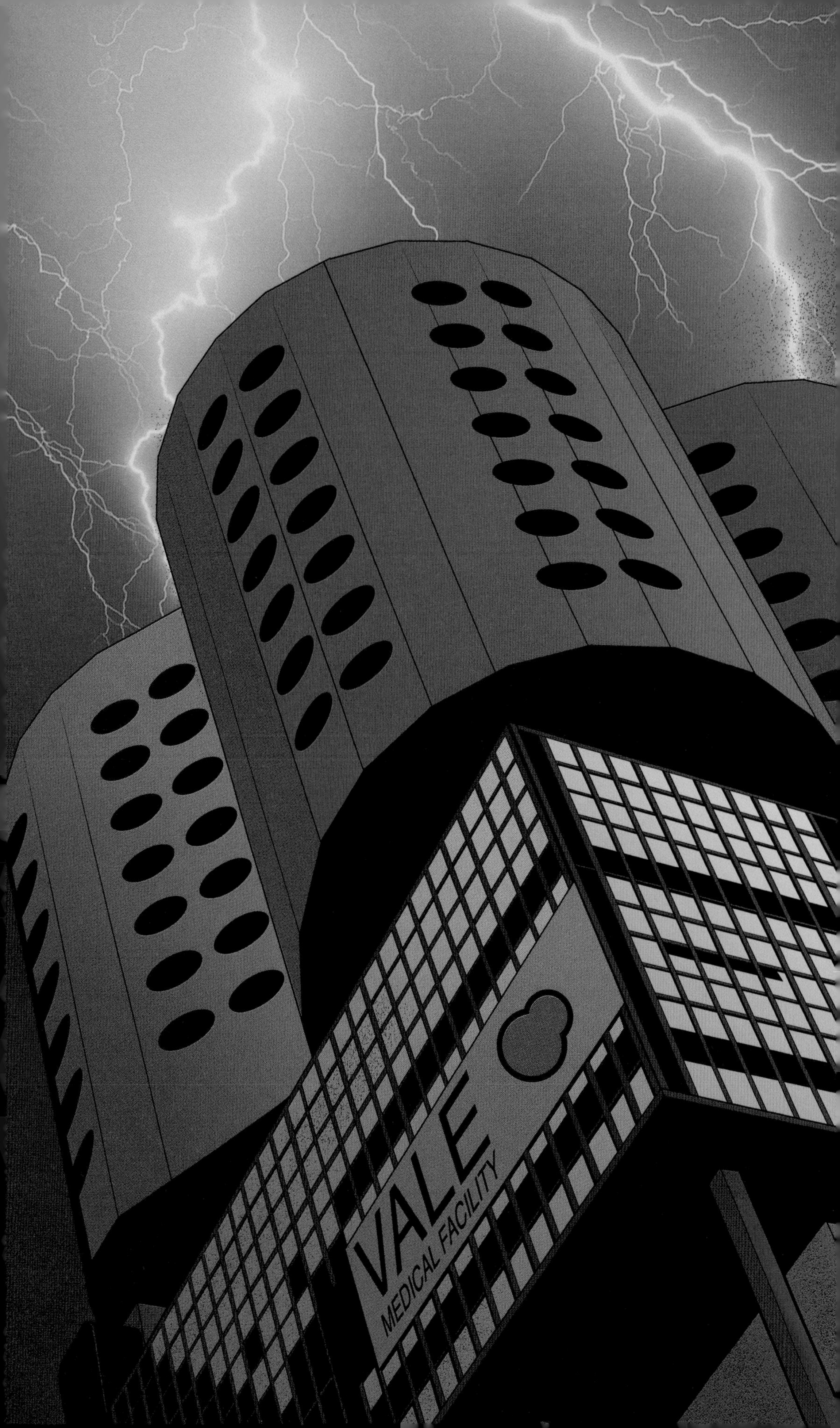
VALE
MEDICAL FACILITY

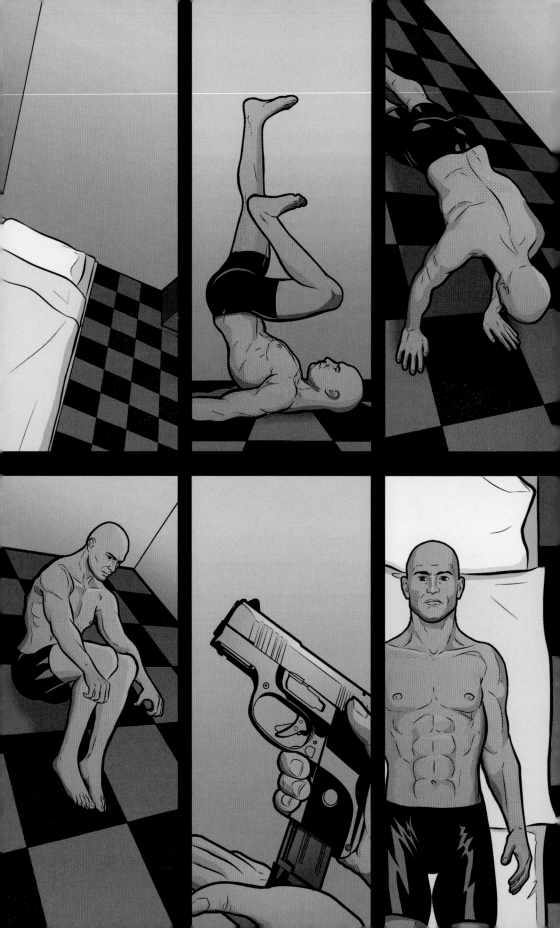

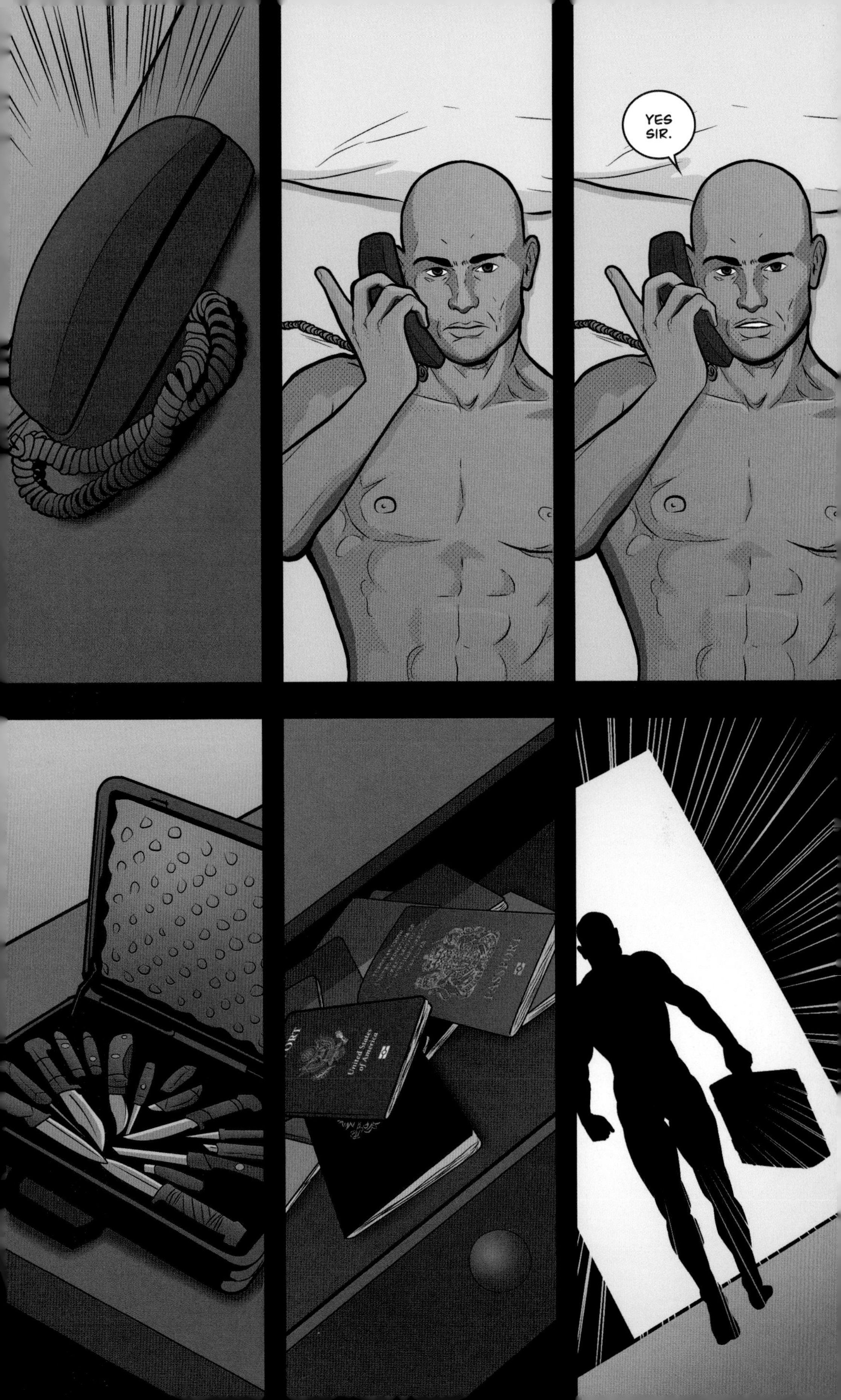
YES SIR.

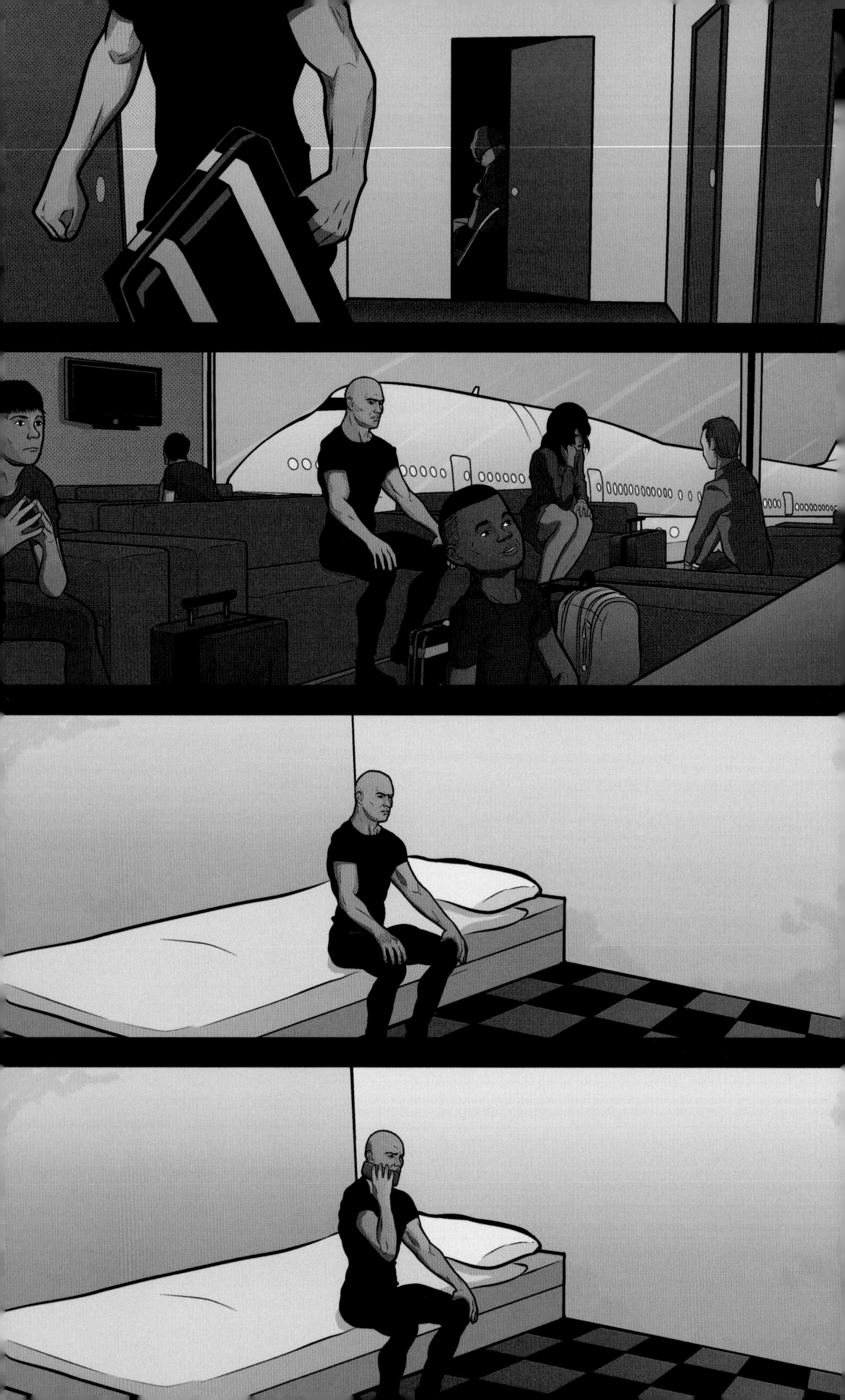

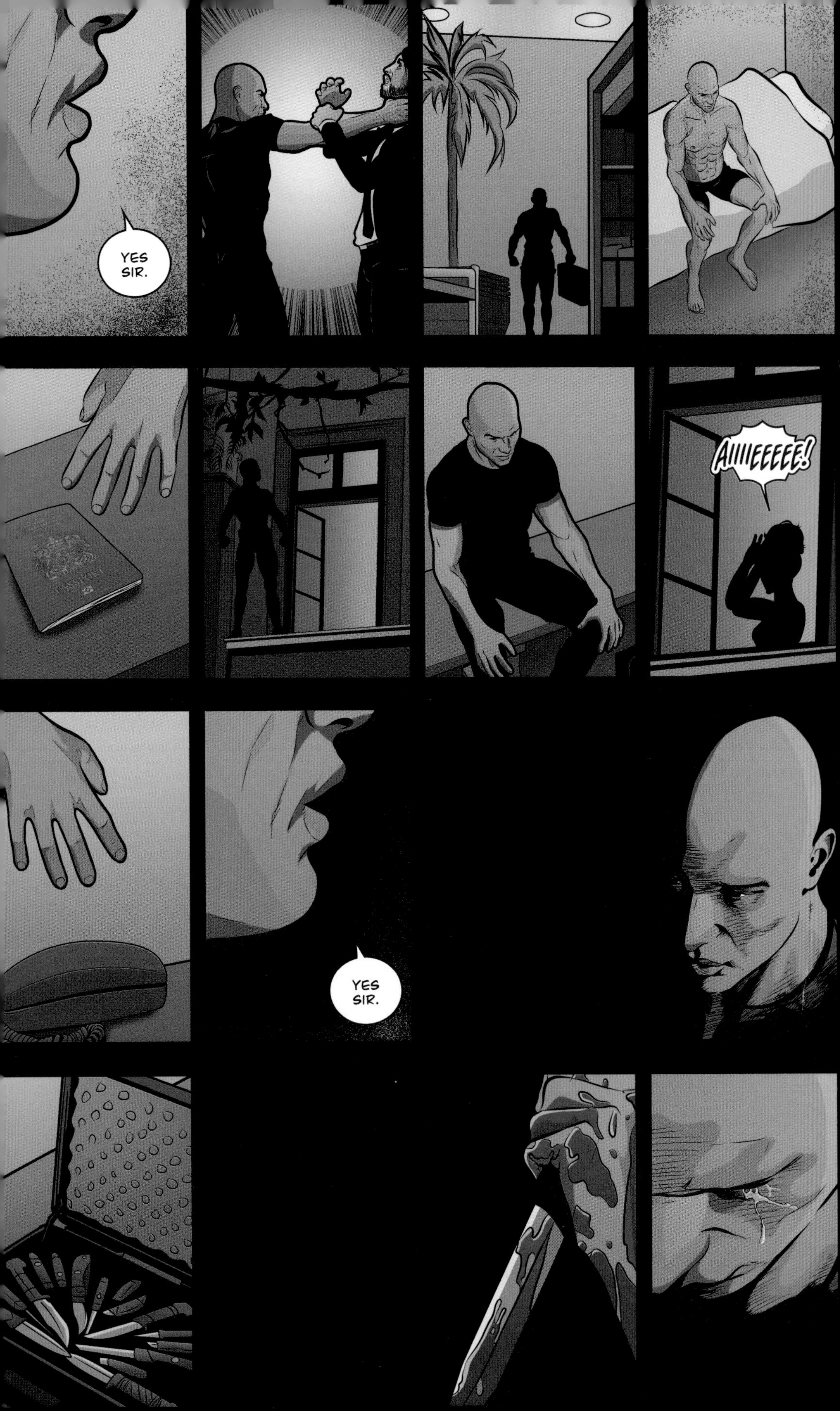
YES SIR.
AIIIIEEEEE!
YES SIR.

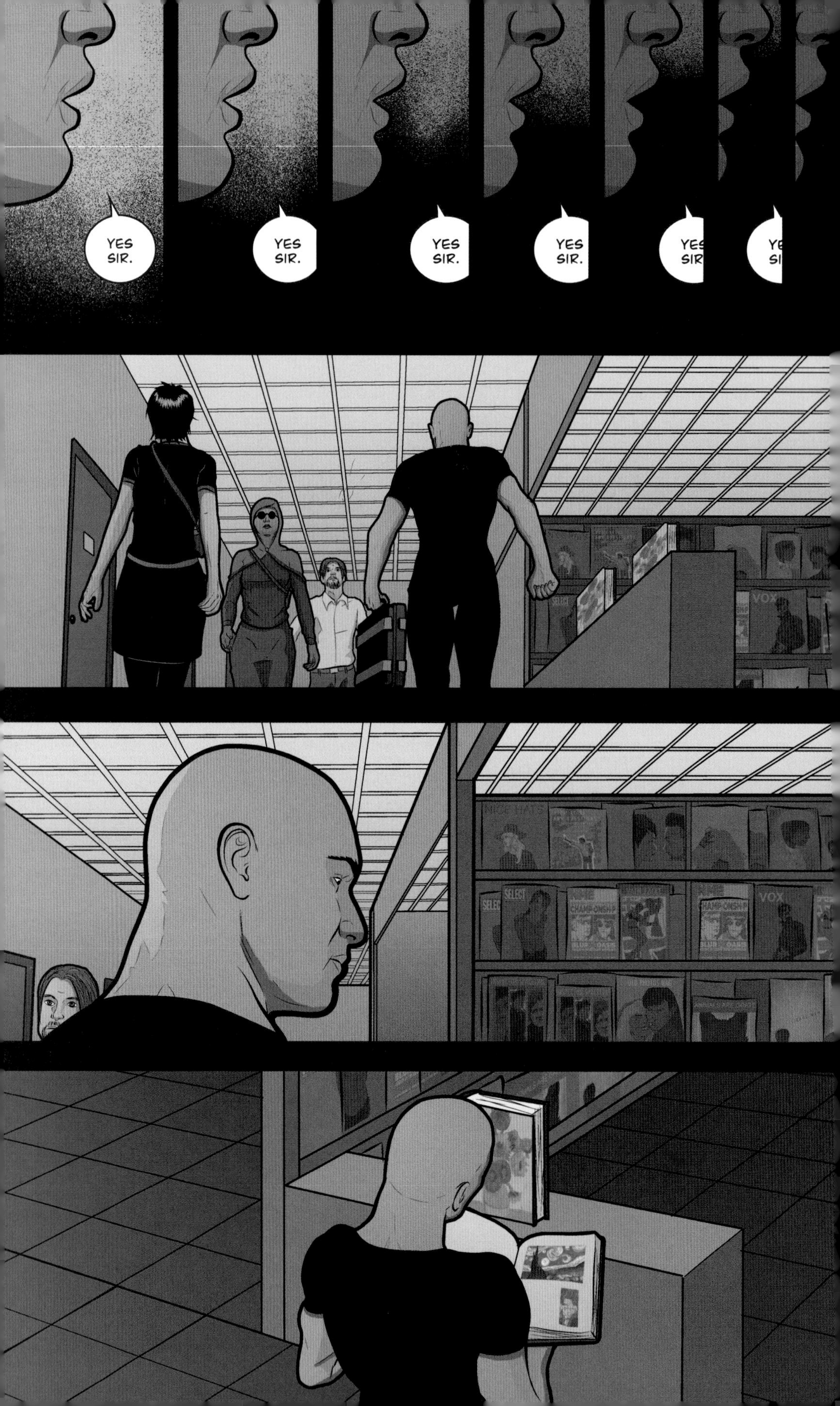
YES SIR.
YES SIR.
YES SIR.
YES SIR.
SELECT
VOX
NICE HATS
SELECT
VOX

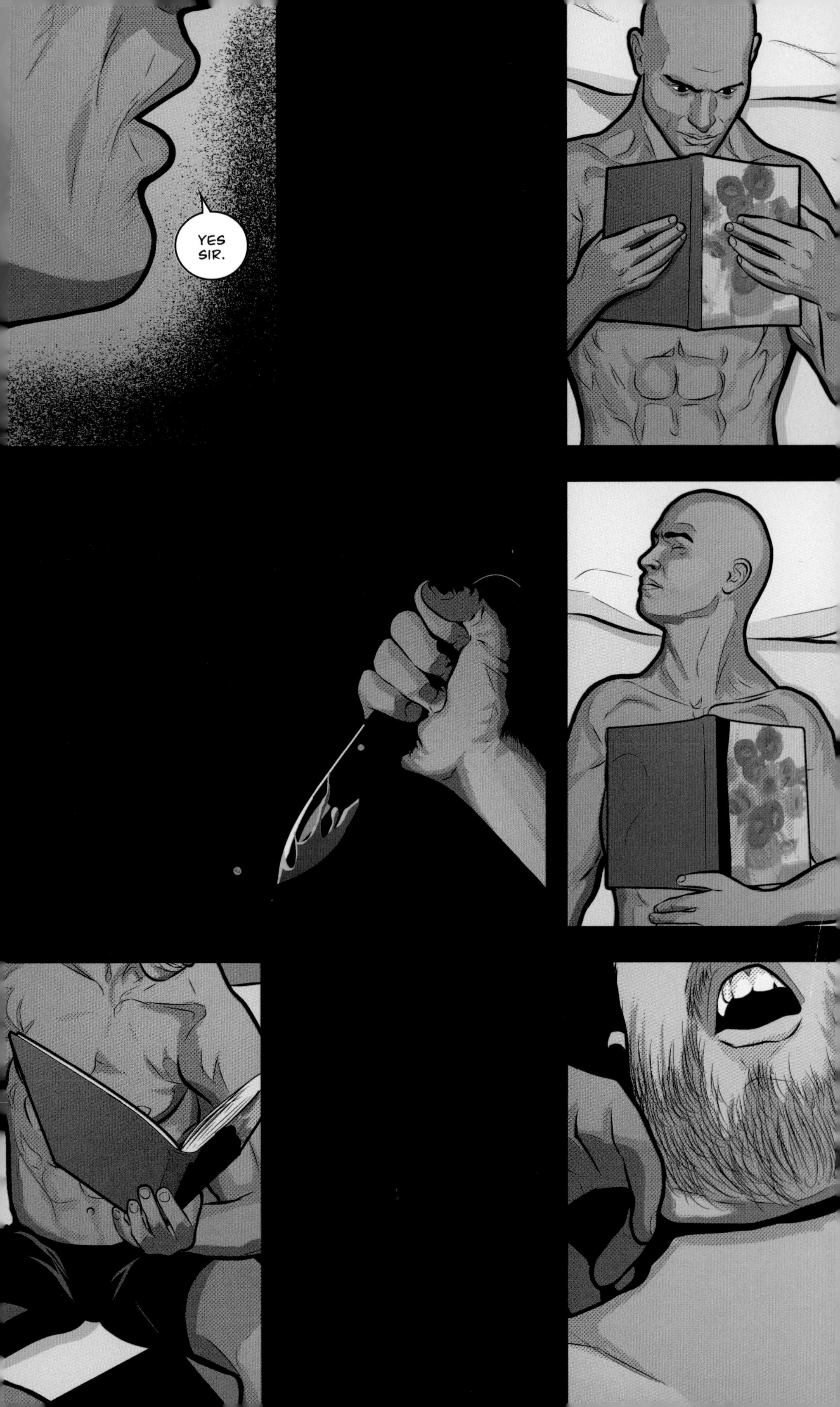
YES SIR.

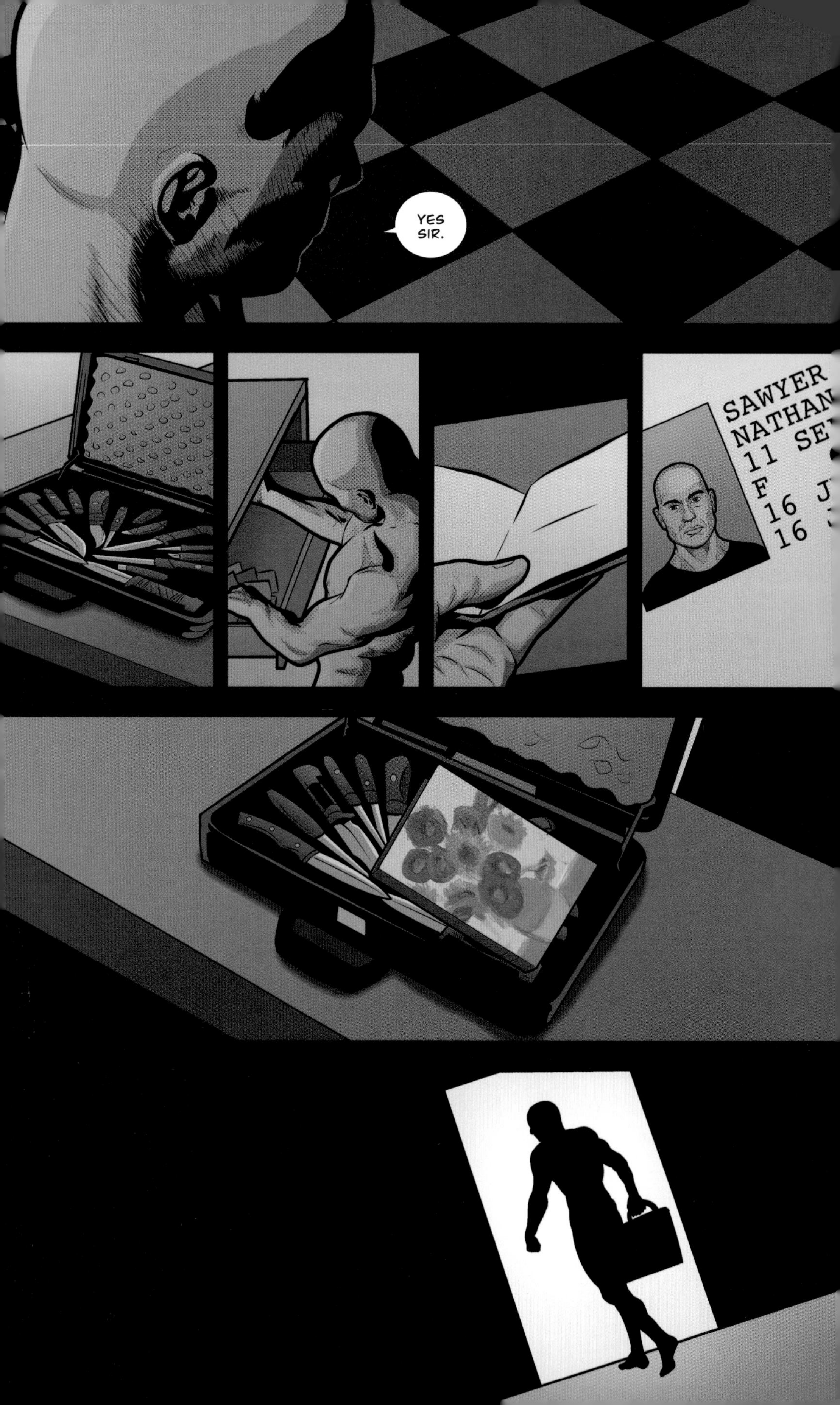

YES SIR.
SAWYER

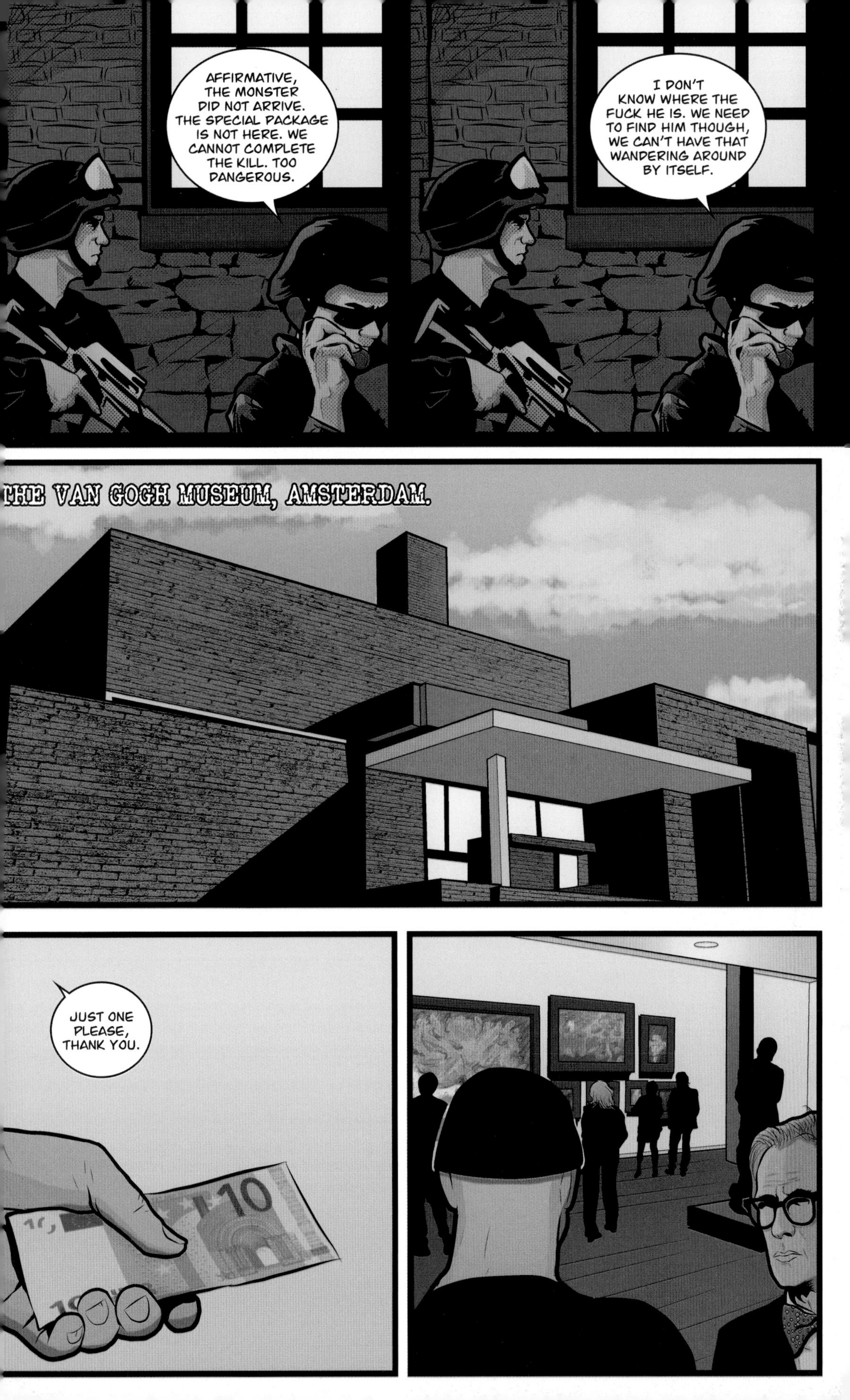
AFFIRMATIVE, THE MONSTER DID NOT ARRIVE. THE SPECIAL PACKAGE IS NOT HERE. WE CANNOT COMPLETE THE KILL. TOO DANGEROUS.
I DON'T KNOW WHERE THE FUCK HE IS. WE NEED TO FIND HIM THOUGH, WE CAN'T HAVE THAT WANDERING AROUND BY ITSELF.
THE VAN GOGH MUSEUM, AMSTERDAM.
JUST ONE PLEASE, THANK YOU.
10

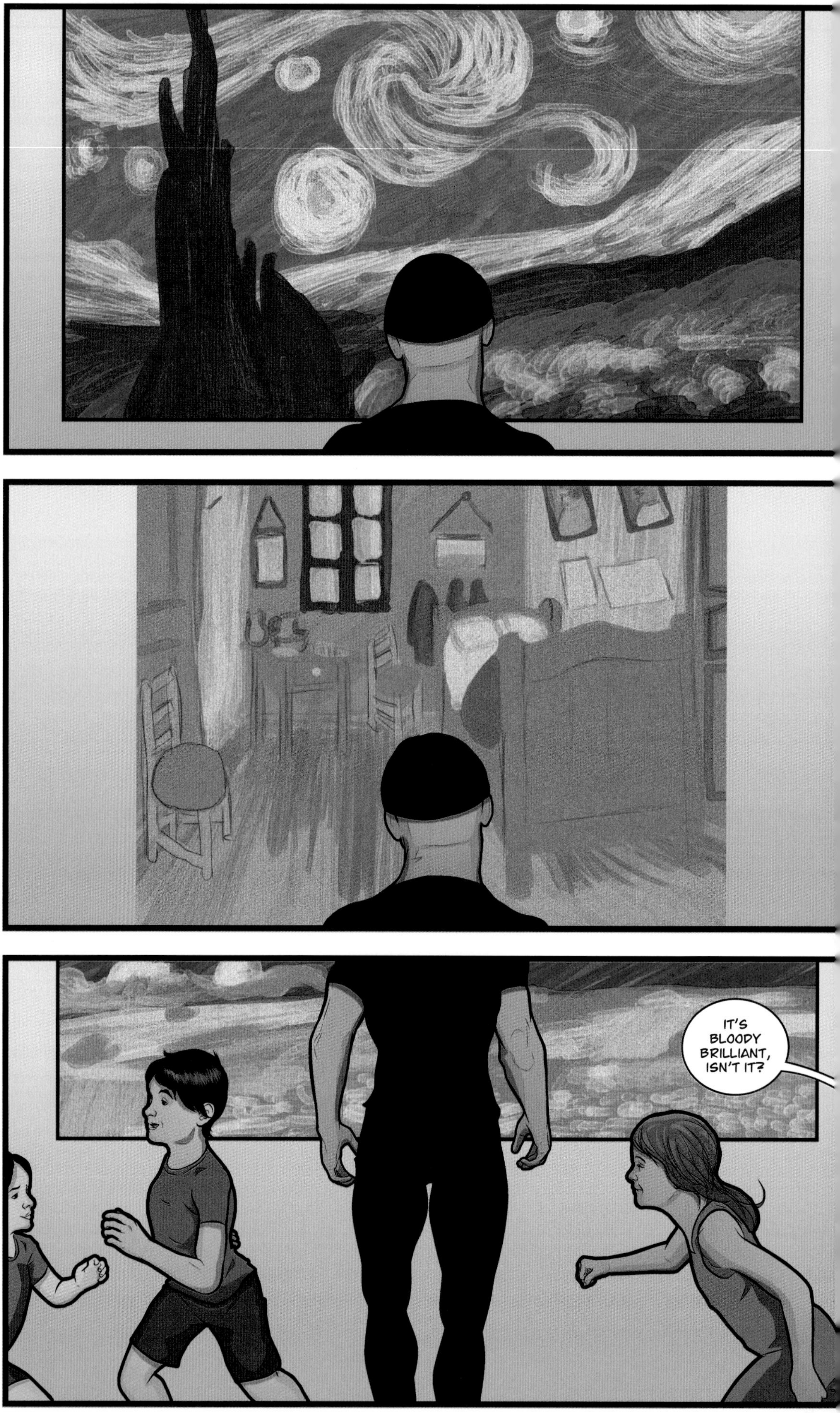
IT'S BLOODY BRILLIANT, ISN'T IT?

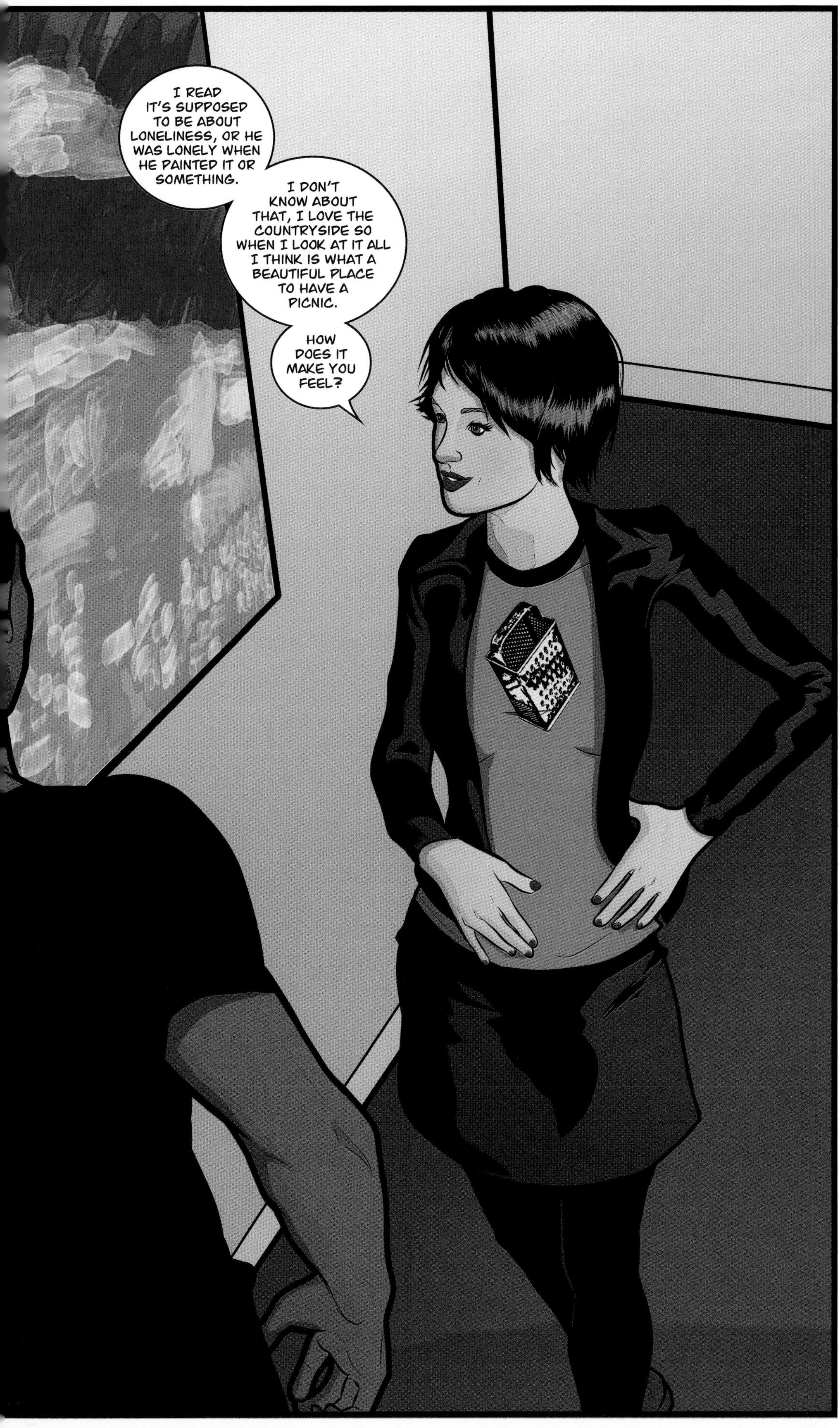
I READ IT'S SUPPOSED TO BE ABOUT LONELINESS, OR HE WAS LONELY WHEN HE PAINTED IT OR SOMETHING.
I DON'T KNOW ABOUT THAT, I LOVE THE COUNTRYSIDE SO WHEN I LOOK AT IT ALL I THINK IS WHAT A BEAUTIFUL PLACE TO HAVE A PICNIC.
HOW DOES IT MAKE YOU FEEL?

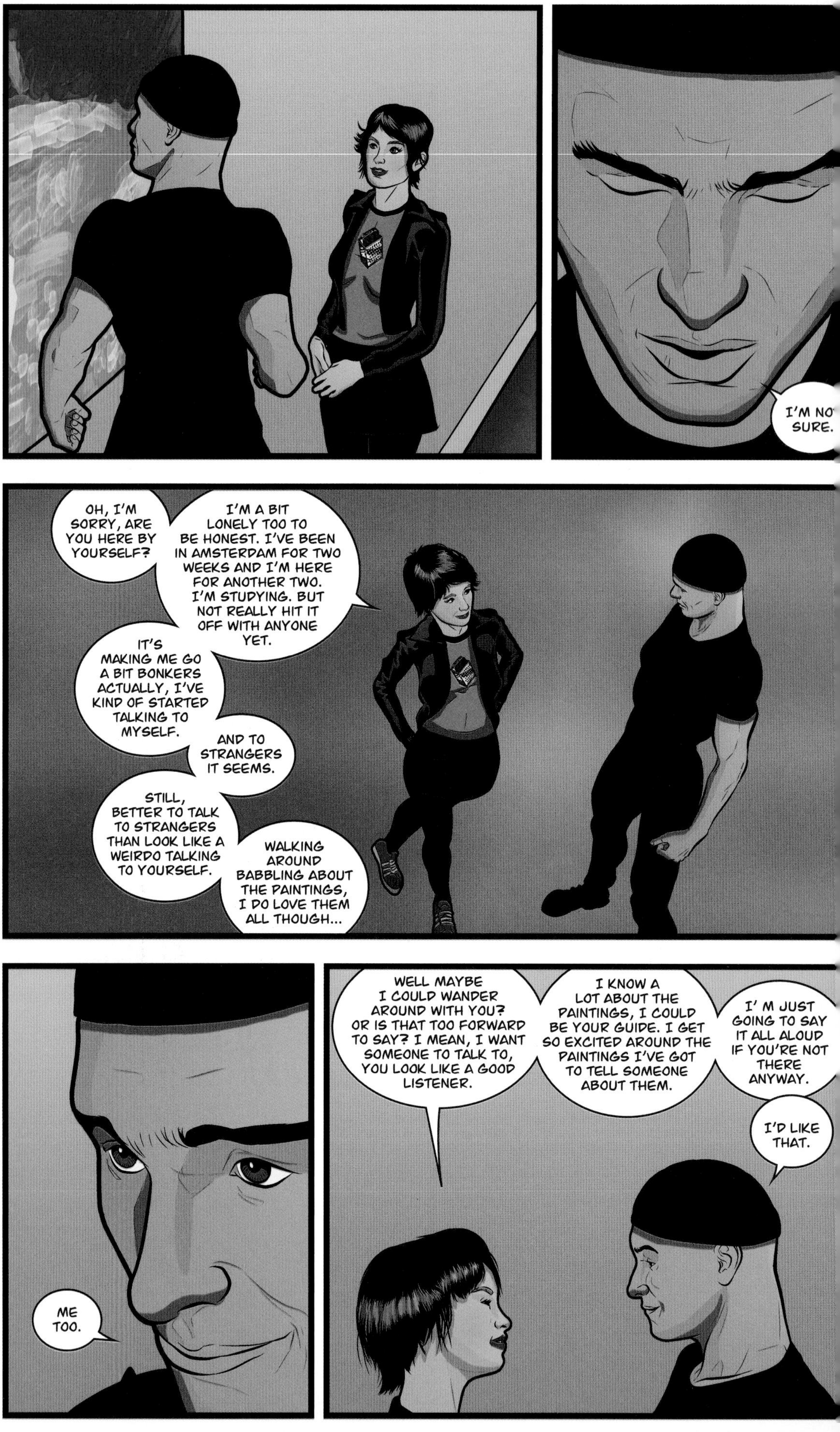
I'M NO
SURE.
OH, I'M SORRY, ARE YOU HERE BY YOURSELF?
I'M A BIT LONELY TOO TO BE HONEST. I'VE BEEN IN AMSTERDAM FOR TWO WEEKS AND I'M HERE FOR ANOTHER TWO. I'M STUDYING. BUT NOT REALLY HIT IT OFF WITH ANYONE YET.
IT'S MAKING ME GO A BIT BONKERS ACTUALLY, I'VE KIND OF STARTED TALKING TO MYSELF.
AND TO STRANGERS IT SEEMS.
STILL, BETTER TO TALK TO STRANGERS THAN LOOK LIKE A WEIRDO TALKING TO YOURSELF.
WALKING AROUND BABBLING ABOUT THE PAINTINGS, I DO LOVE THEM ALL THOUGH...
ME TOO.
WELL MAYBE I COULD WANDER AROUND WITH YOU? OR IS THAT TOO FORWARD TO SAY? I MEAN, I WANT SOMEONE TO TALK TO, YOU LOOK LIKE A GOOD LISTENER.
I KNOW A LOT ABOUT THE PAINTINGS, I COULD BE YOUR GUIDE. I GET SO EXCITED AROUND THE PAINTINGS I'VE GOT TO TELL SOMEONE ABOUT THEM.
I' M JUST GOING TO SAY IT ALL ALOUD IF YOU'RE NOT THERE ANYWAY.
I'D LIKE THAT.

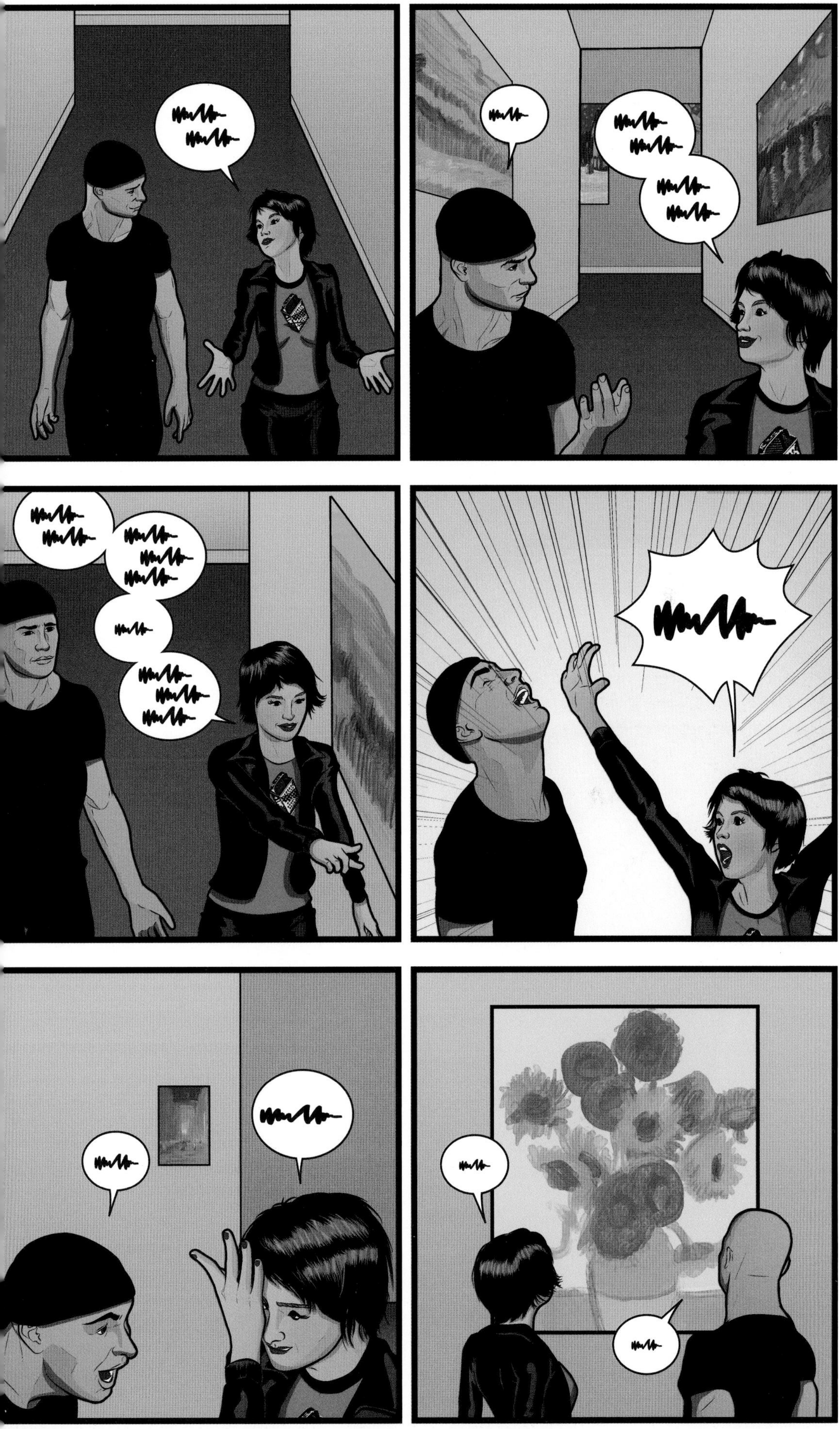

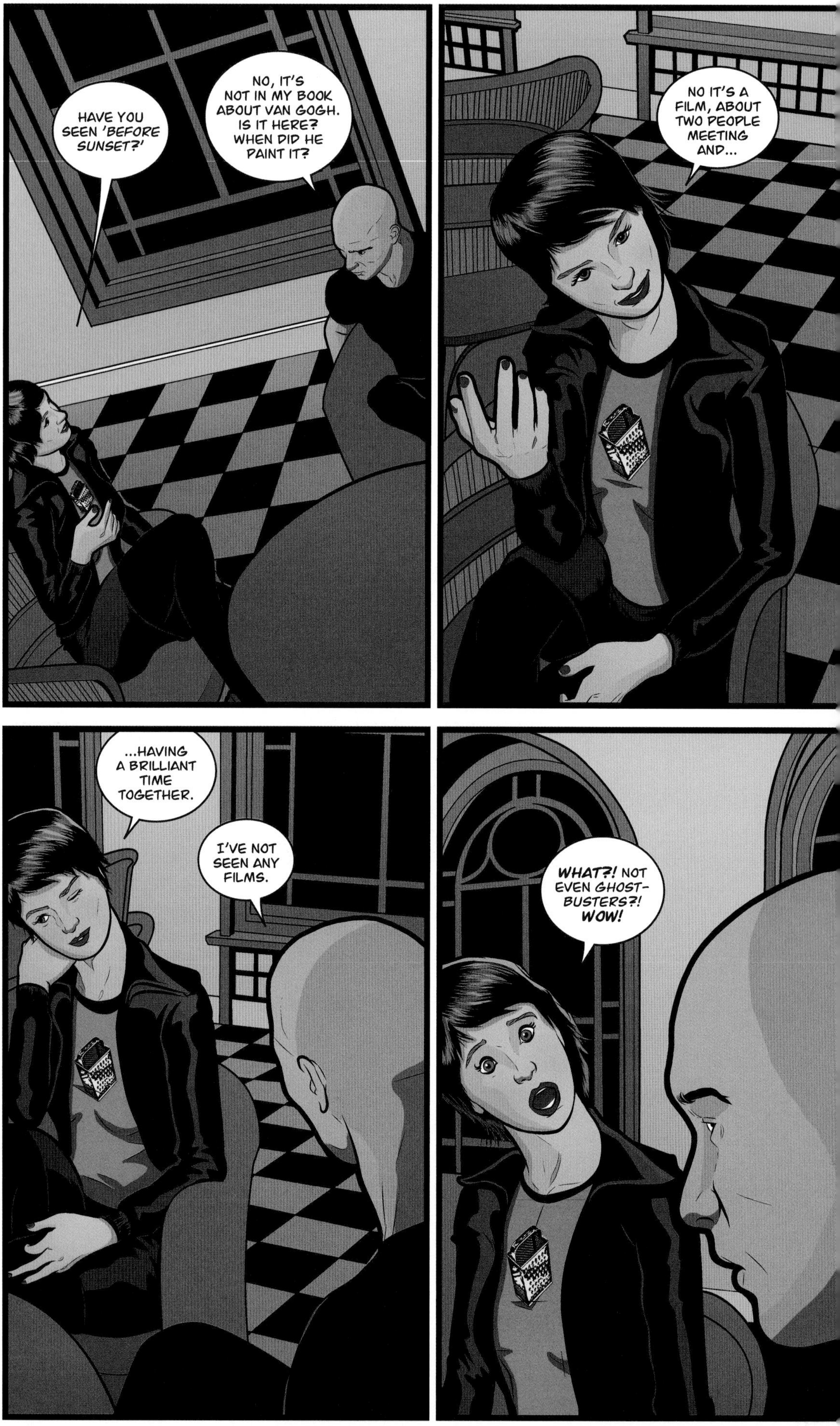
HAVE YOU SEEN 'BEFORE SUNSET?'
NO, IT'S NOT IN MY BOOK ABOUT VAN GOGH. IS IT HERE? WHEN DID HE PAINT IT?
NO IT'S A FILM, ABOUT TWO PEOPLE MEETING AND...
...HAVING A BRILLIANT TIME TOGETHER.
I'VE NOT SEEN ANY FILMS.
WHAT?! NOT EVEN GHOST-BUSTERS?! WOW!

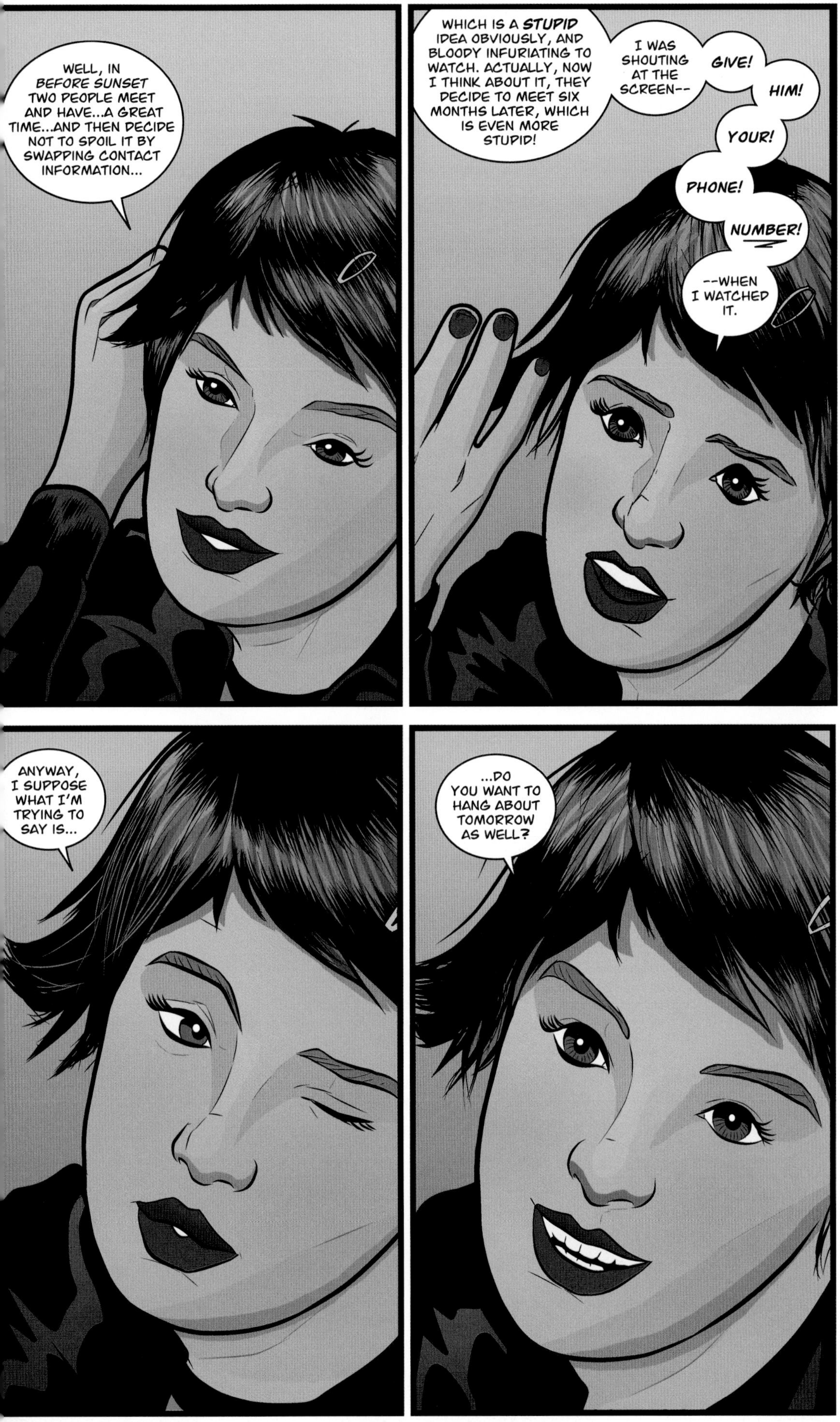
WELL, IN *BEFORE SUNSET* TWO PEOPLE MEET AND HAVE...A GREAT TIME...AND THEN DECIDE NOT TO SPOIL IT BY SWAPPING CONTACT INFORMATION...
WHICH IS A ***STUPID*** IDEA OBVIOUSLY, AND BLOODY INFURIATING TO WATCH. ACTUALLY, NOW I THINK ABOUT IT, THEY DECIDE TO MEET SIX MONTHS LATER, WHICH IS EVEN MORE STUPID!
I WAS SHOUTING AT THE SCREEN--
GIVE!
HIM!
YOUR!
PHONE!
NUMBER!
--WHEN I WATCHED IT.
ANYWAY, I SUPPOSE WHAT I'M TRYING TO SAY IS...
...DO YOU WANT TO HANG ABOUT TOMORROW AS WELL?

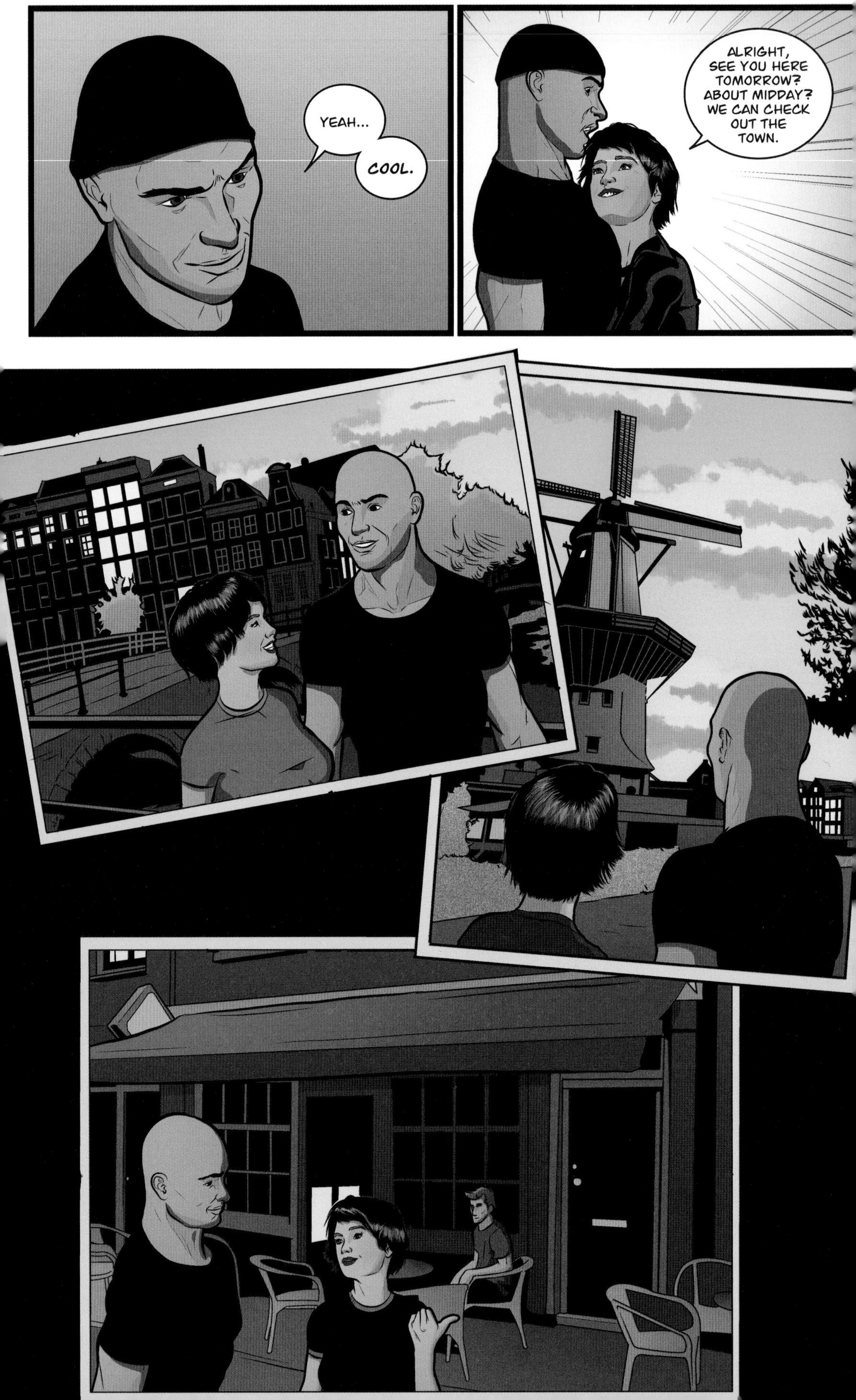
YEAH...
COOL.
ALRIGHT, SEE YOU HERE TOMORROW? ABOUT MIDDAY? WE CAN CHECK OUT THE TOWN.

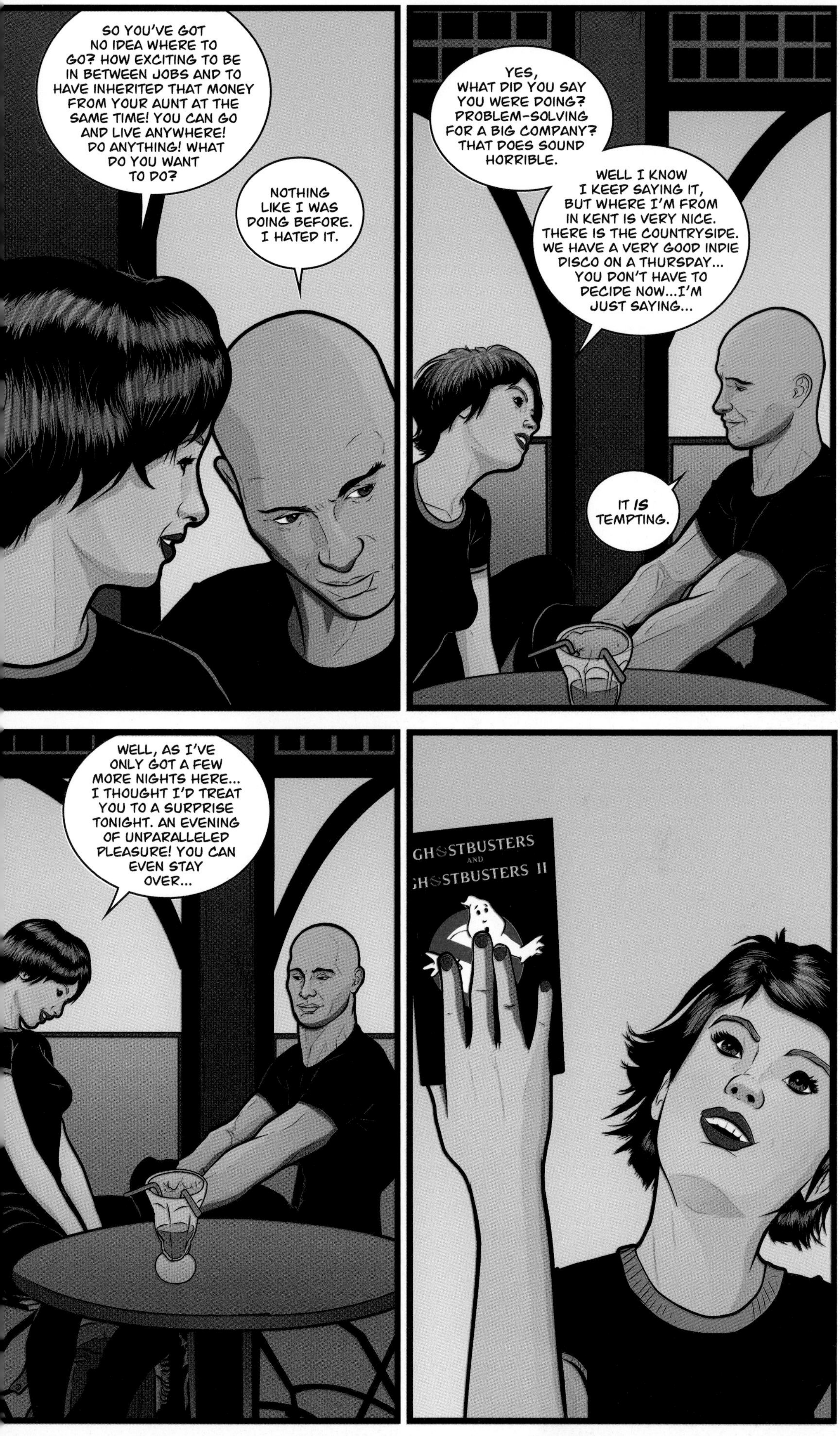
SO YOU'VE GOT NO IDEA WHERE TO GO? HOW EXCITING TO BE IN BETWEEN JOBS AND TO HAVE INHERITED THAT MONEY FROM YOUR AUNT AT THE SAME TIME! YOU CAN GO AND LIVE ANYWHERE! DO ANYTHING! WHAT DO YOU WANT TO DO?
NOTHING LIKE I WAS DOING BEFORE. I HATED IT.
YES, WHAT DID YOU SAY YOU WERE DOING? PROBLEM-SOLVING FOR A BIG COMPANY? THAT DOES SOUND HORRIBLE.
WELL I KNOW I KEEP SAYING IT, BUT WHERE I'M FROM IN KENT IS VERY NICE. THERE IS THE COUNTRYSIDE. WE HAVE A VERY GOOD INDIE DISCO ON A THURSDAY... YOU DON'T HAVE TO DECIDE NOW...I'M JUST SAYING...
IT **IS** TEMPTING.
WELL, AS I'VE ONLY GOT A FEW MORE NIGHTS HERE... I THOUGHT I'D TREAT YOU TO A SURPRISE TONIGHT. AN EVENING OF UNPARALLELED PLEASURE! YOU CAN EVEN STAY OVER...
GHOSTBUSTERS AND GHOSTBUSTERS II

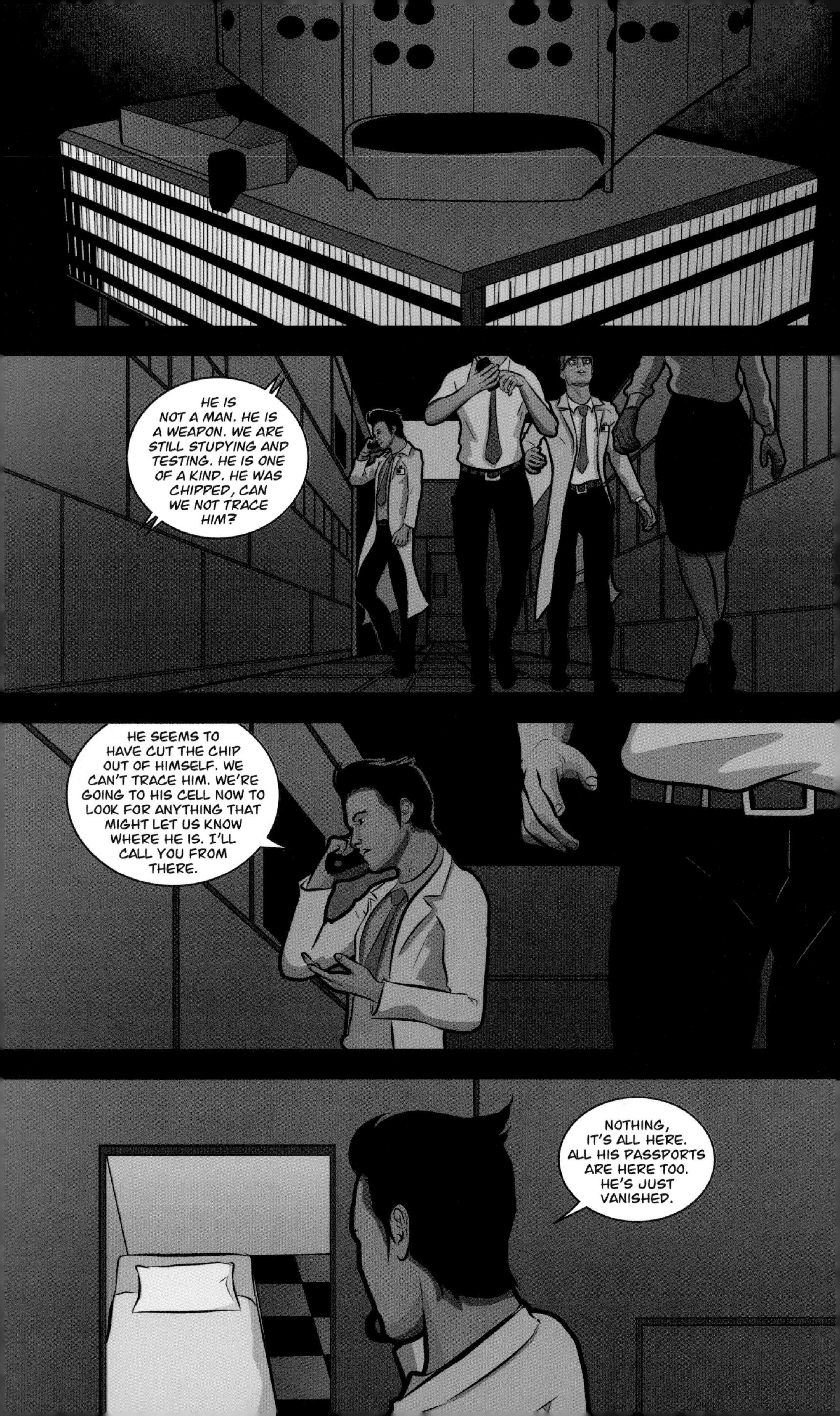
HE IS NOT A MAN. HE IS A WEAPON. WE ARE STILL STUDYING AND TESTING. HE IS ONE OF A KIND. HE WAS CHIPPED, CAN WE NOT TRACE HIM?
HE SEEMS TO HAVE CUT THE CHIP OUT OF HIMSELF. WE CAN'T TRACE HIM. WE'RE GOING TO HIS CELL NOW TO LOOK FOR ANYTHING THAT MIGHT LET US KNOW WHERE HE IS. I'LL CALL YOU FROM THERE.
NOTHING, IT'S ALL HERE. ALL HIS PASSPORTS ARE HERE TOO. HE'S JUST VANISHED.

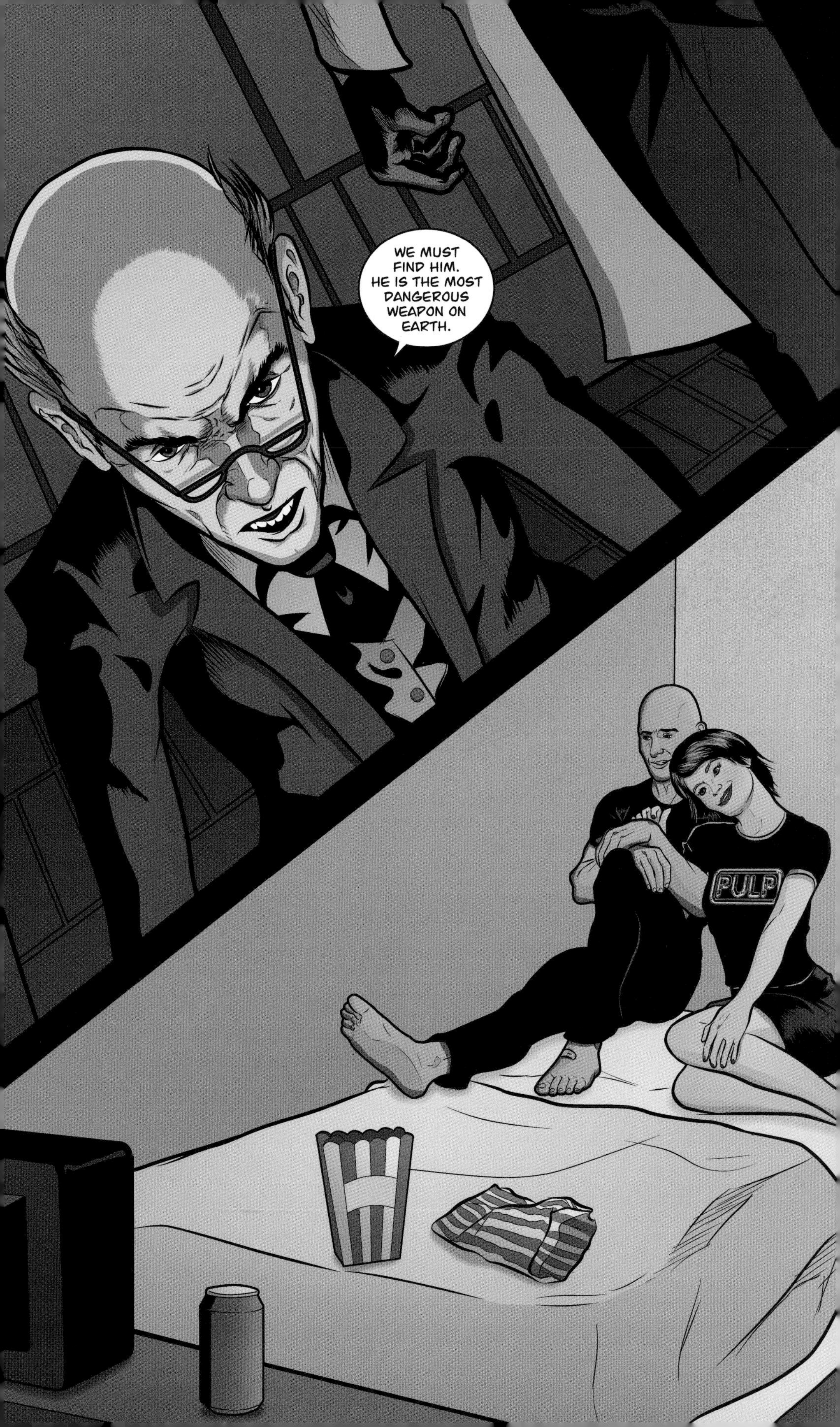
WE MUST FIND HIM. HE IS THE MOST DANGEROUS WEAPON ON EARTH.
PULP

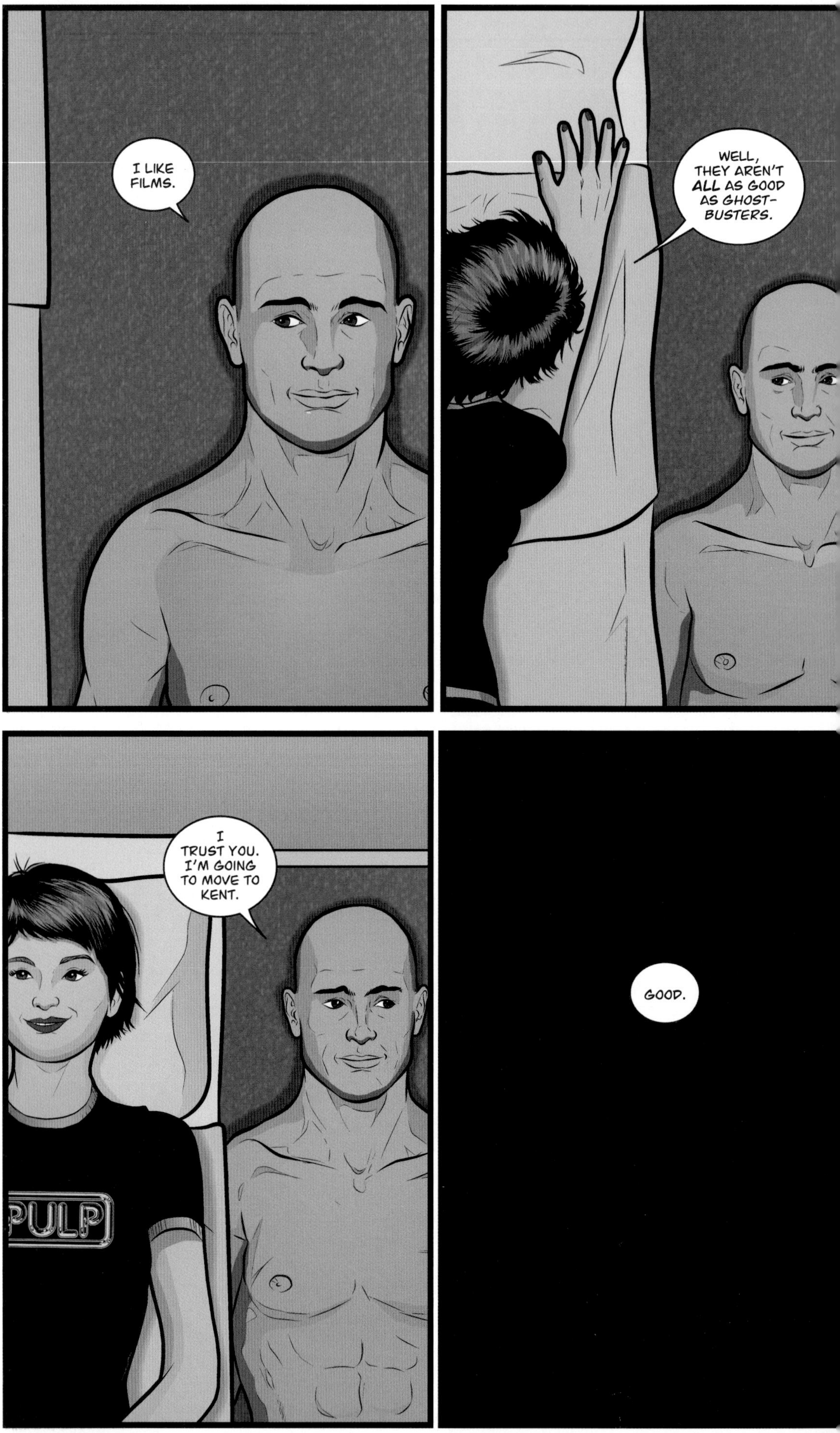
I LIKE FILMS.
WELL, THEY AREN'T ALL AS GOOD AS GHOST-BUSTERS.
I TRUST YOU. I'M GOING TO MOVE TO KENT.
GOOD.
PULP

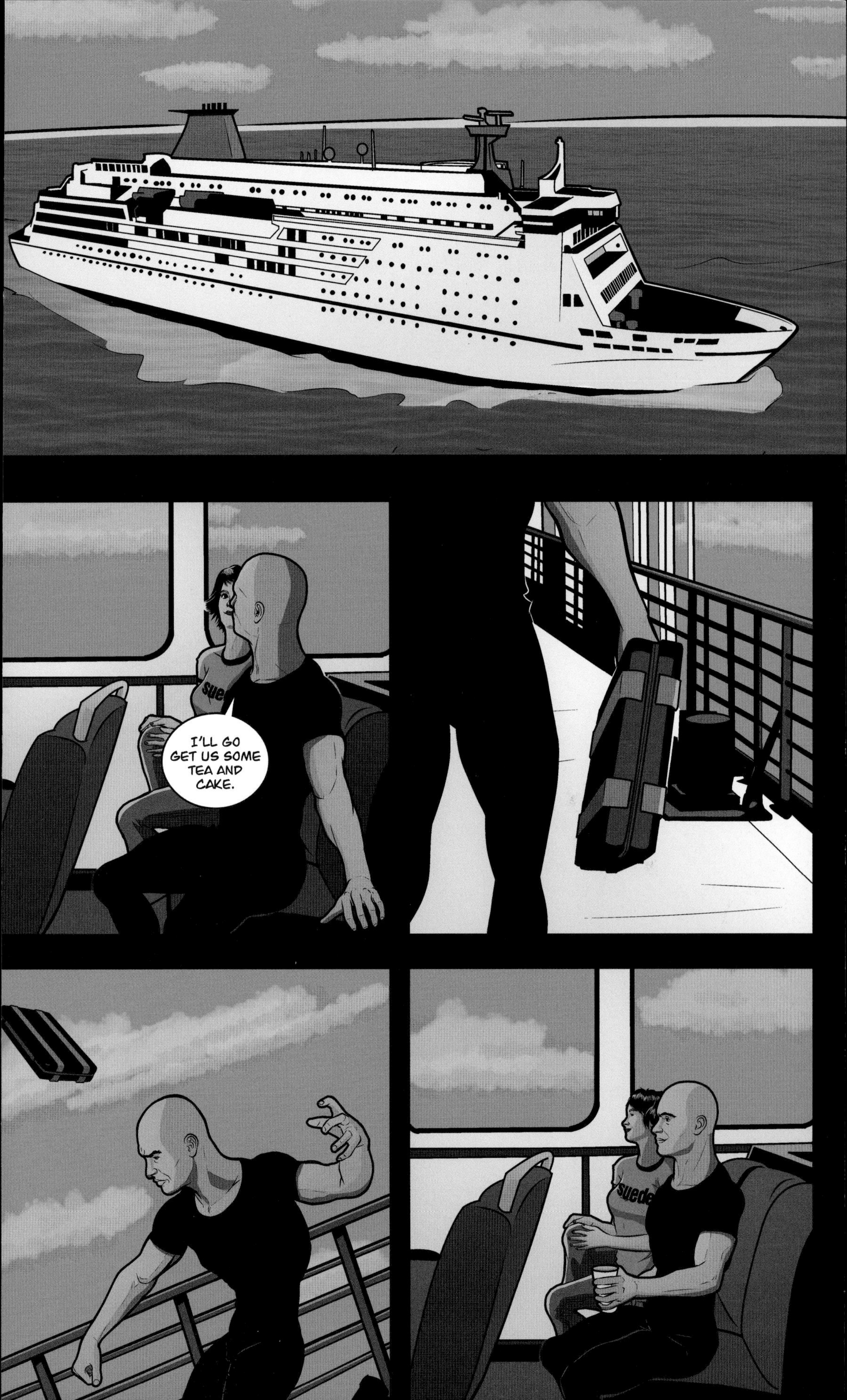
I'LL GO GET US SOME TEA AND CAKE.

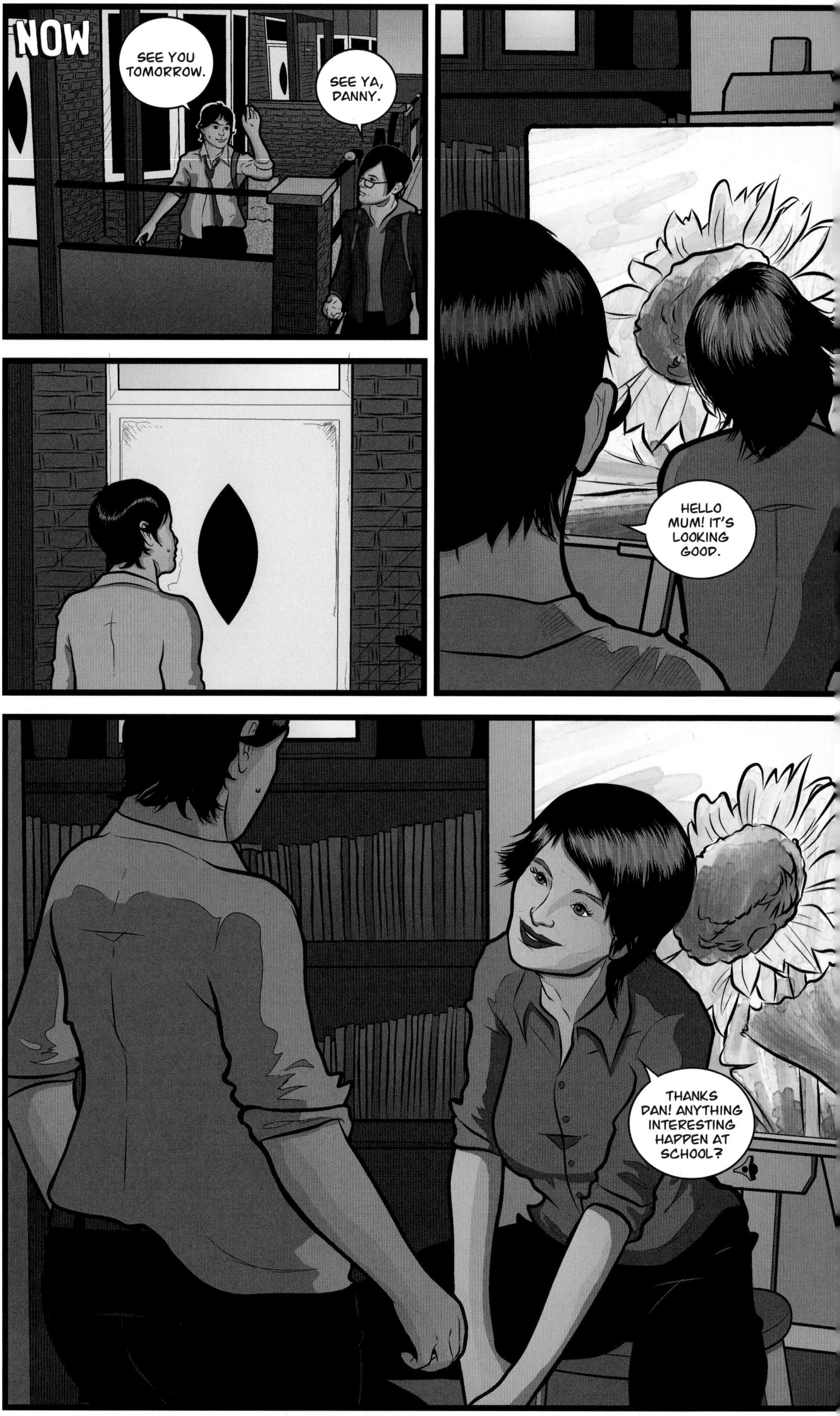
NOW
SEE YOU TOMORROW.
SEE YA, DANNY.
HELLO MUM! IT'S LOOKING GOOD.
THANKS DAN! ANYTHING INTERESTING HAPPEN AT SCHOOL?

CHAPTER 6

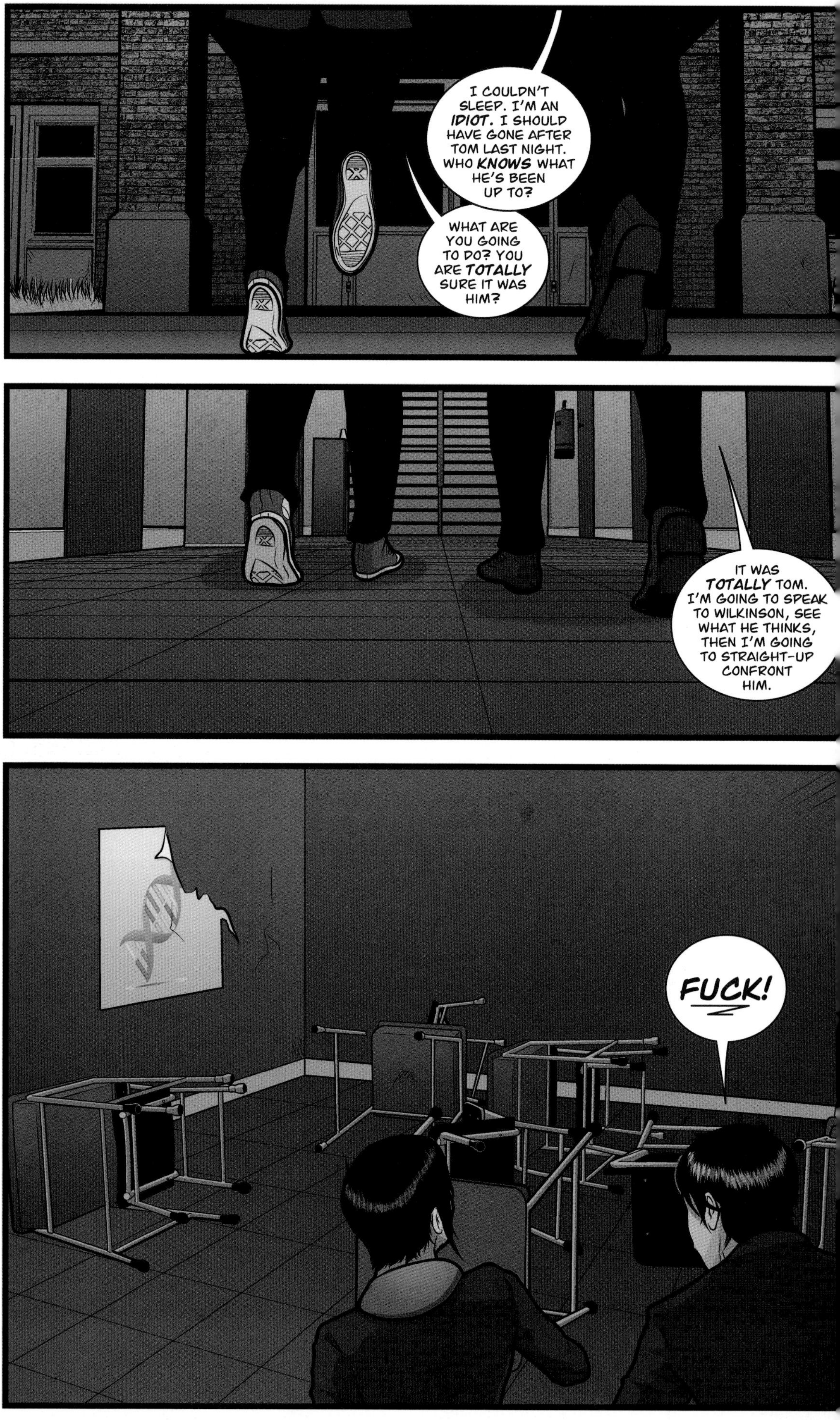
I COULDN'T SLEEP. I'M AN IDIOT. I SHOULD HAVE GONE AFTER TOM LAST NIGHT. WHO KNOWS WHAT HE'S BEEN UP TO?
WHAT ARE YOU GOING TO DO? YOU ARE TOTALLY SURE IT WAS HIM?
IT WAS TOTALLY TOM. I'M GOING TO SPEAK TO WILKINSON, SEE WHAT HE THINKS, THEN I'M GOING TO STRAIGHT-UP CONFRONT HIM.
FUCK!

SHIT!
THAT'S GOT TO
BE TOM, RIGHT?
HE'S SMASHED
WILKINSON! WE
NEED TO FIND
HIM.

AAAAARRRRRGGGGHHH

I RECKON
THAT WAY.

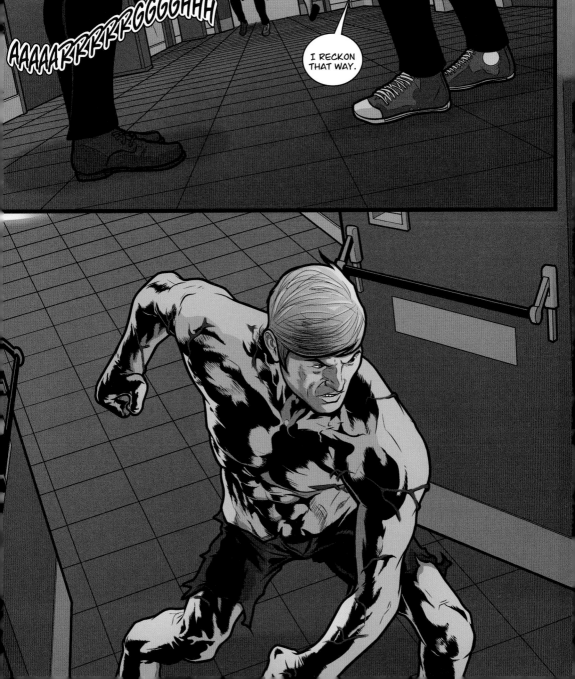

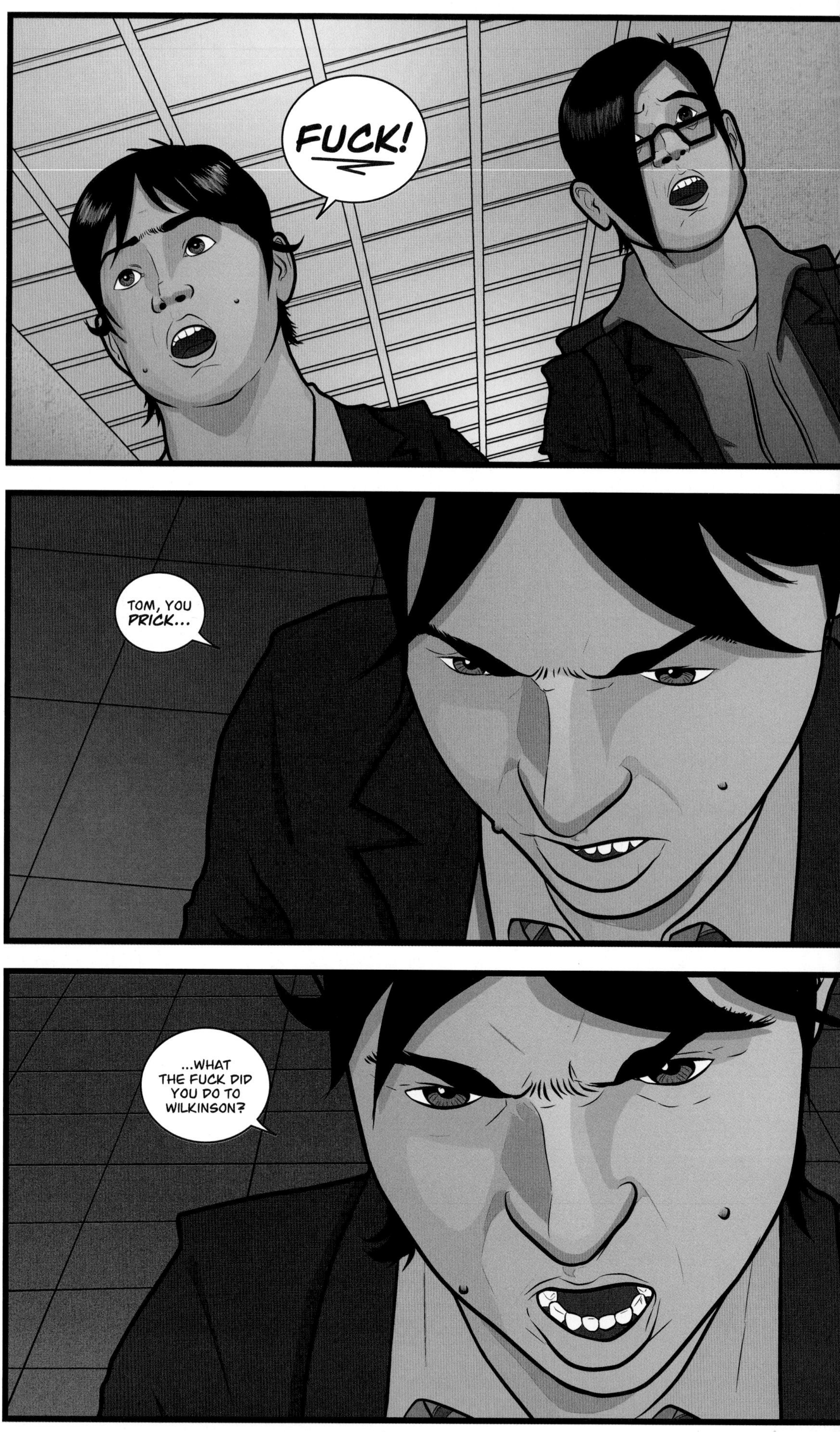
FUCK!
TOM, YOU PRICK...
...WHAT THE FUCK DID YOU DO TO WILKINSON?

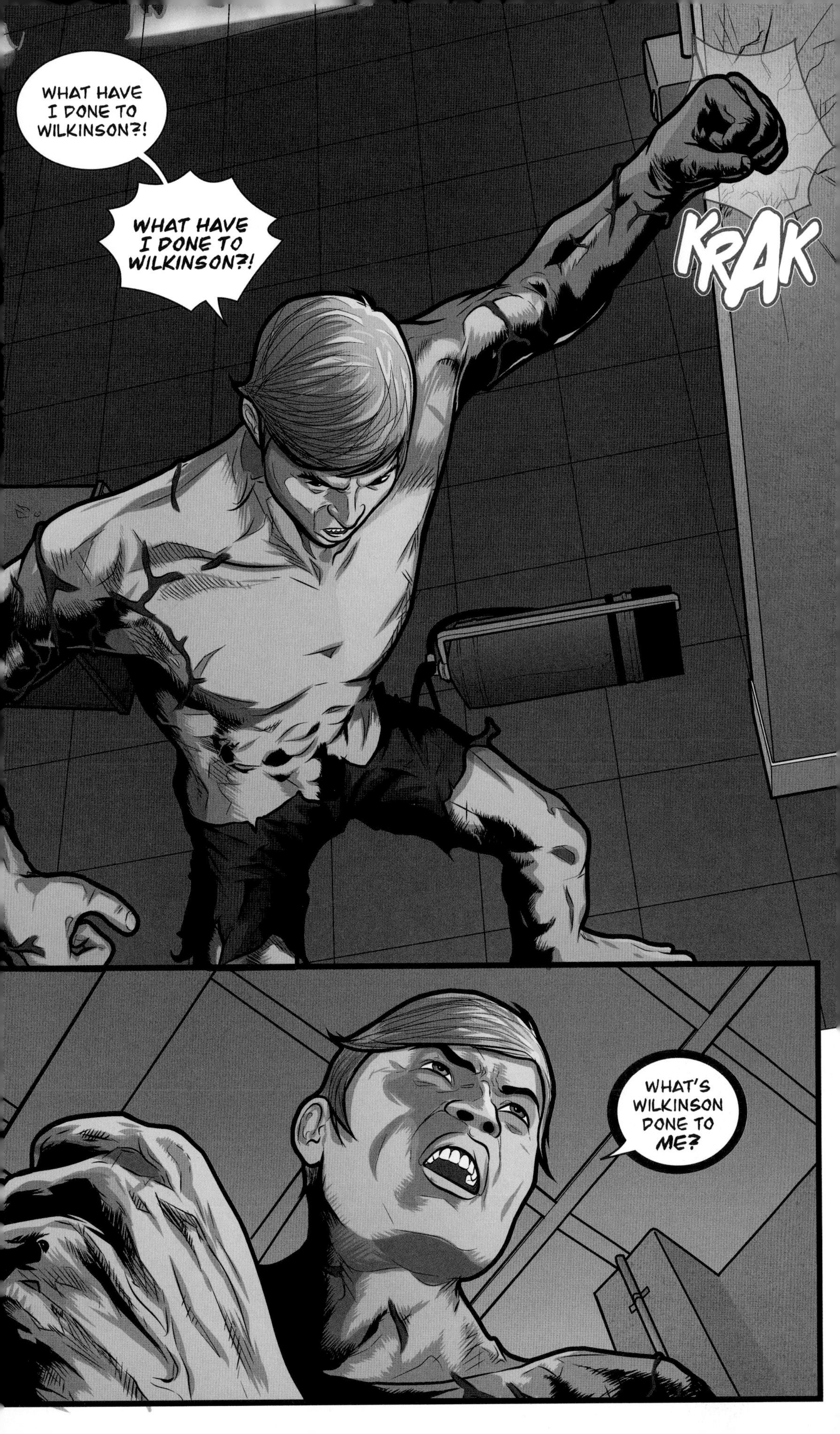
WHAT HAVE I DONE TO WILKINSON?!
WHAT HAVE I DONE TO WILKINSON?!
KRAK
WHAT'S WILKINSON DONE TO ME?

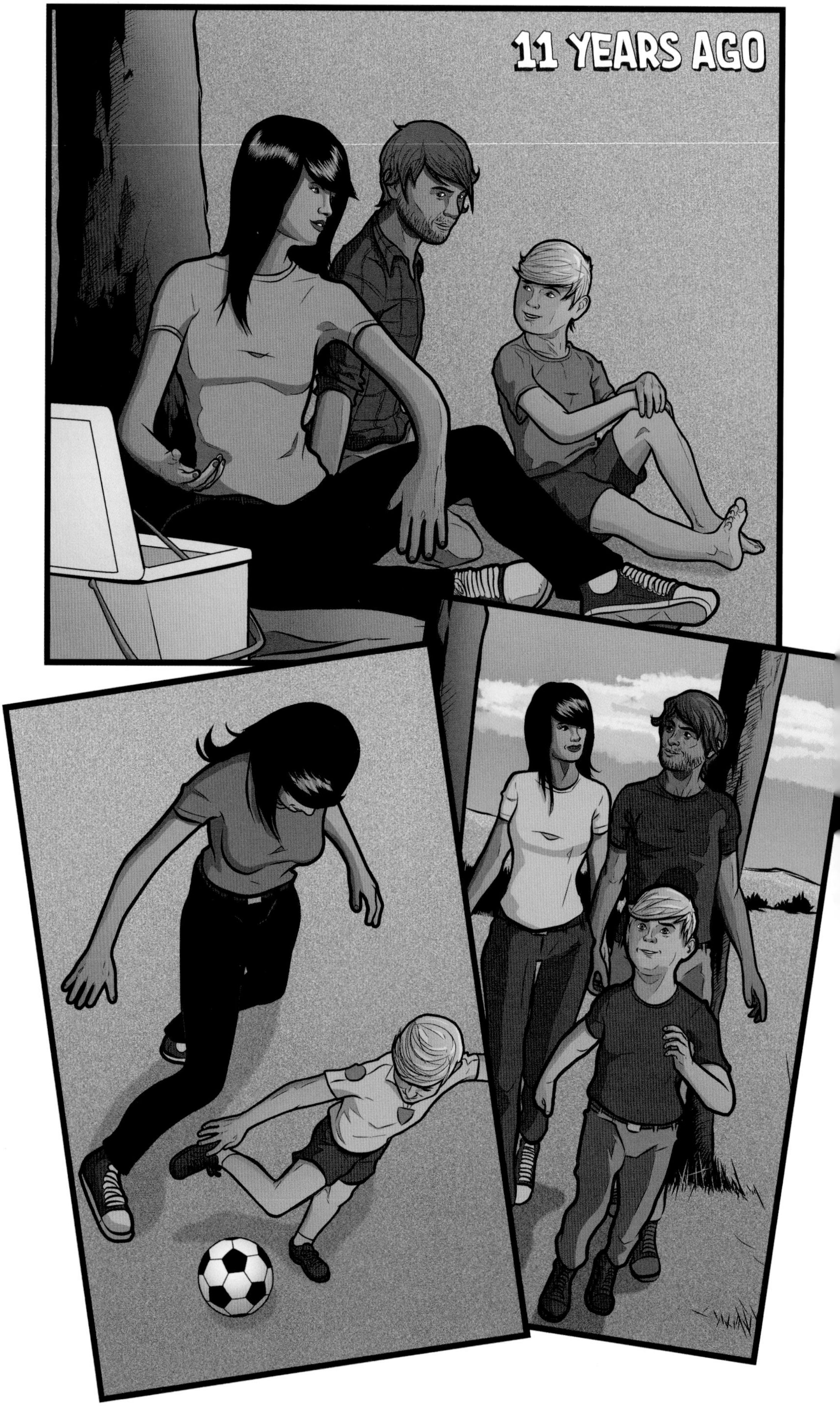
11 YEARS AGO

NHS

LAMBERFORD
HOSPITAL

"TRY NOT
TO CRY."

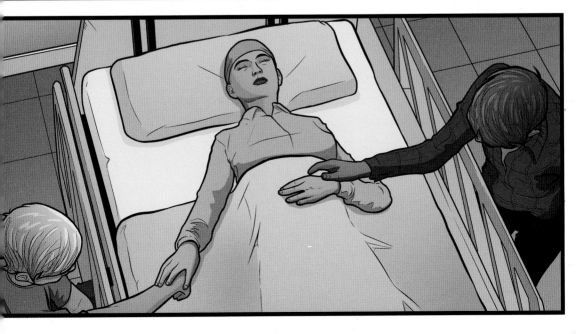

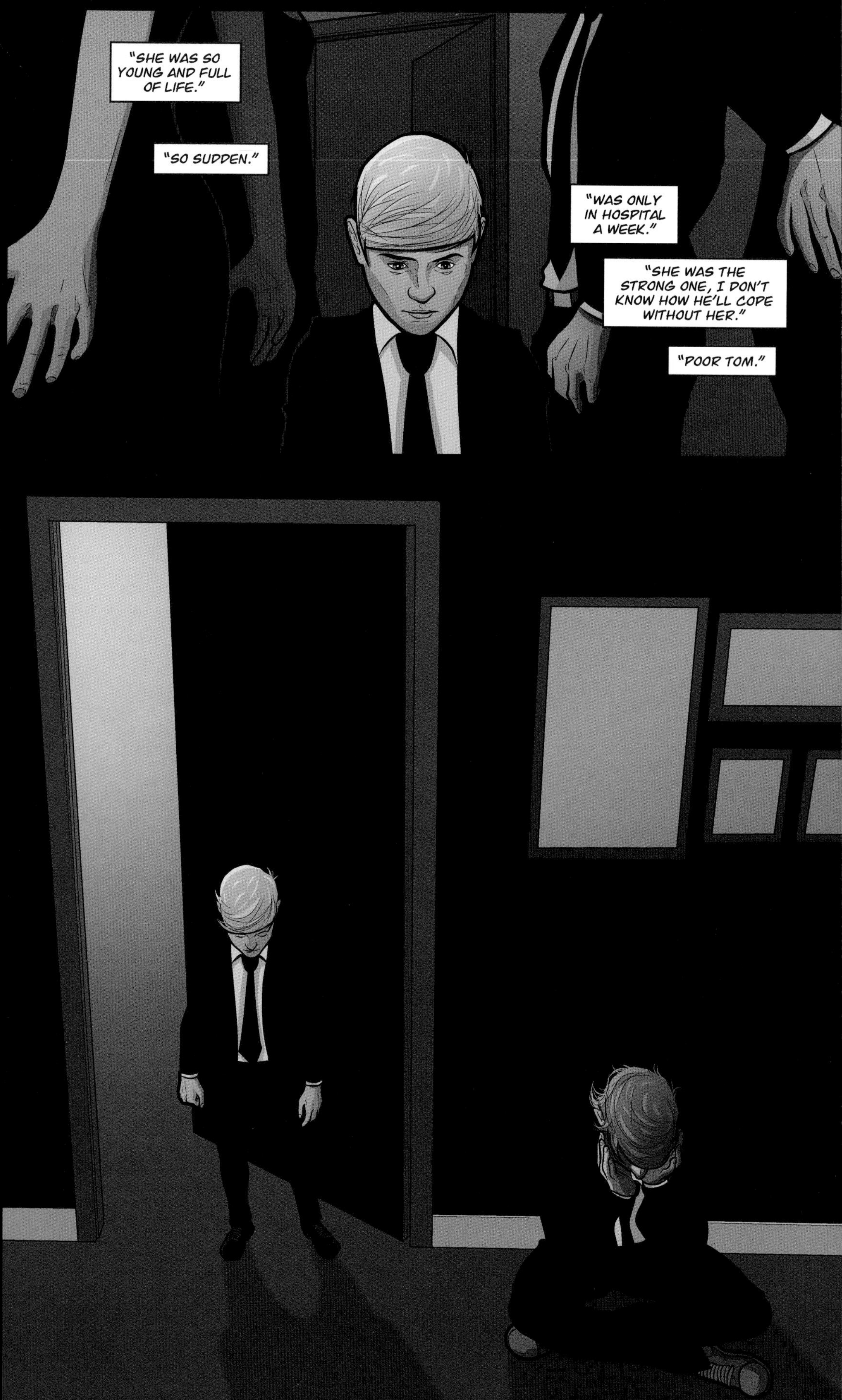
"SHE WAS SO YOUNG AND FULL OF LIFE."
"SO SUDDEN."
"WAS ONLY IN HOSPITAL A WEEK."
"SHE WAS THE STRONG ONE, I DON'T KNOW HOW HE'LL COPE WITHOUT HER."
"POOR TOM."

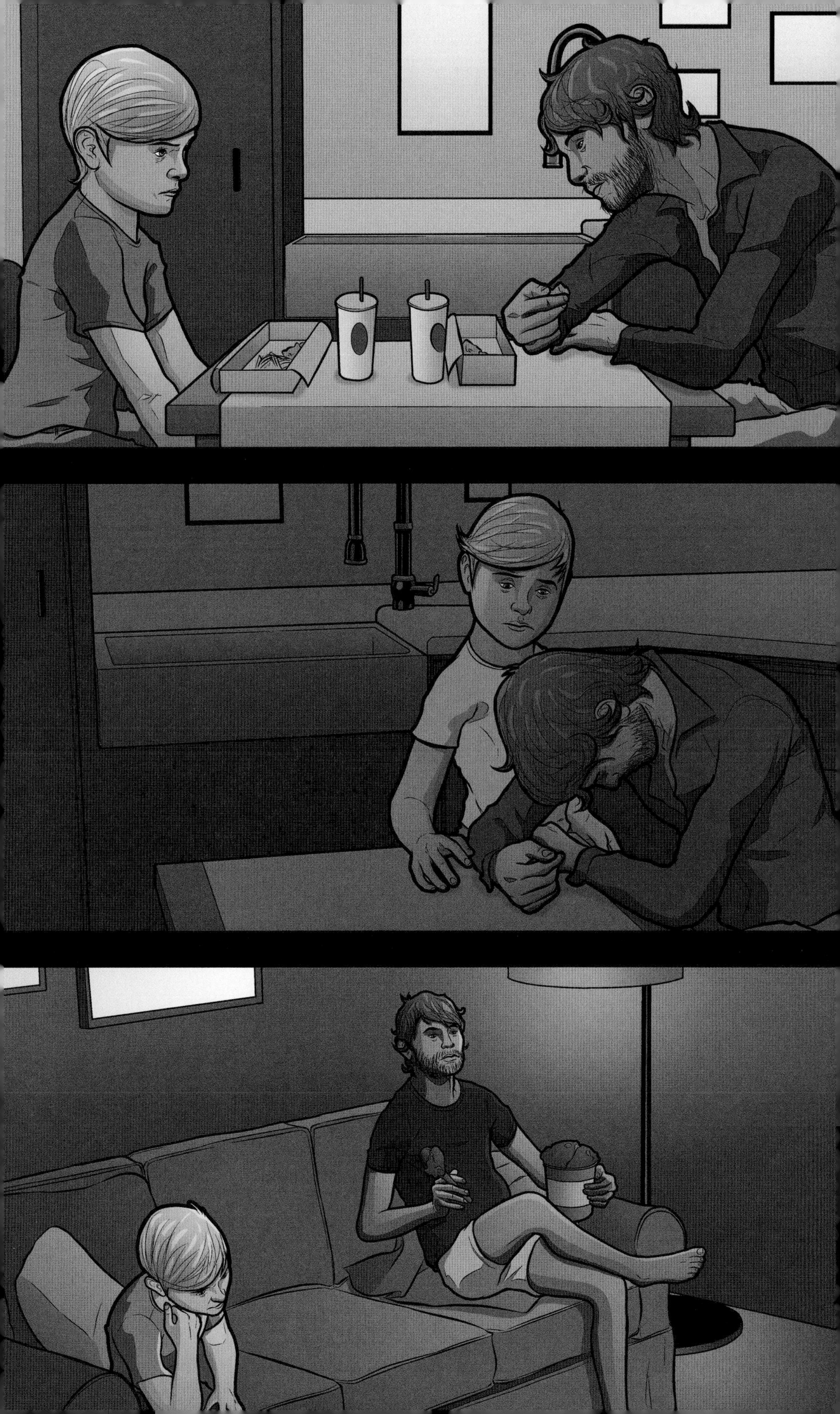

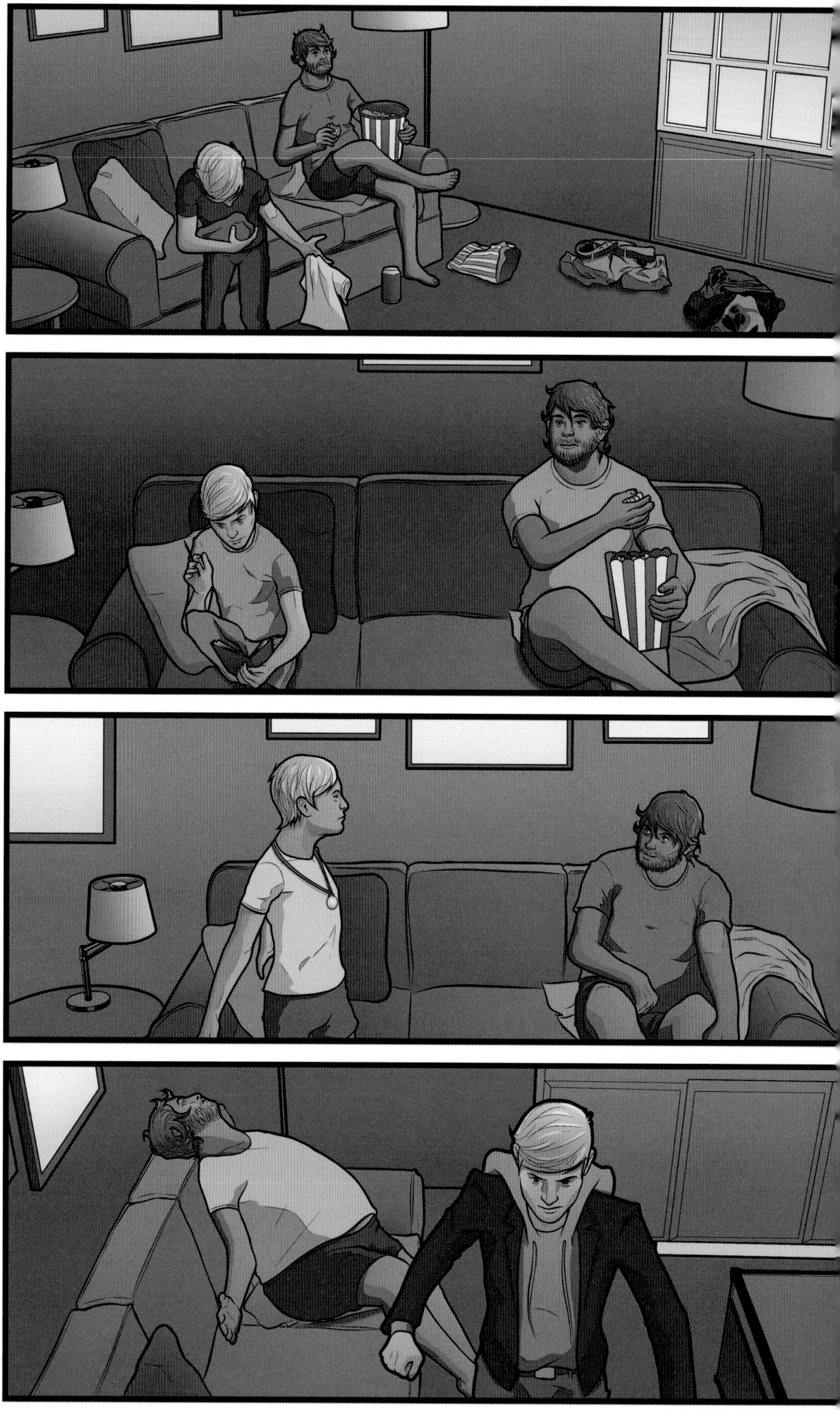

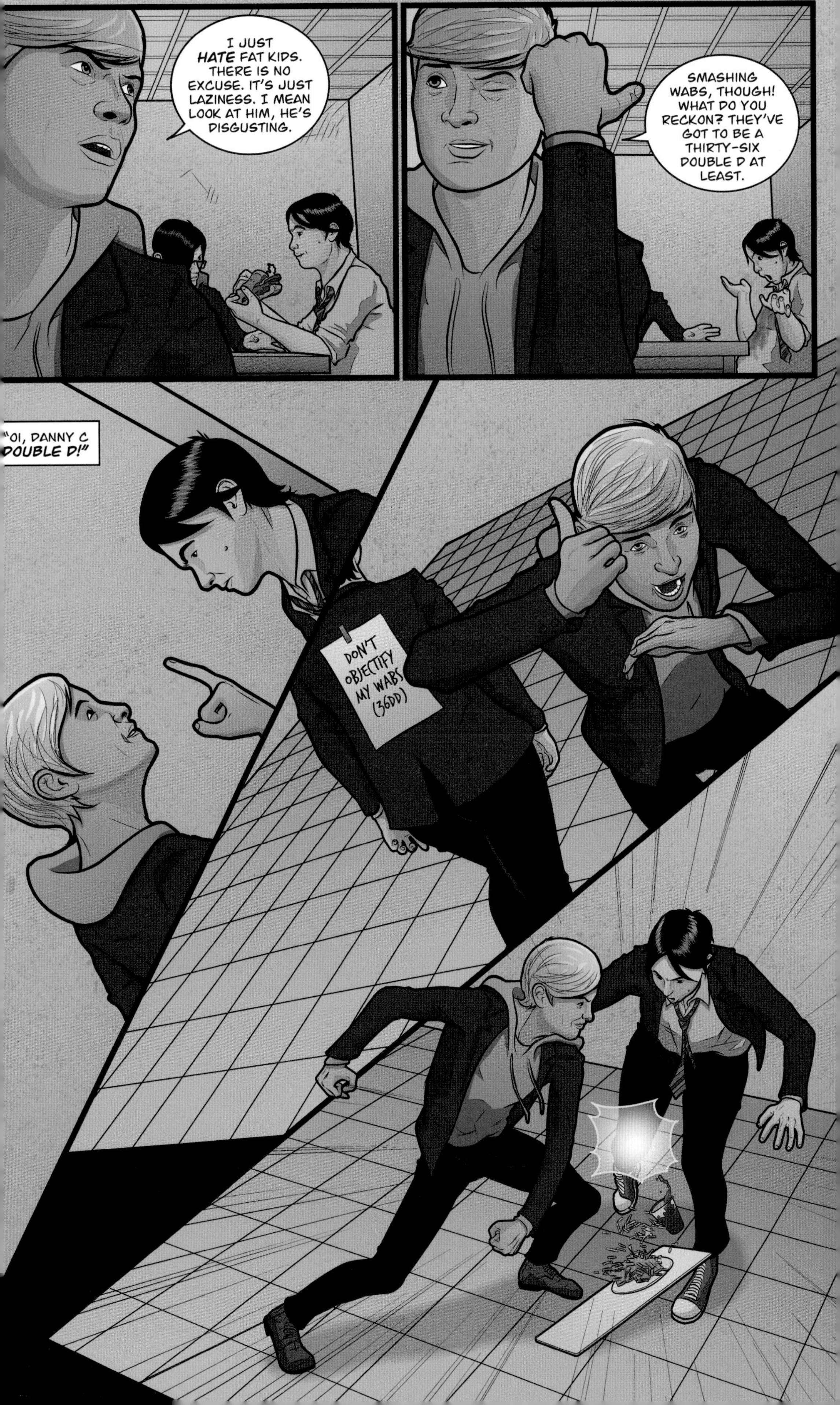
I JUST HATE FAT KIDS. THERE IS NO EXCUSE. IT'S JUST LAZINESS. I MEAN LOOK AT HIM, HE'S DISGUSTING.
SMASHING WABS, THOUGH! WHAT DO YOU RECKON? THEY'VE GOT TO BE A THIRTY-SIX DOUBLE D AT LEAST.
"OI, DANNY C DOUBLE D!"
DON'T OBJECTIFY MY WABS (36DD)

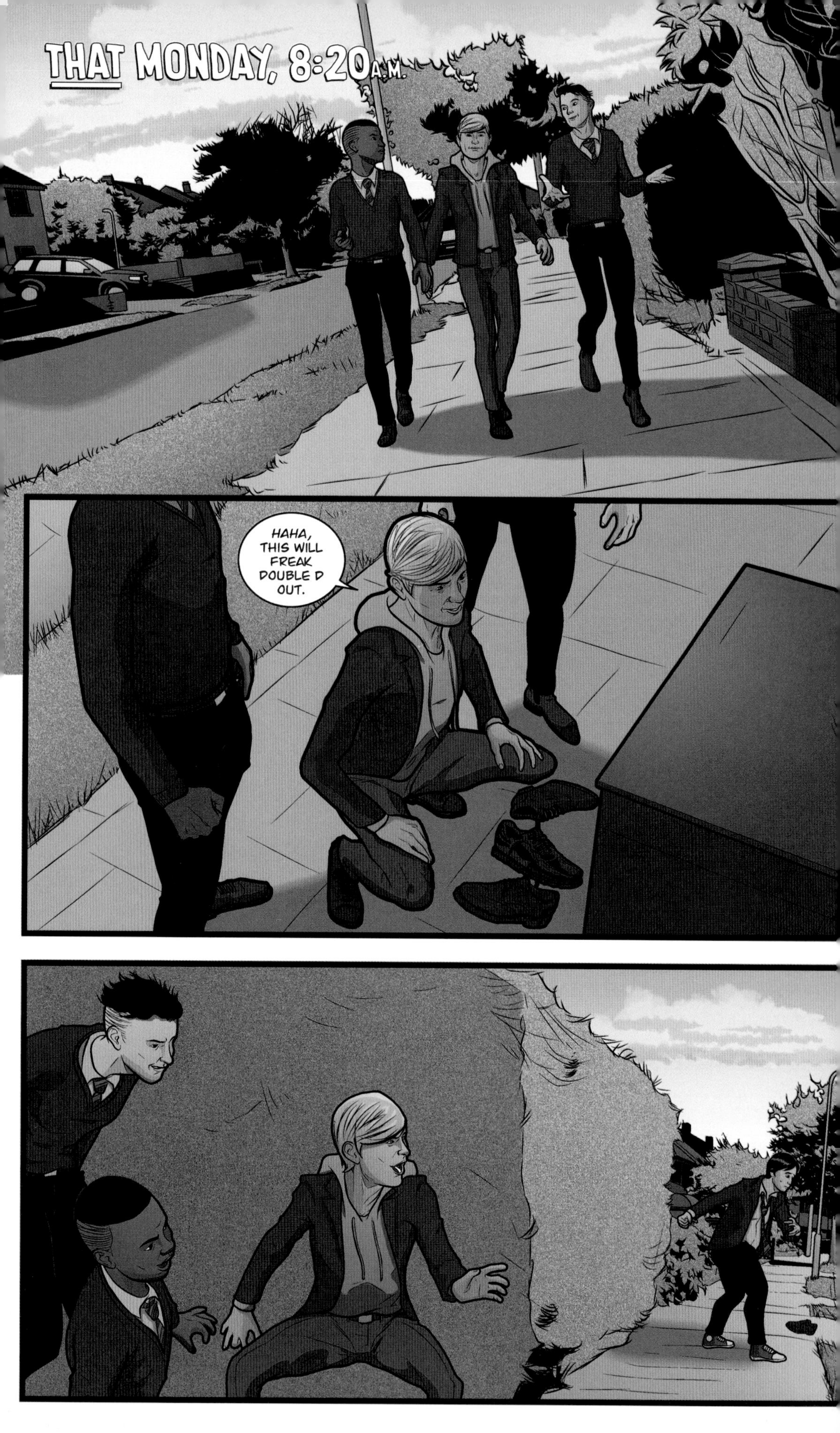
THAT MONDAY, 8:20 A.M.
HAHA, THIS WILL FREAK DOUBLE D OUT.

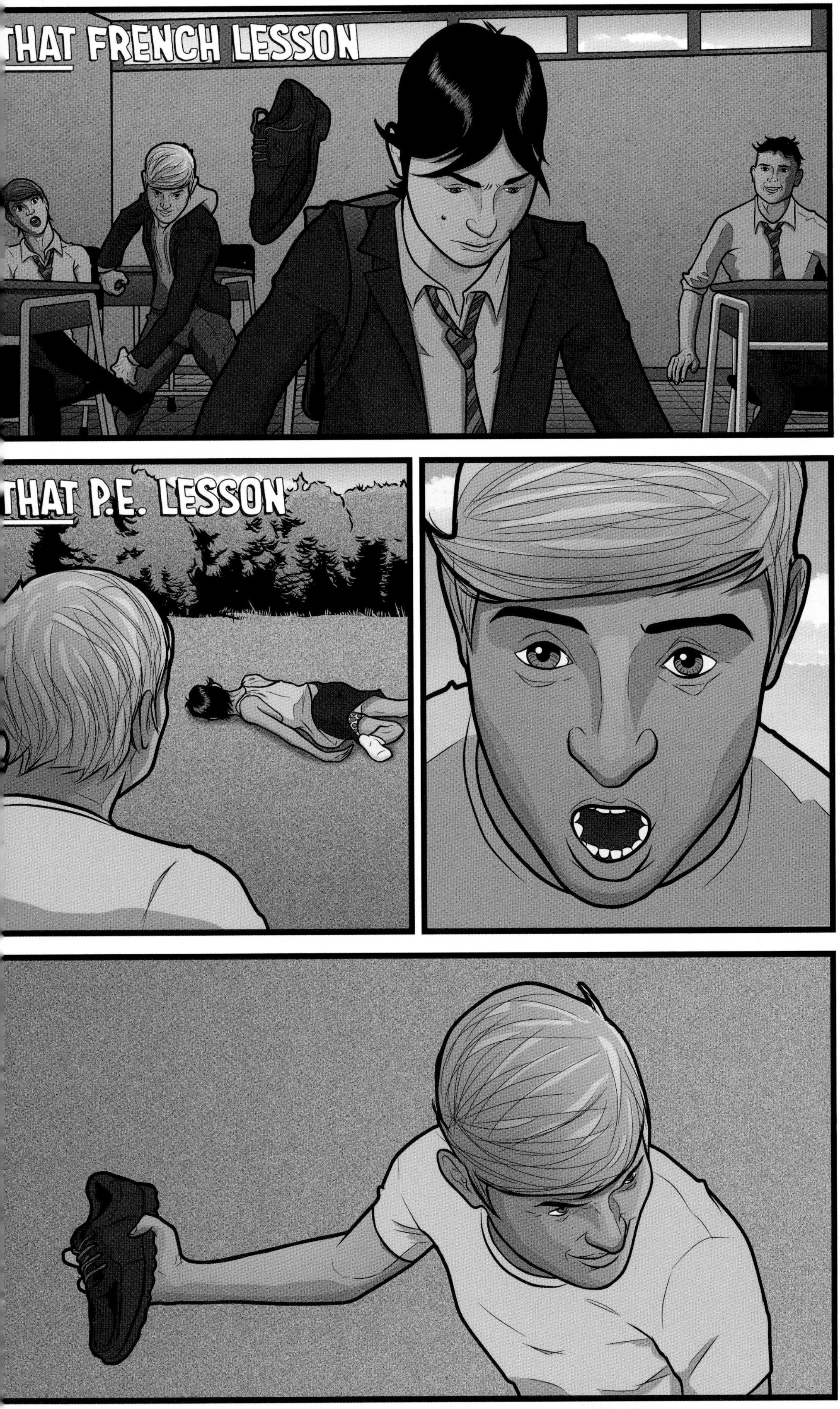
THAT FRENCH LESSON
THAT P.E. LESSON

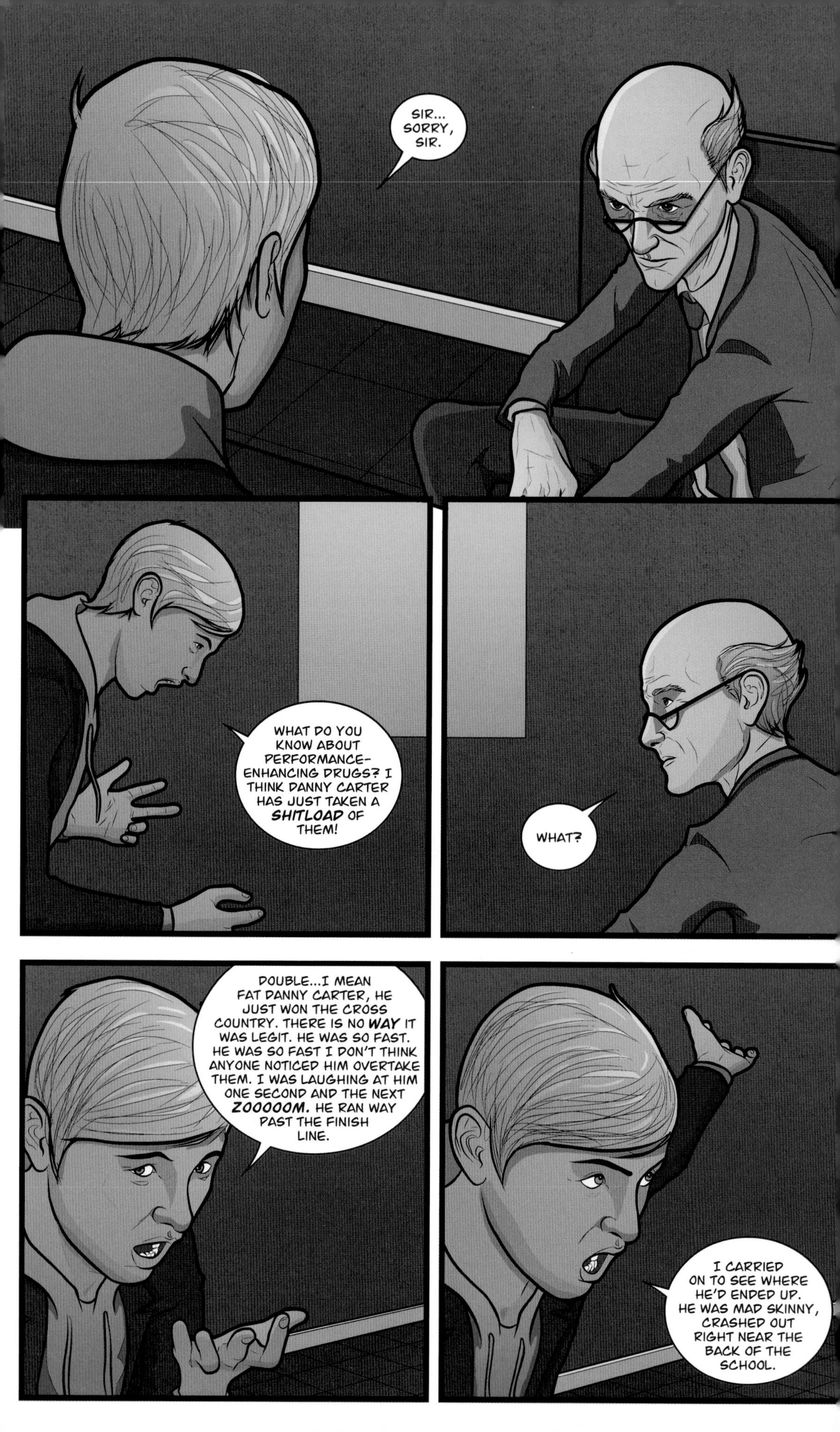
SIR... SORRY, SIR.
WHAT DO YOU KNOW ABOUT PERFORMANCE-ENHANCING DRUGS? I THINK DANNY CARTER HAS JUST TAKEN A SHITLOAD OF THEM!
WHAT?
DOUBLE...I MEAN FAT DANNY CARTER, HE JUST WON THE CROSS COUNTRY. THERE IS NO WAY IT WAS LEGIT. HE WAS SO FAST. HE WAS SO FAST I DON'T THINK ANYONE NOTICED HIM OVERTAKE THEM. I WAS LAUGHING AT HIM ONE SECOND AND THE NEXT ZOOOOOM. HE RAN WAY PAST THE FINISH LINE.
I CARRIED ON TO SEE WHERE HE'D ENDED UP. HE WAS MAD SKINNY, CRASHED OUT RIGHT NEAR THE BACK OF THE SCHOOL.

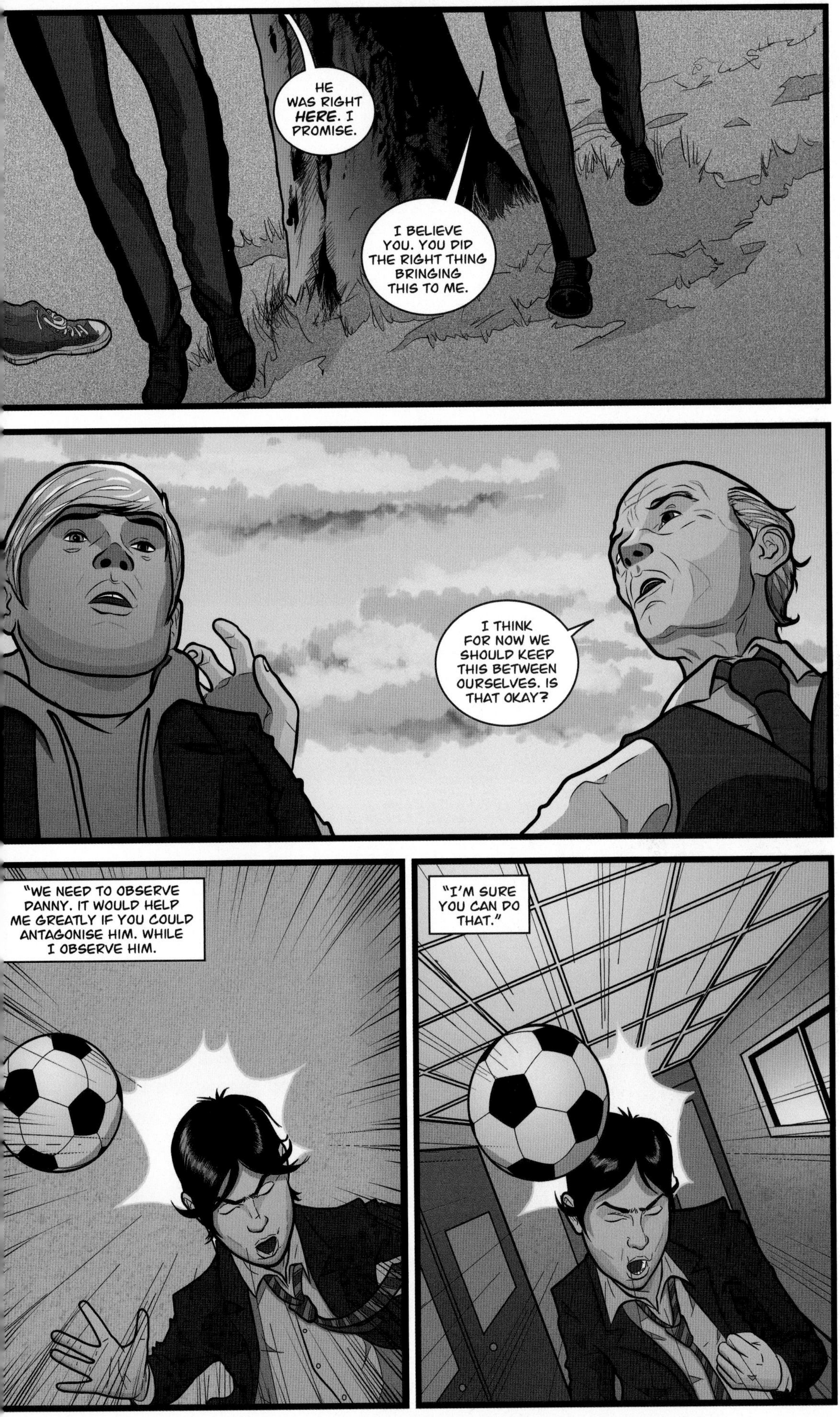
HE WAS RIGHT HERE. I PROMISE.
I BELIEVE YOU. YOU DID THE RIGHT THING BRINGING THIS TO ME.
I THINK FOR NOW WE SHOULD KEEP THIS BETWEEN OURSELVES. IS THAT OKAY?
"WE NEED TO OBSERVE DANNY. IT WOULD HELP ME GREATLY IF YOU COULD ANTAGONISE HIM. WHILE I OBSERVE HIM.
"I'M SURE YOU CAN DO THAT."

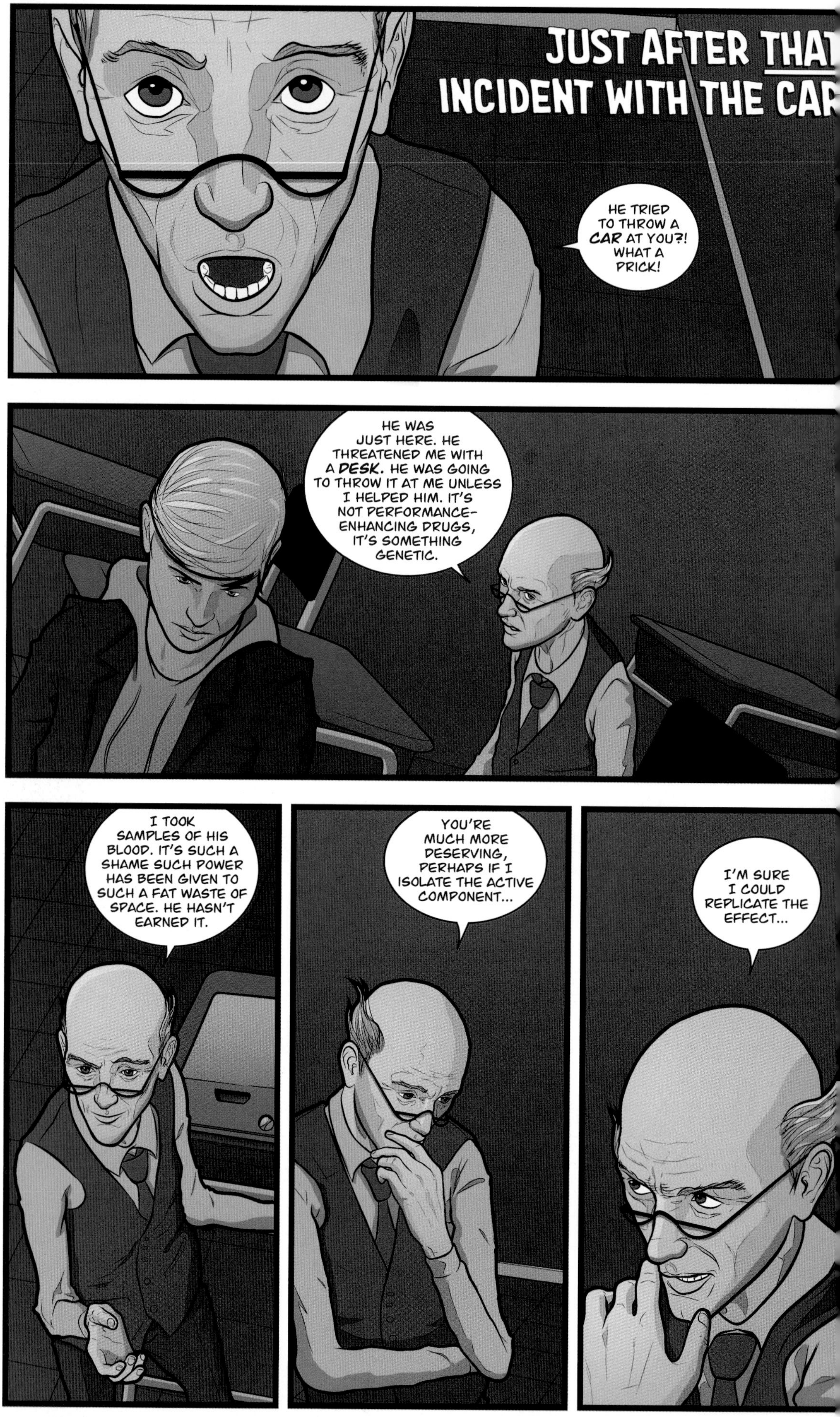

JUST AFTER THAT INCIDENT WITH THE CAR
HE TRIED TO THROW A CAR AT YOU?! WHAT A PRICK!
HE WAS JUST HERE. HE THREATENED ME WITH A DESK. HE WAS GOING TO THROW IT AT ME UNLESS I HELPED HIM. IT'S NOT PERFORMANCE-ENHANCING DRUGS, IT'S SOMETHING GENETIC.
I TOOK SAMPLES OF HIS BLOOD. IT'S SUCH A SHAME SUCH POWER HAS BEEN GIVEN TO SUCH A FAT WASTE OF SPACE. HE HASN'T EARNED IT.
YOU'RE MUCH MORE DESERVING, PERHAPS IF I ISOLATE THE ACTIVE COMPONENT...
I'M SURE I COULD REPLICATE THE EFFECT...

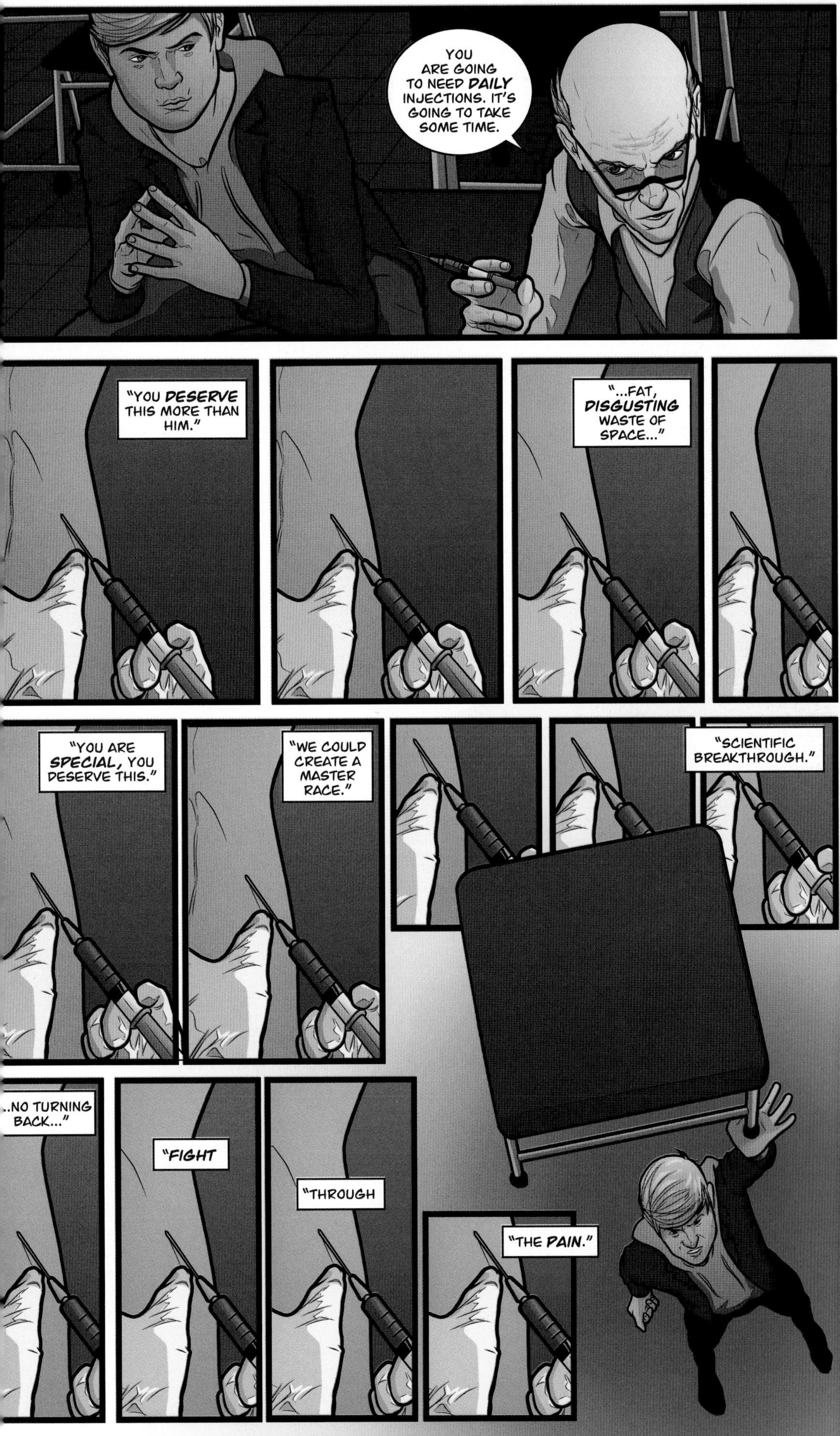
YOU ARE GOING TO NEED DAILY INJECTIONS. IT'S GOING TO TAKE SOME TIME.
"YOU DESERVE THIS MORE THAN HIM."
"...FAT, DISGUSTING WASTE OF SPACE..."
"YOU ARE SPECIAL, YOU DESERVE THIS."
"WE COULD CREATE A MASTER RACE."
"SCIENTIFIC BREAKTHROUGH."
..NO TURNING BACK..."
"FIGHT
"THROUGH
"THE PAIN."

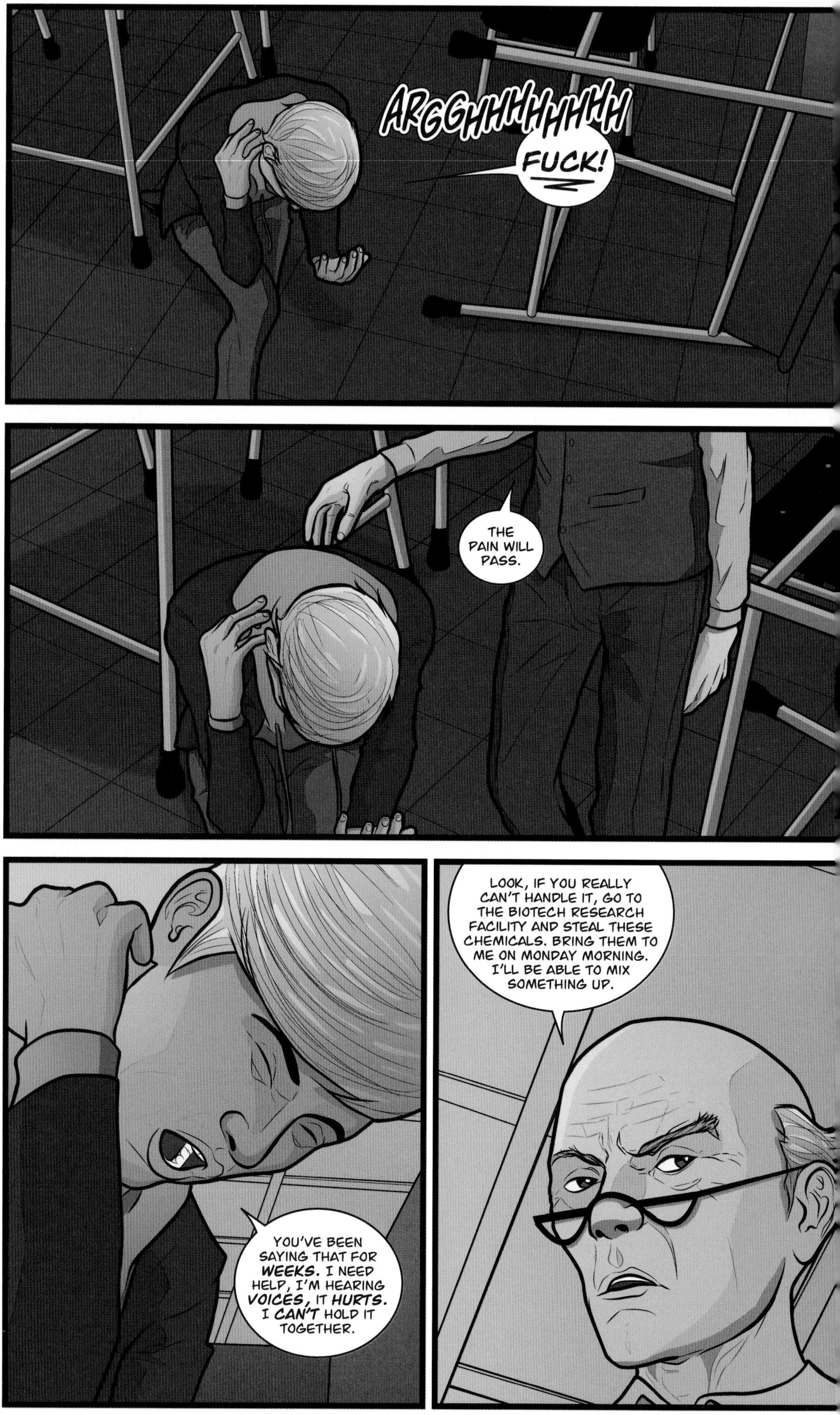
ARGGHHHHHHHH
FUCK!
THE PAIN WILL PASS.
YOU'VE BEEN SAYING THAT FOR WEEKS. I NEED HELP, I'M HEARING VOICES, IT HURTS. I CAN'T HOLD IT TOGETHER.
LOOK, IF YOU REALLY CAN'T HANDLE IT, GO TO THE BIOTECH RESEARCH FACILITY AND STEAL THESE CHEMICALS. BRING THEM TO ME ON MONDAY MORNING. I'LL BE ABLE TO MIX SOMETHING UP.

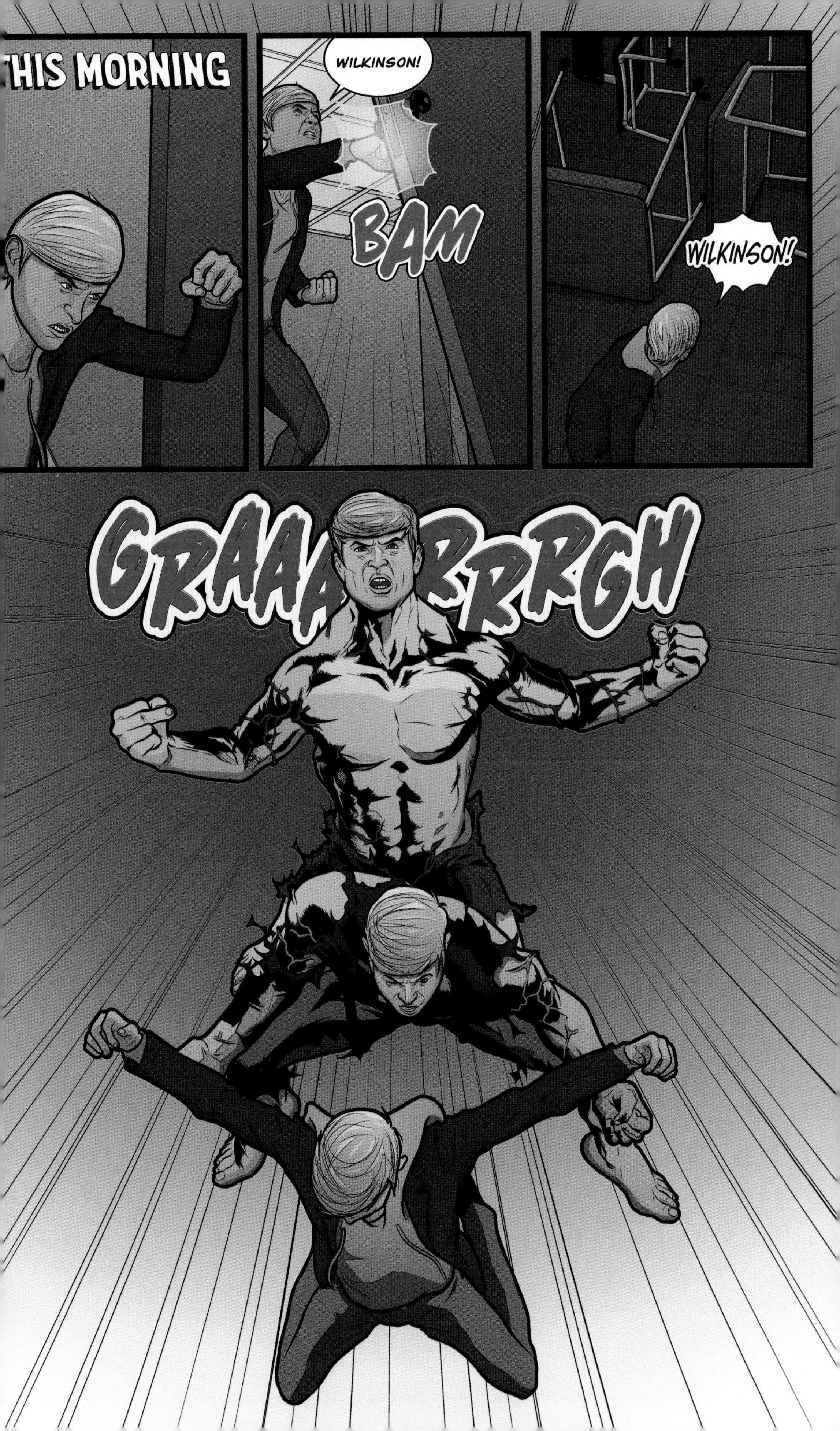
THIS MORNING
WILKINSON!
BAM
WILKINSON!
GRAAAARRRGH

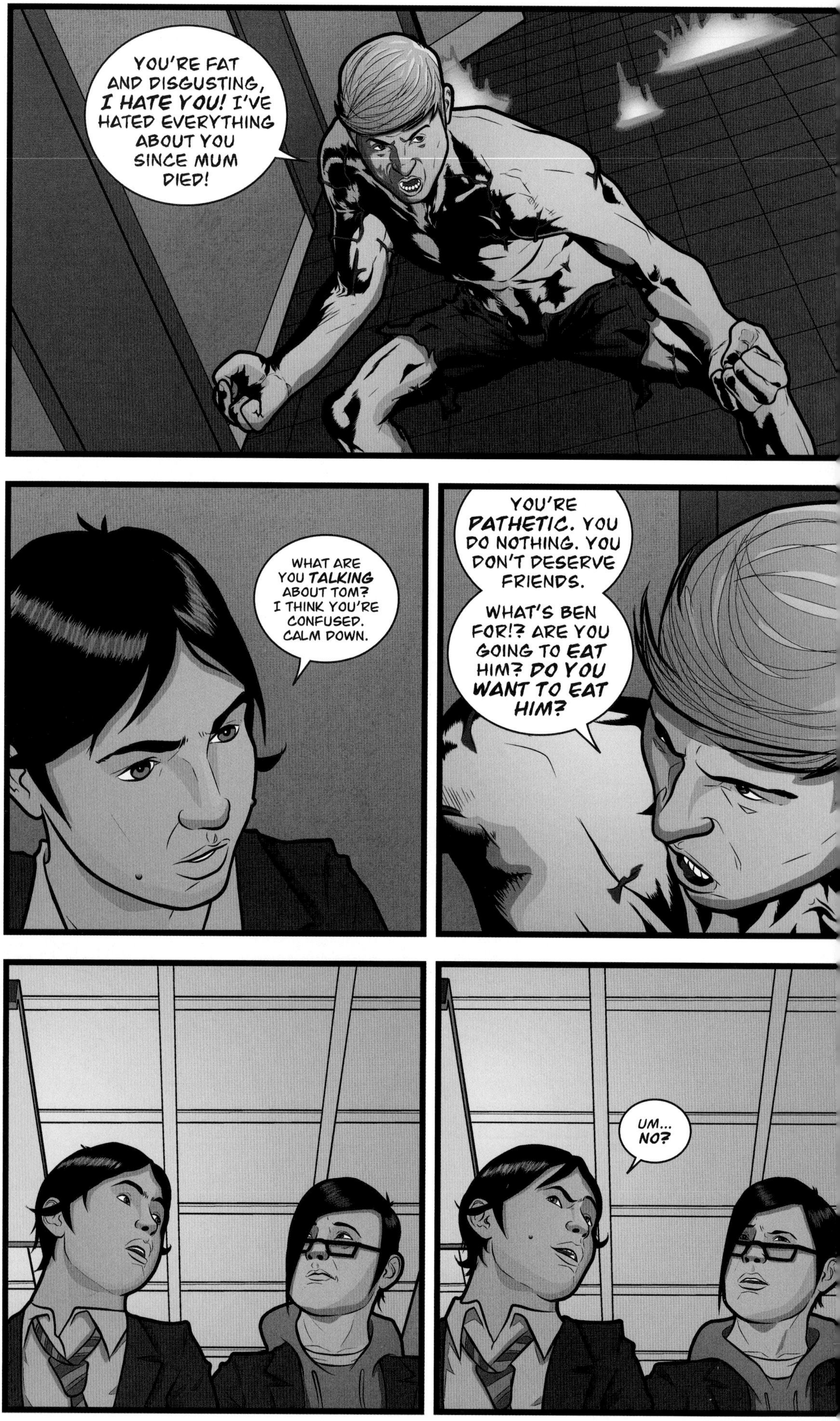
YOU'RE FAT AND DISGUSTING, I HATE YOU! I'VE HATED EVERYTHING ABOUT YOU SINCE MUM DIED!
WHAT ARE YOU TALKING ABOUT TOM? I THINK YOU'RE CONFUSED. CALM DOWN.
YOU'RE PATHETIC. YOU DO NOTHING. YOU DON'T DESERVE FRIENDS.
WHAT'S BEN FOR!? ARE YOU GOING TO EAT HIM? DO YOU WANT TO EAT HIM?
UM... NO?

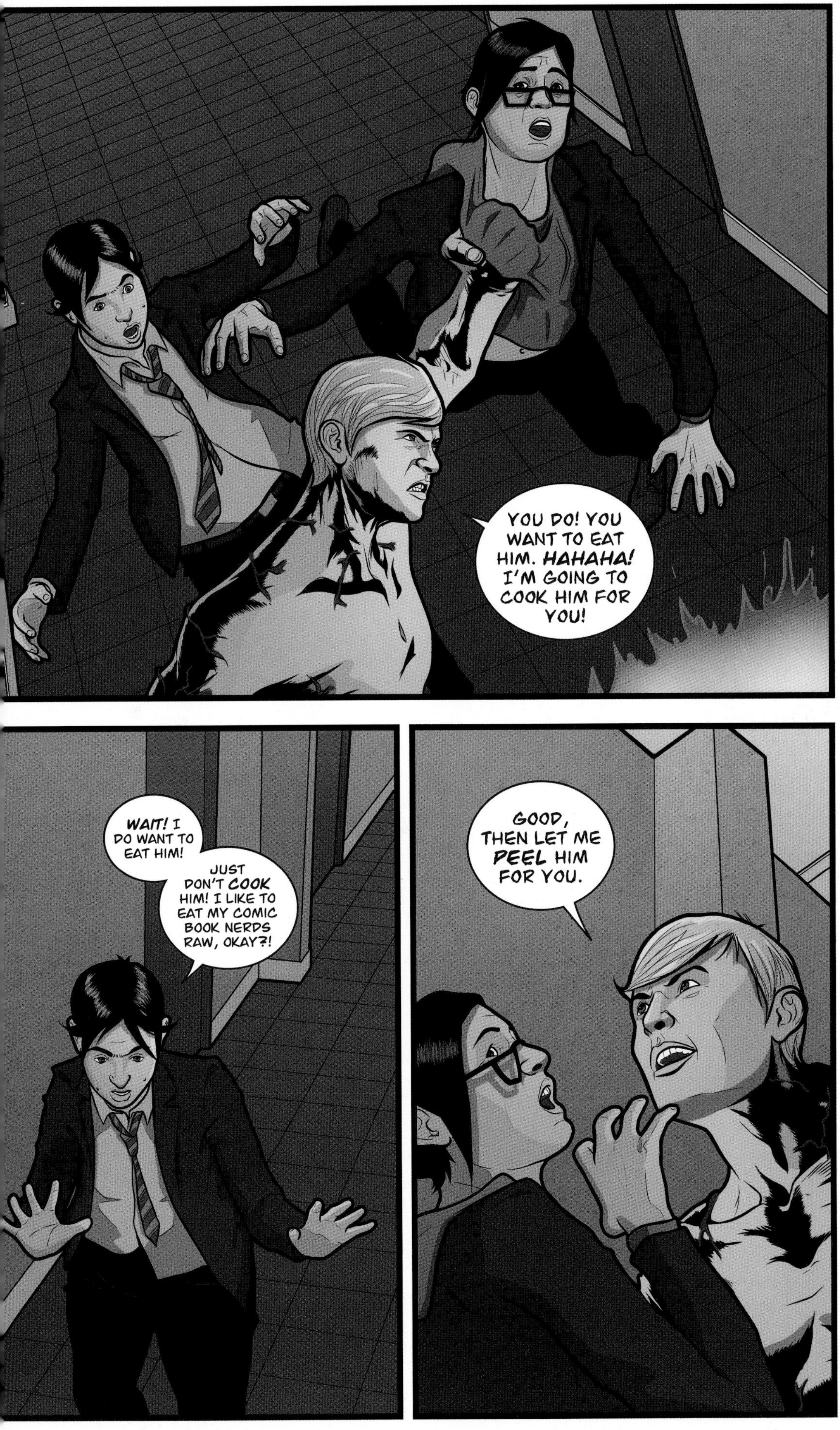
YOU DO! YOU WANT TO EAT HIM. HAHAHA! I'M GOING TO COOK HIM FOR YOU!
WAIT! I DO WANT TO EAT HIM!
JUST DON'T COOK HIM! I LIKE TO EAT MY COMIC BOOK NERDS RAW, OKAY?!
GOOD, THEN LET ME PEEL HIM FOR YOU.

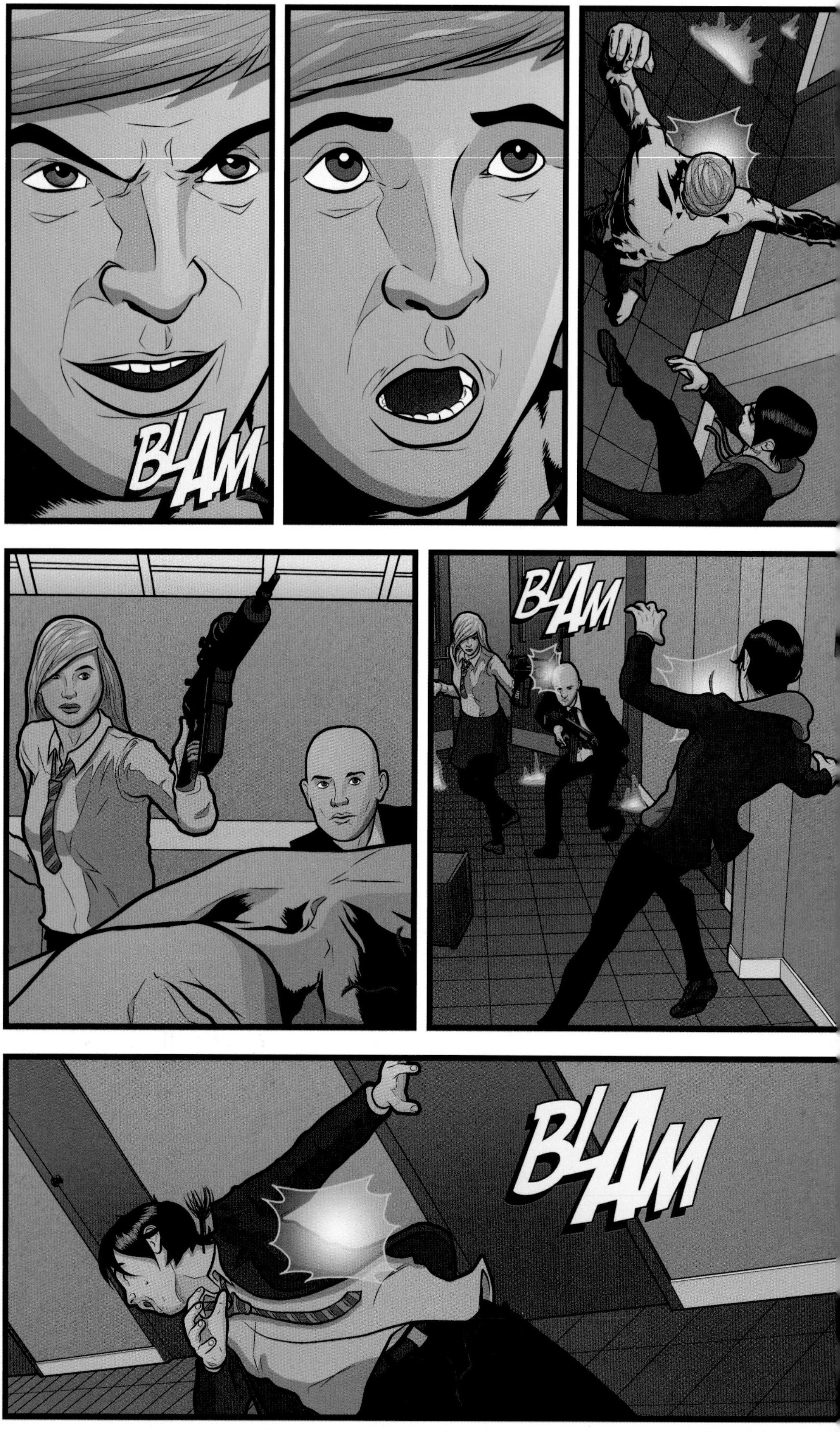
BLAM
BLAM
BLAM

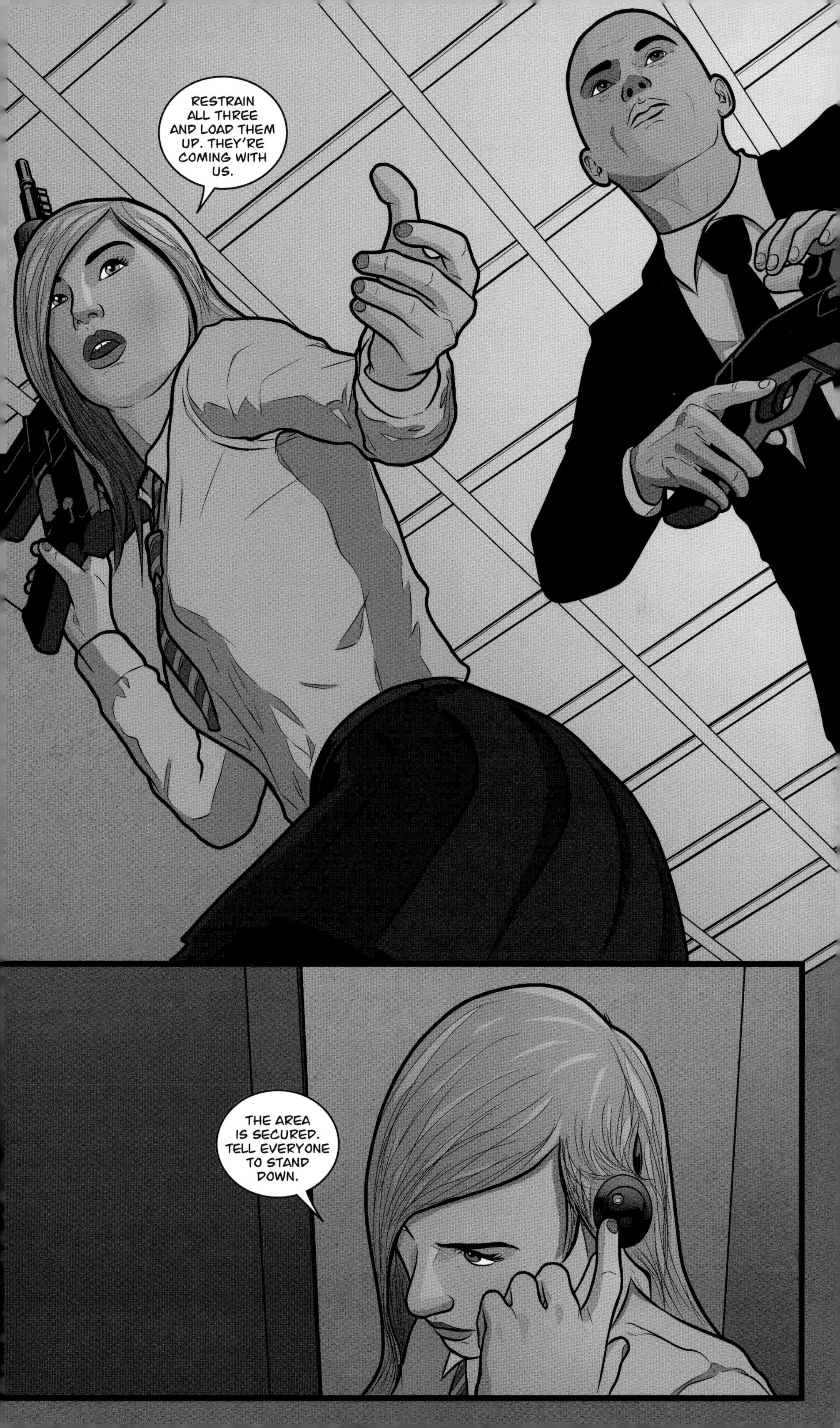
RESTRAIN ALL THREE AND LOAD THEM UP. THEY'RE COMING WITH US.
THE AREA IS SECURED. TELL EVERYONE TO STAND DOWN.

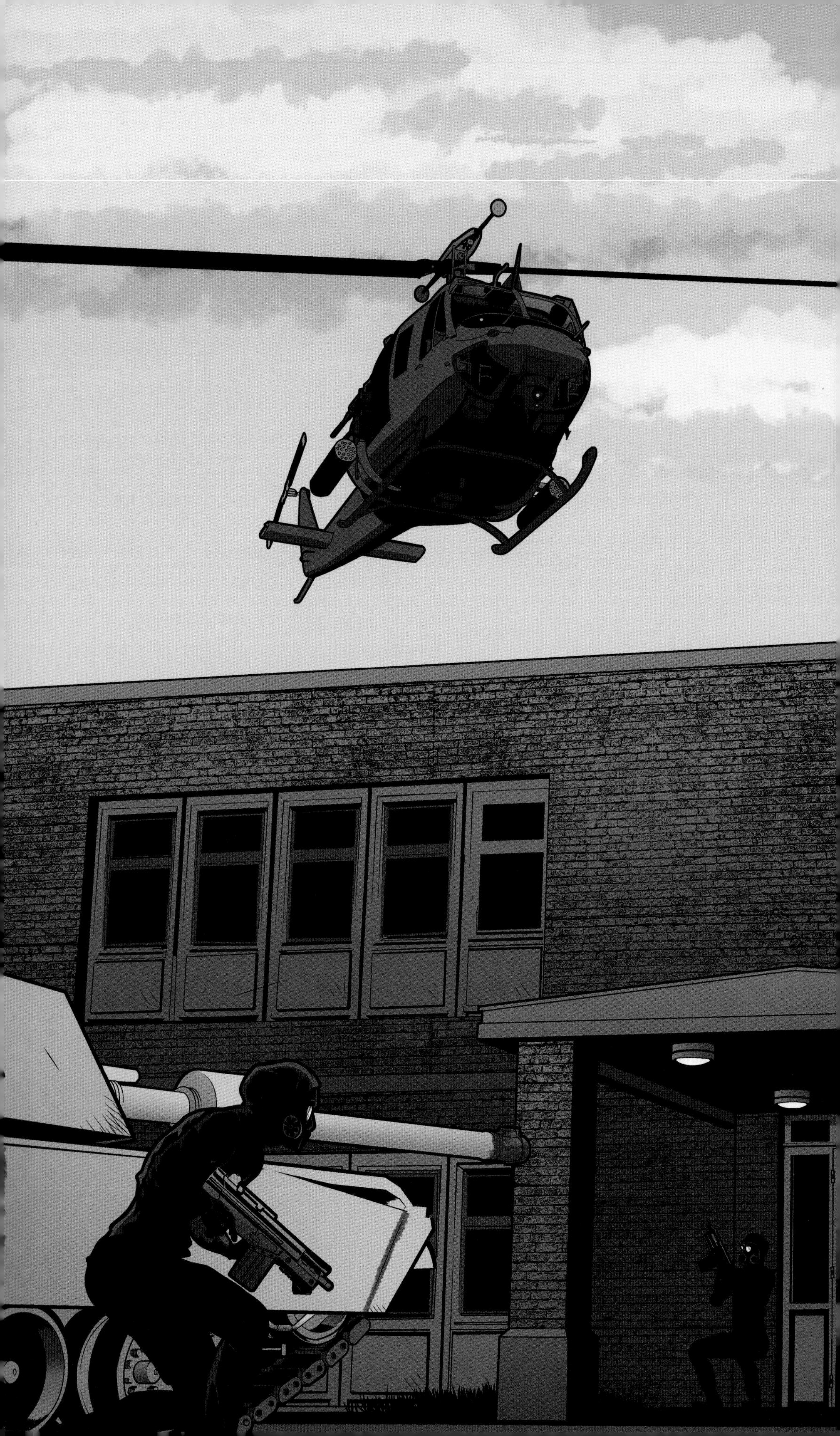

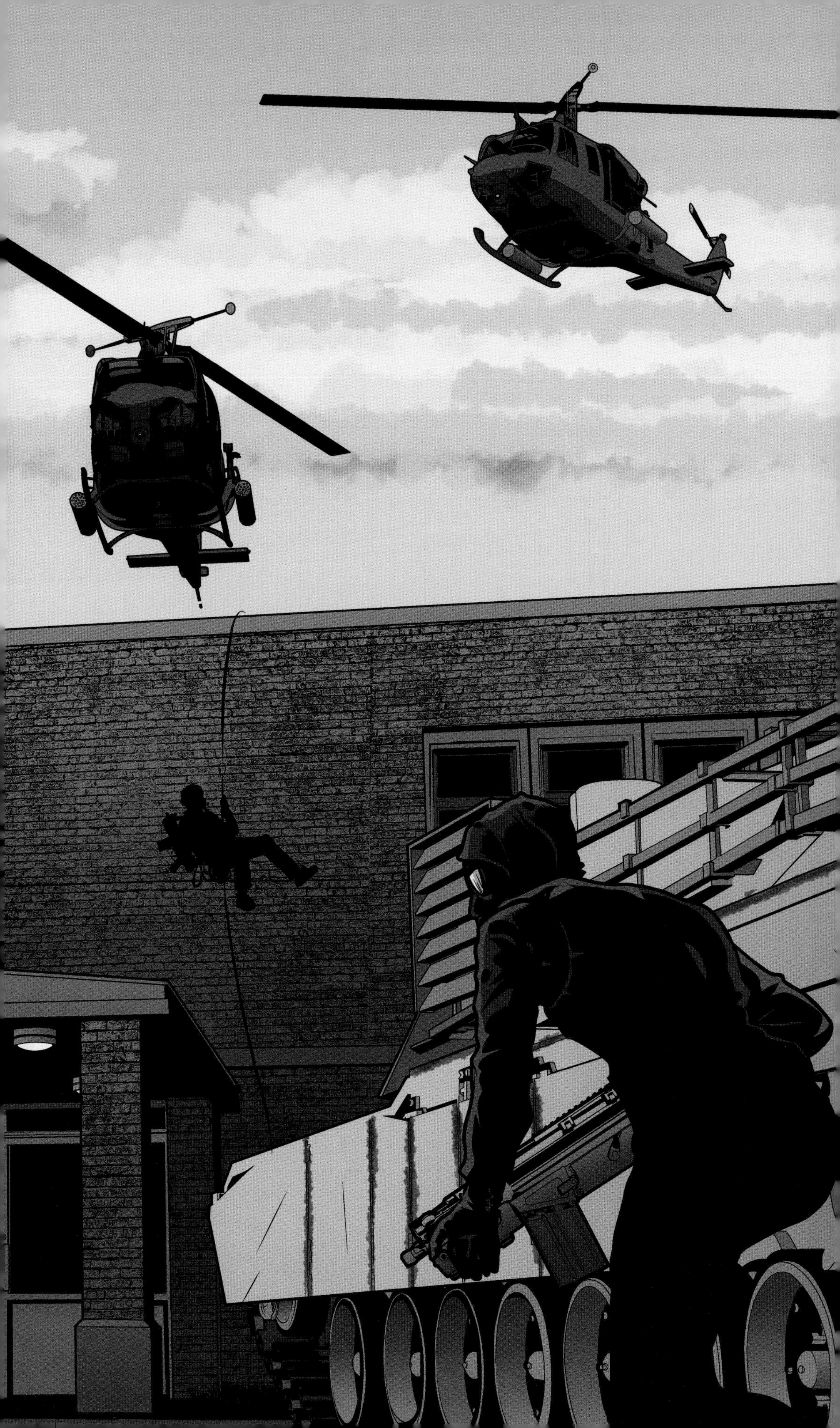

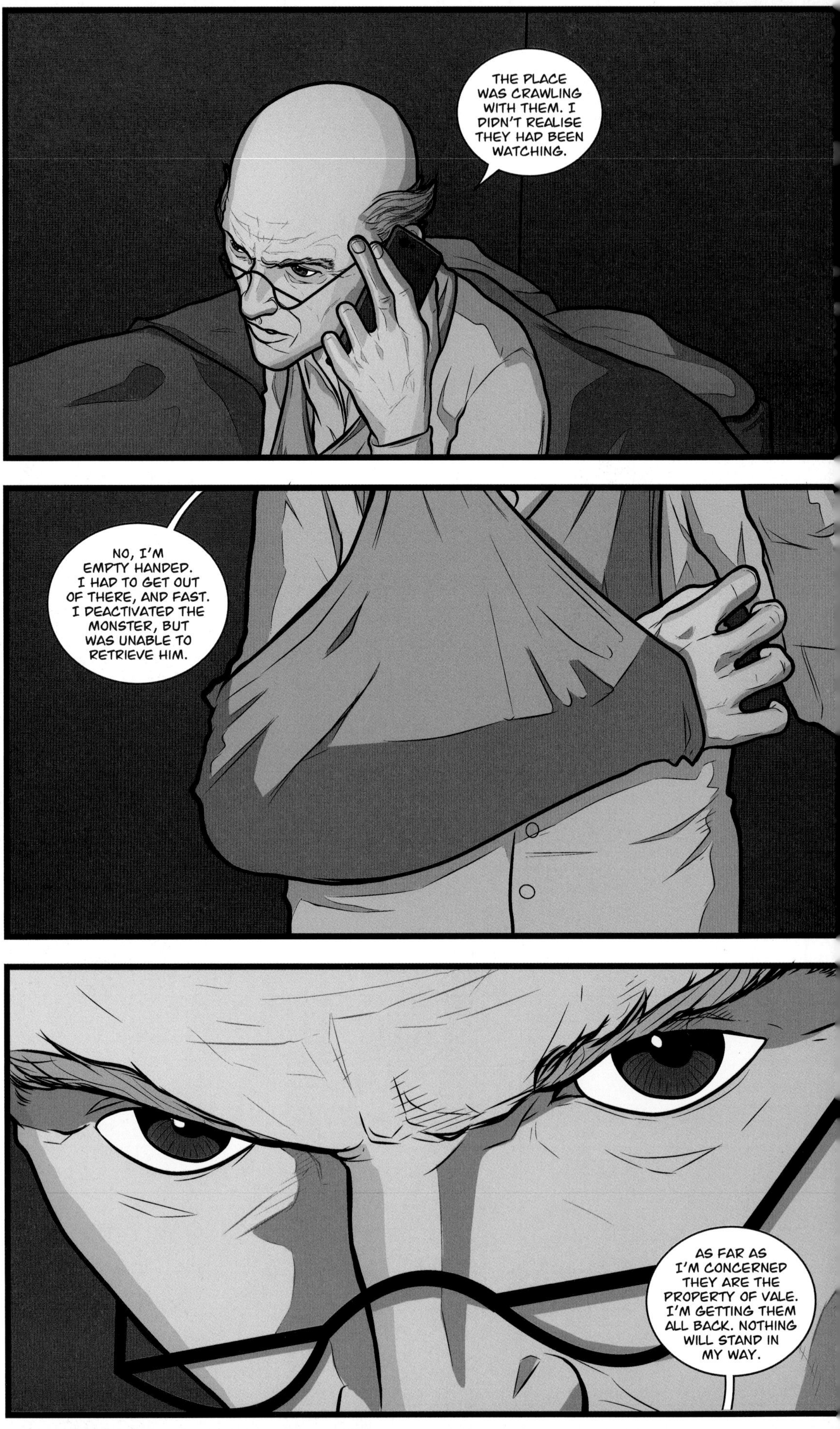
THE PLACE WAS CRAWLING WITH THEM. I DIDN'T REALISE THEY HAD BEEN WATCHING.
NO, I'M EMPTY HANDED. I HAD TO GET OUT OF THERE, AND FAST. I DEACTIVATED THE MONSTER, BUT WAS UNABLE TO RETRIEVE HIM.
AS FAR AS I'M CONCERNED THEY ARE THE PROPERTY OF VALE. I'M GETTING THEM ALL BACK. NOTHING WILL STAND IN MY WAY.

TO BE
CONTINUED...

Unused covers

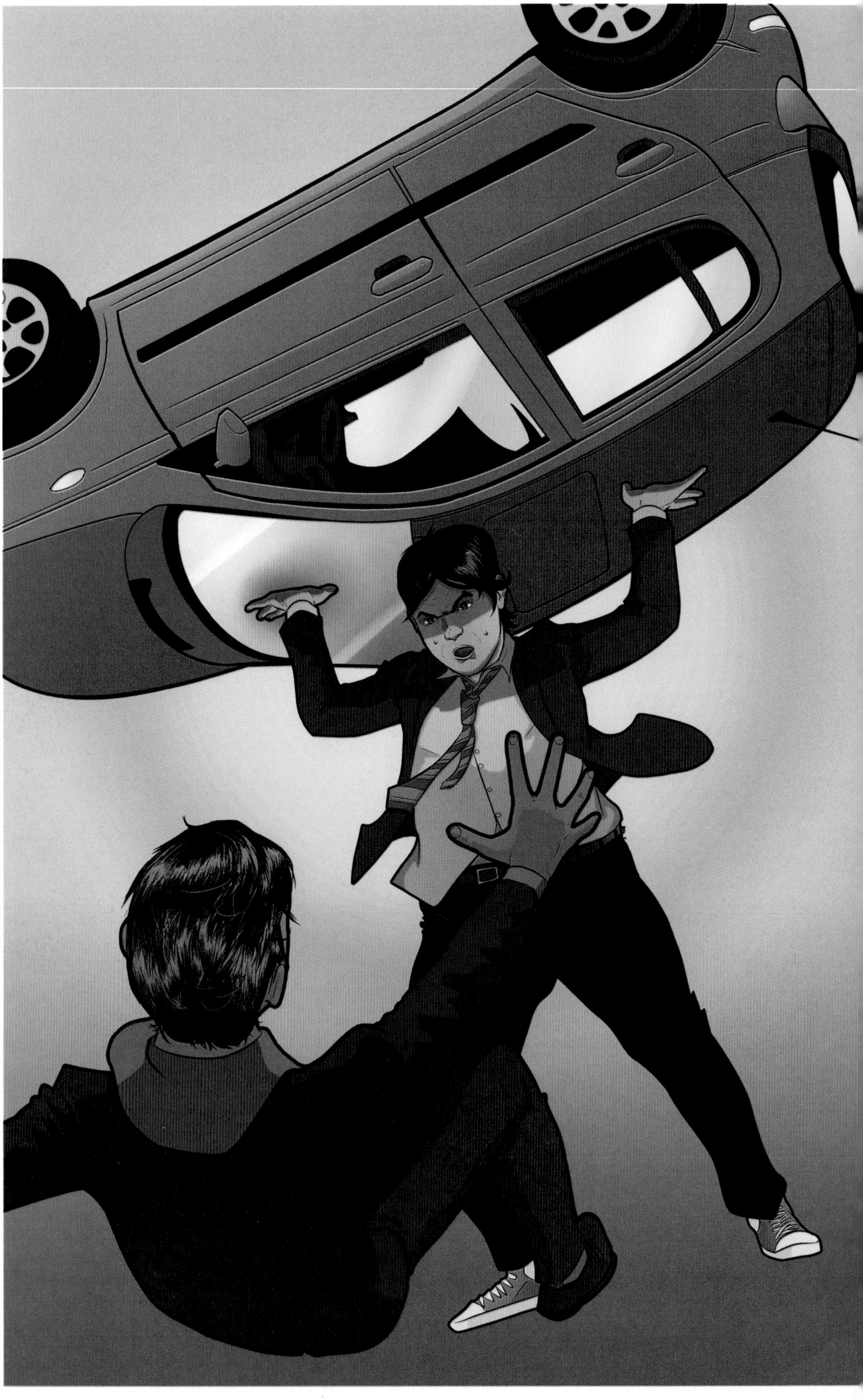

ISSUE 4

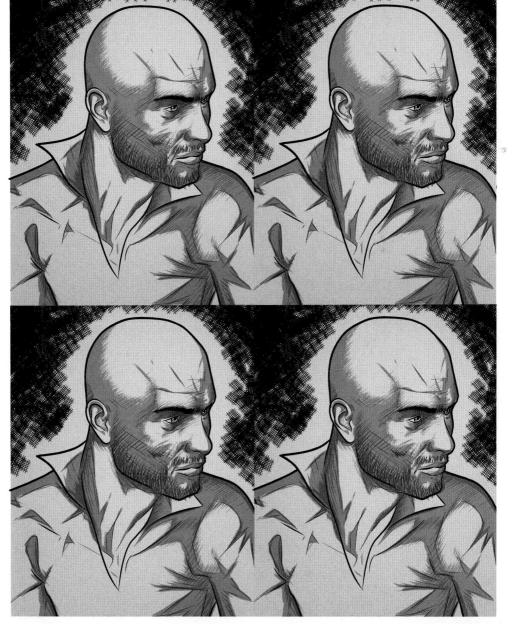

About the creators

EDDIE ARGOS is an artist and writer living in Berlin. He is best-known as the lead singer of the band Art Brut, who have to date released four albums, with the two most recent being produced by Black Francis of Pixies.

He has written for *The Guardian, NME, This Is Fake DIY, Geekweek, Blackbooks* and *Playback:stl* and sees his greatest accomplishment as being placed on the *NME* Cool List TWICE! (He was 46th coolest person in the world in 2004 and 24th in 2007. Not placed 2008, 2009, 2010, 2011, 2012, 2013, 2014, 2015...)

Eddie is a Lo Fi Punk Rock Motherfucker.

STEVEN HORRY draws things. Sometimes he DJs, and at least once a month he hosts intensely geeky pub quizzes in London's Glamorous Camden. His first graphic novel, *The Islanders* (also a collaboration with Eddie), was published by Nasty Little Press in 2013, and since then he's done lots of freelance arty things and contributed to various small press anthologies. He's never been in the Cool List, but he did have a runner-up single of the week in the *NME* once. Do you know who Les McQueen is? That's him, that is.

DAVID COOPER is a Glasgow-based colourist and cartoonist. In addition to colouring comics such as *Dungeon Fun* and *Sleeping Dogs*, he is the creator of long-running webcomic *Perpendicular Universe* and *The Brave & Handsome Squad*. His favourite colour is purple.

Along with his lettering work for comic publishers such as Dark Horse and BOOM! Studios, **COLIN BELL** is known for being the SICBA award-winning writer behind the popular all-ages title *Dungeon Fun* (Comic Book Resources' 61st Best Comic of 2013), and back-up strips for Titan Comics' *Doctor Who: The Twelfth Doctor.* And he thinks you're great!